R<small>ONALD</small> W P<small>ROSS</small>

THE PENNY ENTREPRENEUR

Trafford
PUBLISHING

www.trafford.com

North America & international
toll-free: 1 888 232 4444 (USA & Canada)
phone: 250 383 6864 ♦ fax: 250 383 6804
email: info@trafford.com

The United Kingdom & Europe
phone: +44 (0)1865 722 113 ♦ local rate: 0845 230 9601
facsimile: +44 (0)1865 722 868 ♦ email: info.uk@trafford.com

10 9 8 7

THE PENNY ENTREPRENEUR

A delightful humorous but, none the less, true account of a young boy with a small wartime education but with a big flair to earn a penny or two.

The author begins his story at the age of three years old and relates his pre-teen activities during periods of enemy bombing in London and evacuation to Devon, Lancashire and Buckinghamshire during the 1939-1945 war. His varied places of residence were a result of the conflict and determined by bombing by conventional piloted aircraft, unmanned jet propelled bombs and high explosive rockets that were all targeted on London.

The sprinkling of history from the abdication of Edward V111 in 1936 to 1947 when the author left school to commence work could also serve as an appetiser for further study for those students interested in that period and the Second World War.

DEDICATION

This volume is dedicated to my Granddaughter, Amy Broome, for her continued encouragement to get this book published. With it goes my best wishes and good fortune to her fellow teachers and their students at The Kingswinford School, Dudley, West Midlands.

ACKNOWLEDGMENTS

I have gleaned much of the historical background from old copies of The Daily Mirror and The Daily Express.

The facts and figures of frequency of bombing raids and war casualties have come from the Public Records Office, Kent and HMSO publication 'The Defence of the UK'. Most of the war details, however, are general history in the public domain. I have used only a little licence just for the continuality and I apologise for any inaccuracies that may occur.

A recognition of thanks is also necessary to my daughter Debbie Carpenter for taking a week out of her holiday to correct my errors and to Tony Carpenter for imparting some of his computer expertise.

PROLOGUE

In January 1936, King George V died after a reign of a quarter of a century. Edward VIII, his eldest son, succeeded him. The new King was unmarried and during his term of office as Prince of Wales he had, like his Grandfather, Edward VII, gained a reputation as a playboy.

On 10th December, with less than one year on the throne, King Edward VIII spoke to the nation on the radio.

He announced he was giving up the throne for the woman he loved and abdicating in favour of his Brother George.

'The woman he loved' was the twice married, American born, Mrs Wallis Warfield Simpson:

The relationship between the king and the commoner received very little coverage in the British press and less was known of the fact that she was, at the time of the announcement, still married to her second husband.

Historical commentators labelled 1936 as the year of the three kings.

Much of 1936 Europe was a year of public disobedience and protests: In England there were political marches and demonstrations organised by Oswald Mosley's Fascist Party protesting about the Jewish and rallies organised by The Communist Party protesting about the Fascists. In the streets of London's ' East End', fights broke out whenever the two factions met.

Unemployment was at a high level: In the North East of England 77% of the working population was without a job. In Jarrow, Tyneside, councillors and trade unionists met and organised a march to the Houses of Parliament some 270 miles away. The objective was to present a letter to the government to make politicians aware of the workingman's plight.

Ellen Wilkinson, Member of Parliament, led the marchers from Jarrow. In terms of publicising the plight of the shipbuilding community on the Tyne, the march was an enormous success. To capitalise on their support signatures were collected along the route to London.

The progress of the march was reported daily in the newspapers and more supporters joined along the route. The marchers reached Westminster in an orderly manner and were in good spirit but the delivered petition appeared to have had no influence on the elected members of parliament, the brave men of Jarrow went home dejected. It appeared that, for all the difference their long march had made, they might just as well have stayed at home.

The government had not yet let it be publicly known that the wheels had previously been put in motion for a rearmament programme to begin.

Britain began to rearm, but the government would not concede it was the result of the pressure from the working class wanting employment. Maybe it was, maybe it wasn't but Jarrow did not recover to any reasonable employment level until after the Second World War.

In Spain during the February of 1936, The Popular Socialist Party won the general election and formed a government. It introduced a sweeping programme of social reform including the redistribution of land, much to the distress of the Spanish, over privileged, ruling class, including the Roman Catholic Church and senior military officers.

As a direct result of the election, on July 18th Spanish troops led by General Franco, based in the Spanish possession of The Canary Islands and Spanish occupied Morocco in North Africa, revolted against the legitimately elected government on the mainland of Spain.

The military uprising in Morocco was the opening gambit of the Spanish Civil War. Observers were given an insight of the World War II yet to come.

Wealthy Spanish and a minority of the poor welcomed the rebel force. Germany and Italy, the latter led by Mussolini, supplied men and equipment that had been trained in the techniques of modern warfare.

Spanish Socialists, supported by the 'International Brigade' included men from Russia and the British Isles fought with the elected Government troops to assist the Socialist cause. The war ended when Government forces surrendered in Madrid in April 1939.

General Franco remained head of state until his death in 1975. He became the longest ruling Dictator during his lifetime.

During March 1936, The maiden flight of the "Spitfire" took place from Southampton: Along with the Hawker Hurricane, the Supermarine Spitfire was to become the 'main plank' of the defence of the UK during the Battle of Britain.

May 1936: The 80,733-ton super liner 'Queen Mary' made her maiden voyage.

The Olympic games, the greatest sporting event of the decade, was staged, of all places, in Germany. A spectacular stadium was built on the outskirts of the capital as a showpiece to the achievements of the Third Reich:

Berlin had been the designated city to host the games two years before Hitler took control of the German government in 1933. Many national leaders assumed 'Der Fuhrer' would cancel the Olympics because he objected to competing against 'inferior non-Aryans'

Contrary to this view he decided to turn the Berlin Olympics into a propaganda showcase of technological and racial superiority. Hitler's racist haranguing, however, was muted when Jesse Owens, a black American, won four gold medals. Owens was the super star of the games.

Hitler was furious and though he never shook the black man's hand Owens was well treated by most of the German athletes:

At home in USA one year earlier, Owens broke five world records in one afternoon.

During the Olympic games, there were nine events in Gymnastics. The German team won six of those nine events. Their medals tally were; six gold, one Silver and five Bronze, their coach was Hans Werner:

This piece of information is of special personal interest for me for, fifteen years later, while I was serving in the army in Germany, Hans Werner became my running coach and while stationed in Berlin I had the privilege competing in The Olympic Stadium.

Germany left all other nations far behind in the number of total medals won.

The Olympic Village that had housed over four thousand participants had been designed so that it could be quickly converted to military use.

Also in 1936: The jet engine was invented.

One year earlier Robert Watson-Watt perfected a method of detecting objects in space by the use of radio waves.

From: **RA**dio **D**etecting **A**nd **R**anging the equipment became known as RADAR. It played a very important tool in the air defence of the United Kingdom during the 'Blitz'.

During 1937 the BBC coverage of the coronation of King George V1, was the world's first outside TV broadcast.

Ramsey MacDonald, the failed ex Prime Minister of the first Socialist Government of the UK, died. Neville Chamberlain became Prime Minister.

12 March 1938 German troops ceremonially marched into Austria. Not a shot was fired.

The German strategy, at the time, was not apparent to the rest of Europe but became clearer six months later. Hitler, by his scheming, had been welcomed in Austria and was firmly in control when he turned his attention to Czechoslovakia:

Czechoslovakia had been created as a new state after the 1914-1918 war and had built powerful defences along the Czech/German border but not on its frontier that bordered Austria.

Czechoslovakia was divided by language with one group speaking German, whilst the other spoke Slovak.

With German troops in Austria, the Czechoslovakian border became an open door and one step closer for Hitler's ambition of European domination.

In September, German troops marched from the Austrian border and crossed into The Sudetenland. A cheering, flag waving crowd welcomed them and, again, not a shot was fired:

Hitler's occupation of the Rhineland and Austria had been welcomed by virtually the whole population of those German-speaking people. German soldiers called these occupations 'Blumenkriege', Flower Wars, in which the soldiers received kisses and posies, instead of resistance with bullets.

The Czech's had been outflanked along a two hundred and fifty mile front. German forces entered through the side gate that was Austria.

Hitler claimed he was allowing the people of the Sudetenland, the German speaking Czech's, to join their natural fraternity. Contrary to the 'Volks deutschen', German people, who lived in the border regions, the Slovaks of Czechoslovakia had no love for the Germans.

England and France failed miserably to go to Czechoslovakia's assistance.

The first Earl of Halifax, Britain's Foreign Secretary was an elitist of the old school. He was also a snob of the first order he would recoil and shudder at the prospect of a true democracy. He was an intensely religious man and a former Viceroy of India; he was prepared to go to extreme lengths to appease Hitler. He tried to muzzle the British press from reporting how unruly political mobs were allowed and even encouraged to persecute the Jewish community.

It is a chilling thought to consider how near Lord Halifax came in 1940 to becoming Prime Minister instead of Churchill.

Proudly anti British, American ambassador in the UK, at the time, was Joseph Kennedy father of the future US president John, F. Kennedy. He predicted that in the event of a war against Germany, Britain would not survive.

In the same year Japan launched an invasion on an ill prepared China by bombing Peking and Shanghai, within two months the Japanese army overran most of Northern China. When the Chinese capital, Nankin, fell in December the Japanese massacred two thousand of its Chinese population. At the time it was the worse known atrocity of the century. Later, more was to be discovered. In the following eight years it was estimated that 6 million, mostly Jewish, people died in Nazi gas chambers.

To briefly sum up the 1930's:

Democracy was in decline. Poverty was a worldwide problem but only for those people that had to work for a living.

There was a right wing dictator in Italy and Italy had invaded Ethiopia, now Abyssinia.

Japan had invaded China.

There was a civil war in Spain and Adolf Hitler was democratically elected to be become a dictator with a global ambition.

In Western Europe there was a right wing backlash against Russian communism.

To survive, the majority of the working class had to live by their wits to earn a living.

I hope the discerning reader may question why I have included this condensed history alongside my own. I have done so, for had it not been for world events my story, like every ones, would have been totally different. My adventure is the result of war.

What we are is determined by where and when and from whom we are born.

The scene is set........

ONE

BEFORE THE WAR

My Aunt Lou and Uncle Bill moved to 49 Studley Road one road on from Stockwell Underground Station, South London.

The house was built during the 19th Century to an elegant Georgian style of architecture. The rooms were grand and spacious. The windows, on the inside, from top to bottom had wooden panels on hinges that could be closed and bolted for security. On the outside, at semi basement level, iron railings were cemented into the brickwork and crossed each side of the window frame.

The large gardens at the rear and small garden at the front allowed the occupants to pursue outdoor activities within their own confines, such as gardening and ball games, etc. The houses were also designed to accommodate 'living in servants':

The lowest rooms, on the semi-basement floor of 49 Studley still had the traces and proof that it had, indeed, been occupied by servants: 'Upstairs, Downstairs' was the terminology describing a master and servant relationship.

The 'master and servant' employment situation, however, did not apply in my Aunt Lou's case. When my Aunt and Uncle became residents, I suspect the house had been converted into self-contained flats: The employment of servants by the upper and middle classes began to decline between the two world wars and, with the exclusion of the very wealthy became almost extinct.

When my Aunt Lou married, she became Mrs England.

Her husband, Bill, had between the two world wars, completed a sheet metal workers apprenticeship and had become skilled in nickel-chromium plating.

After he married my Aunt, Uncle Bill was promoted to the grade of Foreman of a sheet metal and plating company in Dorset Road, Kennington.

In 1936 Uncle Bill bought a new AJW motorcycle and immediately dismantled it. When it was reassembled the AJW was a shining showpiece: Every part of the motorcycle that could have been chromium plated, had been. The springs on the saddle, the spokes on the wheels even the smallest nut and bolt had not been overlooked. It could well have been the only one of its kind, of that condition, in the world.

We would regularly travel by motorcycle and sidecar from where we lived in Buckinghamshire to London to see my Grandmother and Grandfather, my Mother's parents, in Arlington Road, SW4.

I had no warm feeling for either of my Grandparents at that time; they were not 'warm people'.

While in their house, my Sister Pat and I were expected to sit and be quiet and not speak until we were spoken to.

My interest in the journey from Buckinghamshire to Lambeth was limited to a small airport we would pass on the Great West Road, A4.

Dad would slow down so that I could get a better look at the rare sight of stationary aircraft on the grass runway. It was a bonus if an aeroplane was in flight and actually coming into land or taking off as we passed. What a thrill!

The two-seater sidecar, attached to the side valve Triumph motorcycle, was mounted on a soft sprung chassis which, when the motorcycle was travelling, had the motion of a rocking cradle and gave a comfortable sleep inducing ride.

Before we started each journey, I have been told I would ask Mum to promise to make sure I was awake so that I would not miss the spectacle as we passed.

The small airport at Heathrow was to be become the busiest airport in the world. The main London Airport at that time was at Croydon:

Croydon was one of the many airfields used by the Royal Air Force, Fighter Command, during the 1939-45 war and played an important role in the defence of London.

After the war it had some limited activity but closed in 1959:

The original control tower and some of the old buildings remain. One of the old administration buildings is now a restaurant and can still seen from Purley Way.

I was four years old when the family moved from Tudor Road to Hughington Road, at the bottom of Missenden Hill, Little Missenden, near Amersham. The house was rented and had the name of 'Alkalane'.

My first school, Hampden Common School, was about three miles from home:

Using 'common' in the title of the school was rather unfortunate. Observers of the young school attendees could be forgiven for thinking it had been so named to label the social status of the parents. I am told, that was not the case.

The school had been built and I use the word 'built' loosely for it was little more than a wooden garden shed on 'Common Land'. The grassy Common doubled as grazing land for the local farmer's cattle and a playground for school children.

On arriving at school each morning, I would play with the other school children on the grass that surrounded the school building until a hand bell rung. With unquestioning obedience, on hearing the bell, we would run to the school door and line up in single file and on the word of command march into the classroom.

During the warmer summer months when the widows were open, a cow would occasionally look in and disrupt lessons.

Any disruption was always welcome and an assortment of laughing, yelling, stamping of feet, banging of hands on desks and laughter would follow, not because the event was that hilarious, it was just a method of expanding the perimeter of our unruliness and thereby reducing the teacher's authority.

Being the age of four, my actions were not a result of cold calculations or planning, as it may read, but even at the earliest age of our lives, even as babies, we are likely to take advantage of any situation to test authority.

Each morning, before we were allowed to leave the school building for our first play break, we were all given a half pint bottle of milk. While the milk was being consumed, the teacher would leave the class to ensure cattle or any droppings the cows may have left behind did not occupy the pathway.

Avoiding the cowpats put real meaning into the game of 'hop, skip and jump'.

One of the local farmers ran a weekday bus service to carry children to and from school. He would 'pick up' and 'drop off' outside each passenger's house. It could have been likened to a taxi service but for one difference he would not stop for latecomers. That is to say, he would stop if he saw someone was making an effort by running but not if they stopped to tie their shoelaces.

Returning home on the bus, after completing my first day at school, I had almost reached my drop off point when, unable to control my bowels, I accidentally made a deposit in my trousers. I gallantly remained in my seat sitting on my firm, but sticky, pile without arousing a comment from neither the driver nor the other passengers.

As soon as the bus stopped at my house I got off and, bow legged like a cowboy that had been many days on the back of a horse. I walked up the garden path.

I immediately told my Mother of my misfortune for I could hardly have kept it a secret. Once in the toilet and I had vacated myself from my trousers, I was pleasantly surprised to see very little sign of my action inside my pants. The evidence, however, was firmly squashed and plastered to my bottom like a present day McDonald's giant beef burger and quite possibly of comparable food value. I was able to peel it of in one piece.

I continued to use the bus, for other than walking, there was no other means of getting to school but I am proud to document I have never repeated my unsocial performance of doing a poo -poo in my pants.

On another occasion, as the bus neared the common and the wooden school building came into view, I noticed a motor vehicle parked on the grass. As each one of us got out of the bus, we joined the remaining children that were gathering around.

A man in an army type but navy blue uniform was unloading small brown cardboard boxes, about six to eight inches square and taking them into the classroom.

There was only one classroom. Did I mention it was a small school?

Like every other morning, when schooling was due to commence, the teacher rang a large hand bell and we all conformed to the ritual of the straight line and the marching into school but, this morning with more zest than usual.

This was to be one of my very special early school days. It was special because it was one of my most enjoyable ones.

No lessons were given but that was not the only reason for it to qualify as a special day. It was because, like all of my classmates, my fun was uncontrolled and I experienced my first 'taste' of defying school authority:

The morning began with the man in the blue suit accompanying the teacher into the classroom.

He walked in front of the teacher's desk, where the teacher usually stood, and spoke to the class.

"I am going to tell you today what is in each of these boxes and how to use them".

Pointing to the pile of brown boxes stacked in the corner he managed to capture and maintain our attention by keeping the contents a secret for as long as he could by commenting about air raids and gas.

"It is expected that one day in the future the British Government will announce we will be at war with another nation. It is feared, as it was in the previous war, twenty years ago, gas will most likely be used. These masks which I am going to issue to you, are to be worn in the event of such a gas attack" he said while pointing again at the pile of boxes. "I am going to show you how to take care of them, how to put them on, how they should be worn and used".

I cannot boast that the above is 100% verbatim but it is not far from accurate because he was reading from a script that was identical to a letter we were told to take home to our parents. My letter remained in my gas mask case, for the duration of the war.

Still not yet having produced the mystery masks, the teacher took advantage of her young attentive audience, an experience I am sure was new to her. Stupidly, she attempted to explain what was meant by 'a war'.

She made the comparison of two boys fighting in the playground with two countries fighting it out on a battlefield.

I thought it a daft likeness; it made little sense to me. War must be much more fun than having a wrestle in the playground. But that did not reduce my anxiety to see the masks inside the boxes.

While the teacher continued talking, the gas mask man walked between the desks and placed a box on each desktop. "Don't open it yet," he said as he passed.

After all of the boxes had been given out the teacher asked, "Has everyone got a gas mask box?"

In chorus, we all replied by happily shouting out "Yes".

But we were still not allowed to open our present. We were instructed to write in large print, some of us with assistance, our name on one side of the box and address on the opposite side. Eventually, after the teacher had walked around the class and inspected every box and having realised that she had 'milked' the subject as much as she could, we were told:

"Children! You have all done very well, now carefully open your box and take out the mask. Now, put your chin into the front and pull the straps over the back of your head".

We all followed her instruction and while we were still wearing our new toy, the teacher continued:

"If war is declared there will be air raids and you must carry your mask with you at all times. Wearing your mask will allow you to breathe safely without being poisoned by gas".

Both teacher and Mr Bluesuit overlooked telling us that if we were bombed, the bombs would have to contain gas for the masks to be any value. It may seem obvious to an adult but not so to a classroom full of four year olds eager to laugh at anything. We were then asked if anyone was frightened and were there any questions?

No one was frightened at trying on the funny rubber masks but all the boys seemed pleasantly excited that with a bit of luck there might soon be a war.

After the teacher had decided she had heard enough questions about war she tried to regain some semblance of control. She clapped her hands.

"Now children! Don't forget what you have been told, If there is a war you must wear your mask so you can breathe without difficulty and without fear of being overcome by gas".

With tiredness becoming obvious in her voice and most likely with her audience, the teacher added, "There will be no more question about war unless it is to do with gas masks".

I hadn't asked a question yet and not wanting to be left out, I put my hand up.

The teacher looked at me. "If your question is to do with gas masks you may ask".

"Please Miss, How can we eat our dinner if we are wearing a mask?"

"Don't ask silly questions boy, sit down and don't be so stupid".

I knew it was a silly question but it got a good laugh so I enjoyed the joke and laughed with the rest of the class.

We had to keep our mask on for long periods during that first day to get used to wearing it, in doing so, after only a short time one boy accidentally discovered that by inhaling deeply and then blowing out, the rubber side pieces would stretch and flap away from the side of the face. The escaping air made a voluptuous sound like that of passing wind but with the additional intensity of going through a megaphone.

The day, from then on was hilarious, it became just one long contest for who could make the loudest and rudest noise.

I enjoyed the day immensely. I felt a happy tingle of excitement at the mass disobedience and rejection of school authority. It was like a party.

When the school day came to an end I could not get home quick enough to show my Sister my new toy. When I reached my front door, my two-year old Sister, who, of course was not yet attending school, greeted me and pointed at her super new blue and yellow 'Mickey Mouse' style mask.

"Ronnie! Look what a nice man as brought me," she said.

The thrill that my, now ghastly, black and brown thing had given me was instantly dashed. What an anticlimax!

Before the week had past, the local county council sent out letters advising all parents that the box and its contents should be carried at all times when, or if, hostilities commenced.

The masks became part of daily dress and although I often mislaid my mask in a box or lost it somewhere it was always returned within a short time:

In Britain, before the year was over, thirty eight thousand gas masks were issued to men, women and children, I should remind the reader at this point that Great Britain was still two years away from declaring war on Germany.

One morning, to check on the weather to consider if it warranted wearing waterproof clothing, Mum stepped out into the garden path from the kitchen side door and held her hand out. I think Mum could not trust her eyes: only if her hand got wet was it raining.

Just as I poked my head out beyond the doorframe, I saw the school bus speed past. With no other means of getting to school Dad got the car out of the garage and drove me:

Dad had bought a large Hillman car a month or two earlier with the intention of advertising his availability for private hire work and also undercut the farmer's school bus price.

In the Hillman we reached Hampden Common and as Dad stopped the car for me to get out I saw the 'tail end' of my peers walking into school and the school door close behind them.

I said goodbye to Dad and waved as he drove away. I ran across the grass field to catch up on lost time but as I got nearer to the school entrance I began to think the situation through. My thinking reduced my sprint to a depressed stroll.

Not wanting the embarrassment of knocking on the door and having to explain why I was late, I acted upon, what I thought a clever piece of deception. I waited in the toilet until playtime but it did not work out to be the clever plan I had imagined.

As soon as I heard the normal uncontrolled happy chorus of shouting and screaming, synonymous to that of a monkey house at feeding time, I run out as I had planned to join the happy throng.

I particularly remember the incident not for the length of time that I waited in the little toilet although, at one time, I did wonder if everyone had gone home. Nor do I remember receiving punishment for my unsuccessful attempt at deception. I remember it for the sudden 'cut off' of noise as I appeared from the toilet and ran onto the playfield. The noise of happy squealing and shouting instantly switched to a frozen silence, as though the whole classroom had been 'tipped off' and had been waiting for me to appear. Within the time of a heartbeat, the stillness of the children's statuesque figures came back to life, not to return to their innocent joyful play but to that of a howling lynching party. It seemed the finger of every hand was stabbing at the air in my direction. Hostile mouths repeatedly shouted, "There he is miss. There he is miss". Each one wanting to be heard above the other as though there was some large reward awaiting the informant for my capture. My only punishment was my embarrassment.

Most of the Buckinghamshire landscape in the area we lived consisted of miles and miles of uninterrupted fields with grazing cattle, rolling hills and woods as far as the eye could see.

Without the knowledge, nor concern, of the laws of trespass, I took it for granted that the woods and the fields were there to be enjoyed by everyone.

From a very early age my Mother and Father gave me a great deal of freedom of movement. I think of them both with affection for my education in that respect. Maybe it was just carelessness on my Mother's part but I like to think my wanderings were a result of my parents wanting not to interfere with me, in my acquaintance with natural surroundings rather than neglect.

I suspect modern council welfare workers would judge more cruelly and suggest the later was the case. For such a lone adventure for two young children to happen today would be regarded as a serious, if not criminal, offence. I suspect that the parents would, if not charged by the police, be cautioned for neglect by the local council social services.

I can imagine reading the report in the headlines in a post war newspaper:

'Two children, a boy aged four and a half with his two year old sister were found roaming miles from home and left all day unattended to gather mushrooms'.

It could also have been called neglect before the war, I don't know but we never felt as though we were neglected, quite the opposite, it was great fun!

When the weather was fine and I don't remember it ever not being so, Mum would make up a picnic lunch for Pat and I and we would set off in the morning for our daily adventure.

Sometimes Pat and I would be gone all day. I remember clearly roaming the fallow fields but time was never important to me, I cannot recall what time we ever returned, we only arrived home when we felt we wanted to, but it was always by daylight. Maybe, being so young, we were not out as long nor so far from home as I imagined.

Pat and I, each with a wicker basket, would walk from one field to another, chase a few cows and then stop to pick a few mushrooms. We would repeat this action until we decided it was time to have our picnic.

Our lunch usually consisted of jam, meat or fish paste sandwiches even condensed milk was not uncommon. Sometimes our food pack would also contain a local grown apple, when one was not included I helped myself, ripe or not, to a couple growing from one of the many orchards.

On no occasion, while we were out on our daily adventures, can I recall ever being approached by anyone to ask what we were doing roaming unsupervised so far away from civilisation, nor was I ever given any cause to consider that we may be in danger. Whether it was due to the scattered country community knowing each other, or it was just good fortune I don't know:

Upon reflection, peoples' actions did seem to be more innocent then than now which was most probably due to the fact that poverty was so widespread and the majority of people had very little on their person to be attacked for.

It was not for mushroom picking alone that I was allowed to roam across the fields. It was normal for my parents to allow me to wander off and do what I wanted to do, for any other reason and for that I am grateful.

Current thinking, regarding the welfare of young people, suggests children are subjected to more danger and crime than before the war.

I would not deny that more crimes by and against children are reported now but could we not attribute some of our anxiety to the communication explosion?

There was no such thing as television and very few people had a telephone in their house and certainly no mobile phones.

Contrary to current belief, maybe a lot more crime against

the person went on than people of my generation would care to admit. Could today's problems partly be a result of there now being different standards, style and sensationalism of present day newspaper reporting? Not forgetting there is now more legislation. An action that could be an offence now, would not necessarily be the case then.

With more than sixty years having passed, maybe comparisons should not be made for we would not be comparing like with like. We now live in a completely different world.

Although I was not a model of good behaviour, I was not, in my view unruly. I never had any strong religious guidance although at my mother's request, I did go to the local Salvation Army Sunday school. But if each of my church visits scored a point, I'm sure I would not have qualified to be called a cherub.

I enjoyed listening to biblical stories when they were read out at Sunday school but they slotted into my category of not being true. I could not mentally grasp and still do not the concept of an all seeing and all caring creator being everywhere for everybody all at the same time. To me, all religious reading fell into the category of fairy stories.

In the garden, at the rear of our house at Missenden Hill, there was a low fence that marked out the boundary line between the garden and a privately owned field and woods beyond.

One lone horse spent most of the daylight hours grazing and roaming the field with no handler and most days the horse was peaceful and would cause no problems.

There were times, however, when for no apparent reason it would kick and race about wildly.

One Sunday morning, Mum, Dad, Pat and I were in the back garden when the horse had one of its crazy spells. It galloped fast along the top of the hill for a short while and then it stopped suddenly and kicked out with its hind legs. It made the movements as though wanting to dislodge an imaginary rider.

We continued to watch the horse performing as it went through his spasm along the edge of the forest; the peak of the hill was about three hundred yards away. Dad read the signs that all was not as it should be and being cautious, instructed Pat and I indoors. Once inside the house we continued watching from the dining room rear window. In a short while, a canter down the hill developed into a frightening mad gallop.

Continuing its downhill track the horse raced downhill, across the field and directly in line and towards our back garden. By this time, Mum and Dad were also inside the house. It then jumped over our garden fence, raced along our path and out of our line of vision from rear window. We heard the ferocious thunder of its hoofs as it passed the kitchen door at the side of the house. We rushed through to the sitting room at the front of the house and from the window, overlooking the front garden, we watched as it jumped over our wooden front gate. It raced across the narrow road, jumped over the bushes on the other side and, without stopping, galloped away into the field beyond.

One morning, a week or two after the first incident, while in the kitchen, we heard the now recognisable vibrating thud of the horse's hooves. It galloped at full speed from the back of the garden but we saw no more than a dark shadow as the horse rushed passed the window. It was a frightening experience. It became common practice to slightly open the side door and cautiously check that it was clear and safe to step outside onto the path to reach either front or rear garden.

I know the nightmares of falling from great heights are very common and I have no problem in wondering why my dreams of falling occurred. I often climbed trees and rocks and looked at scenery from steep cliffs so I attribute my scary nights to my scary daylight activities. But, in addition to those common but sometimes nasty nightmares of falling, I suffered from one particular strange nightmare that disturbed me before I reached school age and lasted for many years.

In my nightmare, I would be carried along in the midst of an endless suffocating mass of, something like, clambering fluffy balls of cotton wool. The small individual turbulent objects appeared to be in a storm as they rolled over and over, bumped into and bounced from another.

I could not see myself but I knew I was among the excitable mass struggling to keep afloat. I was unable to escape and there was no safe harbour to cling to only a restless rushing cluster of something white. The objects always travelled in a uniform direction and always in a rush.

After I left school I realised that I was no longer having the frightening nightmares, more enjoyable X rated dreams had taken their place. I suppose, like many people, I had a dislike for being confined in small places and restricted breathing condition, but I have deliberately not used the word 'claustrophobia':

The inability to breath correctly, due to a small nasal passage, caused me discomfort until I was in my 50's. It was corrected by surgery by having some bone chipped away at the bridge of my nose. It is possible, my poor breathing could have been the link with my nightly childhood fear: I have tried to induce my old nightmare to make a better analysis but without success.

Other nightmares plagued me as a boy but they were, in most cases, explainable because I was only reliving real events of the day.

I once read a book on dreams and in one chapter it described a similar 'fluffy balls' experience to mine. The author speculated that this phenomenon could have been caused by the sexual activities of the parents during the later stages of pregnancy.

If the brain of a foetus was developed enough it could to be capable of remembering activities even though still in the womb.

I wouldn't put a bet on that theory, but who knows. How little we know!

In athletics, during August, 1938, Sydney Wooderson beat the existing fastest time for the mile and set a new world record time of 4.064minutes. It was thought at the time that it was not possible for a human being to run faster. The record would never be broken. Most sports pundits believed it was impossible to run a mile in less than four minutes. A 'four minute mile' was therefore the goal that all world-class middle distance runners set their ambitions on. Another eighteen years elapsed before the 'barrier of the mile' was broken and covered in less than four minutes.

My Father had a wonderful Lancashire humour and a pleasant disposition and from as early as I can remember he was joyful and warm hearted toward us. He would go through many silly routines just to make us laugh. He would set himself up as a stooge and allow Pat and I to play simple tricks on him. One game he introduced to the breakfast table was a 'broken egg routine'.

The first 'egg trick' came about after Dad had finished eating his boiled egg. We were all sitting at the breakfast table one morning when, without Pat or I noticing, Dad turned the empty eggshell upside down in his eggcup, which gave the appearance of being a fresh unbroken egg. He thanked Mum for giving him another one and tapped the top, to peel away the shell only to find, of course, there was nothing inside. He would then ask Pat and I if we had eaten his egg.

We thought that was great fun. Thereafter, whenever eggs were on the table and Dad had finished his egg, he would conveniently look away to allow enough time for either Pat or I to turn his empty shell upside down. The same game was repeated, with variations on the same theme, time and time again that always brought the same amount of amusement as though each time was the first.

Dad never missed an opportunity to relate his seemingly endless store of North Country antics and anecdotes. He would often entertain the family by playing his ukulele banjo, singing and impersonating George Formby. Rob Wilton and Sandy Powell were also among a variety of other radio stars that he mimicked.

Dad was aware of his limited schooling and would regularly emphasise or point, at every opportunity, the advantages of a good education. He wanted Pat and I to concentrate on Maths and English. He was convinced that if we did well, in just those two subjects, we had more than a good chance of succeeding in life.

I hope the reader does not overlook my father's simple definition of success; his view, which may appear naive today, was not far from reality. Having come from a poor working class family, working in an office was regarded as being a reasonable success in life. He would often remind me that if there was anything at school the teacher said that I did not understand, I must always ask for it to be explained again or ask why such a conclusion had been arrived at.

His view was that all teachers like to know that they are not 'wasting their breath' by lecturing to a deaf audience. The response of the listener, by asking questions, was an indication to the lecturer that the students were paying attention and interested enough to want to know more.

To some degree that may be a reasonable hypothesis but I found it was an over simplified one.

While I was in Junior school, I tried to follow Dad's advice but I found that for as many teachers that responded positively there were just as many that did not want to explain any further than they had and accuse me of either not paying attention or being disruptive.

During the period 1935/36 my father was employed as a driver on shift work for The Thames Valley Bus Company. When he was not working. I joined him in some of his outdoor activities:

Once or twice each week in the evening, he took me with him into the field behind our house to set rabbit snares. This was the same field that the mad horse occasionally occupied.

From the rear garden, we would walk across the field and the up rising ground towards the woods and place the snares outside rabbit holes. Dad made the traps from a piece of timber about two inches square and six inches long with a loop of thin gauge wire.

He never took me out to do the collecting, he either thought that I was too young to see dead rabbits with the wire tight around their necks or he went out too early in the morning.

Cows and sheep being too large to put into a sack would account for the fact that we would rarely have beef or lamb. We did, however, occasional have chicken. I wonder where they came from? I think, not bought from the butchers!

While living in Buckinghamshire, before the outbreak of war, I became interested in reading. After reading a number of Janet and John infant books, I starting reading the adventures of Rupert the Bear that appeared daily in a newspaper. I believe Rupert appealed to me because each picture had a short simple rhyming sentence beneath it. Collecting Rupert books and annuals was my first real interest in books:

Rupert Bear was the creation of illustrator Mary Tourtel who introduced him in the pages of the Daily Express in 1920. The hard-back picture books began to appear in the mid 1920s. The famous Rupert Annuals first appeared in 1936 and were illustrated by Alfred Bestall

Purchasing from mail order catalogues was as popular then as it is today: Just before we moved back to London, a large wooden box, similar to that of a tea chest, was delivered to the house.

The chest contained a full dinner and tea set. I am taking a guess, maybe an unfair one but I think it would have been a safe bet to suggest this could have been a mail order purchase and we forgot to let the supplier know we were going to move. I have no reason for the suspicion or to suppose this was the case but 'pay later by post' principle was not an uncommon method for poorer people to gain possession of household goods and clothing. I smile to think it could have had some bearing on the reason why we were always moving house; it was easy to move on from one rented house to another and thereby getting lost from a creditor.

During 1938 we moved from Buckinghamshire with our new dinner and tea service to rent a two-roomed upstairs flat in Elwell Road, off Larkhall Lane, Clapham. The whole length of Elwell Road consisted of an unbroken line of small terraced houses. With no gardens, the front door of each house opened directly onto the pavement. At the rear of the house was a small cobbled yard that contained the only toilet. The house had three small rooms on the ground floor and another two rooms on the floor above. We rented two rooms at the top of the house. We would all eat together in the room at the front of the house I refrain from using the term dining room for that would suggest a degree of opulence. The only chairs we had were those we used while sitting at the table.

The second room was used as a bedroom and shared by the four of us.

There was neither kitchen nor bathroom. Water was obtained from the kitchen in the ground floor flat. We also had to go downstairs to go to the toilet in the yard outside and there were no bath.

Cooking was from an old gas oven placed on a small landing between the two rooms at the top of the stairs. The area was no more than one square yard which was so restricting that a person standing at the cooker would have to move to allow a second person's entry or exit to or from either room or to go up or down stairs.

I was five years old when I first attended Gaskell Street School. My new school was one street along from where I lived in Elwell road.

I was in the infants while my Mother's only Brother, John, was in the junior section of the same school before he moved on to Springfield Road Senior School in Wandsworth Road.

My sister, Pat, now a little over three years old, had not yet started going to school but she usually got out of bed at the same time as me or earlier to wave as I left.

Walking to school took me only a minute or two, which allowed me to come home at midday for a sandwich.

I went to school one morning and because Pat was not very well she remained in bed. On this particular day when I came home for my midday snack my mother told me to be quiet in the house because Pat was still ill in bed with a high temperature. She was waiting for the doctor to call. I went back to school for the afternoon's lessons and on returning home, I was allowed in the bedroom to see Pat asleep.

By the bedside was, what looked to me like something fleshy like a pickled whelk in a jam-jar. Mum told me the jar contained Pat's tonsils and now that they had been removed Pat would soon feel better. There were no complications, after the home surgery, and she was very soon on her feet.

During September 1938 a year before the declaration of war one hundred anti-aircraft guns had been strategically sited to defend London.

From experience, by witnesses of the civil war in Spain, mass bombing raids were anticipated. Veterans of the Great War, 1914-1918, also remembered the airships on bombing raids on London, in which 1413 people were killed:

A fictitious and terrifying example of world war was staged in Alexander Korda's film version of H.G.Wells novel; 'Things to Come'. It was a nightmare vision of warfare at it's worst with bombing, fires and crumbling buildings and mass panic. It was a remarkable piece of prediction.

One Sunday afternoon, Dad and Mum took my Sister Pat and I for a walk to the boating pond at Clapham Common. I was pleased that Dad had chosen my favoured route. The walk up to Old Town Clapham included walking over a railway bridge at the top of Larkhall Rise:

I passed where I had stayed with my Aunt Lou, in the corner house of No 2 Gauden Road, while Mum was giving birth to Pat in 1935.

Not wanting to miss any train that could be approaching I rushed ahead to cover the short distance to reach the middle of the railway bridge just as a train was about to pass underneath.

I was in time to be engulfed in a thick cloud of glorious hot smoke that belched out of the steam locomotive as it thundered along the track below.

I fantasised that I had done something that would be too frightening for most people to contemplate; that is to vanish in the ghostly mist and being wrapped in a magic cloak to make me invisible. I also enjoyed the change from the outside temperature to the sudden warmer dampness and back again to an almost instant cooling off. I thrilled at being momentary alone and totally immersed.

As the train moved on and the smoke thinned out, like an apparition, I emerged to see Mum, Dad and Pat had reached the foot of the bridge. Pat was looking at me in wonder. Dad's face betrayed a grudging smile. From Mum, I sensed I was about to be told off.

"I wish you wouldn't do that Ron, just look at the state of you! You had a wash only an hour ago and now you look as though your face hasn't touched water in a month" Mum said as she continued to walk towards me.

I stood waiting, like a puppy in training. When Mum got alongside me she searched her handbag and retrieved a handkerchief. She spat on it. I don't know if my Mum had considered beforehand that her spit was healthier than a bit of soot, but she applied the wet cloth to my face and wiped away some of the grime, another spit and another polish removed the evidence of my adventure.

"Why don't you tell him Bill", Mum said angrily to Dad.

Dad made no reply, but I could see, by the look on his face, his brain working and trying desperately to repress a smile. I was anticipating his reply and thought he was going to say: "tell him what?"

He didn't. Dad did respond to Mum's request, however, and tried to look stern.

"Why do you do things like that? It isn't clever. You don't see other people running into clouds of black smoke and getting filthy dirty do you? Do you know why most people don't do the things you do?"

I think Dad must have recognised the playful look in my eyes and thought a cheeky answer was about to be offered. Before I could reply he answered for me and told me the answer he wanted to hear:

"It's because they're not all dopey, that's why!"

Being dopey or a fathead was Dad's terminology to describe anybody that done anything that was unconventional or silly. I believe Dad only told me off because Mum had prompted him. I hid a smile and thought the only reason why he didn't join me in the smoke was because Mum would, most likely, have then told him off as well.

Anyway, it was only a short telling off and I don't think it worried Dad a great deal and it didn't bother me; it was like 'water off a ducks back'. We continued walking on past Old Town, Clapham, where the buses terminated and reached the common proper where the grass grew.

Before we got to the boating pond, I had no more than a little interest in toy boats but after a few minutes at the water's edge my interest increased and before we left that day I decided I wanted to be a boat owner.

By chance, we had visited the pond on a day that members of a local adult model sailing club had selected for their day's outing to show off.

Their toys ranged from expensive models of Clipper Ships and Racing Yachts, through to motorised Speed Boats, Lifeboats, Steamers and Paddle Ships and there was even a model Galleon. The selection appeared to represent all types of shipping with infinite detail. In some cases the adult masters of the ships even wore a captain's peak cap.

They were outnumbered, however, by children who had nothing to do with the club. They just had cheaper toy Woolworth's boats.

I noticed, as we walked around the pond, groups of people would form as soon as a vessel reached the water's edge. The owners with expensive models could always be detected for they appeared to be apart from the crowd, not always for their flamboyant dress, for some were quite scruffy, but for their anxiety.

From the moment a ship was placed in the water and given a light push a state of panic would occupy the owner. To a degree their concerns were justified because at the centre of the pond was an area that contained a large mass of weed. Like the legendary, but fictitious, giant octopuses of the deep seas, the weed was the peril of the pond.

At least one toy boat could always be seen trapped in the middle doomed to end up in 'Davy Jones' locker'. The water level at the middle of the pond and the deepest point was chin high to an adult which prohibited any child retrieving their craft if it got entangled.

The serious adult owners, however, were prepared for any such eventuality. Part of their kit was a long wooden rod with a cushioned end and a long pair of rubber waders that reached up to their armpits, which they would often don and wade out.

Another hazard for sailing ships was if a strong breeze caught a full sail. The speed in which a sailing boat could race across the water was sometime faster than their owners could run around the perimeter of the pond. If the boat reached the opposite bank before the owner and crashed into the concrete edge, damage and an expensive to repair bill could result.

As a land locked ship's captain would race around the edge of the pond a panic cry of "make way, make way" was often heard. He would be attempting to beat nature's cruel humour by reaching the end of the boat's journey, at the other side of he pond, before his vessel did.

If a boat owner was lucky he was quick enough to position himself to prod the bow with his rubber-ended stick, and shift his boat's direction to avoid a collision.

Once I had left the pond my thought of owning a boat was not on my list of priorities and took me a number of weeks before I found a suitable oddment of timber to get the project moving:

From the piece of timber I cut and shaped it to resemble a ship's hull and a thin rod in the centre made a mast. I painted it all over with some paint that Dad had no use for. I encountered a small setback when I got a disapproving lecture from my Mum when she discovered what I had used for a sail. It looked very similar to one of Dad's handkerchiefs.

During the Summer I walked to Clapham Common as often as opportunity allowed. I overcame the problem of the obstacle of the boat-trapping weed: I put a nail on the stern and tied strong cotton to it. I kept the other end, on the reel, in my hand so that I could always pull it back if it got stuck. I would expect to be told off as soon as Mum became aware she was missing a reel from her homemade needlework box.

Dad thought, having my boat on the end of a line was a good idea so a little grumble from Mum, now and then, was to be expected.

I became a regular visitor to Clapham Common but on one occasion I noticed, not more than a dozen strides from the boating pond, a low wooden fence had been erected that restricted a large grassed area from the public.

The fence was made of strips of timber about four feet high and held together by wire and had been placed there to reserve an area of privacy rather than for secrecy.

Men in army uniform, on the other side of the fence could be seen going about their duties. I was particularly interested in watching four soldiers handling a barrage balloon that was anchored down and hovering, fully inflated, about ten feet from the ground;

The balloon was coloured silver and appeared to be made of a soft fabric. It was long and fat and looked bigger than a bomber aircraft. On the narrowest end it had an upright tail fin and the same size flaps at each side. The balloon, because of its rounded features, gave the appearance of a soft overgrown cuddly toy and looked more like a cartoon character than an object of war.

There was a small newspaper and tobacconist shop on the corner of the Larkhall Lane end of Elwell Road where I would buy, for my Mum, a packet of five Players Weights cigarettes daily

It was on my second or third visit to the shop that I first saw,

34

on the counter next to a variety of newspapers, an American comic in full colour. This shop was the only one, I was aware of, where American comics could be obtained. I believe English comics, at the time, were printed in black and white only.

The comic was in fact a supplement of a large American Sunday newspaper. The shopkeeper, having noticed my interest, asked me if I could read.

I am not sure that I could do any more than just look at the pictures at that age, albeit I was six years old but I told him I could read so he let me take it home. There was no charge.

On my return home I told Mum that the shopkeeper had given me the comic but rather than her being pleased she told me I was to return it the next day.

I was disappointed with the honesty that was being imposed upon me. I wanted to keep it but, reluctantly, I returned to the shop, with the comic, the next day to purchase another supply of cigarettes.

I thanked him for the loan of the comic and told him I had enjoyed reading it. I must have impressed him, for he told me to take another one. I wondered was it possible he could have thought I was a nice little boy? The fool.

This must have been my earliest example of 'honesty is the best policy'. It didn't change my attitude but it is a good example.

For the short time while living in Elwell Road the comic swapping became a daily routine until I had seen all he had in stock. Not once did he charge me.

In the Spring of 1939 my Grandmother, Grandfather and their two remaining unmarried children, John and Rose, moved from the house they had shared with my Aunt Lou and Uncle Bill, to 49 Studley Road, Clapham, SW4 which now forms part of the Stockwell Estate.

Auntie Lou and 'Unky' Bill moved into a house in Courland Street, SW8 off Larkhall Lane: Courland Street is opposite Elwell Road where we now lived, on the other side of Larkhall Lane.

German troops were also on the move. Without a shot being

fired, Hitler's army marched into the non-German speaking area of Czechoslovakia. The British and French Governments did not act upon their promise to guarantee the security of the Czechoslovakian border.

Intelligence reports were also coming into the Foreign Office in London that Hitler's army generals were making plans to invade Poland.

Four days before my sixth birthday, The Spanish Socialist Government forces, after a bloody civil war, surrendered to Generalissimo Franco's Ultra Right Wing army.

On 31st March, The British Prime Minister made a statement in the House of Commons. He pledged to support Poland if she were attacked and committed the nation to declare war on Germany if Hitler's forces moved into Poland.

The members of the House of Commons responded with cheers to endorse the Government's positive stand.

Many Europeans, however, were not so happy; the tragedy of the Great War (1914-1918) was still fresh in their minds. In less than a week after the announcement was made Italy invaded Albania. A total European war was now looking like a strong possibility.

In England, although we now took the prospect of war very serious, the wealthy were still playing games.

John Cobb broke Malcolm Campbell's land speed record and took it up to 368 mph, while at Lake Conniston; Malcolm Campbell set a new water speed record of 179 mph.

On August 22nd 1939 the world was rocked by the news that a non-aggression pact had been signed between Hitler and Stalin (two very unlikely bed fellows). Everyone had expected, in the event of war, the Russians would fight against Germany. A counterbalance had been destroyed. Russia invaded Finland. It was a major blow for any hopes of peace.

On August 28, the UK Government announced that all children

should be sent to safe places in the countryside.

The findings of a government sub-committee of the committee of defence, led by Sir John Anderson set up in 1924 to consider air raid precautions was re-examined: It is generally believed, and understandable so, that the Anderson air raid shelter was named after Sir John, Anderson, the Home Secretary.

One positive outcome of those meetings was the erecting of corrugated iron air raid shelters, the 'Anderson', in the back garden of every London house.

The construction consisted of fourteen sheets of corrugated iron and when bolted together formed an arch six feet high. It was placed in an oblong trench four feet deep, four and a half feet wide and six and a half feet long. Flowerbeds, prized lawns and vegetable plots were sacrificed to accommodate this new piece family security.

The shelter had a small opening in the front, just enough to allow one average size person access and designed to accommodate six adults: Eventually two and a quarter million shelters were erected.

The galvanized iron shelters lasted for many years long after the war had ended, serving as excellent garden sheds.

The garden shelter was issued free to each household earning less that £250 a year and a charge of £7 for those on higher incomes: The average wage was £3 per week.

The Army and Air Force weekly wage was 14 shillings (70p). The Royal Navy, by tradition, received a little more.

A document, issued in 1935, urged local authorities to plan for action to take against the possibility of air attacks. This preparation brought the initials of ARP, Air Raid Precautions, into the English dictionary.

Some historians have criticised the politicians during the 1920's and 1930's of leaving the country vulnerable and ill prepared for war. The United Kingdom was ill prepared, that is true. I do wonder, however, if the critics that held that view, overlooked the fact that

Britain, in 1939, had still not repaid the loan from America that had financed the Great War that ended twenty-one years earlier.

Taking into account also that, by a vast majority, the British electorate did not want another war, the government planners of the evacuation programme, in my view, should be applauded but for one reservation; arrangements had been made to move three and a half million people from 'priority target areas' but where it went a little amiss was that some Londoners were sent to areas of the South of England where in the event of an enemy invasion, it was expected enemy troops would land.

The month of August had been the hottest and driest ever recorded and the summer had been one of the best in many years. It was no cooler on the political front: On September 1st, 1939, German forces entered Poland from the West while Russians forces entered Poland from the East.

These dramatic actions gave the evacuation plans a boost but not all of the families in the suspected 'danger area' planned in the move, chose to do so.

In London less than half of the children were evacuated. But in spite of its unpopularity approximately 11 1/2 million people responded to the official scheme. Mistakes were made, however, because the operation did not apply to all cities; Bristol, Plymouth and Swansea were designated 'non target areas' and were not included in the evacuation plans but when the war was under way, they were all heavily bombed.

Some children were evacuated further than the English countryside. Some children were shipped to America and Canada and even as far as Australia.

One of the passenger ships, 'City of Benares', on it's journey to Canada, carrying children away from the war, was attacked by a German U-Boat. Of the ninety evacuees on board, seventy-seven were killed.

Most people remember where they were at the time when major news items are made known. For instance: The assassination of President Kennedy in 1963 and the fatal car accident involving Princess Diana. My first big event was when war was declared. I remember very clearly where I was but my reason for remembering the day was not because it was the beginning of hostilities. It was due to the fearful sound of a loud siren:

One Sunday morning I had left my house after breakfast and walked alone to Clapham Common to catch sticklebacks in the boating pond. My fishing net never touched the water. My interest was greater to watch the soldiers digging trenches and filling canvas sacks from the excavated soil around a large anti-aircraft gun. Further inside the fenced area more activity was going on around a large circular piece of machinery that I later discovered was a searchlight. I had forgotten about fishing and I could have watched the soldiers going about their tasks for much longer had I not been distracted:

My distraction was caused by a sudden dreadful high-pitched whine that I had never heard before:

A one note siren commenced, which I now know the time was a little after eleven o'clock. I didn't know what it meant but I was frightened enough to start running home.

I ran over the railway bridge in Larkhall Rise and down the hill without a single thought of trains and with about half the distance covered between Clapham Common and my home in Elwell Road I was stopped by a man dressed in a dark blue army style uniform. Upon his head he wore a black tin helmet with a large white letter 'W', for warden, on the front.

"Don't you know war has just been declared Sony? You should be indoors! Now get a move on and run home as quick as you can!" He said, in a grumpy voice.

Now I knew why I was running but unwittingly, the Warden, later called Air Raid Precaution, ARP, had, by his authoritarian manner, reversed what he had tried to achieve. Before he had stopped me, I was trying to get home as quickly as my legs could carry me but now my fear had been replaced by defiance. I commenced to walk away from him but he shouted "go on, run!"

I broke into a slow trot, and not until I was sure there was a safe distance between us, I shouted back: "You silly old bugger!".

I reached home, knocked on the door and before my mother had the door half open, I excitedly told my news. "Mum, there's a war on!"

Two days earlier the world's first television service closed down. The close down bothered only a very few, for the majority were not aware of the news. It was a luxury, exclusive to the very wealthy.

Not to be overlooked, although it was to have no impact for another six years, nuclear fission was discovered.

TWO

ANOTHER WORLD WAR BEGINS

Neville Chamberlain was the first British Prime Minister to use the radio to tell the population the nation was at war. The message;

"I am speaking to you from the Cabinet Room at No10 Downing Street.

This morning, the British Ambassador in Berlin handed the German Government a final note, stating that unless the British Government heard from them by 11 o'clock that they were prepared at once to withdraw their troops from Poland, a state of war would exists between us. I have to tell you now that no such undertaking has been received and that consequently this country is now at war with Germany".

Neville Chamberlain Prime Minister.
11.15 am. Sunday.3rd September 1939.

For the second time in twenty-five years England had declared war on Germany.

As I ran from Clapham Common, with my fishing net in my hand, the Prime Minister was giving the above, now famous, speech to the nation.

The shrill siren I heard while I had been watching the soldiers doing their gunnery drill coincided with the radio broadcast.

The radio listener was informed that the siren that had just been relayed was a rehearsal but on all future occasions the siren would be a warning that an air raid was imminent and everyone was to take cover. When the threat of danger had passed, the 'all clear' would sound. The whining 'all clear' sound was different from the 'take cover' sound by a distinct wavering tone from high to low and repeated many times.

I believe the earlier plan, to inform the public that danger had passed, was for policemen or ARP personnel to ride bicycles through the streets operating a noisy wooden rattle and carrying a sign displaying 'ALL CLEAR'.

It was fortunate that the country had some brilliant thinking people in government for it didn't take too long for someone to realise that if people were taking cover in shelters the sign could not be seen and the rattle would not be heard.

The apparatus that produced the spine-chilling whine was situated, in most cases, on the rooftop of local police station: A keen eye will notice that some sirens still exist 'in situ' to this day.

After the announcement of Britain's declaration of war, most of the remaining unoccupied European countries placed their armies on alert but nothing exciting happened. It was all very disappointing.

Although there was no arrangement between Britain and the Dominions, Australia and New Zealand also declared war against Germany at once.

Canada did not follow immediately: The Canadian government had reservation that her forces should not again come under the same incompetent style of command the British Generals had shown during the 1914-1918 war. British senior officers had displayed and repeated their disregard for life by the continued slaughter that had taken place on the Western Front.

Canada elected to concentrate on shipbuilding to protect the Atlantic traffic.

South Africa, after an angry parliamentary debate, followed Canada. Incidentally, Canada declared war on Japan before Britain.

The British Government's declaration of war came as no surprise to adults as rearming the services had been going at 'full steam' since German troops had marched into the remaining unoccupied area of Czechoslovakia six months earlier.

To reduce the impact from the blast of expected exploding bombs, sandbags were placed around doorways and windows of public buildings. To limit the danger of flying shards of glass, strips of gummed paper were stuck crisscross on windows.

In London, parks, commons and most open spaces had, at least one detachment of anti aircraft guns and giant searchlights, some had barrage balloons.

On the second day of the war, 4th September, Britain's first bombing raid took place; ten RAF Blenheim bombers attacked ships and naval installations in North Germany at Wilhelmshaven, not all of our aircraft returned.

On the same day, the Monday morning front page of the Daily Mirror had the following headline:

'A British war cabinet of nine members has been selected.

Mr Winston Churchill was First Lord of the Admiralty when Britain last went to war was returned to that post.

Full list of the War Cabinet: -

Prime Minister: Mr Neville Chamberlain.

Secretary of War: Mr Leslie Hore-Belisha.

Chancellor of the Exchequer: Sir John Simon.

Secretary for Air: Sir Kingsley Wood.

Foreign Secretary: Viscount Halifax.

Lord Privy Seal: Sir Samuel Hoare.

Defence Minister: Lord Chatfield

Minister without portfolio: Lord Hankey.

First Sea Lord: Mr Winston Churchill.

There are other ministerial changes. Mr Eden becomes Dominion Secretary.

Sir Thomas Inskip goes to the House of Lords as Lord Chancellor. Lord Stanhope, ex-First Lord becomes Lord President of the council. Sir John Anderson is the Home Secretary and Minister of Home Security'. End quote:

The above list would appear irrelevant without an explanation:

The new cabinet illustrates the 'tight club' of landed gentry and titled people that still governed the country up to the first half of the 20th century. Of the thirteen listed above, there were three Lords, one Viscount and five with the title of Sir.

One, of a number, of early casualties of the war was a lone friendly French aircraft: While crossing the channel it caused a false alarm. Two RAF fighter aircraft scrambled to intercept the imagined threat, they engaged each other in cannon fire and shot each other down.

The first air raid of the war on British soil took place on 15th October. German bombers attacked The Firth of Forth Bridge fortunately all bombs missed the target.

November 8th, Hitler narrowly escaped an assassination attempt. He left a building, in Munich, twenty-seven minutes before a bomb exploded. Several people died in the explosion.

Britain urgently scrambled an Expeditionary Force, BEF, and sent two armoured divisions to France.

The remaining months of 1939 expired with little warlike activity on the ground.

For mariners, Royal Navy and Merchant seaman alike, the war had definitely started with a vengeance. There was nothing phoney about the sinking of the SS Athenia just nine hours after the declaration of war: A German U Boat torpedoed the British liner, 112 passengers died, 28 of which were American.

Merchant shipping, to and from our shore, were an easy target for Germany's E and U Boats. British merchant ships, in the Atlantic, were targets for torpedo attacks and were being sunk at an alarming rate.

The British Isles alone could not support herself with homegrown food and relied on imports from all over the world to 'fill the larder'. During the early period of the war Hitler believed he could starve Britain into submission. He very nearly did.

Within a day or two after the declaration of war, our household received evacuation details. My sister Pat and I were told we were going to spend a while in the country until the war was over. I was looking forward to the journey and the surprise holiday. Four weeks earlier Pat had her fourth birthday and had not yet started school. Mothers of children under school age had the option to travel with their children. Mum chose to remain in London with the rest of the family.

As we arrived at my school and assembled in the tarmac playground we were told the school was being temporarily closed, for as long as the war lasted and the teachers were going to be transferred with us to a safer area.

Parents were given two nametags for each of their children. At the time, I don't believe Mum was aware of our destination but she wrote our surnames and the name of my school on my tags and tied one through my buttonhole on my jacket collar and the second to my small brown paper parcel of clothing. Only a few of the children, of wealthier parents, had suitcases.

The next stage was for us all to get into one of the assortment of transport that was parked outside the school in Gaskell Street, Clapham. The consignment of vehicles that were to take us on to the assembly point must have been called in from various department controlled by The London County Council, LCC.

The vehicles were Ambulances, Council refuge collection lorries, Police vans and many others of all shapes colour and sizes were commandeered for the exercise.

The vehicle that Pat and I were placed in was one of the least luxurious. I use the word 'luxurious' for some of the transport had seats. Dustmen normally used our bus, for collecting household rubbish.

Our transport had not been adapted for carrying passengers by any standard but someone had been thoughtful enough to remove the kitchen garbage from the van before it left the council's depot. After we had been lifted up to the lorry, we drove off in convoy and travelled along Clapham Road. We passed the Underground Station at Stockwell and continued on along the Clapham Road towards The Oval, Kennington. We then turned right into Caldwell Street, crossed Brixton Road and stopped in Vassal Road. Brixton. I was soon disappointed for only ten minutes had elapsed since leaving our starting point when the convoy stopped and we were instructed to get out.

As each vehicle was emptied of their human cargo they drove off to make way for regular buses. We were then ushered off into the main assembly hall of Cowley Road School. This stage of the journey was the main assembly point. Children were arriving from the many other schools in the area for final documentation and the onward journey.

Through a loudspeaker system, parents were told we were to travel on from this point to Waterloo Station and then board a train for the South West Coast. Our destination was Dawlish on the Devon coast.

Adults that were not being evacuated with their children were told to say their goodbyes, as only mothers included in the evacuation would be boarding the vehicles for the onward journey to the railway station.

The announcement started a panic outbreak of cuddles and kisses, followed by Mums crying. Most of the children appeared to be happy and if their feelings were anything like mine, they were more excited to start a new adventure than to be concerned about leaving their Mum behind. After we had been checked again by our respective teachers we were kept in tight groups and ushered out of the school to the pavement outside. The organisers, not wanting a thousand uncontrollable tiny terrors running wild all over the school playground, lost little time in getting us all onto the buses.

As we boarded we were each given a food pack. Once we were all settled in our buses, a final check was made to ensure we all had an identity label on a part of our clothing. Our second label was tied on our paper carrier bags. When the engines of our transport started it encouraged more hand waving and another burst of tears and nose blowing followed from those not 'going on a holiday'.

As we moved off, over the noise of the convoy, the final words of endearment were shouted from loving parents. Assisted by lip reading I heard my Mother shout to me: "Ron! Take good care of Pat". I was six and a half years old.

We moved off, turned right into Brixton Road, thus putting the school out of sight. I felt no sorrow that our parents were being left behind. I was too young to understand the expected invasion was imminent. I was anxious to explore the unknown, just as all explorers do when they embark upon a great adventure.

The second stage of our journey lasted, again, only about ten minutes. We arrived at Waterloo Station from the Waterloo Bridge end of York Road. We stopped again to join another queue of an even larger assortment of transport, each waiting to unload their riotous cargo. As one bus unloaded and moved off another bus would fill the empty space. Our turn to alight came within a short waiting time without one fight having yet taken place.

We were kept under the supervision of our schoolteacher in tight packs of school groups and marched off in military fashion up the concrete steps towards the station entrance.

It was the first time Pat and I had seen a railway station of such magnitude. I had been used to seeing our local station that consisted of just a small platform each side of a pair of railway tracks. Not only was I surprised by the size of The Southern Railway's South London Train Terminal, I was staggered by the splendour. As we marched up the long wide steps, under the tall pillars and the archway high above, I likened my surroundings to the pictures I had seen in the school history books of ancient civilisations. For a brief moment I was transported in time. I became a Roman gladiator marching into a Roman arena:

As an adult and looking back I realise 'William' influenced my thoughts: 'William', created by Richmal Crompton, was my most favoured fictitious schoolboy character.

In columns of three, we entered the main area of the station where the sight and sound of the steam engines brought me back to the present day. The ticket offices had long queues of people each anxiously trying to buy a ticket.

Unlike more recent times, the timetable boards were operated by men standing at ground level moving numbers about with long poles.

The noises coming from travellers moving and talking, horses and carts and Royal mail lorries being unloaded, army lorries and taxi cabs coming and going and railway porters going about their business made the scene like a busy market.

Civilians, rich and poor, the poorer ones were obvious by carrying their own luggage, and people in military uniforms were moving quickly in different directions. Some were heading for the ticket kiosk. Some were dashing to catch a train while others, after getting out of their trains, were hurrying to leave the station. They all had one thing in common; they all wanted to be somewhere else.

Car horns hooted, carriage doors were being slammed shut and while a lady's voice screeched an inaudible message over the loud speaker system, I mimicked a news vender shouting out the newspapers he had for sale; "Star, News an' Standard":

'The Evening Star', 'The Evening News' and 'The Evening Standard' although the newspapers were prefixed with 'evening', they could all be purchased from 11 o'clock in the morning with updated editions coming out all day, mainly to give the latest betting odds and horse racing results.

I noticed that each of the many platforms had a stationary but steaming locomotive up to the buffers with many carriages behind them.

While we stood in a group, waiting for our next instruction from the teacher, the driver of the nearest locomotive gave a blast on the whistle and released a gush of steam that spread across the platform in front of us. As intermittent sprays of steam were released, I watched the driver preparing to back the train out of the station. I watched the large wheels slowly move then slip on the track a number of times before getting a firm grip. I'm sure for the benefit of his audience the driver gave the toggle of the whistle another pull, resulting in the same screeching whistle. As the giant train gradually lumbered out of the station it vanished behind its own curtain of steam, smoke and clinkers. I had not been this close to a steam engine before. What a wonderful start to a holiday.

Meanwhile our teacher/supervisor had been given further instructions and got us moving again to our designated platform but before we stepped on the train, we were given another short, but none the less, boring lecture on behaviour and concluded by saying: "Now, get on the train".

We broke from being a group and with total disregard of her words ran the short distance like maniacs to the carriage doors.

We all piled aboard and rushed for a position nearest to a window. The hitherto harnessed excitement now knew no restraint, what a lark!

Until the teacher managed to get into the carriage we were running about and jumping up and down on the seats like frantic monkeys. A loud authoritative clap of the teacher's hands and a shout of command instructing us to find a seat put a stop to our excited riot. When she was sure of being heard she told us she was very angry and ashamed of us all and demanded we behaved ourselves for the rest of the journey.

Pat, having been quietly and innocently seated throughout the commotion, was upset that she had been included in the 'telling off' but that's democracy!

The guard walked passed checking each carriage that doors were closed and not until the guard had walked the length of platform did he indicate that the train was ready to depart.

He blew his whistle, waved a green flag and we were ready to go! The whistle was also a signal for heads to fill any spare space that was vacant in the open carriage windows.

The train gave a jolt as the heavy chains and hooks linking the carriages took up all of their slack. The train moved off. We were on our way to leave the war and the city behind us.

Our first instruction was to close the windows and not to open them again. We were also told the food parcels were not to be opened until we were given something to drink at our first stop. We could not eat until then. Apart from not approving of the teacher being in charge, I enjoyed the day and I do not recall seeing anyone not getting similar pleasure.

I must not overlook to mention that, statistically, most of the children on the train, unlike Pat and I, would most likely have never been any further than the area they lived in. That is to say that the majority had never travelled to the coast to see the sea or the countryside or seen live farmyard animals.

The exception being a horse: Petrol engines had not yet completely replaced the horse.

After a short while I got restless. It was a terrible strain for any schoolboy with my nature to remain unoccupied for anything but a short time, so I set about devouring the contents of my food parcel.

One uncontrollable wretch, that could have been my mirror image, sitting in a seat opposite, noticed I had started tucking into my food parcel shouted to me "teacher said you mustn't eat your rations yet",

"Sod the teacher, you an' all ".

"I'll tell teacher you said that".

"Go on then if you want a punch on the nose ".

My threat was an empty one, no more than a spontaneous reaction to a challenge. The fearless and threatening exchange of words continued for some time without action taking place. But a scuffle having started further down the corridor diverted interest away from my adversary so I continued to eat with no more aggravation.

When approximately half of the journey had been completed and my packed lunch gone and long forgotten, the train slowed down to stop at a station. As the train came to a halt, a number of trolleys were pushed onto the platform containing bottles of milk and other cold drinks. We were given a choice and one lady in a blue pinafore dress asked us all; "Have you all still got your food packs?"

I was the only one that said "no".

"Why not?" she asked.

I thought if I told the truth, I would be less likely to get another pack. I went for the only lie I could think of.

"I've lost it miss".

I was handed another one, but not being content with one extra pack, like the gambler that keeps betting, while on a lucky streak,

"My sister has lost her one as well miss".

After some "tut, tuts" and a disbelieving look I returned to my seat with a bottle milk, another two packs of sandwiches and two oranges.

I bought off the threats of being exposed, by the potential informer opposite, by giving him one of my extra cheese sandwiches.

Only the passing of time eased Pat's anxiety that we would be put into prison for having had extra food parcels.

The second pack tasted better than the first.

THREE

DEVON GLORIOUS DEVON

"I have never let my schooling interfere with my education".
Mark Twain.

The long train journey came to an end at Teignmouth and after a carriage-by-carriage check had been completed, we were escorted from the platform to an open space outside the South Coast Railway Station and lined up as though for inspection.

Any onlooker observing the amount of physical and administrative effort that was being consumed to establish where and to whom we were going, could have easily come to the conclusion that someone in higher office had, just for a laugh, shuffled the cards.

All the allocations that had previously been arranged, prior to our arrival, had been lost. The potential foster parents were gathered in the railway station area on one side of a white line, while us evacuees remained on the other. It could have been an auction at a cattle market, with children substituted for cows. In all probability the area we had assembled in were cattle pens.

We were lined up in one straight line as though we were about to face a firing squad. When the allocating commenced there was little fuss, but as the distribution progressed and the choice became more limited the potential foster parents dissatisfaction became more vociferous. Although the selection became slower, progress was maintained. When only about twenty of us urchins remained, the selection became difficult. The 'bottom of the barrel' was clear to see:

"I will have that one there, no not him, the one next to the boy with grey cap".

From another potential foster parent: "The girl behind the boy with the torn trousers, yes that one" and so it went on.

It continued until each temporary parent was reasonably happy.

Even at my young but not so tender age I knew what was going on, I felt degraded and angry by the insensitive method of selection.

Pat and I were eventually but reluctantly accepted, I say reluctant because the women that had volunteered to take us had originally requested to care for a little girl only. Pat looked respectable enough and would have suited anyone of our audience but I wasn't on any list of attractions.

The scruffy looking little tearaway brother standing next to her must have looked a liability: I was wearing an old shirt that had once been my father's. To make the shirt fit around the neck, but nowhere else, Mum had cut a strip out of the material from the collar down to the tail and stitched it together to make it fit around my chest. The sleeves were shortened to make the cuffs expose my hands but where the tops of the sleeves should have started at my shoulders the seams were at my elbows, it remained without a collar.

I stood my ground, as much as a six-year-old boy can, I loudly said, "My Mum and Dad said we have to be billeted together". I was firm that we both slept under the same roof.

My determination that I would not be separated from my Sister won through. Before dark agreement was reached between the local allocating authority and our new foster parents.

We were ushered into a car and drove along the sea front, a drive much more comfortable than at the beginning of our journey, through Brixton in a dustcart.

Not until we were led through the side door of our new residence and passed behind the 'bar' did I know we were going to stay in a public house. The publican's doubt of our 'fitting in' proved to be well founded, for I didn't settle down at all well.

From the onset our stay was doomed to be an unhappy one, our foster parents had no children of their own so there were no children's toys to play with and no books to read.

The accommodation was totally unsuitable but as there was a war on, finding a roof and a bed must have been the council's prime objective and the luxury of being happy was, most likely, last on the list of their considerations. The only access to the private living quarters of the 'pub' was from the bar to a staircase that led to the first floor, where our room was situated. There was no front garden. The front door of the pub' opened directly onto the pavement.

Pat and I were not allowed in any room other than the one we slept in. We were not allowed in the toilet in the private quarters. We had to use the customers' toilets in the yard by the shortest route to the side door.

Our only playground was a large concrete courtyard at the rear of the pub where the customers' toilets were sited. The area, something like a present day open sided carport, was packed with barrels and wooden crates filled with bottles.

Had we been granted the privilege of using the occupant's private toilet inside, I guess we would not have had the freedom to visit our 'exercise yard'.

I cannot recall eating together around a table as a family nor can I remember attending school there.

Except for three unpleasant events, I remember little of our stay but that is most likely due to the shortness of the duration. I associate our short stay with barbed wire, playing cards and coming perilously close to drowning.

Had I not have taken a few marbles with me, from London, I would have had nothing to occupy myself.

The publican must have been aware of their shortcomings and tried to compensate by giving Pat and I packs of old playing cards to keep us quite. The value of cards, as an item of entertainment, to children aged four and six years old is limited but we played snap and we also used them for building pyramid houses.

Part of the coastal shore defences around England, consisted of land mines, anti personnel mines and barbed wire, Teignmouth was no exception.

The spiked wire ran along the beech as far as the eyes could see. It was unrolled from large heavy coils about fifteen yards out from the promenade that allowed pedestrians a narrow safe path when the tide was out.

The sight of the barbed wire along the beach, that became submerged when the tide was in, was obviously to hinder the advance of the expected German seaborne invasion. For people that usually went for a swim the mines buried in the sand on the seaward side of the wire had a persuasive influence to discourage the sport:

Even the least inquisitive reader may question the wisdom of the government transporting children, to escape the bombing, to an area where it was considered vulnerable as an attractive site for the enemy to make its expected invasion. It's a question for which I have no answer. But good fortune prevailed and England was not invaded, the German army did not arrive.

The only adventure that I can remember my Sister and I were involved in during our stay in Teignmouth was getting trapped between the sea wall, the barbed wire and the incoming tide:

We had walked down the steps, from the promenade to the beach, to play on the sand. The tide was out and the sea was a long way beyond the other side of the barbed wire barrier. As we played and built sand castles neither of us were aware of the length of time that had elapsed. I only became alert that we were in any danger by hearing shouting above us. I looked up and saw a small group of people leaning over the promenade, shouting excitedly and pointing towards the sea.

I had no need to understand the words they were shouting, being distracted from our play was enough. Neither Pat nor I had noticed the incoming tide. Immediately our attention was drawn to the water, I saw we were playing on a small island of sand. I had unwittingly chosen a raised area for us to play on. I grabbed Pat's hand and we both ran through the shallow water that was, in places, splashing against the promenade wall. At the deepest point the tide had come in to a height that came above my knees and before we reached the steps we were both soaked from head to foot.

Although the event is still clear in my mind, I am confused how it became possible for us to escape from the pub' to be there.

In addition to the playing cards we must have also been supplied with writing material, for I remember writing to Mum and Dad telling them we were not happy with our foster parents and our temporary home. I would not have been surprised to have later learnt that the publican had also written a very similar letter telling of our escape of near drowning and included his desire for our departure.

After being away from home and with our foster parents for no more than two weeks, Mum and Dad arrived one day at the doorstep. It was like a dream, I could not believe it was real. I wanted us all to leave immediately and have a cuddle but I was to be disappointed. It seemed there was more urgent business for Mum and Dad to deal with. Talking to our short-term foster parents was more important than for a friendly family greeting.

After a short conversation, however, Mum asked Pat and I if we would like to go home. What joy the memory brings.

The answer from Pat and I was displayed by our enthusiastic jumping up and down excitedly. Mum accompanied Pat and I to our bedroom and quickly gathered up our small quantity of clothing. I looked out of the window overlooking the street and saw Dad still talking to the publican.

With a few packs of playing cards in a paper carrier bag, I followed Mum and Pat and walked out of our room for the last time. I was last as we walked down the stairs and as I walked passed the bar I picked up a packet of cardboard beer mats and slipped them into my coat pocket. I didn't want them I just wanted to take something.

We walked out into the street from the pub's front door, to see Dad standing by the open, near side, door of his 'cab' still in serious but not unfriendly, conversation with the pub' owner.

As soon as we had arrived back on the scene Dad's attention was diverted to Pat and I and their conversation came to an end with them shaking hands.

Dad lifted me by the waist and placed my feet on the mudguard, above the large front wheel with a push he helped me on to the seat. I slid along to the middle of the bench seat that stretched the width of the cab. In the same manner from the kerbside Dad assisted Pat, Mum managed without Dad's assistance.

I watched Dad as he walked around the front of the lorry and climb into the driver's seat. We all squeezed up together and as Dad moved to close the door by his side, I inhaled the splendid warm, almost anaesthetic, cocktail of his sweaty smell of body odour and diesel oil.

In addition to my own tingling happy excitement of being rescued, I was pleased for Dad I sensed the pride radiating from him now he had collected his 'flock' around him again. I enjoyed the closeness of the four of us cramped together, in a space designed for two, as we excitedly exchanged news. I sat nearest to Dad with the gear change lever between my parted legs.

He started the noisy Diesel engine, rearranged my legs to move the gear stick and without looking back, at the two people standing in the pub doorway, we started moving.

Above the noise of the engine Mum told us that London was no different. The expected air raids had not happened and even though the fear of an immediate aerial bombardment had diminished we were not yet going back to our two rooms in the capital.

Dad informed us we were going to live with Mum and stay in a house of our own. Had I heard correctly? We were going to live together again and in our own house.

We spent only a short time in our cramped positions in the lorry, for our new home was only ten miles, or so, away in Topsham:

I believe Topsham was too large to be a classified as a village but, at most, it was only a very small town. The population eight years later in 1948 was 3,500.

Due to the war, Topsham had an increase in population from the pre-war era because the dockside warehouses had been partly converted to billet soldiers that worked on the docks:

Topsham had a dockside served by the fast flowing River Clyst and a small quayside. There was a lot of commercial activity on the dock by fishermen, with their privately owned assortment of boats and trawlers, also local fishermen and seamen employees of owners of larger sailing ships.

The River Clyst was ideal for rod or line fishing and with little more than a five minutes walk away from my new house I very soon took advantage of a cost free pastime. The riverbank and the dockside accounted for most of my daylight activities. A large portion of the waterway area remained outside military control.

The local railway station was five minutes walk away. Exeter, to the North, and Exmouth to the South were only a short journey away by train. A spur line ran to the quay where The Navy, Army and Air Force Institute, NAAFI, warehouse was sited.

During the period I lived in Topsham, The NAAFI was guarded by the military. I am guessing but I believe it to be sound that while Dad was making one of his regular deliveries or pick-ups to or from the NAAFI at the Topsham warehouse, he gained some information regarding an empty house and secured a tenancy.

Our new address was: 29 Monmouth Road. Topsham. Exeter. Devon.

The outside of the small three-bedroomed terraced house had a 'mini' grand Georgian appearance with an imposing pillar each side of the front door:

The pillars supported an open sided roofed vestibule to give shelter while 'key fumbling'.

An oddity of the interior of the building that I had not seen elsewhere was the layout of the three upstairs bedrooms: One of the bedrooms was situated behind the other with no corridor. That is to say the third bedroom could only be reached by walking through the second bedroom.

My room, the third and end bedroom, although as wide as the second, was not as long but I was happy with the arrangement because it allowed me an extra minute or two in bed each morning.

The main feature and luxury, for a short time at least was the fact that Pat and I had our own room.

There was neither hot nor cold running water: Water was drawn up from a natural well by a hand pump situated in the yard just outside the kitchen door. That alone would not be so unusual for country dwellers except for the fact that the well was under the floor in the kitchen. Fifty years on, it is difficult to imagine a kitchen sink with no water taps but household domestic problems were not mine. My only daily consideration was how much fun I could squeeze into one day and Topsham had all the ingredients for fun.

It was a schoolboy's dream; it had a railway track, a bridge, a tunnel, two rivers, a dock, a quayside and a water mill.

Moving down river, within one hundred yards, before reaching Fisher's Bridge Mill, the River formed a whirlpool. The river passed the mill, under the road bridge and skirted Topsham to, eventually, join the River Exe. All of this was my playground.

I am sure it was not by chance that the London evacuees were scattered thinly throughout the town. I make this point because the small influx of Londoners were regarded as thieving gypsies and foreigners by the inhabitance and the local authority wanted to avoid 'alien' ethnic gangs being formed:

I know from experience what it is like to be a foreigner and most probably why I have sympathy for asylum seekers, of any nationality, seeking residency in foreign surroundings.

When I got involved with any activity that was not socially acceptable it was a result of being in company with other local boys. When I was alone, I was able to keep out of trouble:

Some of my adventures were with school acquaintances but most times I made my own entertainment. It made little difference to me, however, I did what I wanted to do, with or without friends.

That is not to say I was a devout 'loner'. I could share my fun with anyone. While I lived in Topsham, I did not have a 'best friend' or any friend that I knew well enough to knock on their door, or vice versa, nor did I seek company. I didn't give it a thought then but I don't think I was the exception.

People didn't travel anything like today and many were ignorant of what was beyond the area outside their own walking distance.

Most of the locals regarded the evacuees with suspicion. But I have read documentation that suggested many evacuee children were greeted by their foster parents with 'open arms' and made welcome. That may well be true but my opinion is based on my own experience, which I found to be totally the opposite.

Although most of the time I was alone, there was plenty of fun waiting to be had. I had no 'hang-ups', playing with children I knew from school and the local dopey children with funny Devon accents. They couldn't even talk proper English.

I remember my first Christmas in Topsham not for snow or bad weather but because I mistakenly found, in a cupboard, my Christmas toy, that Dad had made, beating Santa Claus by about two weeks.

Because of the wartime restriction on nonessential items, most of our toys were home made and many children had to be satisfied with an apple and a new penny, the more fortunate could have even got an orange. As a statement of fact that is true but in our case we always had at least one toy.

Dad was ingenious at making 'something out of nothing'. He made all of our toys, Christmas or not. The scarcity of money was the greater problem.

Generally, at any given time, there was always a toy in the process of being made. His list of completed handy work projects included; A toy garage, a dolls house with furniture (not for me) a skittle board, a bagatelle board, a fort, a galleon, hoopla board, an archery set, croquet and the list goes on.

The feared mass air raids on the cities of the British Isles by German bombers had not yet begun.

After the invasion of Poland, the next warring activity came from Russia when in November, she invaded Finland. The Fins' defended fiercely and put up a magnificent show of resistance. The fighting continued for over three months and ceased only after a treaty was signed on 13th March 1940:

The Russian Foreign Secretary's name, at that time, was Vyacheslav Molotov and for the obvious reason he was known only by his surname. It was during the Finnish/Russian conflict the petrol bomb 'Molotov Cocktail' was first used.

The idea of the cheap but very effective bomb was made from petrol being poured into a glass bottle and sealed at the neck with a piece of waste cloth. The cloth was then ignited and thrown. On hitting an object, preferable the target, the bottle broke and the spilt petrol then ignited.

Brave soldiers and civilians climbed onto Russian tanks and throwing the fragile incendiary inside the turret made an effective use of the new and cheap weapon.

This simple petrol bomb has been used world wide ever since and of course has retained its name.

In spite of the setback by the escalation of the Russo-Finnish conflict, there was still hope that peace talks, between Britain and Germany, would take place before the war started proper. Optimism was such, in December 1939, of those children evacuated from London and other potential target areas, approximately fifty per cent had returned to their homes by Christmas. The winter of 1939 went by with no bad weather to restrict any of my activities and the 'peaceful war' carried on.

In the new year of 1940, everyone was issued with a food rations book. Not only did food become rationed there were controls limiting the consumption of a variety of everyday commodities. Coupons were required for Coal, Clothing, Petrol and Furniture: Newly wedded couples were given extra furniture dockets to furnish a flat. Not rationed was a glass of beer at sixpence a pint.

Pat and I were too young to absorb the importance and the implications of the perilous situation the country was facing, we walked to our school daily without interruption, or concern that anything would happen to change it.

Outside school hours I happily went fishing along the riverbank or from the quayside without fear.

I had a preference for the quay for as I sat on the edge of the small jetty, I watched the fishermen as they repaired their nets and lobster pots and I felt part of their industry.

In the High Street there was a shop that sold fresh fish during the morning and fried fish and chips in the afternoon and evening.

One afternoon, after using all of my worms, I was in need of some bait for my fishing hook. I walked into the fish shop and not knowing what to expect, I asked the man behind the counter if he had a free fish head for bait for fishing.

The cheerful shopkeeper, without giving me a bag or wrapping paper, put two slippery herrings heads in my hand.

"Come back tomorrow", he said "and I will save some large cods heads for you".

From then on, with my own small sack, I regularly went into the shop. I did not have to ask, a mere "hello" and he would put a quantity of fish cuttings in my small canvas holdall for the cost of no more than a "thank you".

The journey from the High Street was only a short distance of two or three minutes walk to my fishing spot in 'The Strand'.

One day I went fishing down 'The Strand' and like any other day I started out alone. While I sat fishing I was joined by some school acquaintances and as time elapsed and the tide ebbed our interest in fishing also began to recede. For a reason that I cannot remember something steered me towards some 'horseplay' with one of the locals that ultimately turned into us having a serious fight. As we wrestled on the rotting wooden planks of the short pier we rolled off the jetty and both fell onto light shingle over a soft muddy bed ten feet below.

I walked home covered from head to foot in mud and a very painful right arm. Mum was not very happy with me standing at the doorstep making the place look more untidy than normal. But it took little time to walk through the house to the pump in the yard and get clean.

I awoke the next morning to learn that Dad had returned during the night from a long distance delivery. My arm was still very painful so instead of going to school I was taken to see the doctor. I got pleasure from hearing the doctor tell Mum that he suspected my arm had been broken. After the doctor made a phone call, he handed Mum a note and told her to take me to the hospital in Exeter that day: This was pre National Health Service days and because the hospital existed by charity, no ambulance was supplied and Mum had to arrange our own transport. We took a bus to the hospital and were directed to the X-Ray department in the Exeter Royal Infirmary. The X-Ray confirmed, the doctor's diagnosis. I had a compound fracture.

Mum remained with me during the short time it took for the wet plaster bandage to be applied and get rock hard.

On the bus during our return journey to Topsham I was delighted to display my plastered wound.

Dad was still in bed sleeping off his all night driving when we returned home. I ran upstairs to the bedroom and woke him,

"Dad I've got a broken arm. I've got a confounded fracture and I didn't cry. I fell off the pier. I was unlucky the tide was out Dad wasn't

I?" I said excitedly.

He made no reference that my break was confounded.

Although I didn't think I was unlucky at all. I was proud of my arm covered in plaster. Dad was fully aroused but made no effort to lift his head from the pillow but I was pleased he wanted to talk to me.

"'Why do you think it was unlucky to break your arm because the tide was out Ron?" Dad asked, looking baffled that I had linked my broken arm with the outgoing tide.

"Well, if I had fallen when the tide was in, I would have fallen into water and the water would have broken my fall and I might not have broken my arm"

"Have you learnt to swim then?" Dad asked.

"No, not yet, but I am trying. I can nearly" I said, pleased that Dad was still interested.

"Well, that's a bit daft then isn't it? If you can't swim you could have drowned. You could also have broken your neck but it wouldn't have mattered then would it. I think it was lucky for you the tide had gone out!"

I was disappointed that Dad had so quickly found a flaw in my silly logic. I had not impressed him. I had wanted Dad to tell me I had been very brave but he had only told me I was a bit daft. I did not pursue his reasoning but I thought he had made a quick observation and a good one at that. I hoped, when I grew up, I would get out of the habit of making stupid statements.

I went to school the following day eager to display my new super cast. I was the centre of attraction. I felt so pleased I wasn't looking forward to it coming off.

After being the centre of attraction for a week, I returned to hospital and the plaster was cut away and unceremoniously discarded into a waste bin.

The only other restriction to my activity, while I was in Devon, was again a short term one:

As the summer came to and end my eyes became sore and after

a few days they started to weep. The discharge became so sticky that after a few more days elapsed, upon waking, I was unable to open them. To release the adhesion I had to bath them with warm water and as the problem did not improve Mum took me to see the doctor. The doctor diagnosed conjunctivitis: and prescribed an ointment to use in each eye at night and bathe in water each morning but after another week went by there was no sign of improvement.

On returning to the doctor, he made an appointment for me to see an eye specialist, again at Exeter Hospital, the next day. We had to walk down Monmouth Hill to catch the bus and while we were waiting at the bus stop by The Lighter Inn an army lorry came out the quayside army warehouse, pulled up and the driver offered us a lift:

Mum was an attractive slim young women then, still in her twenties and able to get a second look from a man as she passed. Mum took advantage of the offer and accepted but put me in the cab first so that I sat between Mum and the driver.

The journey was uneventful and the driver dropped us off outside the main entrance of the Exeter Royal Infirmary, said "good bye" and drove off.

Once inside the hospital we took a seat and after a long wait we were shown into an office. While a doctor examined me he asked Mum some questions and took notes. A nurse came into the room and while Mum remained with the doctor, she took hold of my hand and led me along a corridor to another small room at the end of a ward.

The small room was a linen cupboard. The nurse selected a pair of pyjamas for me to wear, not until then was I informed that I was to be admitted and my Mother had left the building. I could not understand why Mum had not told me. Either she had been advised by the doctor not to do so, or she just did not know how to handle it. At the time, however, I wasn't looking for any reason that would excuse Mum from deserting me. I felt a lonely prisoner and angry because I could do nothing, Mum had left without saying goodbye. I cried for a long time. I had been abandoned but after I had been bathed by a nurse and dressed in pyjamas I felt better.

While a nurse held my hand and I stood at the entrance of the ward I noticed it was very long with, what looked like, an endless line of beds on each opposing walls. Boys were on one side and girls on the other.

All of the patients were about my age and all watched me as I was led, by the hand, to the middle of the ward to my bed.

The bed felt very strange, it was so high. I had never been in such new, clean white, starch stiffened sheets before it was also the first time I had worn a pair of pyjamas.

I began to cry again as I climbed into bed and a young nurse tried to console me by telling me I would be going home in a day or two. I cried myself to sleep.

I cannot say, for sure, why I should have been so upset. It had not bothered me to say goodbye when Pat and I had been evacuated. Considering the situation and my character as it is now, maybe I was angry that I had not been asked to stay.

I awoke the next morning with all of my anger from the day before gone and my objection of being abandoned was forgotten. As I had not been confined to my bed a nurse told me to wash and dress and showed me where to go for my breakfast. After I had eaten porridge and a couple of slices of bread with jam on, I was told I could get a book out of the library.

I cannot remember the treatment I received but on that first day I learnt, from one of the boy's in my ward, the hospital had a garden. The garden had well kept flowerbeds and lawns but more important than the flowers it also had an orchard.

The orchard was separated from the flowers and grass by an inner brick wall and the whole fruit growing area extended to the hospital perimeter wall. The orchard had many apple, pear and plum trees with their fruit ripe and after tasting one of the apples I decided I would pick some to take home. I began storing them along the side of the wall, where they would not be seen, and covered them over with long grass. Mum visited me the next day and I told her to bring with her two carrier bags on the day before I was to be discharged.

The second evening in hospital, when we were all in bed and no nurses were in the ward, one girl, almost opposite me sat up and suggested we should all play a game.

Her idea of a game, I was soon to discover, was not what I had played before. The game involved each one of to us stand on our bed and expose our private parts.

She told us the rules and she volunteered to go first if the boy in the opposite bed went second. There were no objections so the 'game' began. Without any sign of modesty, she stood up and lifted her nightgown. After exposing herself in a bold pose, with her nightgown held high up to her chest for a couple of seconds she sat down, it was now a boy's turn. The boy repeated the process. The next girl to her went third the boy opposite the second girl going away from me went fourth and so on along the ward. The action was repeated, from the middle of the ward down to the end.

Because the peep show had started in the middle, after reaching the end of the ward the 'lifting of nightgowns and dropping of pyjama trousers' continued at the other end of the ward working towards the centre. Some of the children were shy and the 'lifting and dropping' was little more than a blur to the onlooker, others confidently took their time and displayed their charms with a twist of the hips or a little dance. Each illicit showing brought my unwanted turn nearer, it arrived too soon.

I was the last to stand. I dropped my trousers just as the others had but that wasn't good enough for the girl opposite that had suggested the game. She said she could not see me properly and instructed me to hold my pyjama jacket higher. I did as I was instructed and at that precise moment, with my trousers around my ankles and my jacket up to my chest and boasting a full frontal exposure the duty nurse entered the ward.

All of the children had done exactly what I had just been caught doing but the nurse only saw me!

When the nurse had entered the ward, my fellow partners in the crime that had been sitting up in their beds gradually slid down into a sleeping position and kept quiet. As the nurse's attention was focused entirely on me, in her eyes I was a lone offender. No one else had done this obscene deed. The horrible little 'scruff' evacuee from London was corrupting her innocent little country cherubs. She was very cross and handled me roughly while tucking me back into my covers.

"You might do things like that in London but you don't do that sort of thing in my ward and If you continue to act like that you are doomed to walk with the devil" she said.

I made no comment but I knew that it was the girl opposite my bed that had caused the trouble. It had nothing to do with the devil:

Probably because many hospitals, before The National Insurance Act, 1946, had a reliance on charity they appeared to have a strong relationship with the church. Framed prints of Jesus on the cross and pictures of saints in wards were not an uncommon sight. Many hospitals were named after Saints, some still are, and the nurses' dress style were not very far removed from looking like a nun.

I knew boys shouldn't look up girl's clothes nor anywhere where knickers are worn and most important, when they were not worn!

It was daft playing with girls anyway. It wasn't proper fun like, being chased off an orchard by the farmer or knocking on doors and running away.

Had it have given me some pleasure maybe I would not have felt angry. My only reason for joining the junior exhibitionists was because I didn't want to be seen as being a killjoy. I was annoyed because girls had nothing to look at anyway. Boys did have something hanging that could be seen and another thing, girls can't pee over the school playground wall.

The nurse interrupted my sulking thoughts and told me she was going to report me to the matron, who in turn would tell my mother:

Matron was the nursing equivalent to the army's Regimental Sergeant Major.

I spent an agitated night dropping in and out of shallow sleep. I was angry being the only one that got caught and therefore the only one that was told off. I was also anxious about the outcome in the morning.

My mother visited me the next day and I was relieved that she made no mention of the nurse's threat and, to my knowledge, no more was said of the matter but I still felt I needed to get my own back and it was a good excuse for me to 'pinch' as much fruit from the orchard as I could manage.

Each day for the remainder of the week, I wandered to the end of the hospital garden, where the fruit trees were, and made a separate pile of apples and pears and stacked them against a brick wall ready for collection on my departure day. I hid them behind some bushes and to make the camouflage complete I covered them with grass.

On the sixth day Mum told me my eye infection had been cured and I would be going home the next day. I asked Mum to bring a carrier bag with her, whether she brought them I cannot recall, it wasn't necessary anyway.

The next morning before Mum arrived, I walked to the end of the garden to inspect my apple store and found them to be either all going rotten or covered with slugs and wasps and partly eaten. None of them were worth taking; the insect life had already had their dinner from them.

During the journey home I spoke to Mum of the pile of fruit that I had stored and how it all came to be rotten. I cannot remember Mum making any comment but I am sure had I have been with Dad he would have responded with an educational lecture but even without a lecture, I still learnt something about gardening.

A few weeks after I was discharged from hospital, Pat had an accident that required a visit to the doctor:

Sometimes Dad, while working for NAAFI, would drive all

night and other irregular hours and therefore returned home and slept at odd hours.

One morning Pat and I heard Dad arrive home and rapidly seeking somewhere to hide we scrambled over the top of the settee. As Pat dropped over the back, without wearing shoes, she caught her foot, or one of her toes, on a nail that was sticking out of the wooden frame. The nail, like a knife, gave her a nasty cut that bled profusely. The sight of blood around Pat's foot and on the floor took away all the excitement that usually followed Dad's return home. During the time that Pat was at home with her foot bandaged, a school inspector came to the house to check her absence from school was genuine.

The fact that Dad was unable to bring home an income to bring us above the poverty line was not an unusual situation. Wages were designed to keep the working class at that level. Dad was one of millions but I do wonder how many more years would have elapsed before the social structure was to change had the war not have intervened.

The poverty that still remains as normal over some parts of the world today is a good reminder of how it was. But the situation was normal to us. I was not aware we were deprived of anything.

One item, in particular, I knew was not 'up to scratch' and I didn't boast about, was our shortage of crockery. At one time, my substitute for a cup was a small jam jar with a 'Robinsons' golliwog label. I called it my wolligog cup:

A golliwog, not a wolligog, was a doll of an imaginary character with a black face and black curly hair. The doll is believed to have originated in an American childrens storybooks that was first published in 1895.

In 1910 Robinsons Jam's adopted this character as its trademark. Robinson's withstood a lot of bad publicity from racial equality groups but eventually dropped the last three letters to take 'wog' from the name and introduced a new name of Mr Golly.

In 2001 the image of a black doll was scrapped.

FOUR

A NEW PRIME MINISTER AND THE GREAT ESCAPE

"I have nothing to offer but blood, toil, tears and sweat. You ask what is our aim? I can answer that in one word: Victory.
Victory at all cost,
Victory, in spite of all terror,
Victory however hard and long the road may be,
For without victory there is no survival".
  Winston Churchill, 1874-1965,
  House of Commons,
  May 13, 1940.

On 23rd February 1940 my parents had their fourth child and my sister, Bebe, was born. I failed to mention previously my mother had her first child in 1932. He was born premature and because he was so small he was referred to as Tom Thumb but actually Christened William Henry and only saw two days of life.

On May 10th, German forces launched an attack on Belgium, which resulted in Belgium's capitulation on 23rd May. In the same action Rotterdam was virtually destroyed by German bombing raids to 'soften up' resistance against the German army crossing the Dutch border.

Within five days of German troops entering The Netherlands

(Holland) she was also overrun and surrendered on midnight 27th May.

The attack on The Netherlands coincided with the first attack of the war on English soil by one lone German aircraft.

The same day, resulting from the German initiative on the continent, the British Parliament put pressure on Neville Chamberlain, now seventy years old and dying from cancer, to resign. He did so and at 6 o'clock that evening Winston Churchill became the new Prime Minister.

Winston Churchill, now already renown for his stirring patriotic speeches, on June 4th gave a memorable broadcast on the radio. The content should have quashed any idea that Hitler may have held that Great Britain was about to surrender. His characteristic slow, dramatic and slurred speech inspired the nation.

"We shall defend our island home and outlive the menace of tyranny, if necessary for years, if necessary alone.

We shall not flag nor fail.

We shall go on to the end.

We shall fight in France.

We shall fight on the seas and oceans.

We shall fight with growing confidence and growing strength in the air,

We shall defend our island, whatever the cost may be.

We shall fight on the beaches.

We shall fight on the landing grounds.

We shall fight in the fields and in the streets.

We shall fight them in the hills.

We shall never surrender."

With the French armies in full retreat, the British Expeditionary Force, BEF, made their way to Dunkirk.

By 4th June, after five days of frantic activity, over 226,000 British and over 123,000 French troops were lifted off the beaches and saved from being taken prisoners of war by the German army. All of the heavy guns, ammunition and vehicles, large and small, were left behind in France.

The evacuation at Dunkirk, 'Operation Dynamo', was the greatest escape story of all time. Dunkirk concentrated the minds of the nation that the war was now very real and all thoughts of phoniness came to an end. The evacuation of Dunkirk stimulated new thinking. With such a desperate shortage of men at home the evacuation of such a large force from Dunkirk was a blessing.

At the outbreak of war, in 1939, two fifths of the world's land surface was part of the British Empire.

The British Empire was the biggest empire the world had ever known and most of the British army was still serving in the colonies in Hong Kong, The Pacific Islands, Singapore, Ceylon, India, Burma, South America, Africa, Palestine, Aden, Egypt, Cyprus, Malta, Falkland Islands and Gibraltar and if I haven't covered the world that is my mistake.

The path was clear for German forces to continue their advance and cross the English Channel, or so it seemed, just one little precursor remained to knock out The Royal Air Force and gain superiority of the sky over England.

On June 10th Mussolini, the dictator of Italy, to be on the winning side, decided to join Germany and declared war on Britain and France.

The French government made an unsuccessful appeal to the US President for help. Four days later the victorious German army entered Paris.

Continuing his triumphant move south, Field Marshal Erwin Rommel was joyfully quoted, in a broadcast in Germany as saying "The war has turned into a lightning tour of France".

The French military position was now hopeless and a new French government, led by Marshall Petain asked for an armistice. The terms of the armistice divided France in two, one controlled by the German military and a French puppet government led by Pierre Laval administered the South of the country.

During the following twelve months Great Britain was in constant fear that an invasion of the British Isles was imminent. The British war cabinet believed a large force of airborne soldiers would precede a sea-borne invasion.

The English coastline 'sprouted' dense rolls of barbed wire, concrete gun emplacements, anti-tank pillars, scaffold poles and many other items all designed for the purpose of repelling, or at least making a landing difficult for, an invading sea-borne enemy.

In spite of Britain's such obvious defiance against the aggressor, it was not discovered until the end of hostilities, that Hitler was still hopeful, at this point, that Great Britain would 'throw in the towel'. It was not until July 2nd, 1940, some nine months into the war, that Hitler ordered a study plan of the feasibility of an invasion of The British Isles.

Why did he leave it so long? The answer, in the view of many historians is that Hitler was convinced there was a large enough anti Semitism in influential places in Britain that would force the government not to fight against his anti Jewish views and seek peace terms.

On 18th June in the House of Commons, Winston Churchill gave another inspiring speech:

"The whole fury and might of the enemy must very soon be turned on us. Hitler knows that he will have to break us in this island or loose the war. If we fail, then the whole world, including the United States and all that we have known and cared for will sink into the abyss of a new dark age made more sinister and perhaps more protracted, by the lights of a perverted science. Let us therefore brace ourselves to our duty and so bear ourselves that if the British Empire and its Commonwealth lasts for a thousand years men will say this was their finest hour".

More wonderful stirring words!

For Dad's 34th birthday present, Mum bought him a new ukulele banjo, to replace a rather old instrument he had possessed for many years. Later, when the Blitz started, he practiced regularly while we were taking cover from the bombing in the garden shelter: Dad always played and having a Lancashire accent helped with his impersonation of singing like George Formby. The only other home entertainment was the radio.

By the end of June, with the exception of Portugal, Spain, Switzerland and Sweden, which remained neutral throughout the war, the Mainland of Western Europe was occupied by enemy Forces. Britain stood alone and isolated to face the mightiest war machine the world had ever seen.

The British Expeditionary Force was back home from Dunkirk and still had the will to fight but what weapons could they fight with? All of the artillery, ammunition, equipment and vehicles were abandoned in France.

Britain had only 500 field guns and very few anti-tank weapons left to defend our island. The ground of the expected German invasion area covered about 800 miles of British coastline.

It was revealed, after the war, the military were so short of small arms, machine guns in particular, that had the invasion of the German army come during the summer of 1940, we would have had only one machine gun per mile to defend the entire English coastline.

The weather was glorious but mines and barbed wire along the English coast discouraged a summer beach holiday!

Although there had been constant bombing raids on ships passing through the Straits of Dover, bombing on the mainland did not commence until the summer:

The official date for 'The Battle of Britain' is from July to October 1940. But, the official dates could be misleading for they are the dates that qualified fighter command pilots for the award of a medal 'The Battle of Britain Clasp': The importance of the Battle of Britain was the battle of control of the skies and it was critical to stop Hitler achieving his required precondition for the invasion of England.

There is general agreement among British military historians that the precise date The Battle of Britain started was on 10th July and came to an end 31st of October 1940. The residence of the Channel Islands, however, could be forgiven for thinking The Battle of Britain started two weeks earlier for it was bombed on 28th June: Through a quirky piece of history dating back to the Norman Conquest, 1066, although the Channel Islands are part of Great Britain and the British Isles they are not part of the United Kingdom.

Had Hitler remained alive after the war, he also could have argued that the end date was incorrect. Having his finger alone 'on the button' knew different. Two weeks earlier on 17th October he had postponed the invasion of England and deferred it to The Spring of 1941.

When the first German soldiers were dropped on Guernsey 30th June, the British garrison had already pulled out with all equipment. Jersey fell the next day and by the 4th of July all of the Channel Islands were under German occupation. There was no resistance.

This was the first time since the Norman Conquest an invader had occupied any part of The British Isles.

The first of the 'heavy' air raids began in July and during August the first daylight air raid on London began. 'The Blitz' was to come later.

'Blitzkrieg', Lightning war, was a successful tactic used by the German military to 'soften up' their enemy by using aircraft in dive-bombing raids before sending in ground troops. When the bombing over London in 1940 became an every night occurrence British newspapers shortened the German word' blitzkrieg to 'Blitz'. The word became synonymous with this particular part of the war and has remained in the English dictionary ever since.

Hitler's *'Adlerangriff'*, Attack of the Eagles, began by concentrating his bombing on mainland England's airfield's ground organisation. The plan was to destroy all aircraft while still on the ground and disrupt communications, thereby knocking out any resistance in the air from the Royal Air Force.

Had the plan been successful it would then have allowed the Luftwaffe their *'Adler Tag '*, Eagle Day, the freedom of the sky.

It was a tactic that had been tested and proven successful by the German Air Force in the Spanish Civil War and in Poland. True or not, it was reported that one German bomber, strictly against his orders, dropped some bombs on London. In retaliation the RAF bombed Berlin the following night. It was an action that Hitler had promised the German people would never happen. In anger, Hitler discarded the wisdom of relying on a sound and well tested strategy. He halted his plan, to 'knock-out' the airfields in England that was on the brink of succeeding and diverted his rage towards London.

Had Hitler not changed tactics, his precondition for 'Operation Sea Lion', the German code for the invasion of England, to commence would almost certainly have been fulfilled: The German intelligence network, by remarkable good fortune, also got their homework wrong.

Our aircraft losses had exceeded the safety level for our defence and our bombed airfields were in a critical need of repair. The Luftwaffe strategy to divert from the original plan and bomb the docks and the civilian population in London began on 7th September. This action gave Britain the time that it so preciously needed to repair the radar systems and the runways on the airfields.

British Chiefs of Staff believed that the heavy bombing on 7th September was the final indication that the German invasion of England was about to commence. On that night, 300 German bombers, escorted by 600 fighters, dropped incendiary bombs. Their main target was the docks in the East End of London. It was estimated between 430 to 450 London civilians were killed. Deep shelters and the underground railway system helped to protect many lives. Casualties in London for September and October were high – 13000 were killed.

On 15th September it was reported that 185 enemy aircraft were shot down. The correct number was in fact 56 but still a creditable amount. Not until the night of 3rd November was the sky over London quiet again from air raids.

The bombing had continued on the capital non-stop for 57 nights. But that is not to say there was no more bombing. During November,

Coventry was very badly bombed. Services were so badly damaged that all water had to be boiled before drinking. The civilian death toll for the month of November was nearly 7,000.

Meanwhile as the 'Blitz' continued over England, the war was just over one year old and the outcome looked very one sided in favour of Germany winning. The rewards of such a large, potential, victory encouraged El Presidenti Mussolini, The Dictator of Italy, to join in the conflict:

On September 13th Mussolini decided to chance his luck and attacked British troops in Egypt. The Italian army crossed, from the border of Libya into The British Protectorate of Egypt and advanced towards the port of Alexandria. The main objective was to command the shipping in the Mediterranean Sea and through the Suez Canal. The assault lasted three days after which British held the line and the offensive came to a halt at Sidi Barrani. The North Africa campaign had begun.

Summer was now in the wane and the invasion of England, Operation Sea Lion, remained, tantalisingly, just out of Hitler's reach.

When 'The Blitz' started, Grandmother Bridger, my Mother's Mother and my Uncle John, came to stay with us at Topsham. Within a week or two of her arrival, in spite of the heavy bombing still raging in London my Grandmother returned to her home in London; 49 Studley Road, Clapham.

Uncle John, aged twelve, settled in and remained until 1941 when the bombing raids over London became less frequent.

While John lived with us we had a common interest in line fishing and there were times when we would go to the quay together and fish from the River Clyst.

I use the term 'line fishing' in its truest sense because that is all it was. We had no rods, just line. We used fine strong twine with a fish head on a hook and just threw it out as far as we could from the quay into the river below. The weight of the bait took the end of the line out a good distance.

On most occasions the time we waited for a 'bite' was short but we always caught more crabs than fish. Because the crabs clung to the fish head, by pinching with claws and not caught by the hook, they often dropped off before the line was pulled back in. This suited me fine because I didn't like crabs and I never took them home, I always threw them back into the river. I was fishing for eels.

My catch for each session usually consisted of half a dozen or so and would measure between eight to twelve inches long and about an inch across.

Because of their long, thin and slippery nature it was always a fight to disentangle the eel from the hook, but that was all part of the fun. Eels always seemed to have a reserve of energy, they appear to stay alive much longer out of water than most other fish are able and they put up a longer sustained resistance after landing to get them detached from the hook. It was not unusual to struggle for a minute or two to release the hook that the eel would take advantage of being released and slither out of my hands and flip back into the river.

That what made the whole episode of my eel fishing worth remembering is due to just one event:

Early one afternoon, I was sitting next to John on the quay, both of us with a line, when he told me he had a 'bite'. After the usual sudden pull on the hook, the strain on the line ceased and for a minute or two caused no more excitement. The catch must have swum toward us for a longer time than usual but we assumed the fish had got free. John remained sitting casually 'pulling in' thinking he would need to put another head on the line:

Our normal rest position was sitting on the edge with our feet dangling over the side of the quay high above the water line; Like any other dockside there was no safety rails, not that we ever considered they were needed, there was only the occasional bollards. By good fortune it so happened we chose to sit next to one. Suddenly! John gave a lurch forward. I am sure that by instinct only, his hand 'shot out' and grabbed the bollards at his side. I do not know how he didn't get pulled down into the river ten feet below.

The incident remains, to this day, a snapshot in my memory; his bottom jerked up from a sitting position and both arms stretched outright, like a policeman on point duty halting oncoming traffic. It was a split-second reaction, one hand shot out and gripped the iron bollard his other hand still held onto his line. The danger was over in an instance, it had happened all to quickly for me to give John any assistance.

What had he caught? Whatever it was it was at first appeared to have got free as the line again went slack. I can still smile now easily reliving the situation, after all the years that have passed I can still hear John words "Sod it! I've lost it".

But the line suddenly tightened as the fish jerked and slapped against the concrete edge. He hadn't lost it! It was still on the end of his line. He had the determination not to let go of his catch and the wisdom to immediately regain a safer position by securely tying the line around the bollard by his side. It could be argued, it would have been safer for him to have the wisdom to let go but that was not his consideration. John continued to shorten the distance between him and his catch. Pull by pull he wound the line in around the sturdy metal ring of the bollard.

There were other school lads also fishing nearby that were attracted by the commotion of John's struggle. What John had on his line became a greater interest to them. They came to watch.

I stretched myself out full length on my tummy and looked over the edge to see what John had caught.

After a time he managed to get just the head of his prize out of the water, to relate I was alarmed by what I saw would be an understatement. The head was so big at first glance I thought it was a dead dog. It was the biggest eel I had ever seen.

Where as fresh water fish, like carp or roach are a beautiful clean silvery looking creatures, this big black shiny thing looked so evil I wanted John to let it go. Only after a lot of effort and manipulation the end of the eel had cleared the water was it was possible to judge its length. It must have been at least five foot long. Eventually John managed to land it onto the jetty but his early attempts at trying to release it from the hook were unsuccessful. It flapped and wriggled about and at one point of the struggle, when John managed to get a firm grip, it curled all over his body like an anaconda, up his arm and around his neck, it looked as though he was wrestling with an animated inner tube from a motor car's tyre.

Had the fish been able to sink its teeth over John's wrist I am sure it could have taken his hand off. It was a spectacular fight, worthy of being included in a Hollywood movie but he eventually managed to overcome the beast and unwind it from his body.

He won the struggle by being able to get a grip of the tail end and, driven by a mix of fear and anger, with a wide swing brought the head of the eel in contact with the jetty's concrete floor. He furiously repeated this action many times before the swift movements of the fish began to subside. The resistance of the eel had weakened and when the eel, having lost the fight, lay motionless we threw our remaining unused cods heads into the river, packed up our fishing gear and made our way home.

We passed the Lighter Inn and walked up Monmouth Hill and within ten minutes we stood under the porch in front of our street door. I knocked and at the same moment, we both turned and looked at each other and burst out laughing. We were still laughing when the door opened which was just as well for it eased the shock that confronted my Mother. With John's trophy over his shoulder, the eel's head and tail almost touched the pavement, John stood in front of her, stinking like an abandoned fish shop, covered in a shimmering, sticky slime. John took the eel through the house and placed it in the large dry terracotta sink that was sited next to the hand water pump in the yard. The fish stayed there all night. After breakfast, the following morning, I accompanied John out to the yard to assist in washing off the sticky slime before he cut it up. As John pumped water into the sink the eel started to move. I could not believe what I was seeing was real, we had both thought it was dead. It had survived the vicious head banging that John had inflicted and ten hours out of water. The eel's reincarnation, however, was short lived. After cleaning it under the pump, with one clean cut and without the slightest hesitation John chopped the head off. While it still wriggled John slit it along the belly. He pulled out and discarded a handful of the eel's 'inner working parts', with his hands covered in blood, he cut the body up into about two inch lengths and put them into a saucepan ready for stewing. I felt sick.

This was the first time I had witnessed the preparation for cooking and I wished I had not, but it did nothing to spoil my appetite for stewed jellied eels.

It was one of the few fishing evenings I spent with John but it is my most treasured. Most of my fishing was spent alone and I was happy doing what I wanted to do. When I packed up at the end of each day, I was always pleased even with a modest catch. I left the gutting to someone else.

John was twelve years old and during the short time he lived with us he made friends with a small group of local lads about his age and seemed to spend most of his 'out of school time' swimming.

About a mile from where we lived was a water mill. A little distance away from the mill the width of the riverbank narrowed which caused the water to run rapidly. Beyond that point between where the river began to run fast and the paddle of the mill, a whirlpool was created.

John and his friends spent most of their school summer holiday in their trunks in the river. Being all good swimmers one of their antics was to dive from the riverbank, one at a time and swim into the whirlpool to deliberately get caught in the drag. The velocity of the current would snatch them into a spin, when they were half way around they would swim furiously to break the pull and return to the riverbank. They always succeeded while we were living there; in this particular event there were no fatalities.

The stupidity of the act is almost too unbelievable to be true but true it is. Because I could not swim I watched from the riverbank envying their confidence and ability.

Further down river, as it flowed towards the River Exe it got wider. The teenagers performed their diving tricks without fear. It became a competition to achieve the most spectacular.

Another stunt they performed was to somersault while diving from a concrete ramp. The ramp was used as a slipway for small fishing boats into the river. One local fourteen year old dived into the river when the tide was going out consequently the water was not deep enough. He cut into the shallow water and plunged head first into a bed of mud. He was dead before he could be pulled out.

Like the 1914-1918 war, the German U boat had been a terrible threat to our shipping on the high seas and came near to starving Britain into submission.

By the end of the first month of the war in September 1939, a similar pattern to the First World War was emerging. Fifty-three British, Allied and neutral ships were sunk.

During October another twenty-seven ships when to the bottom of the sea with vital food supplies and materials that were so desperately needed to carry on the fight.

Both sides knew the power of the submarine and its ability to knock their supply lines. After the war Churchill stated that the success of the German U-boat, 'Unterseeboot', had been the only thing that frightened him.

Odd then that by the outbreak of war, Hitler had not paid more attention to the production of these awesome craft. In September 1939, at the outbreak of war, Germany had only 56 U-boats. Maybe Hitler was confident that Britain would not go to war and he would not need them.

Strange as it may seem, it has been recorded, that of all the U-boats that were launched, less than 50% fired a torpedo at a ship. Stranger still of the 870 U-boat on active service, 550 of them sank nothing.

The nature of Dad's job did not allow him to work normal hours, he would arrive home at all odd times of the day and night.

In times of peace, foodstuff would normally have been stored in warehouses at the docks. The warehouses were now scattered all over the country to smaller and safer inland storage depots. Sometimes Dad would be away, night after night, delivering food supplies, like a tramp steamer with no home port, from the docks to an army barracks or a warehouse.

Because petrol was in very short supply, lorries were not normally allowed to travel empty. This often frustrating order, meant that a delivery to anywhere in the country had to coincide with a pick-up. If after making a delivery, there was no load for a return journey to the lorry's home depot, the driver would have to wait or load up with a consignment to go somewhere else. Sometimes a day or two could elapse until something was available to allow a lorry to move. In some cases travel permits were issued to drivers to allow a lorry to be driven empty to another collection point or for the return journey home.

Timetables were also difficult to adhere to. The docks and barracks were target areas for enemy aircraft that meant schedules were largely determined by the accuracy or inaccuracy of enemy bombing.

One night Dad arrived home and parked his lorry outside the front door. Hanging over his shoulder he had a large white fish covered by a white muslin cloth. It was approximately eighteen inches across and six foot long in two separate halves. It had so much salt in, for a preservative, it was as stiff as a plank of wood. Dad hung it from a large hook on the kitchen wall but he was always very cautious of bringing 'Black Market' food into the house. In this case, he was uneasy about it being so blatantly on display and wanted it to be used as quickly as possible. Mum cut off four strips, put it in a pot and boiled it until it was cooked.

The fish was so salty it was inedible and not knowing how to eliminate the extremely high salt content it had to be disposed of. Dad dug a trench in the rear garden and buried it:

It was six years later, while I was helping Dad, as he worked on an engine in the garage, he spoke of the salty fish.

"Ron, do you remember, when we lived in Topsham, those two large stiff salty pieces of fish I brought home?" he said from underneath the car.

"Yes, I do. I also remember you buried it by the cherry tree".

"That's right! Well, somebody told me while I was at work today that it only had to have been soaked in fresh water for twenty four hours before boiling to remove the trace of salt and it would have been suitable for eating".

We didn't go back to Topsham to dig it up!

In addition to our legitimate weekly rations the 'Black Market' was not the only supply of extra food.

The local fishermen would often walk the streets during the evening with a costermonger's wheelbarrow trying to sell their day's catch. Accompanied to the clang of a hand bell, to make their presence known, they shouted out:

"A bob a basket, fresh fish, eels 'n crabs":

A basket of fish contained a varied assortment of sea creatures.

For a meal I had a special liking for stewed eels, mashed potatoes with parsley sauce and plenty of vinegar.

One afternoon in the late autumn, Pat and I returned home together from school and to our surprise Mum's youngest sister, Rose, was there; Rose had joined the army a few weeks previously and had come to spend a few days leave with us.

She was dressed in khaki and wore the uniform of the Women Royal Army Corps, WRAC.

Rose could not have been stationed very far away because after seeing her the first time in her uniform, she visited us regularly for short periods and many times she would get a twenty four hour pass and stop overnight.

When Aunt Rose's overnight stop coincided with Dad not being at home, Mum and Rose would walk down to the 'Lighter Inn' and spend most of the evening there.

Dad drank beer very little and I believe he never drank spirits but if he was at home during a period when Rose was on leave on a weekend pass they would all walk to the pub together.

We had no bathroom in the Topsham house and the only toilet was in a small brick built washhouse outside in the yard. There was no connecting door between house and toilet so entrance could only be gained by going through the kitchen and outside the house.

Our bathroom was a portable one, that is to say, it normally hung on the wall in the shed but we bathed in the kitchen. The shed was built onto the rear of the house that made our bath night a major operation. Dad was also the only one strong enough and tall enough to get the bath down from the wall and carry it from the garden to the kitchen. A bath, therefore, could only be taken when Dad came home.

To prepare for bath night all of the kitchen saucepans and kettles were collected and filled with water from the pump outside. A cast iron cooking range, the Grandmother of the present day Agar, was stoked up to boil enough water in the kitchen utensils to give us a sufficient supply of hot water.

The lucky one had the luxury of having the first bath.

There was never any question that clean water would accompany the next to get in. The cooling water in the just vacated bath was topped up with more hot water only if necessary for the next occupant. The guiding factor for the next body to enter the bath was the heat of the water. If it was hot enough, it was good enough. We bathed separately but the cleaning process was the same for each of us. I cannot be sure of the method of selection but Pat was always in the bath first. It made good sense for the smallest to be first and the dirtiest to be last. It was more than likely John or I would be last. Who would have wanted to get in after us? Each time the bath was vacated a coat of scum was skimmed from the top with a large saucepan in preparation for the next body to enter. The scum was not always attributed to grime from a body. The soap was responsible for much of the muddy effect on the water. I don't know if because of the war there was no other type of soap available but the only soap I ever saw in my house was a cheap unperfumed 'scrubbing soap', made from animal fats and antiseptic carbolic.

Comparing taking a bath to present day standards it could be considered an ordeal rather than a pleasure but Dad made bath night fun. After soaping and washing our hair he would prepare us for the rinsing by telling us to hold a flannel up to our eyes and then pour a saucepan with the water from the bath and pour the contents over our heads and finish off with the last rinse with clean water. Dad would also have a towel warming by the fire for when we were ready to get out of the bath, stepping out of the bath was accompanied by a hot wrap around and a rub down.

The drying of feet always brought a lot of laughter; Dad would cover one of his fingers with the towel and poke it between each toe and wiggle it around, the whole bathing routine was to extract as much fun as possible. When we had completed our bath there was the problem then for the disposal of the water that of course had to be emptied by the reverse process.

The bath had to be carried back out to the garden and hung on its position on a large nail in the wall of the shed, where it usually stayed for at least another week.

On one occasion, after returning home from school Mum let me into the house, I followed her down the hall until she turned off into the first room which was the sitting room at the front of the house. I continued on passed the staircase and into the dining room that led to the kitchen by a door with just a latch catch. The door was usually left open, on this occasion it was closed but I thought no more of it. I opened the door to walk into the kitchen to get to the back garden as I did so I was halted in the doorframe by a scream. It was my Aunt

Rose, standing upright and naked:

At the precise moment I had chose to enter the kitchen my Aunt, having completed washing herself, had just put one foot out of the bath. The other foot was still in the water. In panic, by trying to cover her vital parts with her hands, she lost her balance. She tried to save herself from falling but failed.

Her arms fluttered outwards as though attempting to imitate a bird flying. She neither flew nor corrected herself from falling. Both legs went upwards. She slipped over on her back and landed on the stone floor.

Winded for no more than a second or two, she posed brazenly exposing herself with her left leg hanging over the rim of the bath. I was surprised when I noticed was she wearing a pair of brief black knickers. In an instant, as she regained he senses, she broke her pose and rolled over to get both of her legs on the ground.

As she turned away from me, to hide her private parts, I realised it was not a piece of underwear she was wearing at all, it was her own pubic hair I had seen.

The two lumps on the front of her chest looked so large I wondered why they did not stick out so obviously when she was dressed.

Unfortunately for my Aunt's modesty she is on my list of only two, real life, naked adult females I have ever seen.

Fortunately, for my education, I learnt that day that when girls grew up, they were not just taller versions of little girls like those that lifted their nighties to me in Exeter Hospital. They grew things outwards as well as growing upwards.

As my Aunt's scream tailed off, I heard my mother running closer behind me. She shouted out:

"Ron what have you done now?"

I realised I would not be able to explain my innocence quick enough before a wallop came my way.

Wisdom, I am told, being the better part of valour, I made a dash for the kitchen door that led me outside to the garden. I ran into the toilet hut and locked myself in.

I reasoned that it was safer for me to explain to my Mum what had happened with the thick wood of the lavatory door between us. I came out only after I heard a tap on the door, it was my aunt Rose.

"It's all right Ron it wasn't your fault I have explained what happened to your Mum. You can come out now"!

I attended a small junior school for a short time in Majorfield Road, Topsham. The school was sited in the same road as the Town Hall's Community Centre.

I remember little of my education at school in Topsham, most of my education was out of school but there were a couple of exceptional days:

On one occasion, during a leisurely period, the teacher broke the seal on a large cardboard box. The box was full of smaller boxes of an assortment of colours of modelling 'Plasticine'. Every one in the class was given three small boxes each box contained a different colour. I, like the remainder of the class, modelled something of our own choice. When the lesson was over, we were all told to return the modelling plastic to the large box. In turn, I walked to the box and went through the motion of returning the clay. It went into my pocket. When the last lesson of the day was over and we were dismissed, like every other day I ran out of the school playground. My running caused the 'Plastacine' to fall from my trouser pocket and although I knew I had dropped it I didn't stop for fear of being caught with the incriminating evidence.

There were exceptional days, because of the movement of munitions or food to and from the Topsham dockside warehouse, when I was unable to get to my favoured fishing spot nor onto the harbour jetty. It was on one such day that armed soldiers guarded the harbour and barred passageway for civilians even for little boys wanting to fish.

As I could only return in the direction I had come from, I began to walk back to my house. Walking back up Monmouth Hill I met two local Devon boys that I knew from my class at school. After having a short discussion, we decided to go along the river, to the whirlpool, behind Fishers Bridge Mills. To get there we had to pass my house and cross over the railway bridge in Elm Grove Road. We stopped at the bridge and while looking over and down at the railway trucks carrying military equipment towards the harbour one of us noticed a thick swarm of wasps in the hedgerow on the far side of the bridge.

As we walked nearer we saw the wasps were a constant moving mass emerging and entering a large nest. Fun too good to miss! We threw a few stones at the nest and not until one of the missiles hit the target did the activity around the nest increase.

The swarm got larger as it started circling in a greater area but remained close to the nest and still at a safe distance from us. Not letting the fun stop there, we scouted around until we had each acquired a long branch for further provoking and prodding.

We returned to our stone throwing area but now we started poking the nest with our long sticks. The wasps, or maybe they were hornets, did not give us enough time to enjoy our fun before they strongly objected. Within seconds, after a couple of pokes, the small busy swarm transformed from a melodic happy buzz into a thick angry droning cloud that zoomed straight towards us. In an instant a thick cloud surrounded us and fell upon us like a black blanket being dropped from the sky. We could not run fast enough to avoid their wrath. We ran and scattered in panic in different directions. After frantically running for some distance downhill towards the river I realised I was alone in a field.

Through exhaustion, my running slowed to a trot. It was only then that I became aware that the wasps were not settling on my skin. They were only flying around me in circles, getting no closer to me than a few inches. It was as though an invisible barrier protected me.

I took my jacket off and started waving it haphazardly warding them off until their numbers had reduced to, no more, than half a dozen. I continued in this manner while slowly walking back up the grassy hill until my starting point came into view. I reached the top of the hill by the railway bridge and sat down with my back against a large old oak tree.

I rested while my breathing returned to normal and watched the, still angry, but regrouping wasps on the opposite side of the road. The oak tree that I chose to recover against was one of a small number of oaks, sycamores and horse chestnuts that had grown haphazardly from seed and had obviously not been a planned planting. The trees grew around the top of the railway bridge and thinned out before they reached lower ground to make way for rolling fields and hedges.

From the spot where I sat I could just see the top of the mill at Fishers Bridge.

After a while my two school acquaintances reappeared and joined me by sitting and talking excitedly about the chase.

We were at the age where we still dressed in short trousers and one of the boys claimed to have been stung on both of his legs. It is possible due to my body scent being far removed from that of a flower, I escaped the experience without damage.

The danger having passed, allowed us to regain our normal rhythm of breathing and allowed us to laugh and lie to each other at what good fun it had been. With plenty of time still to spend before returning home, we started climbing the large tall tree we had rested against.

After having climbed a few branches, I noticed something I had not observed before. Still climbing, we saw above us planks of timber positioned horizontally across an area where the main branches parted. The three of us quickened our pace, each accepting an unspoken challenge to reach the mystery first. As we got nearer, I spotted a more obvious foothold and easier route on the other side of the tree, I moved around and thereby established a good lead on my two pals. I stopped again, took another glance up and called to the other two to follow me.

There in front of me just a few more steps up was a circular cut out. The gap was large enough to allow the passage of a man.

I continued my climb alongside the main trunk until I reached the entrance and crawled onto the flat boards. It had a strong floor and a roof and the sides, from the floor up, were covered halfway, the remaining area to the roof was open. There were two crudely made benches, one on each of two sides with a matching table in the centre. There was nothing else inside the hut. The branches had been cut away to give unobstructed vision of the countryside.

I stood up and walked around and imagined how Robinson Crusoe could have felt on his desert island.

I looked Eastward to my right. The view was spectacular! I could see acre upon acre of golden wheat sheaves awaiting collection in the fields. I could see both sides of the Topsham Road that came from the Topsham army depot to the junction of the Exeter and Exmouth Road.

In the far distance, I could see a convoy of army lorries heading south towards the coast and the A376. Immediately behind me, the trees were scattered thinly that gradually increased in density to form the forest that covered about a quarter of my view.

From north to south, I could see the River Clyst as it threaded its way through the countryside to join the River Exe.

I excitedly called down and was explaining how super it was as I assisted the next one up. When the three of us had calmed down we pledged a bond of secrecy that our discovery must remain known only to us.

Not once did we mention, and I did certainly not consider it, that as we hadn't built it, somebody else knew about it. Nor did we wonder what it was used for. The three of us met twice at school, after our discovery, to decide our next visit to our tree top hut but the thrill was in the find and the enthusiasm of just looking out at the countryside soon waned.

Our last tree meeting was on a Sunday afternoon, as had been all the previous ones.

As we walked across the field I started picking mushrooms that were growing which allowed the other two to get in front of me. By the time I had reached the tree they had already climbed to the top and were calling me to come up. I started to climb, as I would have done without their invitation. I was more than half way up the tree before I had a clear vision of the opening in the floorboards that was also the entrance.

I climbed a few more steps and heard my two companions laughing excitedly. I looked up again but this time I saw one very white bare bum filling the gap, within a second of my upward glance he emptied his bowels.

With no place or time to dodge, the foul missile caught me square on the head and splattered down onto the shoulders of my shirt.

My hurried descent, with head and face covered in a mask of human excrement, was hilarious to my onlookers. They were delighted with the spectacle. They jeered at me and applauded my retreat.

I reached ground level crying with rage and ran down the hill towards the river, about two hundred yards away, to wash. I must have looked as though I had been used as a cleaning brush for the inside of a sewer pipe. As I ran, crying, across the field and down to the riverbank, I slipped on a pile of fresh cow droppings. It was an ideal substitute for what I had just received.

I wondered how I could use the cow dung on my 'old friends' to return some of the treatment they had dropped on me.

When I reached the river, I removed my shirt and while I hurriedly washed away the foul remnants of my attacker's missile, I scrambled together a plan of revenge.

I dried myself, as best I could, on the bottom half of my shirt and left it off. I looked a little cleaner now, but only a little, I still looked as though I had just been retrieved from the muddy river.

My anger was so intense I was trembling. Had I have been in the possession of a gun I could have easily shot them both, which could be used as an argument for everyone not to carry firearms.

As I walked back to the scene of their crime a clear plan of attack developed in my mind. I ruled out fighting them both at the same time, I wasn't that brave. My opportunity for vengeance was totally dependent upon my two adversaries being still up the tree and coming down, not knowing I was waiting in hiding, surprise was critical.

Using my folded soggy and foul smelling shirt as a shopping bag I hurriedly collected two large wet portions of 'what the cows dropped behind them to help make the mushrooms grow'.

When I reached the tree, to my delight, I heard the two of them talking excitedly above on the observation platform. I wanted them to believe I had gone home, so as to catch them off guard I kept silent and positioned myself on their blind side when they came down.

There was only one way down for them on the lower part of the tree that allowed only one at a time to reach ground level. I wanted to inflict more than the same punishment, I wanted to hurt them physically. I was not expecting to satisfy my anger without receiving more punishment but that didn't matter, I just wanted revenge. As time was on my side, I quietly searched the surrounding area for a weapon. I soon found the ideal tool, a thick heavy branch of a tree that resembled a large baseball bat but with it came a bonus, it had knobs on. I waited in ambush.

I didn't have to wait too long before I heard one of the boys coming down the tree.

By good fortune, my timing was perfect. As my unsuspecting victim hung on the lowest branch, with his feet only a short distance off the ground and about to drop, I swung my club with all of the strength that was in me.

It caught him on the back of his legs at the crease of his knee joint. He let out a scream and fell to the ground.

Before he became aware of what had happened I swung my club at him again. This time my second blow was aimed at his knees. My club made contact before he had time to put himself in a more defensive position. He let out another scream and cried unashamedly as he rolled over to clutch both of his legs, as though trying to rock himself to sleep. My third and last blow went across his right wrist that was protecting his knees. My onslaught was vicious:

"And that's for afters" I said, as I emptied a generous helping of squashy cow dung on his face.

I felt instantly satisfied when some of the almost liquid dung, mingled with his tears, went into his open mouth. His screams had alerted his ally that had been some distance behind him and still coming down the tree. As he dropped from the lowest branch my first swing at him landed too high, I caught him across his back, just below his shoulder blades.

He had landed on his feet and remained upright but as he turned to face me, before he could steady his balance, he received a second wallop, like his mate, across his chins.

He rolled over on the ground in pain, clutching both legs and crying loudly. His vulnerable position allowed me to enjoy giving him the same treatment as I had done to his fellow conspirator. I emptied the remains of my selected cow dung over his head and face and rubbed it in vigorously. I also emptied and repeated my full range of swear words on them.

Upon reflection my frenzied attack had been without restrain and bordering on insanity. I do not consider myself a violent person, in fact normally the opposite is true but it is an example of what anyone is capable of.

They were both heavily built boys and I knew I would not have had a chance to get my own back without that element of surprise. My revenge was sweet but my delight did not last. As I ran away, one of them was still screaming in pain. Concerned, I looked back and wondered if my violent reaction had gone too far. It was over but now I became frightened. As I sprinted towards the safety of my home my worry had turned into fearful concern. Could I have broken their legs?

I didn't stop running until I reached my front door in Monmouth Street. I cannot remember what happened to my shirt which is rather odd for my wardrobe was rather limited and would have most surely have been missed.

Very sure that trouble would follow from the day's event, I went to bed that night in a disturbed state. My mind raced thinking of various lies I could tell in my defence when questioned. I slept in shallow restless fits with thoughts of squads of policemen knocking on my bedroom door and dragging me away. In the dream, I kicked and screamed out my innocence. While I was being taken away my mother looked on unconcerned.

I went to school on Monday, the next day, uncertain of what awaited me. I reflected on my action. I was still worried that I had over reacted because I had convinced myself that I had caused at least one of them serious damage.

It took all of my courage not to feint an illness and stay at home but I reasoned my absence would only imply my guilt. I had options:

I could face the issue and slant the event more in my favour and bluff my way out of it, or tell my Mum and Dad the whole truth. Or tell a complete lie which was not quite the same as the first choice but from experience, I knew that lying only brought on more problems by having to think of more lies to support the first lie. I decided in favour of my first option and let the day take its course.

I walked to school, with the same fictitious permutations, that had plagued me the night before, of how I could present my innocence went through my mind.

I fully expected that a policeman or, at least, the headmistress would be waiting for me. As I got nearer to school I had made a firm decision; when I was confronted by anyone of authority, I would tell the truth as near as possible. I would concentrate on the fact that there were two of them and they both attacked me first. All I had done was to escape and all of my action was in self-defence.

It so happened that all of my anxiety was for nothing. Neither of the two boys arrived at school that day. I was intoxicated with joy. My relief was indescribable.

One of the boys came to school the following day with a bandaged leg. He looked away from me as I proudly held my head high and sneered at him. As an excuse for his absence he produced a letter from his mother. He told some of his friends he had fallen from his bicycle. By learning that he felt the need to lie, my victory over him was now more than physical. All that day I wallowed in a smug glow of superiority of being a Londoner. The concern for my victim's welfare was now totally erased.

The other boy returned to school, after being absent for the whole week. I was pleased no one had been aware of the anxiety that taunted me during the first night of the incident. It allowed me to openly display my contempt for both of them.

Their legs still showed scars, which was a reward for me in itself. What gave me the warmest gratification and the longer lasting, however, was to hear the gossip that circulated the school.

The rumour was they had been involved in a fight that was nearly true, but against each other! It also gave me great delight in helping to promote the rumour.

That skirmish, of course, put an end to our threesome treetop adventure and many weeks elapsed before I again thought of the tree hut.

Being no more than a short walk from my home and armed only with an undaunted sense of adventure I paid another visit to the treetop house.

This time I was alone and all appeared normal and deserted as I climbed the tree. When I reached the hole in the platform and about to clamber in, I looked up and saw two men. They could not have heard me climbing for they had their backs to me looking out over the side towards the meadow.

One of the men was pointing at something and talking while the other man was writing in a notebook. Naively, I saw this tree as mine and these strangers had no right to be there.

With just my head appearing above the flooring boards and feeling indignant, instead of using my head I used my mouth, I called out; "Oy! Whatcher doing up here?"

With startled looks on their faces, both of the men turned around and without hesitation one of the men walked towards me; "clear off!" he said.

"Clear off yourself! This is my gang hut".

"Listen sonny, if you don't clear off now, I'll throw you off".

He walked another few paces forward and deliberately trod on my fingers that were gripping the topside of the hole and level with my chin.

The other man, aware that his companion was getting annoyed with me, joined him and mumbled something like not doing anything that would make me fall.

Defiant in my retreat, as I descended, I shouted back that I suspected they were two rotten German spies. That was the last time I visited my tree top house.

By chance, when I got home Dad was there. He had returned from his deliveries for that day and still wanting to get my revenge on the two men I mentioned the incident.

With my schoolboy inventive imagination working 'overtime' and with emphasis on the binoculars and notebook, I told Dad of my theory that they could be German spies. My exciting story must have been convincing because Dad said he would go to the police station and report it. He did so and on his returned, told me that the two men, because of my accusation, had also gone to the police. They reported what had happened and humorously included that I suggested they were spies. Their story was not as colourful as mine however. They were two old men, too old to be 'called up' for military service and most probably too old to be spies.

I could have made my two spies think they could have looked just a little suspicious. But the laugh was on me. They were not 'rotten German spies' at all and were never likely to have been. The 'odds' were most likely for them to have been bird watchers and, of course, that is exactly what they were. They could hardly have been anything else!

There was no purpose built cinema in Topsham, the nearest was in Exeter four miles away. There was, however, a film show twice a week in St Mathews Hall, in the main road. Although I went to the cinema regularly the only film I recall seeing there was a James Cagney film I think it was called Strawberry Blonde. The hall also had other uses. It was an occasional Theatre and a Community Centre where ration books were renewed. A Women's Voluntary Service group, held weekly handouts to the poor that consisted of clothing, household goods and furniture. Children's health checks by dentists and inspection of heads for fleas, during school hours, were also held there. One day, my class was marched there from school to have an extra filter fitted to our gas masks.

In the same hall, every Sabbath morning a church sponsored Sunday school was held. In the afternoon a couple of free documentary films were shown, always with a moral, war propaganda or religious theme. I attended the hall for Sunday school at irregular intervals only to get a ticket and a programme of the forthcoming Sunday afternoon free film shows.

The water mill at Fisher's Bridge was on the other side of the railway and downhill from the 'bird spotters' tree hut. It was one of my favourite spots for all sorts of activities.

The road was raised a little higher than the fields on each side, most probably to allow rain to drain off. Along the length of the hedgerow, between road and field, wild blackberries grew.

During the fruit-picking season I spent a lot of time 'scrumping' in private orchards, ravaging chestnut trees for 'conkers' and picking wild fruit and nuts also took up my time.

On one evening scrumping raid alone I could gather twelve apples that I could sell for a penny each in school the next day. By filling both trouser pockets and both jacket pockets I could collect about 4lbs of fruit.

On one raid, I had managed to climb over some spiked railing to get into an apple orchard without mishap. I collected enough fruit to fill all of my pockets but on my return journey over the railings my shirt got caught on barbed wire and interrupted my movement. Through the waistband of my shorts a bard cut along the side of my stomach. By good fortune the wound was a long scratch rather than a deep cut. Stealing the apples on that outing could have been at a greater expense than I had bargained for.

Another occasion, Pat and I and a school friend went picking blackberries together, this time legally, along the road that past Fisher's Bridge:

The summer had been dry with long periods of sunny weather. The grass verges on each side of the road were sun scorched and gave the appearance of straw and the fruit on the blackberry bushes were meagre and shrivelled. Due to the lack of a decent return from our labour after a short while, our collecting ceased. 'Fed up' with such a small quantity of fruit available to pick, we sat down by the edge of the field wondering what to do next.

We started tucking into the few blackberries we had just picked but after a very short time I noticed the area we had chosen to sit was near a busy ants nest:

With total disregard of my mother's order, I played with matches and like most other boys I knew, I often carried a box in my pocket this day was no exception. For a while I watched, with interest, two long lines of ants purposefully rushing to and fro. In one line all of the ants were carrying pieces of leaf. The ants travelling in the opposite direction had no load. I placed a thick twig across the path of one line to see how they would overcome the obstacle.

It did not stop their traffic nor did they go off in another direction, they just went up one side of the piece of wood and down the other. I then surrounded the nest with dried grass. I wanted to see that, if by putting a lighted match to the grass ring, they would change their routine and go through the safe gap I had provided. I struck the match and put it to the strips of grass.

Due to the strong sunlight, I saw no flame. The grass just made a crackle and turned black. The flame appeared to have died. Unfortunately the 'crackling and the blackening' did not stop spreading and the fire had not withered but I could still see no flame. Within seconds, before I had time to gather my wits, the fire took hold and flames now became visible. The flames burst from my little grass ring and reached out like long arms and spread to the nearby long grass and bracken.

The small flames within no time became large flames and started to wrestle and devour small shrubs. The flames leaped to larger surrounding bushes and within seconds left them charcoaled and withered.

My Sister and my school friend, who had not been aware of my little experiment, were more surprised than I, In a panic, the three of us scrambled up the side of the bank, from the edge of the field and ran to the road in terror.

Once we reached the tarmac footpath, we ran about two hundred yards to reach and then pass the mill on our right, on the opposite side of the road. We continued running over the bridge that spanned the river and didn't stop running until we got half way up the hill. When we stopped running, it was not because we felt safe but through total exhaustion.

For the first time since commencing our run from the field we all looked back. I was astonished and terrified at what I saw. Both sides of the road were now ablaze. Black smoke and flames were swirling from the banking, down the side of the road and spreading across the dry field.

Vehicles that were on the road became caught in a point of no return situation. It was just as dangerous, or more so, for them to turn around as to continue forward. The vehicles vanished from our view in the dense black smoke. The fire had travelled evenly from its epicentre until it reached a natural firebreak of the river we had just passed but the fire was still raging furiously. It raced away from us on both sides of the road, towards the junction of the Exeter/Exmouth road.

We had run about a quarter of a mile but in spite of our distance from the fire small pieces of burning embers and charcoal were raining down on us. Grey ash, from burnt grass, leaves and twigs, were floating about and descending like confetti at a grand wedding.

As if glued to the pavement we all looked on. I felt a little relieved when I saw, travelling towards us, a lorry safely emerge from the choking black curtain:

Even now, so many years later I think of my stupidity and the damage that a small boy with a small box of matches can inflict. Although the event played no part in my future nightmares, I was haunted, in my daydreams, by the scene of a fire in all of its ferocity and the fear of what may have happened had the fire not stopped at the river.

The docks and a large food warehouse were about a mile away. A company of soldiers guarded it and it is very possible that live ammunition could also been stored there.

I realised that if I had been an adult and if found guilty of committing the same offence I could have received a prison sentence. Had I have been caught, at the age I was, it is possible I could have been seen as a budding young arsonist and taken out of my parents control and put under the supervision of the local council. But then I wondered that about a lot of silly things I did.

It was during the early stages of the war that I began to take note at what was going on. At first, I was just interested in the newspaper maps of the individual battle zones:

My Mother bought The Daily Mirror newspaper every day and as with all national newspapers the front page reported on the war.

To support the written words, the articles were always illustrated with maps showing territorial losses and arrows pointing to objectives, in the same manner as today. I had a preference for the maps in The Daily Express, but neither Mum nor Dad bought that newspaper because it was politically a conservative 'right wing' newspaper. It was, however, by far the better paper for my new hobby because the maps gave much more detail. I managed to obtain a copy most days from various sources, like a waste paper basket or dustbin.

From the newspaper's maps and additional help from my school atlas of the world, I made a large copy from the map of the North Africa coastline.

I started my new pastime when the news that the British Commonwealth forces had made a successful counter attack against the Italians. Not only had the enemy been halted, they had been turned and were in full retreat.

It was the first piece of success of the war for The British and Commonwealth forces and a much needed morale boost for public consumption.

I began to remember the names of the villages along the coast of the Mediterranean Sea and sites inland that were no more than watering holes. Some of the place names such as Benghazi, Tobruk and El Alemein etc, in peacetime were of little significance but later became known worldwide for the heroic battles that took place there.

While I was making my first home made map my Sister was cutting pieces of coloured paper into short strips to make paper chains for Christmas decorations.

In previous years, I had contributed but the birth of my new interest coincided with a British Commonwealth offensive that had just commenced. It was 9th December.

Nearly all of the reported main battles in North Africa were for possession of railway halts and small coastline towns.

Each day, I listened to the news on the radio and read the latest reports in the newspapers and transferred the information to my wall map. Some mornings I was disappointed with the news when there was not enough activity for me to do any updating. On other days news would be released of an advance of hundreds of miles. My method of recording troop movements was simply to colour in the British and Commonwealth troops advance in red coloured ink.

There were no air raids during the Christmas of 1940 but the 'take cover' siren sounded again over London on Sunday 29th December at 6pm and the 'all clear' siren was not switched on until midnight. The bombing was the most ferocious yet:

The East End Docklands and The City area were almost one mass of fire. Six firemen were killed and many more were injured. It did not help matters that the River Thames was at an unusual low tide and in some areas the firemen's hoses ran out of water. Of course, it was not London alone that took the punishment for standing up to Hitler. England's second largest city, Southampton, received bombing raids on two consecutive nights. The target was the Supermarine aircraft factory where the extremely successful Spitfire fighter aeroplane was built.

During the Battle of Britain cities from North to South of Britain took a pounding, the worst damaged were Liverpool, Manchester, Portsmouth, Plymouth, Sheffield and Birmingham.

During November one bombing raid on Coventry, lasted twelve hours, much of the city was destroyed, including the cathedral. Over 500 civilians were killed and 400 wounded:

After the war it was revealed that Prime Minister Churchill had known via the code breakers at Bletchingley, of the pending bombing raid on Coventry but forbade the information to be passed on. British intelligence gatherers had broken the code of the German Luftwaffe Enigma coded message machine and to have allowed the information, regarding the Coventry air attack, to be made public knowledge would have alerted German intelligence their code had been broken.

It took just six minutes for aircraft to cross the English Channel but they were 'picked up' by radar before they left the French Coast thus giving Fighter Command enough time to be airborne and waiting. The bombing raids were not all one-way traffic, however, British aircraft were also pounding the German capital on nightly tit-for-tat bombing raids.

While British bombers were flying Eastwards, to targets in enemy occupied Europe, German bombers were flying Westwards to targets in England. Thousands of Londoners, some totally homeless, others just in need of a good night's rest, began sleeping on the platforms of the underground railway. I was still living in Devon at this time.

Many smaller towns were on Hitler's hit list and did not escape the aerial bombardment. But in spite of the grief and misery that war brings it is remarkable that humour still prevails

After one German air raid, many of the bombs fell on a wide area of grazing land. After one such raid the BBC news broadcast reported most of the bombs were dropped at random:

German intelligence monitored all the BBC broadcast's, as British Intelligence did theirs, but on this occasion the German monitors misinterpreted the meaning of 'random'.

Thinking that 'random was a name of a town, the following day, a radio transmission to the German people, announced that Random had been heavily bombed. This German report was in turn picked up by monitors manned by British Intelligence and as a result a hasty piece of propaganda was put together by the British government moral boosting team at the 'Crown Unit' film studio and released their version of the event.

The following week, the cinema newsreel showed a duck-pond with the caption "maybe this is Random".

Another piece of 'tongue–in–cheek' cinema fun came from one occasion when the Royal Air Force had dropped leaflets on German cities.

The leaflets message was intended to encourage German civilians to sue for peace and not to co-operate with the German war effort. To impress the British people that we were fighting the war according to the rules, like a game of cricket. The story went something like this:

The British pilot flying the mission to drop leaflets on one particular German city returned to base two hours earlier than he was expected. Reporting back to his Commanding Officer, the pilot was asked how he had completed his flight so quickly. The pilot explained that he had just tipped the bundles of leaflets over the side.

"Good god man, do you mean you didn't untie the bundles" his C.O. angrily reprimanded, "You could have killed somebody!"

It was during this period that Winston Churchill delivered another one of his, so many famous, speeches to the nation. It was a tribute to the fighter pilots of the Royal Air Force. One passage went:

"Never, in the field of human conflict, has so much been owed, by so many, to so few".

Obviously, there were many important battles during the 1939-45 conflict where the outcome was critical but by the end of October 1940 the German Air Force, The 'Luftwaffe', had lost more than 1,700 aircraft in an attempt to destroy Britain's defences.

'The Battle of Britain' ranks, not only high, but as one the most decisive battles in world history.

Roy Jenkins in his book 'Churchill' makes a contribution. I quote: The Battle of Britain was at least as decisive in its consequences as Blenheim or Waterloo, but was a much less precise event...Both sides grossly exaggerated the others losses and their own victories. The result was a draw but it was one of those draws that were more valuable to one side, the British, than to the Germans who ought to, on the form, have won overwhelmingly. A draw was all that Britain needed... end quote.

It was not just in the air alone, however, that the battle was being waged. There were still many others of critical importance, on land and sea, to be fought before the war was over.

FIVE

THE DEPUTY FUHRER VISITS SCOTLAND

By February 7th 1941 British and Commonwealth soldiers had recovered all of the previous lost ground in Egypt and the main body of the Italian army, while in retreat, were out manoeuvred and having been surrounded had nowhere else to go but into the sea. During the two months offensive approximately 130,000 Italian soldiers were taken prisoner.

The 'seesaw war 'in the desert had now taken a decisive turn for the better. Not content at stopping at the Egyptian border allied troops carried on Westwards into Libya and on 22nd February took Tobruk. The good news was 'beefed up' when reported in the newspapers. It was composed to make excitable reading. The euphoria was, however, short lived. A little over a fortnight later Field Marshal Erwin Rommel arrived in Tripoli two days ahead of his German Afrika Corps.

On my eighth birthday Rommel launched his first offensive in Cyrenaica, in the Libyan Desert, and forced The British and Commonwealth troops to retreat.

As our forces had advanced, I coloured in the recovered ground, on my wall map, with diagonal red stripes in permanent ink, I had not considered the likelihood that our forces would be forced to retreat. My map was spoilt and obsolete so I set about making a larger one. My new war chart was an improvement on the previous map. I used a large piece of plywood and covered it with a reversed sheet of plain wallpaper.

My latest effort was more flexible because I had now introduced an allowance to move new front line positions, backwards or forwards, as they occurred. I used drawing pins and thick cotton and moved the pins, according to each reported activity. I must have got the idea from a wartime documentary film I had seen. The movement of British and Commonwealth troops, for the remainder of the year, was one way only, backwards!

The radio and newspapers reported some minor successful skirmishes and were presented in a manner to make the news appear hopeful without telling lies. But for me, wanting to use my system to register British gains, I was not impressed. The news was not good. It was a long wait for anything to happen to be cheerful about.

The Commander-in-Chief of British and Commonwealth forces was replaced in July but the change did little to alter our fortune. The main force of our army retreated all the way back to Egypt.

During the early days of my charts, Mum and Dad paid little attention to my hobby of charting the gains and losses of the war. The interest I had for my maps were regarded as a joke in the family. Dad often made light-hearted jokes about my interest. He once made a 'tongue-in-cheek' comment to suggest; "maybe we are losing the war because you are not drawing your maps properly".

The care that I took to produce the maps was disregarded. They must have been seen as little more than the modern equivalent of primitive cave drawings but it suited me for my own bit of fun. In reality, to be fair to my parents', some of their humour was well founded. But they did not, nor did I, at the time, realise the additional education I was getting.

As a result of my interest, I was giving myself history and geography lessons and no less important I was getting a complete up-to-date picture of the news as it was released. As the year progressed my interest expanded into recognising different types of aircraft, tanks, field and handguns. By the end of the war, I was most probably more knowledgeable in world geography than anyone else in the family.

Dad must have noticed my sustained enthusiasm had broadened my knowledge and gradually, both he and Mum began to make more serious comments about my maps. Dad's first serious comment, as I recall, was regarding his previous doubt of my accuracy in copying information from radio and newspapers and his offer to assist me.

One evening, while we were all sitting around the table having our last meal of the day, usually bread and jam and listening to the news on the radio, Dad questioned me on the location of a certain place that had just been mentioned. I told him where it was and proved I was correct by taking Dad into my bedroom and showing him the area and the place name on my wall map. I showed Dad where the conflict was taking place and the position of our allied troops and the enemy lines. The enthusiasm Dad began to show encouraged me to tell him more than he had asked. I pointed out the gains the Commonwealth troops had made by pushing the Italian army into retreat.

When the German 'Afrika Corp' arrived in North Africa, they not only halted the rout the Italians had received, they inflicted the same treatment upon the allied army and drove them back to the position now shown on my map. I believe I had impressed Dad with my accurate recording of the news, for many times after, Dad would mention a news item he thought I could have missed. Throughout the North Africa campaign in particular, Dad would engage with me in a more adult conversation, or as adult as any eight-year-old can with his father. He encouraged me, with his enthusiasm, to keep my maps up-to-date.

Dad was still driving his NAAFI lorry all over the country to and from docks and to army barracks, carrying food and other vital commodities.

One day, Dad's lorry was found on its side in a ditch with Dad inside the cab unconscious. He had been driving a consignment of ammunition, from a factory in the Midlands to a barracks in

Plymouth's dockyard. Dad's official report of his interrupted journey was the result of a lone enemy aircraft having strafed his lorry. Although the German fighter may not have used its machine guns, Dad was forced off the road. Dad claimed he could not remember anything after that until he recovered in hospital.

He told me some years later the story he had told the police was fiction for insurance reasons only. The event that caused the accident was not as he had told the hospital staff and the police. Dad told me not to say a word to anyone. The true story was to be kept a secret just between the two of us:

It is true, he told me that his lorry went off the road and rolled over down into a ditch but he had fallen asleep while driving. The enemy aircraft story was fiction. Dad calculated, had he told the true version, he would have admitted to having committed a driving offence that could have involved a summons. Dad also feared there would have been the question that the insurance company may not have paid the bill for the repair cost of the lorry, which, without doubt, would have displeased Dad's boss, he would also have had to pay the ambulance bill and receive no wage while he was recovering and not at work.

After being found unconscious, he was taken to hospital by ambulance. Because he had been 'knocked out' he was admitted and remained there overnight.

Mum received the message that Dad had been involved in an accident and he had been admitted to The Exeter Royal Infirmary.

His injuries amounted to only a large bump on his forehead and a cut cheek and accounted for his head and face wound by suggesting, when his vehicle turned over the lorry's starting handle, that was loose in the cab, could have dropped on his head.

This little yarn, which could have been serious, had a humorous ending. When Mum went to the hospital the next day to accompany Dad home she was told he was not allowed to leave until the ambulance fee of five shillings had been paid. Not having enough money to pay the bill, Mum had to travel back to Topsham and borrowed the money, as an advance from her wages, from her publican boss for whom she worked in the Lighter Inn. Mum then returned to Exeter, four miles in each direction, to pay the bill. The insurance company later reimbursed Mum the five shillings.

Uncle John had moved back to London earlier in the year and as the bombing had not ceased I wondered why he made such an unwise decision. I have looked at the records to confirm it was reckless: I found by the end of April 1941 bombs had killed 28,859 British civilians. By the early spring air raids were still taking place but the nightly bombing became less frequent.

A feeling of greater safety must have been the deciding factor for Mum and Dad to return to London.

My Mother's family, Gran' and Grandad Bridger, had moved into a rented three storey terraced house, 49 Studley Road, Clapham, S.W.4. We became subtenants and rented three rooms on the top floor and attic.

My attic bedroom was 'running alive' with bugs and in the winter it was also very cold and damp.

Cold and damp housing went 'hand in hand', as it does today, for people on poverty level incomes.

I slept in my vest, shirt and socks and learnt to live with the bugs: I did not experience the luxury of owning a pair of pyjamas until I went into the army.

Sometimes these miniature vampires, without wings, would find a soft and warm part of my body, under my armpits, creases of elbows and knees and groin, without disturbing my sleep. They would settle down without interruption and feast until they had their fill. The next morning their visits were obvious by the large bite marks that remained on my skin, after their departure they would then return to their hiding places in the mattress, the woodwork or the wallpaper and start over again the next night:

Mattresses were not like the modern sprung interior type of today, my lumpy mattress was made of flock and horsehair and very firm.

All of my bedding was dusted regularly with an insecticide powder but the success in their total eradication was almost impossible. Some of their hiding places were in the tongue and groove joints of the floorboards where the powder could not reach. Although common to most houses, nobody spoke of their private bug problems. I think it was generally accepted that poor housing had bugs and attempting to eradicate them was fighting a losing battle.

There were times, after a session of mattress dusting that I believe contained sulphur, the lingering smell of the powder was worse than going to bed with the bugs. Another form of trying to eliminate the pests was to release DDT Bombs: The bomb was a small circular metal canister similar to a 'Vick' menthol inhalers: DDT was banned in the 1970's

The walls that divided the rooms were also unlike today's construction; Where the modern internal wall divider is made of brick, blockboard or plaster board, the buildings of days gone were of interwoven thin strips of timber with layers of horse-hair and covered, for a smooth finish, with plaster: The timber and hair was a haven for bugs and vermin to breed and survive.

There were times when John would share my attic bedroom with me but only when my Aunt Rose came home on leave and she would use his bedroom downstairs, on the first floor.

John had a 0.22 Webley air pistol he used for, among other things, while laying on his bed, shooting the bugs on my bedroom wall, the ammunition he used for his pistol was lead pellets or feathered slugs.

The lead slugs made easily repairable dents and holes in the wall, but a very permanent result upon the bugs. The damage to the wall at the point of impact, depended upon there being a firm wooden joist, a softer lathe, or softer still, a wad of hair beneath the thin layer of plaster. If the area around the targets were soft, the lead pellet, on striking the target, would go through the wall, take a lot of plaster with it and leave a hole about than the size of an eggcup and no remains of the dead bug. If, on the other hand, the bug in John's gun sight was on a part of the wall where a strip of wood was immediately behind the plaster the pellet would just damage the plaster and leave a small hole the size of a shirt button. If a joist was immediately behind the point of impact, the slug would be flattened but remain visible in the timber. The overall pattern on the wall was one of small holes and indents. As a result of John's marksmanship the indents in the walls were coloured in varying shades of red through to dark brown, depending how long ago the death of the bug had occurred and the accuracy of the hit. The red, of course, was some of my previously drawn off blood and the compressed remains of the bug.

John's gun was powered by a spring and compressed air but it was a surprisingly powerful weapon.

Shooting at cats and birds, from my attic bedroom window, was a favoured sport of John's. A slug fired at a cat from a distance of thirty yards would be felt and make it run for cover. I think I would not have known of his pastime had it not have been for him sharing my room.

This little bedtime story may read just too grotesque to be believed but I have not exaggerated any part, every word is true.

Adults living in those conditions did not, generally, talk about their bed bugs and rats, they were on the same unwritten list of 'unspeakable' subjects, such as: incest, pregnancy, illegitimacy and women's monthly periods.

John was not a character of respectable deeds, nor was he a good teacher to anyone wishing to become a model citizen or a member of the church going community. In simply terms he was a lot of fun to be with. He influenced my early years a great deal.

Many times when I was in John's company, he would show me the best methods of breaking the law and getting away with it without recrimination. He taught me how to fire his gun and become competent at shoplifting. I practiced firing his pistol when he allowed it and joined him in the art of thieving as often as the opportunity presented itself.

The most popular training ground for stealing was from Woolworth's. Woolworth's stores were the easiest shops for apprentice shoplifters to practise. Pears and apples, in boxes on display, outside greengrocers' shops were also easy pickings and came a very close second choice. Shoplifting from the counter of the Woolworth's store at Brixton was a large source of increasing my foreign postage stamp collection.

Having returned to London and living at a different address, I resumed my education, I use the term loosely, at the same school I had attended twenty months earlier. Now we lived in Studley Road the normal walking time to Gaskell Street School had increased to about ten minutes. I write 'normal' for the want of a better word. What is normal in war is not necessarily normal in times of peace:

If an air raid had taken place during the night, my walking time could very easily extent to an hour or more. The extra time was not always due to the aftermath that the hazard of bombing could bring more often than not it was due to my insatiable need to collect pieces of shrapnel.

I would start off heading in the main direction of school each morning, but I was too easily distracted by the odd cartridge case of fighter aircraft's cannon shells. I lost all sense of time but I was not alone in being late for roll call, some of my class mates arrived after me.

My eyes would scan the roads, pavements, gutters and front gardens for any small piece of twisted metal. Scrap metal was in great demand to help the war effort and had long been gathered up so any metallic object, seen in the streets, would almost certainly have been something that had been delivered out of the sky during the night.

Shrapnel, the metal fragments of shells or bombs, was instantly recognisable for it was always jagged, partly split and dull silver in colour.

It would have been either a part of one of our exploded shells or the remains of a piece of an enemy bomb. Top place in my collection was a complete fin of an incendiary bomb that I retrieved from a front garden. During this period swapping' pieces of spent artillery was my most important reason for going to school, even more highly placed than cigarette card or postage stamp collecting.

My collection of pieces of twisted metal and cartridge cases got to such a quantity that I made a large wooden box to keep them in. I kept the box under my bed.

The second most important reason was setting out each morning was to see if the school was still 'standing' and hoping that it wasn't. I suppose most children that are generally backward in their learning skills at school, like myself, held the same view.

Living in London during the bombing did not disturb me but I missed the excitement of fishing by a riverbank or climbing trees and most of the things that girls don't like doing.

I must not exclude my contribution to the science and nature lessons; I took the tops of a carrot and a parsnip to display in the school classroom to watch them grow in a jar of water.

Shrapnel, Army Badges and stamps infected me for life with the incurable disease of 'collectivitis'.

The worst of the bombing had taken place during our twenty months absence from the capital and although some very near misses were in evidence No 49 Studley Road had survived and was still habitable.

Along the whole length, on the opposite side of the road, only three houses remained with a roof. Of the odd numbered houses, those on the side of the road that I lived, more than half of the houses had been totally destroyed but a house did not have to have had a direct hit for it to be totally ruined. The blast from explosions caused enormous damage. I believe our house was protected from some of the blast by a large solid built church on the opposite corner of a narrow road, Stanley Villas. There was no protection, of course, for the other three sides of the house.

The nearest anti aircraft detachment to Stockwell was the one that I had watched being set up at Clapham Common the day that war was declared where there were; Anti-aircraft, Ack-Ack, guns, searchlights and barrage balloons.

In local conversation the Ack-Ack detachment at Clapham Common was always referred to with a sense of pride in the possessive tense as 'our guns': "Did you hear 'our guns' going off last night?"

Not only would one have been deaf not to have heard them but also been void of all sense of feel. When 'our guns', about two miles away, started firing the earth trembled. The sound of the guns sending anti aircraft shells upward, were as loud and just as frightening as the explosion of the bombs that were coming down. I have done only a little research on the wartime value of anti aircraft guns and balloons but I do know they were not as effective against enemy bombers as being met by The Spitfire fighter aircraft.

But to hear that any action was being taken against the enemy, whatever it may be, was a good morale booster, or so we were told!

The barrage balloons in the sky became as normal to see as the clouds. They did not appear to be part of the war machine at all: They looked like tokens of joy as if they were floating in the sky to cheer people up. The silvery grey balloons lazily drifted on their steel anchored cables like soft and friendly fairy elephants. I was unaware of the barrage balloons' proper function until the pilotless aircraft came on the scene in July 1944:

I had assumed the balloon itself was designed to be the obstacle for aircraft but that was not the case. It was the numerous steel cords that hung down from all sides of the balloon that presented the hazard. The theory, it would seem, was a good one, for if an aircraft flew below the balloon, the dangling steel cords would be unseen by the pilot before it was too late to take evasive action. Upon impact the hanging steel cords could sever an aircraft's wing.

To avoid the hanging steel cords the aircraft flew above the balloons but the higher altitude the enemy then had to fly, to deliver their bomb load, made their targets more difficult to hit. German documents, found after the war however, tell that German pilots reported the great pleasure they got from flying above the balloon and firing their machine guns at them. On being hit, the balloon would burst and float down to earth in a mass of flames.

In more recent wars, aircraft and bombs have been developed that are larger, heavier and more accurately delivered and with the potential to destroy a much larger area than the bombs used during the Second World War. In addition to high explosives there was a great emphasise on the use of incendiary bombs, which could not only leave a house 'gutted' from roof to basement it could cause a fire that could spread and cause damage far beyond that of the initial impact. By good fortune our house did not receive a direct hit from an HE bomb but due to the blast from a number of previous bombs that had been dropped on the surrounding area, it was not a safe house to live in. The church played only a small part in the protection business.

Because of the seemingly endless requirement for raw materials, scrap metal collection was needed to meet the targets demanded by the war. A national campaign was launched to encourage people to salvage their rubbish; old tin cans, unused kitchen utensils, prams, bicycle frames, jam jars, newspapers, magazines, empty toothpaste tubes etc, etc, all were recycled. In London, and maybe many other places, even the cast iron railings around parks and private front gardens were pulled up and taken away for melting down. It appeared that almost everything in daily use could be salvaged to help with the war effort.

My playground, being most often bombed ruined houses, was exciting for there was the element of danger in their unsafe condition. Not knowing what we may find next added to the thrill. Stealing from unoccupied houses, albeit bombed, was called looting which carried a heavy penalty and could lead to imprisonment to anyone caught. My two friends and I called it exploring and made it mentally easier to engage in but, nevertheless, it was still illegal.

I was eight years old at this time and, upon reflection, I had already begun to acquire my credentials to go on my criminal curriculum vitae. Being subject to good and bad influences in particular during periods of war when we are young displays the fine 'tightrope of life' we all walk. I believe it is only a matter of good fortune that we are either guided by wise and law abiding people or the stupid and criminal.

Anyone that lived through the 1930's and 1940's would, most probably, listen to the radio with the same regularity as watching television today.

For me, the news was important to listen to enable me keep my maps up to date. I rarely missed listening to the news at least once a day. The newsreaders: Alvar Liddell, John Snagge and Bruce Belfrage are synonymous with the war years and were as well known then as television celebrities are today. Although it was radio, the BBC imposed a dress suit and bow tie dress code on all newsreaders:

On 13th May, the most extraordinary news on the radio and in the newspapers was released regarding Germany's Deputy Leader, it didn't matter that the news was three days late.

It was reported that Rudolf Hess had left Augsburg, Germany, by aircraft and landed in Scotland near a small village called Eaglesham.

There was newspaper speculation but denied by the government, that a meeting had been scheduled to take place with The Duke of Hamilton, or more English aristocrats to negotiate a peace plan. If that was the case the plan went very wrong for Rudolf Hess was arrested and remained in an English prison for the remainder of the war.

Considering that Germany was winning the war and if there was nothing sinister going on, why did Deputy Fuhrer Hess, the English equivalent of our heir to the throne, mysteriously risk coming to the U.K?

If some people in government were not aware of his intention, why was his aircraft not discovered by radar and intercepted as it approached our shores like any other aircraft?

Could Hitler have been driven by a blind arrogance to believe that the British government would not dare to do anything other than accept his deputy to our shores? Was Hitler really that foolish? Well, he certainly wasn't foolish but depending upon who is doing the measuring he could have been insane. It also appears on captured German records after the war, that Hitler did believe he could avoid going to war against England. It was also claimed Hitler was unaware of his deputy's peace mission.

I join those with the view, not that my view adds any credence to the story, that most likely there were unofficial secret negotiations being conducted behind Churchill's back, as the newspapers suggested. It was known there were a number of titled nobility: Earl Halifax and The Duke of Northumberland, for instance, were known to be sympathetic to Hitler's cause.

Sir Oswald Mosley, leader of The British Fascist Party, 'The Black Shirts', also supported Hitler's anti Semitic views.

Many British citizens in powerful positions would have willingly discussed peace plans and allied The United Kingdom with the Third Reich not least, ex King Edward VIII.

It was suspected, by British military intelligence but not revealed to the British public until many years after the war, that Edward was passing military secrets to the Germans.

There has also been, in more recent years, speculation and supported by some circumstantial evidence that Edward had secretly agreed with Hitler to accept the British Crown, as a puppet, once the UK ceased to be at war with Germany.

Also, why after the war was won, did Hess, answerable only to Hitler, survive the Nuremburg War Crimes Trial? He out lived, except for those not traced, all of the Nazi leaders. Albeit he lived in captivity but unlike his senior colleagues he escaped execution.

Being in the majority group of the population that is only ever 'fed' a limited amount of information, from government, one can only make logical guesses but I am happy with the view there was a plot to ally Britain to Germany.

I believe some of the British aristocracy and some of the ruling class were concerned with preserving their life style. Democracy was allowing more power to the working class, thus reducing influence through wealth. I speculate that those that favoured Hitler sought to look after themselves and felt safer with a dictatorship, like Germany, that was anti Semitic and totally opposed to the, very possible, spread of Communism in the UK.

Will we ever know? I should not exclude that at this stage of the war the horrors of Hitler's 'final solution' for the Jewish race and the mentally handicapped were not known to the British and German public.

May 24th was a day of mourning: The pride of the British navy, HMS Hood, the biggest battleship in the world, was sunk:

She was hit by one shell fired from the German battleship 'Bismarck'. A freak shot struck 'Hood's' ammunition magazine. There were one thousand, four hundred and twenty one men on board. Only three survived.

The German warship responsible was hunted down for three days in a combined effort between the navy and the air force. It gave the nation a wonderful tonic when it was reported on BBC's radio news that the 'Bismark' had been sunk. The nation wallowed in a feeling of 'getting its own back'. Britain had levelled the score.

One thousand seven hundred of the two thousand five hundred German seamen were killed during the action. Eight hundred survivors were in the water nine hours before a British warship began picking up survivors, but a message warning of a German U boat was approaching forced the rescue to be abandoned after only one hundred had been taken aboard. Seven hundred were left to perish in the water.

A lesson had been learnt on both sides. The big battleships proved too vulnerable for modern warfare. Battle giants, such as these, were never built again.

The next day, 28th May, the evacuation of British troops from Crete was reported.

To feed the war in Northern Africa, it was necessary to keep the supply lines open. Both allied and axis forces depended upon supplies by convoys of ships 'running the gauntlet' across or through the Mediterranean Sea. The safety of shipping was paramount to maintain that supply.

The Italians introduced a remarkable two man electric underwater 'chariot' ridden by frogmen in scuba suits. They sat astride outside and steered a high explosive warhead to a target. Once the mine was released, the timer set and attached to the hull of an enemy ship the frogmen returned to base. I believe the ballpoint pen was born at this time: The 'Biro' was invented for the purpose of allowing the information that was gathered, to be written in ink while still underwater,

Once a week, a nurse would attend school and class by class, examine every child's head with a steel comb looking for head lice. As the nurse entered the classroom our teacher would rise and tell the class to stand-up and say good morning to the nurse. The class would stand and comply but hidden within the greeting of thirty a few young voices would chorus "Good Morning Nitty Nora" that came with a snigger from my colleagues and I in the back row. One at a time, each child had to walk from his desk to the front of the class to have a steel comb run through his hair. After each inspection the comb would be 'wiggled' in a glass of surgical spirit and cleansed ready for the next inspection. It was another part of school life that I disliked for it was usual for the nurse to find fleas on my head or hair. The finding was not as disturbing as the lack of privacy. The whole class would be aware the nurse had made a 'find' by the route in which one was directed after the inspection. I was not alone, however, only a minority of the class returned to their desks without a 'letter', but, naturally, I would have preferred to have joined the 'clean ones'.

One morning, during assembly, I was sitting in the main hall with the rest of the school children waiting for a teacher to finish reading from the bible when I began to feel an ache that within a minute or so developed into a sharp stabbing pain in my stomach. I had felt similar intermittent pain in the past but during the past few days it had become more severe. It was now almost unbearable. In addition to the pain I now felt hot, weak and dizzy. I moved from my cross legged position to stretch myself out on the hall floor which, as well as easing the pain, was sleep inducing. Although I was aware of my action and embarrassed that I may be seen, my need for some form of relief felt greater than conforming to convention. Being amid other children and nearer to the rear of the hall, I was not noticed by the teaching staff sitting at the front.

The last I can recall of the incident was feeling very tired and relaxed as the pain began to recede. Maybe I fainted or just went to sleep, I do not know but I remember nothing more until waking on a bed with a blanket over me in the school medical room. My mother was sitting by the side of a desk talking to a doctor. A considerable time must have elapsed between being stretched out in the hall and becoming aware of my surroundings again for my next recollection was being at home in bed.

The following day, Mum took me on a 34 tram to Kings College Hospital. Denmark Hill. Camberwell. I had misgivings about going to hospital again after being the star of the fiasco while I was in Exeter Hospital but while we waited, Mum assured me I would not be admitted and told me I had only come for an examination.

Eventually my name was called and Mum escorted me into a small office. The man was sitting and writing at a large office desk, to my surprise, was wearing a suit, it made him look like a School Teacher. As we entered he stood up and beckoned Mum to take a seat, he then took a white linen jacket from a coat rack behind him and put in on. Now he looked like a hospital doctor.

I was told to take my clothing off and he sounded my chest. My examination started with getting weighed, followed by being measured. Then my temperature was taken.

He then instructed me to take a deep breath while he tapped his fingers on my chest and back. I then followed his instruction to get on to his couch where he then pushed, prodded and poked with cold hands on my stomach and terminated with a tap on of my knees with a rubber hammer. After his examination, the doctor returned to his desk and while I was getting dressed, began writing again. As he wrote, without looking up, the doctor explained to Mum what he believed was causing my pain. We returned home with the knowledge that I had grumbling appendicitis.

The day after I had attended hospital, a nurse welfare worker visited our house. After she had left, Mum told me the visitor was the result of my medical examination at the hospital. The home visit by the nurse was to confirm the conclusion of the doctor that I was undernourished and was suffering from malnutrition. On seeing my Sister, the nurse concluded that Pat also should be included in the doctors recommendation. With my stomach problem officially confirmed the school doctor visited me at home and legitimately excused my absence from school. From then on until I moved to a senior school, at the age of eleven, I remained on the Council's child welfare list:

Being placed on the council list of 'children in need of special care' granted me having, free of charge, extra nutrients.

During school hours, before I commenced my lessons, I would join the queue at the school medical room to be served a large sticky spoonful of Cod Liver Oil and Malt and vitamin pills. This special treatment was in addition to a free bottle of milk a day given to all children. There is no doubt in my mind, the reason that warranted Pat and I to attend the local London County Council Welfare and Malnutrition Clinic was the result of our living conditions

We attended the clinic in Wansdworth Road every Thursday afternoon during school hours for a sulphur bath, I learnt later the purple ointment was the standard treatment for ringworm and impetigo, both skin infections.

I was not told if the chemical bath we were subjected to was to reduce cure of the visibly obvious bites from the bed bugs or to deter the parasites from putting me on their bedtime menu. After the bath, a thick sticky brown paste, somewhat like heavy-duty grease used on motorcars was spread on various parts of my body with a wooden spatula then covered with a bandage.

Other parts, not touched by the paste, including my face, were painted with the purple ointment. In spite of the attention I received the next day at school, after my first session at the clinic, with dabs of mauve paint on my face, I looked forward to Thursday's:

After having a school dinner, Pat and I would walk from school to the clinic, about a mile away, have the bath and 'cosmetics' and then go straight home without having to return to school. Pat's treatment was not as drastic or as visible as mine but as she didn't sleep up in the attic, she was not getting eaten alive each night. I also think she was not in the same underweight condition as I.

It was after one visit by the nurse, at school, that I was reported for being in an unhealthy dirty state. I was sent, with a note from my teacher, to see the headmaster.

The note informed him that I had come to school with a grimy neck and dirt underneath my fingernails. Maybe I was too young for the cane. For a punishment, I had to write one hundred lines; 'Cleanliness is next to Godliness'.

Although the cost for being unclean on this occasion was not a painful one I had taken the initial step of being out of favour with the teaching staff. It was a position I found I was unable to reverse.

Less frequent than the inspection of heads for fleas by a roving nurse, that until more recent years were dressed like nuns, was teeth inspection by a dentist.

One visit by the school dentist resulted in my mother receiving a letter advising that an appointment should by made for me to attend a dentist for treatment. The appointment was made and I attended a dentist in Clapham Road, opposite the Stockwell war cenotaph.

All teeth extractions were carried out either by gas or cocaine. Most probably there was a higher charge to have cocaine. I remember vividly the ordeal of having gas.

I had no prior memory of going to a dentist for treatment it was a new experience for me. I sat in the dentist chair not knowing what to expect, or how a tooth was extracted. A bib was placed around my neck as the dentist told me to close my eyes and relax. Up to that point it was no different from today. I obeyed his instruction. By closing my eyes, I didn't see the mask he was about to place on my face. Once the mask was put in place I started to struggle to free myself because my air supply had been shut out and I couldn't breathe properly.

I was not aware the purpose of the mask over my mouth and nose was to induce sleep for me to have a painless extraction; I just thought that something had gone wrong. I was given no explanation of what to expect.

Had the dentist told me to take deep breathes and forewarned me I would have had no problem. I will never know if my muffled cry of "I can't breathe! I cant breathe!" was heard through the mask but my anxiety must have been noticed as I struggled to free myself. My plight, however, was totally ignored. As the gas began to send me off to dreamland the soft suffocating rolling fluffy balls, I had seen so many times in my past nightmares, returned.

The extraction may have been successful, in as much I had one tooth less in my mouth. I did not have my teeth attended to again for another ten years.

I passed the same dentist premises in the 1960's. As I passed, my thoughts of the torture returned. I hoped he had 'gone out of business, rather than the likelihood he had moved on to a more attractive address. The vacated shop had become a restaurant.

It is strange how attitudes have changed towards professional people. It is not just my own personal point of view that Doctors, Dentists, Solicitors and even Policemen were shown more respect than they are today. People in authority were rarely challenged, due to the general belief that because they were wealthier they were also wiser. I believe challenging authority became more acceptable and widespread after the 1939-45 war.

I have made more than a hint of the poor standard of low cost accommodation available for rent, for which I make no apologies. There were no options for manual workers. Anything other than renting was not a consideration. It would have been seen as being boastful if one claimed to work in an office, more so a person working in a bank. Bank employees had an added advantage of gaining height on the social ladder for they had the opportunity to obtain a low cost mortgage. Bank workers, although having an advantage of a low interest rate to buy their own property, were caught in the trap of being tied to their job. If the bank employee decided he wanted to seek new employment he had to consider if he could afford to continue buying a house at a higher rate of interest.

The best hope for someone on a low income was to rent a house or flat from the London County Council, LCC or the local Borough Council, they even had a bathroom! Unfortunately there were just not enough new houses erected to cater for all of those in need. The opportunity to get to the top of the waiting list and offered a flat was very limited.

I am not making a gripe because we were not in either category as a family we were not alone being 'caught up' with shabby housing. We were in company with the majority of other families experiencing the same squalid conditions. It was normal for low income working people so I never considered myself as being deprived. There were still many more millions that would have improved their conditions by living in a house like the one I lived in. I come back to this matter to refer to many winter evening treats that my sister and I enjoyed. Dad used a simple piece of psychology to get us into bed. He would take a pillow from each bed and warm them in front of the fire. "First one in bed gets the warmest one!" he would announce. It was, of course, a veiled order to go to bed but it was a pleasant and exciting one and it always worked. We would make a mad dash to our respective bedrooms and await the luxury of a hot pillow. The few minutes taken for the pillow to be in front of the fire also helped to dry it.

While living in Studley Road I had two constant school friends and another local boy less consistently.

John Bennett was two months younger than me and lived in the same terraced block about ten doors along from my house. John's nickname could not have been anything other than 'Benny'. His father was a sergeant in the metropolitan police. Part of his family was a frisky and lovable Cocker Spaniel. Benny promised me I could have a puppy from her next litter.

My other constant companion was Patrick Beauchamp, his nickname, Beechy, was also obvious.

The other school friend made up the quartet at school but was not in the gang outside school hours. His surname, Trevor Leftwhich, fitted nicely to have the nickname of Lefty: Lefty was also the name of a character in the Tommy Handley show: ITMA. (It's That Man Again).

My nickname was just Prossy. Not a very original adaption but what can be done with a surname like Pross?

Because the mothers' of Benny and Beechy and Lefty spoke of their displeasure regarding nicknames, the three of us always used our full Christian names when we were in the company of parents, just to keep them happy, although it did make us sound as though we were trying to talk posh. I believe the parents suspected we went over the top by referring to Benny as Jonathon and me as Ronald. It just didn't fit, sometimes we even laughed while saying it.

Beechy lived at the junction at the end of Larkhall Lane in Landsdowne Way. His father was serving in the army overseas.

The three of us, Benny, Beechy and myself, were all born in 1933. We lived within close proximity to each other and all attended the same school and sat in the same classroom.

Our only form of transport other than our feet were home made wooden scooters.

The no cost shopping list for the materials required to make these magnificent machines were; two planks of timber, each approximately 2 foot long, my mistake, 600mm, to make an upright and the foot board: These materials were easily obtained from old floorboards of bombed houses.

One 120mm square piece of timber 200mm long, known as the steering block came from a joist that supported floorboards. The block was nailed to the front of the footboard section and held two screw eyes which made up part of the steering.

One 50mm square piece of timber about 400mm long, made the handle.

Two industrial Ball Races for the wheels, were obtained from local motor repair garages: The two wheels, were usually discarded from lorry big-end engine or wheel bearings; After our local supplier was bombed and moved to premises further afield we obtained our bearings, always free of charge, from any motor repair garage.

Four large screw eyes, two were screwed to the block the other two were screwed into the upright.

One 20mm coach bolt, slid into the four screw eyes thus allowing the upright to articulate the foot board to allow for steering. A nut, for the end of the bolt stopped it vibrating out of the screw eyes.

Two pieces of timber were required for the wheel axles, the size being dependent upon the internal size of the bearings.

Home made wooden scooters were owned by almost every boy in the land, certainly in my area. Their numbers exceeded, by far, that of all the skateboards and roller skates owners of today.

Most boys, in working class areas, formed scooter gangs from the street they lived in and put markings on the front of their scooter. The front upright of the scooter, for steering, would normally be decorated with either coloured metal milk bottle tops or just painted. Some of the designs, spelt out the name of the street the gang resided in. Although something in the region of a hundred houses had been erected in Studley Road very few houses remained habitable. We were a small gang. Benny and I were the only other two boys left in residence. Beechy lived two streets away.

My scooter and those of my two friends proudly displayed the sign 'Lightning Gang'.

It would not have been unusual to see a gang of as many as ten boys scootering together and causing havoc and dispersing pedestrians on the pavement.

Because of the aggravating noise and the general nuisance the hardened steel wheels would make on concrete paving, understandably, we were not welcome on the pavement, nor anywhere else for that matter.

For some people, too old to own a scooter of their own, the noise was unbearable they would curse and angrily complain as we passed.

One old lady, a recluse living alone in a house two doors along from my house in Studley Road, disturbed by the noise would often run out of her house shouting and shaking her fist at us as we scooted passed her front garden. A few weeks elapsed after her first show of displeasure, her patients failed her, for on hearing our approach she resorted to arming herself with knives and forks and throwing a handful at us each time we went by.

The anti social rating of our scooter gang could be compared today with someone cycling fast between costermongers' stalls on market day.

The sight of a scooter catapulting its rider over the top of his ferocious machine at high speed as the front wheel came off was not uncommon. Such an accident, to many observers, would bring a smug silent sense of pleasure rather than assistance.

The hours of fun we had on our scooters was immense and for a historical record I would rate myself, albeit I was only eight years old, as a forerunner of one of the present motor cycling 'Hells Angels'.

Every generation believes children are more ill mannered and less disciplined than when they themselves were young. My small gang and I did our best to help maintain that belief but it is a myth. It is documented that even during the 'high days' of the Roman Empire, over 2000 years ago, the same comments were being made of their youth.

Benny's Cocker Spaniel had her litter of pups and I spent a couple of weeks trying to convince Mum and Dad to let me have one of them. I don't think they really had an objection they just wanted to make sure that I was going to be responsible in looking after it if they agreed. I promised that I would feed it, make sure it didn't do its business in the house, take it for walks, keep it clean and look after it properly.

When the pups were ready to be taken away from their mother I brought one of them home. It was a lovely little thing and everyone in the house fell in love with it. It instantly became part of the family and for a short while it controlled most of my out-of-door activities.

Because his ears were almost as long as its legs, I named it after a fictitious, big eared, elephant in a Walt Disney film.

A week or two later after I had explained to someone why I had named my dog Jumbo I was promptly informed that the cartoon elephant, with very large ears, was called Dumbo. By this time however, I had got accustomed to calling it Jumbo and the name remained.

Jumbo slept in the house during the night on the couch, which was placed by the window.

Immediately the 'siren' sounded, to indicate that enemy aircraft were approaching, we stopped whatever we happened to be doing and made a dash downstairs to the air raid shelter in the garden. Within a very short space of time Jumbo associated the one tone whining siren to 'take cover' with running to the shelter. The intermittent wavering tone of the 'all clear' he associated with leaving the shelter and returning to his couch.

It soon became normal for Jumbo to give us advance warning to vacate the house and take cover. Before the siren could be heard by anyone in the house, Jumbo would prick up his ears, bark twice, jump off the couch, run down the stairs and wait at the door leading to the back garden. There were times, if the back door was open, he would continue his run until he made himself comfortable on his blanket in the shelter.

I believed Mum's theory that my dog must have been born with the gift of a sixth sense; but before I was not much older I'm happy to report I became a little wiser. Sooner or later wisdom usually comes at a cost. To be ridiculed by my teacher, in front of my classmates, was my cost:

During an English lesson the class was given the task of writing a story from a wide choice of titles. My choice was 'Pets'. The title of my essay was 'My Dog, Jumbo'.

After completing my story, my paper was handed in at the end of the lesson with all of the others. A few days elapsed, before the marked papers were returned at next English lesson. The teacher walked around the classroom returning the marked papers. As my piece of handiwork was placed in front of me, I could not avoid seeing the teacher's comment. Written across the top of the page, in red capital letters was 'SEE ME'.

With all of the papers circulated, the teacher returned to his desk. With apprehension I raised my hand to attract the teacher's attention. He must have been waiting for me, before I could utter a word he spoke.

"Oh yes! Come to the front of the class Pross so that we can all see you. The Dog Story" the teacher said with vicious enthusiasm.

I left my seat, walked up to the teacher and told him he wanted to see me.

"I know I want to see you! We all want to see you, and we all want to hear you"

He stood up, tapped a ruler on his desk and addressed the class.

"Listen children! Ron Pross is going to entertain us and read his essay to you".

I had mixed feeling, more fear than pride. My fear was due to not being able to read very well. Reading to myself was one thing but reading to an audience was a different proposition. But I was fortified by the thinking my story must have been better than I had previously thought but I would have been happier had my story just got a 'star'. Reading it aloud to the class, I could easily have forfeited. But for all of my trepidation I was not expecting what followed:

I started to read, but before I got passed the first sentence, in a severe manner the teacher said: "Stop! Stand up straight. Face the class and start again, properly this time and start by telling the class the title".

I now had an unhappy feeling that I was the proverbial Christian in the Roman arena and the teacher was going to be the lion. This was not going to be a pleasant experience.

I started again but I was beginning to show symptoms of being a nervous wreck.

"The title please": The teacher urged with irritation creeping into his voice.

"My Dog Jumbo" I started but I stumbled over the next few words, as though I was trying to read a manuscript in Braille with fur gloves on. Instead of excusing me, after having a little fun the teacher constantly interrupted me with comments to make the class laugh and made me read to the end of my story. Not until I had finished did he send me back to my seat.

To add to my humiliation, my desk was in the back row, which allowed all of the class to have their eyes upon me as I walked back. I knew of no reason why the teacher decided to pick on me. Maybe to ridicule anyone would have suited his twisted mind and I was just unlucky. Maybe my story really was the worst.

But with theatrical timing, he waited until I was seated and the laughing had finished before he spoke.

"Well class does anyone have a comment?"

Total silence.

"Come on now surely someone has something to say"

He didn't get the response he was expecting. Still there was a deathly silence, I imagine, from the collective fear, that the next to speak could well be his next victim.

"Well! Let me say it for you then. It's a total nonsense "

Still there was no reply.

"Yes! Of course it is" the teacher answered. "Why is it nonsense?"

The class still remained silent. None of the boys wanted to raise their heads above their desk parapets and be in his firing line by giving a wrong answer. Maybe they were all as dopey as I and they didn't know either. But there was to be no other victim to satisfy the teacher this day.

The teacher had used my essay and mine alone, to use it as an introduction for something he had decided was a good subject to talk about.

For all of his faults as a teacher I must not omit I did learn something from the lesson: He told the class what was wrong with the logic of my theme:

"Canine hearing can detect a higher pitch than the human ears".

This piece of science was new to me it allowed me to understand why Jumbo had heard the warning before we did.

The teacher went on to explain why it had nothing to do with, as I had suggested in my essay, my dog's Super Sensory Perception, SSP. Jumbo was just hearing the sound of the sirens going off further away, no different to any other dog.

What a disappointment this information was. I would rather have been told officially there was no Santa Claus. But later I reasoned the teacher also had a flaw in his logic. It had nothing to do with 'pitch' either. The sound being more distant than our local siren only made the sound more fainter not alter the pitch. Maybe my dog just listened better after all he did have big ears, even bigger than mine.

I came to the conclusion that the teacher was no better educated than my mother.

Because my English was poor, it seemed to me, the teacher always picked on me to be the victim of his ridicule. He must have looked forward to each lesson and the fun he could have at my expense. The teacher's verbal bullying made me dislike the rotten lessons. It would have been better for all, had he forgotten his ambition to be a comedian.

During another English lesson, the same teacher gave a brief talk about boiling an egg. Before the talk commenced, the teacher said he was expecting us all to write an essay on the subject after he had finished talking.

Anyone with an ounce of common sense would have taken some notes. I didn't. After he had finished talking, we all set about writing.

I got the title correct: 'How to boil an egg', that was written on the board!

At the end of the lesson, as I left the class, I put my essay on the teacher's desk, as did the rest of the class. A few days elapsed until I was again sitting in the next English lesson. The teacher applied the same routine of distribution: He walked around the class, returning all of the essay papers. He missed me, and continued until he reached his desk. One piece of paper remained in his hand. Yes, it was mine.

Standing at his desk, the teacher held my one page essay and waved it above his head. It reminded me of the famous 'Peace in our time' newspaper photograph of the pre-war prime minister, Neville Chamberlain, when he returned to England after his talks with Adolf Hitler.

"I have a gem of a piece of literature in my hand children. I must not deny you the benefit of hearing the contents. I will read it to you".

My discomfort was eased a little when he said " I will read it to you".

I was pleased, also, that he had not given me the credit for the work, but that came later. He read my essay as I had written. Every grammatical error and every spelling mistake he wrote on the blackboard. He criticised every line, as was his job but he gloated. His manner was belittling. In addition to my many mistakes an extra depth of laughter came from my colleagues as he read out that I had suggested it took thirty minutes in boiling water, to obtain a soft boil egg. An understanding teacher, or at least a teacher whose prime interest was to educate, may have encouraged a little more eagerness in me to improve. I hated teachers. He should never have been one.

We had now been at war for two years and, although not every night, there were still bombing raids all over the country.

I rarely saw Grandad in the garden shelter for most nights he would be 'fire watching' at the Southern Railways at Nine Elms goods yard at Wandsworth. That doesn't mean he watched fires burn. It was the duty of all men, not in the services, to keep a look out at their place of work for fires breaking out during a bombing raid and put them out if possible. Their fire watching duties commenced after the finish of the normal days work that meant not all employees were able to go home every night.

After the many bombing raids, the 'grapevine' of information, if that's what gossip is still called, was remarkably swift. Within minutes of hearing the 'all clear', regardless of weather conditions, someone would be at the door of our Anderson shelter telling of the nearest street that had been damaged, what type of bomb had caused it. Who had been killed or hurt and a wildly exaggerate number of enemy aircraft that had been wishfully shot down. .

Despite the fact that John was still of school age, he was also often missing when an air raid was in progress.

Because we could never be sure of any one night we would not have an air raid it became normal for our family to sleep in the back garden shelter. I was happy with this new routine I likened it to camping. When it was time for bed, rather than being aroused in the middle of the night, we didn't wait for the siren to commence, we went to the shelter every night as we would normally have gone to the bedroom.

There were times when the raids were distant enough to enable us to have an undisturbed night's sleep other times we were awake most of the night. Dad would join us in the shelter when he wasn't working away from home.

Mum and her eldest sister Lou were very proud of some of their young brother John's brave public spirited exploits, Aunt Lou still told of his adventures at regular intervals even after his death in 1976.

One of my Aunt's favoured stories of her brother's heroics was of how he once escorted a woman from the top floor of a blazing house:

An incendiary bomb had hit a house in Studley Road and John rushed into the burning house and assisted a lady, too frightened to move from her bedroom, to the safety of a concrete shelter in the street.

It wasn't until after the war that John told me what he really got up to. He preferred me to think of him as a rogue rather than a hero. When I questioned him about the particular incident of the lady in the burning house that Aunt Lou had told me, he told me he had gone into the house thinking it was empty. He was hoping to rescue, not a female in distress but items of value like jewellery and money. I could not have told my Aunt Lou what really happened. I am glad she died not knowing the truth.

At the outbreak of war my Aunt Lou had worked in an electrical engineering company as a coil winder and making armatures. During the war, she was directed to work like everyone by the Ministry of Labour. In her case, she had to work in a factory spraying lead paint on heavy oxygen bottles for use in aircraft. The vaporised particles of lead paint affected her stomach and badly damaged her lungs. In 1949 it was necessary for her to go into hospital for treatment but even after having a stomach operation, she never fully recovered from the affects of lead poisoning.

The German invasion of Russia, 'Operation Barbarosa' in June 1941 brought the end of the continuous heavy night bombing. That is not to say that it was the end of the air raids over England. Occasional night attacks still happened.

A little over six months must have elapsed since our return from Topsham when during one bombing raid we experienced a very nasty fright, most certainly our nearest miss:

After going to sleep, one night, in our garden shelter I was aroused by the wailing of a distant air raid siren. As the droning engine noise of the enemy aircraft got nearer so did the firing sequence of the guns in the next line of defence. The distant sound of bombs exploding and the gunfire seemed to be upon us within seconds. As the enemy aircraft came within range of the anti aircraft detachment sited on Clapham Common they started firing. The noise was deafening.

On previous occasions we had been given more warning and our local siren would have had time to have run through it's timed warning sequence before the bombers were overhead but this time the siren was still wailing when we heard the noise of the bombs exploding and defence guns began firing.

It was unusual for the men folk to be at home together on any one night. This particular night was an exception because the bombs were exploding much nearer than we had previously experienced. The adult males were inspired to take cover and join the women and children with more enthusiasm. Bombs were falling all around us but Dad had remained in the garden just outside the shelter. Suddenly Dad pushed open the door, rushed through the small entrance and avoiding the few steps jumped. As he did so, John appeared at the entrance and like Dad positioned himself about to jump the small distance. Suddenly there was a blinding white flash. John, still poised in the door space appeared as a silhouette against an ultra white background. The bomb had exploded so close it felt as though a giant hand had violently shaken our small corrugated iron garden shelter. The blast from the explosion propelled John, as though he had wings. He flew from the top of the shelter steps to the far end of the bottom bunk bed. Grandad followed but his entrance was, although spectacular not so elegant. He appeared as though bouncing on a diving board and about to perform a double somersault, in fact it resulted in the worst kind of belly flop. John fell on to Dad and Grandad fell onto both of them.

The vibration from the blast had been so great that soil sprinkled in through the bolted metal joints of the shelter and floated down covering us all in a fine dust. We all looked at each other stunned. The noise had been so loud I was momentarily deafened and my ears were ringing. I could see Mum was talking but I couldn't hear her words. Her voice was muffled as though she was speaking through a mouthful of cotton wool. Within a few seconds my hearing became partially restored and aided by lip reading, I managed to reason John say: "Jesus that was a bit too blasted close. That was a bloody land mine! I'll bet that's the church next door done for".

The church John spoke of was the grand building I referred to in a previous chapter. How much nearer the bomb needed to be to have killed us all, I don't know.

Grandma' was in a dishevelled state she looked as though she had just got home from an all night drunken rave-up. With great Victorian female dignity and unaware of her dishevelled appearance made no comment on the explosion or danger that had just passed but readjusted the position of her hat back on her head and told John not to swear.

Dad also caught by the blast, was lying spread eagled still underneath John on the floor and level with Pat lying on the bottom bunk. Dad quickly came out of his stunned state, looked around and pointed a finger at my Sister,

"Look at Pat".

Mum and I on the same ground level, looked across to the bottom bunk that Pat always slept on, It was unbelievable, She was still asleep!

She was on her back with her mouth wide open. Her face was covered with soil and dust that was still trickling in through one of the joints of the side panels of the shelter. Pat, in a sleepy state, opened her eyes. She looked as though a fairy prince had awakened her. She sat up, gave a cough, spat and dribbled the soil from her mouth. With her hands, she wiped the dust from her face and said: "What are you all laughing at?"

Her question and total ignorance of the event that had just passed made the moment funnier. Pat was then six years old. She had not been disturbed by the noise of the explosion but by our almost hysterical laughing. I think the shock and the relief that we had all survived caused our hilarity.

After the 'All Clear' siren had sounded and daylight came, we all climbed out of the shelter to investigate the damage. To the surprise of us all, our house and the church were still standing. The explosion had occurred on the furthest side of the church and demolished a block of terraced houses at the rear of the church in Paradise Road. The church, again, had supplied us with protection from the blast. Without a doubt and without a prayer it was religion that saved us that night.

Good fortune again remained with us when during another night's bombing raid a large bomb exploded about two hundred yards away in Paradise Road.

On the morning after this second near miss, we all climbed out of our shelter to see the garden carpeted with empty paper seed packets. The air was full of a very strong smell of curry and lavender.

Later that morning, I left my house, as I set off on my way to school by the garden side gate in Stanley Villas, I witnessed what should have been no surprise to me. The main casualty of the bombing raid was, in addition to the surrounding houses, a lorry repair shop with a garage and a factory/warehouse that belonged to Pannett and Needen's:

P & N before the war was one of the country's biggest supplier of kitchen herbs and garden flower seeds.

Dad parked his NAFFI lorry in the bombed garage in Paradise Road. The motor repair shop had, until now, supplied the bearings for our scooter wheels.

My path to school that morning was littered with house bricks across the roads that would have made it impossible for any wheeled vehicle to pass. The spicy aroma remained thick in the air, seeds, herbs and empty seed packets were everywhere. I crossed Paradise Road and passed the demolished P&N building on my left into Clarence Walk and while doing so I collected as many different titled packets as I could find. Having walked the length of Clarence Walk I crossed Jeffrey's Road into Bromfelde Road, passed Elwell Road, where I had lived two years earlier and reached school in Gaskell Street:

When the school was built, little more than half a century past, it was surrounded with a ten-foot high brick wall. The entrance would normally be gained by two separate wrought iron gates of a similar height, one for infant boys at one end of the school and at the other end for junior boys. Thus keeping the two age groups separate.

A large section of the wall was now missing and although it was not necessary I automatically walked through the hole where the gates had once been. As I entered the playground I was surprised to see it to was covered with the P&N seed packets and children were kicking the packets about like the fallen leaves in August.

I think it must have been the result of the experience of our lucky escapes that prompted Mum and Dad to reconsider their wisdom of our return to London from Devon.

I cannot remember the actual date of our next excursion but Pat and I were evacuated to the North of England.

We must have travelled by train to reach Flixton.

Flixton was near Urmston, in the suburbs West of Manchester, this was to become our third evacuation home. Although I remember little about the house, I do recall it was terraced which I would now consider to have been built in the late thirties so at the time it was only about three to five years old.

One feature of the house I remember was the lavatory. It had a proper roll of toilet paper on a proper holder attached to the wall!

Pat remembers the owners of the house where I can remember nothing about them. In one of Pat's many regular letters she has written, since living in Australia, she referred to a Mrs Williams and her three months old son. But my most vivid recollection of our

Manchester visit is the school that I attended. It was magnificent. It made a lasting impression on me because it was not like any school I had seen before:

Many years later, while on holiday in The Canary Islands I was in conversation with a native Manchurian, after I had described the school I had attended, I was told the school was the Stretford Technical School.

Nearly all the schools in inner London were built in the previous century, during the reign of Queen Victoria. This school, like the house we were staying at, was also relatively newly built. It was a large impressive building, set back from the main road. There were lawns and flowerbeds on each side of a long wide path that led to a wide main entrance. The playing area was grassed and sited at the rear of the building and unseen from the road.

Through a minor misdemeanour, regarding leaving school ten minutes before finishing time, I only had one visit to the headmaster's office, This came to nothing because I was able to convince the head' I had misunderstood a piece of information I had been given by my teacher. My excuse was only in part honest: As my first day neared the end of the last lesson an alarm above the classroom door began buzzing which alerted the teacher to the time. He looked at his watch

"All of those catching the early bus may leave now".

I was catching a bus and as I had no objection to leaving early I thought that would do me nicely. Leaving the class ten minutes early, however, was only allowed to the children travelling on one particular bus route and towards the centre of Manchester.

A few children got up out of their seats and walked out of the classroom. Applying the dictum 'don't ask the question if you don't want to know the answer', I boldly followed them. As we walked along the corridor, we were joined by children from other classes, all wanting to catch the same bus. When we reached the bus stop I was the only one that continued walking and crossed the road to catch the bus going in the opposite direction. As I was the only one to cross the road and going away from town, it took little brainpower that I should have stayed in the classroom. But I got away with it, so I continued to do so for couple of weeks until I got 'rumbled'.

For the rest of my stay I obeyed the rules and I was a good little lad, well no worse than the rest. There was a downside: good little lads don't earn dodgy pennies.

Grandad Bridger's hobby was breading cage birds; canaries and budgerigars, chickens and 'Chinchilla Giganta' rabbits for show purposes. To say that his interest in animals was his only pastime would be an understatement. It was a passion he was totally immersed in.

From my observations, animals seemed to be his only reason for living. Regardless of the weather, sun, rain or snow and with no exceptions for a Sunday, he would get up early in the morning to attend to his 'fur and feathered friends' before he went to work. When he returned from work in the evening his first task was to allocate the cooked bran and potato peelings, sprinkled with other nutrients, into small dishes and serve the rabbits individually. He repeated the procedure, with different ingredients, for his birds and chickens. Not until all this was done would he come into the house to feed himself. To say the smell of boiling potato peelings, barley and bran was rather unpleasant would be misleading. It was vile.

The smell was at its worse during the winter months it polluted our three-storey house from top to bottom. When it was cold outside the house, water ran down the walls on the inside, but not from rain. The steam from Grandad's brew would be absorbed by the wallpaper like an invisible alien and remained there until the house began to dry out in late Spring.

With only one exception in 1946, to my knowledge Grandad never had a summer holiday nor for that matter even a one-day break. He would not trust anyone to care for his large family of animals. The exception I refer to in a later chapter.

I include that observation not as a criticism but as a compliment. It was a common sense approach on his part. He could not trust a delegate to come up to his standard of care and responsibility. I doubted that anyone in South London could equal his comprehensive knowledge.

He went about his daily life as though he was a lone inhabitant on a desert island, he limited himself with talking as though speech was a valuable commodity and was saving it for an important function.

I never heard him swear or engage in normal casual conversation or waste time with pleasantries, like "good morning" as one would normally do in passing. He could ignore anyone in his presence as though they were not there. To his credit, on the rare occasions that he would speak, it would be information giving, educational and worth listening to, that is assuming the listener was interested in Rabbits, Birds or Chickens.

I think of him now as though he lived behind an invisible barrier in his self-inflicted isolation. He never spoke, nor touched me to cuddle or even to playfully ruffle my hair. If the reader comes to the conclusion that I did not like my Grandfather, I have used the wrong words for my description of him. At the time, I never considered whether I liked him or not. We had nothing in common even his unsociable manner didn't bother me we were worlds apart.

One oddity that I could not figure out however, he would nurse his creatures with loving care and tend to their needs as though they were his own children. He fed them before he went to work in the morning and as soon as he returned each night. If, however, they did not come up to his high standard, for show purposes, he could finish their lives 'in the blink of an eye'. In the case of a chicken by one short twist and a sharp pull he could wring its neck without the slightest hesitation. A rabbit that was not likely to win a competition rosette, was also quickly terminated:

The area that was used for his animals ran the whole width of the garden along the back wall. Because of the hay, straw and other animal food he kept there it was also a haven for stray cats to give birth to their litters.

I once observed him, from my bedroom window, gather a litter of small and pink skinned kittens and bundle them all into a sack. The sack also contained a brick. He then dropped the sack into a bucket of water to drown them. As soon as he became aware that I had been observing him, he appeared to get agitated. He called to me and invited me to come into his half of the garden. When I arrived at his side he offered me a reason for his action:

"If I had not done that the rats would have had them. You have to be cruel to be kind," he said.

Over time he appeared to become aware that I was taking notice of his knowledge and enthusiasm for natural science. He must have recognised a potential junior friend as I began to show an interest in his activities. He also gave me 'snips' of information on gardening.

He encouraged me to care for a small plot of soil to grow various vegetables and flowers from seed that he supplied.

The two years anniversary since the outbreak of war was approaching and soldiers, sailors, airmen and civilians throughout the world were being slain, dying of malnutrition or being taken prisoner weekly in their thousands. Many of the civilian prisoners were used for slave labour.

Because so little appeared to be happening in the area of the Mediterranean war zone no adjustments had been made to my wall map for months. I decided to use part of the opposite side of my bedroom wall to hold another map where plenty of action was taking place:

Part of Africa that I had not included on my war map was the area that was known as Eritrea and Somaliland. During Mussolini's brief period of empire building in the 1930's, both countries had been grouped together with Abyssinia, now Ethiopia, and renamed Italian East Africa

During December, Commonwealth forces, with the help of Ethiopians troops, drove the Italian army out of their country and regained their independence.

My new action map was of the war zone of Poland and Russia and referred to as 'The Eastern Front'.

The invincible German forces were gaining ground and racing

into Russia from The Baltic Sea in North Eastern Europe to The Ukraine in the South. A strategically important objective in the South was the oil rich area of the Black Sea. However, even with the remarkable speed of the German army's advance, they could not beat nature. Hitler commenced his initial summer offensive too late.

So confident was Hitler of a swift success on the Eastern Front his troops were equipped with only one thin summer issue of clothing. Hitler's plan was to make a lightning assault to install his Eastern army's headquarters in Moscow before Christmas:

Hitler made the same mistake Napoleon had made one hundred and twenty eight years before. He underestimated the ferocity of Russia's sub zero winters. During the battle of Stalingrad temperatures were recorded as low as 35 degrees below freezing. The big guns froze and the tanks failed to start. German sentries accidentally falling to sleep and thereby stationary were found the next morning frozen to death. At the furthest point of their advance, German forces had come within twelve miles of the Kremlin but it was not quite near enough. Hitler's mistake in his timing was to prove fatal.

German forces on the Eastern front were freezing to death in the Russian winter while in North Africa they were seeking shade from the sun in the desert.

The German bombing raids over the British Isle continued.

The 7th December will long be remembered, if not by the world, certainly by all Americans. Without giving a declaration of war, Japanese fighter and torpedo planes attacked Pearl Harbour in Hawaii:

Five American battleships at anchor were sunk and 2,344 men were killed. Understandably, the next day, America declared war on Japan.

In a broadcast to the American nation, President Roosevelt said it was: "A date that will live in infamy".

After the bombing one senior Japanese officer that opposed the attack of the American Pacific fleet told the military government "You have woken a sleeping tiger".

On Christmas Day, 1941, Hong Kong, a peninsular on the Chinese mainland, surrendered and became the first British possession, of the war, to fall to the Japanese. While the raid by Japanese aircraft against the American Pacific Fleet on Hawaii was taking place, the desert war on the other side of the world, continued.

German forces fighting the Russians, on the Eastern Front went on the defensive. After some bloody battles, with heavy losses on both sides, German troops started to withdraw. Joy!

The seesaw swung in the Allies favour. I got my cotton and pins to work again. Bad news came after Christmas. The German army counter attacked. I had been too hasty.

Since Churchill became Prime Minister, eighteen months earlier, he had been involved in a secret meeting with Roosevelt to encourage him to come into the war against Germany. But there was a powerful political lobby in America that did not want a repeat of the Great War in 1914-18.

Britain was bankrupt. It had not yet paid back the loan it had acquired from the USA to finance the Great War of 1914-1918. New agreed loans were now piling up on top of the old.

One of Churchill's lesser arguments, to encourage the United States to enter the war, was that America should join in the fight, if only to protect her investment. Churchill was delighted when he informed the government and the British people that Germany had declared war on The United States of America.

Great Britain and the Empire were no longer alone.

SIX

ROMMEL SPOILS MY MAP

Erwin Rommel opened his second offensive on 21st January 1942, by capturing the coastal town of Benghazi, North Africa. On 7th February he came to a halt.

In Britain on 26th January 1942, the arrival of the first American GI's, General Issue, added to the growing amount of uniformed service men and women serving in the armed forces. There were also civilians, having fled their homes on the mainland of Europe and came to England because there was nowhere else for them to go.

It was a period that servicemen from all over the Empire came to Britain. People from other distant Commonwealth countries and those with no special allegiance to the United Kingdom arrived to help fight for the allied cause. They were people of a variety of skin colour, religions and customs. But they all had, at least, one thing in common. They had a desperate passion to fight against an evil regime.

Most men and women of service age that had not been resident in the United Kingdom before the war were formed into their own national fighting battalions and brigades with their own country's officers and battledress insignias. All of which came under the command of the British army. The French, for example, that had escaped with the British Expeditionary Force, BEF, during the evacuation of Dunkirk, formed their own 'Fighting Free French' unit under the command of a young General DeGaul.

In most cases before the war, unless one lived near a large port area like London, Southampton or Liverpool Docks where foreign seamen spent their shore leave, for instance, black people would only have been seen on rare occasions. It was so rare in contrast to today it was considered lucky to see a black African but good luck would only be effective if the observer touched their own collar, spat and made a wish.

The influx of nationalities into the country gave a wonderful boost to my collection of foreign matchboxes, cigarette packets and chewing gum wrappers.

In addition to the increased potential for my hobby of collecting various scraps of junk the war was not all one sided.

The year was one of changing fortune from a most humiliating defeat inflicted by the Japanese on Commonwealth troops in Asia, to sweet victories over the Germans in Egypt and Russia. In the space of less than three years, from the outbreak of war, the 'civilised world' was at the edge of a precipice. The 'Axis' forces, the German and Japanese, had almost complete command of The Atlantic and The Pacific Oceans.

German troops came 'within a whisker' of controlling the oil fields in the Middle East. Almost half of the world had become subservient to two ruthless military regimes.

The news of the surrender, on February 15th, of British forces in Singapore was a terrible shock. It will, most likely, register in history as one of Britain's most disgraceful acts of senior officer incompetence. It is a fact that the fall of Singapore ranks as the biggest defeat ever in British military history. It is reputed that the Japanese infantry came through the, so-called, impenetrable jungle on bicycles to engage an enemy that outnumbered them by three to one.

One troop carrier, bringing Australian forces in to support the garrison had just docked at the harbour when the surrender was announced. They walked straight off the boat to become Japanese prisoners of war. Not only had Singapore been lost to the Japanese, Burma had also been overrun.

From Odessa, the Russian port on the Black Sea, nineteen and half thousand Jewish people were deported in cattle trucks to Gestapo controlled concentration camps.

Before the end of the year evidence appeared in newspapers that many Jews in Eastern Europe were being exterminated.

The Northern and Eastern coast of Australia was on alert from fear that the Japanese would launch an invasion.

During May 1942, a combined effort from the British and American navy met the Japanese flotilla and, after a monumental battle, destroyed the enemy. That mighty historic sea battle is known as the 'Battle of the Coral Sea'.

In North Africa the battle continued. The seesaw of fortune swung backwards and forwards and claimed heavy casualties on both sides.

My new map began to look like a pincushion. I stuck pieces of fresh paper over previous territorial gains and losses to allow the pins to stay firm on the board. Britain was in a desperate position to maintain morale and needed a big victory. Anywhere would do!

In Eastern Europe, the German army was still threatening Moscow and our ships carrying vital supplies to Russia were being seriously disrupted by German U Boats and aircraft attacks. Losses in ships and men sometimes amounted to three-quarters of the convoys.

From the outbreak of war in 1939 to 1942, one in five British merchant seamen lost their lives. During that period, up to 1942, their casualty rate was greater than any one of three fighting services. In March 1942, 273 Allied ships were lost through enemy action. It was to be the worst monthly total of the war.

Although I had no less interest in the war going on in Asia and the Pacific Islands, I did not record the activity in the same manner as I did for the North Africa and European campaigns. There is a good reason for this omission there was not enough space around my bedroom to record all the war zones.

From newspapers, I cut out all of the maps I could get my hands on and stuck them in scrapbooks. For scrapbooks I used old bound ledgers that I picked up in empty houses and for the adhesive paste, to stick the maps onto the pages, I used flower and water.

It was about this time a new plan was introduced by the Ministry of Food. The campaign was called 'Adopt a Pig'. The plan was for households to collect kitchen scraps and waste table food to feed pigs.

The object of the exercise was that each person anticipating in the scheme became a shareholder in a pig. There were only a limited number of shares in any one pig because at end of each year the idea was for the animal to be slaughtered, cut up and distributed between the shareholders for their Christmas dinners.

The idea 'caught on' and was well supported but there was a difference of opinion when December came. Many pig minders had become so attached to their animal they were seen more as pets than a dinner and objected to the idea of them being eaten:

A couple of swill bins were placed at the end of many roads in the capital and maybe in many other towns and emptied daily.

Some employees of commercial organisations were attracted to the idea and made use of unused plots of land belonging to their employers to set up a pigsty. The policemen at Brixton police station in Gresham Road, where Grandad, (Stylo, my Father's Father) was employed as a 'special', had their own club.

On Clapham Common, where the children's swings are now sited, was an area cleared for the construction of a pigsty. In a short time, a number of young pigs were being cared for and fed in their new home. But only until Christmas.

Pat and I soon returned to London, physically none the worse, from our Manchester trip, in fact I think it was for the better. The school may not have taught me anything to improve my education to pass exams but it was a mental education, in as much that, I learnt not all teachers were psychopaths or sadists.

Living in a clean, tidy and well furnished house also left an impression on me that it was not only in houses where rich people lived that had decent toilet facilities with rolls of toilet paper instead of old telephone directories nailed to the toilet wall but, most important they did not all have bedrooms with bugs.

Back in the capital, life returned to normal, in spite of the occasional air raid.

While I was in the garden one day, Dad came down the steps from the house, walked up and spoke to me. He asked me in a very tired voice and an unconvincing interest "what are you doing Ron?"

Before I could reply, he put his hand on my shoulder and told me to walk to the end of the garden with him. Surprised at his unusual request, I turned and looked up at his face. His eyes were watery and had a fixed glazed stare and his manner was very solemn. With his hand still on my shoulder, we slowly walked down to the end of the garden. This was one of the few times I felt uncomfortable in his company. His mood was such that I had never seen before I sensed he also felt ill at ease. Neither of us said another word until we turned the path that took us behind the air raid shelter. Out of sight from the house, standing between the long row of Grandad's rabbit hutches and bird cages at the rear of the air raid shelter we stopped.

I could see tears in Dad's tired eyes as he turned towards me to speak. "Ron, you have got to be a brave boy now".

He turned his head away from me, took a deep breath and gave a strained cough. He remained staring silently at the back of the corrugated metal shelter for a while as though hypnotised. The suspense was too long for me to be just waiting and doing nothing. I felt a need to speak. I broke the silence. "What's the matter Dad?"

"You won't be able to play with your Sister Bebe anymore Ron".

I replied with little understanding or sympathy: "Is she dead?"

My unemotional question shocked Dad back to a more controlled state and helped him to continue.

"Yes! I am going to tell Pat that Bebe has gone to play with the angels so don't say anything to her about it".

The next day, I overheard Mum and Dad talking about inviting family, friends and neighbours to see Bebe for the last time. When Mum and I were alone, I told my Mother I also wanted to see Bede for the last time. Her response was a very firm no but I didn't let the answer rest at that. I continued to pester her and eventually she suggested we should wait to hear what Dad had to say.

The following day Aunt Rose, still in the Women's Royal Army Corps, WRACS, came home on compassionate leave from her barracks and took Pat and I to Clapham Common.

This, I thought about later, was a plan devised by the 'grown ups' to keep us away from the house while the undertaker delivered the coffin with our dead baby Sister from the funeral parlour. To my surprise, when we returned, in the late afternoon, Dad was home. He looked better and a little more like his normal self.

Out of hearing from anyone else Dad told me he knew I wanted to see Bebe for the last time. "Ma'm is not sure because she thinks you are too young but I think you have been so brave I am going to let you see Bebe sleeping but you must be on your best behaviour" he said.

The next day, Mum and Dad took me downstairs to my Gran' and Grandad's flat. We had to pass through the door on the landing that had once, before we lived there, divided the master quarters from the servants and walked down the stairs.

The thick pungent mouldy smell of stewed potato peelings and bran, being cooked for the rabbits, filled the air.

The funeral event had not interfered with Grandad's timetable to feed his furry friends. I did not consider the smell could have been anything other than what was cooking.

We descended into the gloomy basement and Dad led me into my Grandparents front parlour. I had been downstairs in my Grandparents kitchens before but it was the first time I had ever been inside this room, I am happy that it was also the last.

Once inside I was surprised to see, not only relations but some folk that I did not recognise.

The curtains in the room were drawn and two large flickering candles dimly lit the room.

The flat, being in the basement, had a damp mouldy smell and in addition to the cooking added to the overall unsettling atmosphere. A clergyman was standing furthest away from the door with his back to the curtained window at the head of the open coffin. With both hands crossed and holding a black book in front of him he looked in my direction.

"Ah! Here's the little chap," he said, as my father and I walked into the room.

I took an instant liking to him because he had a gentle soft pink face. Then, looking at Dad, the clergymen said "Father bring young Ronnie over here and let him stand next to me".

Dad obeyed and the clergy' took my hand and indicated for me to stand next to him. He then transferred his right hand to my shoulder, drew me close to his side, looked down at me and smiled. He transferred, from both hands, to his left hand, his book that I assumed was a bible. Before I walked towards the clergyman, all of the people in the little room had been quiet. I noticed some people began to cry, I didn't get a great psychological hang-up over it but it looked to me that the family was more upset at seeing me alive than seeing my Sister dead.

I looked up and watched him as he turned his face towards Mum and Dad. With a permanent soft smile, he began to read a passage from his book. I did not hear what was said, I was too numb. I was already wishing that I had not been so stubborn by wanting to attend.

Too frightened to move anymore than my eyes, while the vicar was still reading, I looked downwards into the small open white coffin in front of me: If hearts can miss a beat through shock, then I am sure mine must have done so. At that moment, I wanted to object that it wasn't Bebe. I could hardly believe I was looking at my dead baby Sister.

She looked like a small creamy white wax doll, much smaller than when she was alive. My eyes, still without moving my head, wandered around the walls; I observed many old sepia photographs of more people I had never seen. It was a frightening experience. I hope I will never have to witness seeing a dead person again. For many nights, I relived that haunting sight although I never admitted Mum was right in her first judgment to refuse my request. I never told Pat that Bebe was dead.

I have a black bordered 'In loving memory card' my Aunt Lou gave me thirty years later. On the front page the card is headed with the words:

Suffer* little children to come unto me.

The passage inside the card reads:

'There's a home for little children,

Above the bright blue sky,

And all who love the saviour,

Will reach it bye and bye'.

*For many years, long into adulthood, I thought, the biblical quotation 'suffer little children' was brutal and at odds with the philosophy of Christianity.

It was not until I checked in Chambers Dictionary and discovered that 'suffer' also meant ' to allow' or 'permit' did it make sense. 'Allow' little children to come unto me, reads much better.

The bombing continued throughout the year all over the British Isles during the summer. In addition to the cities, the Isle of Wight was targeted. Seaside resorts along the East and South coast and small farming villages including Storrington and Petworth in Sussex, were also hit.

On the Mediterranean coast on 21st June German troops, in a 'whirlwind' assault captured Tobruk.

154

Nearly 33,000 British and South African troops with vast supplies of arms and equipment were captured. German forces built on their success and advanced well into Egypt but were held at the perimeter of El Alamein.

A paradox of the desert war was the supply of food and equipment: The distance between German and British Headquarters were over twelve hundred miles apart. The major difficulty of the advancing army, was keeping a longer supply line secure. The greater the distance became between depot and front line, the more vulnerable it became from enemy bombing because it was more difficult to protect. On the other hand, the retreating army had the advantage of a shorter supply line.

On 23rdOctober at ten o'clock on a cloudless night the Battle of El Alamein commenced:

Alamein is two hundred and fifty miles inside Egypt. It was only a small desert railway halt but it was vitally important. It was the last defence before Cairo, only two hundred miles away.

To support a counter-attack of one hundred thousand Commonwealth infantrymen, sixteen thousand big guns roared into action firing on German and Italian positions. A massive all-out offensive began.

A week after the battle of Alamein American marines made a successful landing in French North Africa, 'Operation Torch'. The British Commonwealth forces continued to attack the German 'Afrika Corps' front line while the fresh, newly arrived, American army threatened the German headquarters from the rear. The American landing made Rommel's position hopeless. His supplies of everyday needs having to cross The Mediterranean from Europe were constantly being disrupted by air attacks and placed him in a position which made any thought to counter attack impossible. He had been out manoeuvred and out gunned and placed in a situation he could not possibly win.

In spite of the enemy air raids on London live stage shows continued and cinemas remained open.

One theatre, 'The Windmill', off Shaftsbury Avenue, in the West End boasted that it never closed during the war.

Going to the cinema was the main form of family entertainment, which in London at least ran continuous performances. If an air raid started while a film was in progress, the film would stop being shown for a minute or two and the words; 'There is an air raid alert. The film will continue for those patrons wishing to remain in the cinema' would be displayed on the screen.

A collection of desert battle scenes on film were put together by the Government controlled Crown Film Unit and was released through the cinema circuit a short time after the Battle of Alamein. The film was called 'Desert Victory'.

One sequence, I recall, was of Commonwealth soldiers, silhouetted by moonlight, walking forward in a crouching position. The minefields in the sand were seen being cleared by 'Sappers' in front of them.

They advanced with long bayonets fixed to the end of their rifles against a background flashing gunfire that looked like strobe lighting at a present day disco.

The newscaster proudly speculated: "This time there will be no more retreating"

The words and pictures were very inspiring to keep the home front spirits up. At the time the artillery bombardment was the heaviest in history

One cinema news film, covering the Alamein battle, was an illustration of the extreme range of temperature: During the hours of daylight, it got so hot a soldier was able to fry an egg on the mudguard of a lorry. While during the night, stationary vehicles had to have the water drained from their radiators for fear of the water inside freezing and damaging the engine or splitting the radiator:

In the event of a surprise attack, a fleet of vehicles with no water in their radiators was in a vulnerable situation. To remedy this handicap a mixture of Methanol and, or, Propylene Glycol was added to the radiator water, which allowed water to remain in a liquid state at a much lower temperature below the normal freezing point.

It has been used commercially ever since. We now call it anti-freeze.

On 1st November, the German army disengaged and withdrew from the battle. The victory at El Alamein is regarded as one of the many significant battles of the war.

It is held in such high regard because before the battle the Allies had encountered nothing but defeat on land. There was anxious concern that a victory of substance was long overdue. Encouraged by newspaper speculation that, at last, the war had swung in our favour and there would be no more defeats, I set about drawing my third new map with revived enthusiasm.

There were three main film distributors, each with their own chain of cinemas; Associated British Cinemas, ABC's, Odeon Cinemas and British Gaumont. ABC cinemas distributed Metro Goldwyn Meyer pictures. MGM, movies produced the most lavish musicals. 'Paramount' films could only be seen in an Odeon cinema and 'Universal' films were distributed throughout the British Gaumont network.

All of the main London cinemas belonged to one of the above groups and, in most cases, would show a new film for a period of one week only.

All films would be shown in the West End cinemas before going on general release. If the movie was successful it could remain in the West End for months and remain there until another was ready to take its place or the attendance figures began to slip. In addition to there being three main distributors there were also three London areas of distribution which were divided into three groups; North London always got the first week of release from the West End. North East and North West London on the second week and South

London on the third week.

Cinema seats were priced like the theatre, Stalls, Circle, Upper Circle etc. The price range was 6d, 9d, 1/-, 1/3d and dress circle 1/9d. Unlike the theatre, the stalls were the cheapest.

The cinema show consisted of an 'A' and a 'B' movie, each of about ninety minutes in duration. The main feature film was the 'A'. The 'B' was usually made on a lower budget. The two movies were separated by an interval in which the latest news, information films and trailers, of forthcoming programmes were shown. In addition to films, it was not unusual for an organist to be included in the show and play popular wartime songs. The audience was encouraged to sing along. The words were shown on the screen and a small ball bounced along the top of the words in time with the music.

Unlike today cinema programmes, films were shown as a continuing performance, which allowed anyone to begin seeing a film at beginning, middle or end.

'British Gaumont' newsreels were shown, obviously, at British Gaumont cinemas, while 'Pathe News' was shown at Odeon cinemas.

Sometimes I went to the pictures with Mum, Dad and Pat, as much as twice in one week, but the frequency was very much dependent on Dad's NAAFI delivery schedule. I did not rely, however, on going to the cinema with my parents, sometimes I would go with a friend and 'bunk in'. To my school friends it was seen to be a sissy to pay. The method we most often used was getting in through the emergency fire exit doors:

There were times the emergency exit door would not have been closed properly by people using it as an ordinary exit door and we were able to just walk in. All of the fire doors were of the push bar type but when closed properly could only be opened from the inside. When the fire doors were closed properly one of us would have to climb onto a friend's shoulder and climb in through an, always open, toilet window. Toilets, for a reason I cannot explain, were always next to fire exits.

158

Once inside the toilet, the one that had got in through the window would then walk to the fire exit door and push the emergency door open. But it was not always an easy task, it took cunning and good timing.

Sometimes the wait, on the outside, for the door to be opened, could be lengthy. The push bar, when used was a noisy piece of mechanism and it was wise for the one on the inside to wait for the soundtrack on the film to reach a noisy section before pushing the bar on the door. Once we were all inside, without a ticket, it was wise to disperse as quickly as possible. Boldness was the safest ploy. To avoid arousing suspicion we had to find a seat as quickly as possible. The safest seat to seek was an empty one next to an adult couple where it was easier to blend in. I think, if the person I chose to sit next to became aware I was alone he must also have assumed correctly I had no ticket but had most probably done the same thing when he was younger and 'turned a blind eye'.

Once seated, I was never informed upon by a ticket holder nor discovered by an usherette. Not having to pay to get in the cinema was a great incentive to use the back door. But, because of the strict censorship laws, unless accompanied with an adult, children were not allowed to see many of the film released. The law actually encouraged children, unaccompanied by an adult, to 'bunk in'. To see an 'A' rated film there was no option, cinemas were not allowed to sell minors a ticket to see an 'A' film.

Hollywood dominated the film industry during the war, when did it not? There was great rivalry between the film studios and each spent a lot of money in promoting the popularity of their respective actors and actresses.

One hobby that was very popular with my school colleagues was that of collecting signed glossy photographs of the 'stars'. Swapping film studio addresses was an active pastime at school.

I had a collection which included signed photographs from idols such as Alan Ladd, Clarke Gable, Edward.G.Robinson, Bing Crosby, Bob Hope, Paul Muni, Humphrey Bogart, Fred McMurray, James

Cagney, Betty Grable, Dorothy Lamour and many more.

From the time I had posted a letter to California, requesting a photograph the reply containing a prized photograph could take many months, sometimes a year could elapse, before receiving a reply. When it did arrive I had long forgotten I had made the request,.

To ask for a photograph from the British studios was not so popular, they always asked for a receipt of a donation from a charity.

By December 13th Rommel's army was in full retreat. On December 21st, the British Commonwealth 8th Army reoccupied Benghazi and pushed the German Afrika Korps back beyond the positions that the British forces had held on two previous occasions. Total victory in Africa, however, was still another five months away. But the territories that Hitler's army had under its control reached its peak during 1942.

I lived in a corner house on the end of a line of terraced houses and our back garden ran half of the length of Stanley Villas: Studley Road between Clapham Road to Larkhall Lane. Half way down Studley Road was a small side street, Stanley Villas. Stanley Villas linked Studley Road to Paradise Road. A road it was. Paradise it most certainly was not. From an aerial view Stanley Villas would have looked like the horizontal that linked the two verticals of the letter H.

Each daily walk, to and from school, necessitated the fearful operation of crossing Paradise Road. The houses in Paradise Road were unlike the, once large elegant, houses in Studley Road. They were much smaller homes and built for the less wealthy. It was also home for two large and very violent families.

One family in particular that aspired to being the most feared was the Boyler family (name changed for fear of reprisal from the descendants). They were an infamous mob, it was rumoured that, before the war, all of the adult members of the family were continually in and out of prison.

From my point of view, however, the activities of the adults of the family did not concern me. It was a couple of the young Boylers, going to my school that terrorised me and every other schoolboy in the area. The whole family was lawless anti social animals. They were a law unto themselves. The two youngest members of the family demanded a toll, with a threat of violence, to enter their road: I had to cross Paradise Road to get to school. Money, marbles, cigarette cards, catapult's, penknives, anything that could be found in a school boy's pocket, to enter 'their road' would be an acceptable token. On one occasion, when I was alone, I was not brave enough to deny their demands some of my valued possessions changed hands. I would like to relate a fairy tale ending where I got my own back and they never pestered me, or anyone else again but that didn't happen. It only happened to me once, however, I had learnt from my first encounter, I had to move faster crossing the street and not to become a victim again.

A lone member of any other local gang that unwittingly roamed into the 'Paradise' domain was subjected to the same demands. Very often a small single incident provoked a full-scale gang war when a victim would return with his own gang in full force for retribution.

While making a dash from Stanley Villas, across Paradise Road to the opposite side turning in Clarence Walk, it was not unusual to see the aftermath of a war of rival gangs that had taken place. The road would be littered with broken milk bottles, bricks and other items that had been used as missiles.

After an air raid a street battle would only be noticeable by the quantity of broken milk bottles. Street fights, however, were not always the reserve of school children. Grown men, usually as a result of being drunk, staged their own violent performances.

The Paradise Road family remained a gang of anti social terrorists until they were eventually bombed out by enemy aircraft. Perhaps even the Germans had heard of them.

During some of my school holidays, Dad would take me with him on his NAAFI distribution runs. On one occasion when he took me with him, we 'loaded up' his lorry at Okehampton, Devon and delivered our load to an army barracks in Plymouth. It was early evening when we arrived and after Dad had made the necessary arrangements to get the lorry unloaded, I followed him to the stores where we were allocated a bed each. After Dad had signed for our bed linen we carried our pillows and blankets to our assigned billet.

Our sleeping quarters were in a long corrugated iron shed, like a shrunken aircraft hanger, with about fifty beds. Most of the beds had sheets and blankets but empty of people. We chose two adjoining empty beds with just a mattress, dropped our bed linen on them and went off to the army canteen for a meal. Because it was outside the normal mealtime the place was empty except for a cook that supplied us with a feast. After we had finished eating and seeing a film in the crowded camp cinema we returned to our allocated sleeping hut.

I was out of place as I followed Dad in and saw that it was now fully occupied with soldiers. Those not in bed, were either reading, playing cards or cleaning their equipment, others were just standing around occupied in talking.

I watched intrigued as one soldier meticulously cleaned his stripped down rifle, he noticed my interest and told me they were all waiting to go overseas. I soon became the topic of the soldiers banter all on the theme of being so young to have been 'called up' for military service. They all enjoyed their foolish jokes about me that continued after 'lights out'. I thought they were all a bit daft and felt disappointed that Dad had joined in with their simple humour.

With the lorry unloaded we then spent the best part of the next boring day waiting for the lorry to be loaded up again to transport a fresh load to a food storage depot inland. By early evening, having completed the loading, we went over to the canteen and had a last evening meal before setting off. We left the barracks at Plymouth late in the evening just as it was getting dark. It was not long after we had left the city houses behind us and got into the countryside that Dad said "there's a vehicle behind us that keeps blinking his lights, I wonder what's wrong?"

The 'blackout' applied to vehicles as well as buildings and street lighting. Vehicle headlights were 'hooded' with a metal cap with a small horizontal slit covering the glass area that allowed just enough light to be seen by approaching traffic. A 'blink' was from dimmed light to no light. It also became an offence to drive a vehicle without white painted bumpers and running boards. Offenders could be fined up to a £10fine.

I suspected much later, that Dad knew exactly what he was stopping for and the meeting, about to take place, had been prearranged.

We pulled into a lay-by and stopped. As he did so an army jeep pulled up along side and then reversed, so as to face the direction it had just come from and backed up behind us. Dad got out of the cab and walked to the back of his lorry. I looked through the 'wing' mirror and saw two uniformed men get out of their jeep and start a conversation but it sounded as though the soldiers were doing most of the talking. I came to the conclusion by their accent they were American. Whilst the talking continued, I heard something being moved and one of the tailboard pins on the back of our lorry being drawn out of its holder. The chain clattered against the bodywork, followed rapidly by the second pin and chain and board. In contrast to the silence of the night, as the tailboard banged against the bodywork, it sounded like a bomb had exploded. I did not have a clue what was going on but I realised that speed took priority over sound. I heard someone jump up on the back of the lorry accompanied with more talking by the 'Yanks'. I wanted to get out to see what was going on but Dad had told me, before he had got out, to stay where I was. During whatever was 'going on' in the back of the lorry was between Dad and one of the soldiers, the other soldier walked around to the front of the cab.

I noticed he had a bright multi coloured insignia on the top of his sleeve and further down, just above his elbow, he was wearing a red armband with the letters M.P. I knew the initials stood for Military Police so I thought, as we had only just left the barracks, the police were carrying out a random search. The soldier facing me from the other side of the door had a grumpy looking mournful face and a manner to match.

He put his head halfway into the cab' and spoke in a miserable drawl, he sounded like a movie cowboy:

"Thars war's gonna take a dang lot longa than mose piple wanna thank about. Ar hopes eets all over fore you all gets ya r 'call up' son".

I did not quite understand all what he was saying but the words seemed to suit his message. He didn't want to have a conversation he just made the statement. I remember his miserable looking face to this day

As he turned to walk, away he gave me a packet of chewing gum. Perhaps he was not as unpleasant as he appeared to be. Later I wondered if he survived the war. The action of the previous few minutes went into reverse order. I heard the sound of someone with hob nailed boots jump from the back of the lorry and onto the road. The heavy hinges on the tailboard squeaked as it was lifted up and then banged as it was swung to its closed position against the uprights of the bodywork. I recognised the familiar sound of the tailboard chains and the safety pins being dropped back into their slots. More rapid unintelligible whispering followed as the noisy engine of the jeep was switched on.

The engine revved up and down, in response to an anxious jerky foot movement on the accelerator as though the driver was waiting for the 'go' light at a race meeting.

As the driver 'clunked' the vehicle into gear I heard Dad say: "OK Pal" and, with his colleague now aboard, accelerated off.

Dad walked up to my side of the lorry, poked his head through the open window and asked if I wanted to 'stretch my legs' for a minute:

When we were travelling 'stretching legs' was a term that Dad and Mum always used to replace 'do you want go to the toilet'.

I jumped down from the lorry, watered the hedge, at the side of the road, buttoned up my trousers and returned to my seat: Zips were patented in 1915 and had been in use for many years but I believe they had not been used on trousers until many years later certainly not on mine.

Dad smiled when I told him that the soldier had given me some chewing gum but his smile changed to a look of concern when I asked him "what have the soldiers put in the back of the lorry Dad?"

As we drove off, I thought Dad told me he had bought a 'ciderham' from them but it was to be kept a secret so I must not tell anyone. It sounded too heavy for it to have been a few bottles and as I didn't have a clue what he was talking about, it would be very easy for me to have kept it a secret.

"Ciderham, what's a ciderham?"I asked.

"It's half of a whole one you daft a'puth"(half a penny) Dad replied, thinking he had now made it clear to me and that was the end it.

"I don't understand what you mean!"

"What d'you mean you don't know what I mean? You know what a lamb is. Well this is half of a whole one"

"Oh. I thought you meant cider to drink".

I was quite for only a minute or two. I thought: if it is only half it must be dead. A lamb would have made a nice pet but it wouldn't be much good if it wasn't alive.

"What do you want half of a dead lamb for Dad?"

"What do you think it's for? It's to eat you fathead!"

There was no humour in his voice and what could have been a comical conversation, in fact was hostile. I felt he was regretting he had responded to my curiosity. I knew he was getting irritated that I had asked him to explain the purchase.

I was yet to see a joint of meat of lamb, beef or pork. I had only ever seen dead chickens or rabbits. I now fully understood what Dad had told me but I thought I ought to say something humorous to help his grumps go away.

"Dad, wouldn't it be funny if we had half of a lamb for a pet. It would keep falling over" I said laughing.

My joke didn't help. Dad gave me a sidelong glance, as though I was only confirming I was a fathead. I felt uneasy believing he would have preferred me not to know, we spoke no more for the duration of the journey.

When we got home, the next morning, Dad told Mum all about the incident. His account of the event made it sound funnier than it had seemed to me and we all had a good laugh. I joined in the fun, albeit at my expense but I was pleased that Dad and I were friends again.

Refrigerators would not to be seen in working people's homes for at least another ten years to come, so it could never have been Dad's intention for the family to eat the side of lamb, it would have gone rotten before we would have been able to have eaten it all. I imagine Dad must have sold it to a restaurant or a butcher, for none of it was to be seen on our table.

To my knowledge that was the only illegal transaction that Dad got involved in while I was with him. It could have been that, due to my inquisitiveness, Dad became more cautious. That is not to say that was the only occasion 'black market' food came into the house. We had an Aladdin's cave of tinned food stacked away under loose floorboards in the front room.

While living in Topsham we always had either a case of thirty six tins of mackerel in tomato sauce, a case of pilchards in tomato sauce, Corned Beef or American 'Spam'. The sight of 'Spam' on our dinner plates appeared with sickening regularity. But compared to what we were only allowed to buy with our ration books I should have regarded anything extra as luxuries. Mum and Dad most probably did.

In an attempt to ease the monotony of what we were eating and make the meat content of a meal look different from the day before Mum would present slices of Spam in many different ways:

It would be grilled one day, fried in a batter, another day, in a jacket potato, as a hash mashed into cream potatoes, fried with a bubble and squeak, yesterday's 'leftovers' of cabbage and potato. For a summer meal it could be served up cold with a salad or just between two slices of toasted or plain bread. Cans of dehydrated eggs and sardines were also regular item of our extra diet. There were usually thirty-six cans in any one case and each case of the same item lasted about a month.

Dad made sure that each case of meat was consumed before he brought the next one home.

Cases of dried apricots, figs or sultanas were also always stored away, all hidden under the floorboards in the front room of the house. Because the fruit was dried, I believe Mum had to soak them in water overnight, it would be eaten the following day with custard.

A few weeks after I had accompanied Dad on his trip to Plymouth Docks, he informed me the barracks that we had slept in had suffered a torpedo attack by enemy aircraft.

49 Studley Road, being a corner house, gave access to our garden from a side gate in Stanley Villas. On the side wall of the house that was in Stanley Villas, Grandad had a wooden board fitted. From the street I watched the sign writer screwing the board into position, it read:

'Studley Stud'

Prop; H.Bridger.

-FOR SALE -

Breeder of High Class Prize Winning

Budgerigars, Canaries and Rabbits.

Gold Medal winner of Blue Chinchillas Gigantus,

Apply at basement front door.

When the signwriter had finished and commenced walking down his ladder, I asked him "What's a Blue Chinchillas Gigantus mister?"

"I dunno fer sure cocker! I fink its a rabbit. Looks posh dunnit?"

167

He put his ladder over his shoulder, got astride his bicycle and pedalled away. I walked into the garden, through the side door in the wall. Down the far end of the garden, I saw my grandfather cleaning out one of his many rabbit hutches behind the air raid shelter.

I walked up to him and asked; "Grandad! A man has just put a sign on the wall outside with your name on. What's a Chinchilla Gigantus?"

This was the first time I had approached him to engage in a conversation.

"A Chinchilla is a furry animal that looks like a cross between a rat and a squirrel and comes from South America but in this case Ron the Chinchillas I have are very special rabbits. Come with me and I will show you one".

I was to become one of the privileged few to enter his private kingdom. Other than my grandfather, I had never seen anyone, not even a member of the family tread on this sacred ground and, I suspect, nor did they want to.

He took me into his world of birds and animals where entrance was by strict invitation only which I imagine was normally reserved only for serious buyers. He led me into what outwardly appeared to be just a long shed but it was more than that. It was as long as the house was wide covering the entire width of the garden.

Once inside Grandad's menagerie, we passed row upon row of rabbits in wooden cages all under one long roof. As we walked along the centre isle, I noticed half of the length was allocated to hutches on both sides. They were placed on top of each other, three high, making six rows. At a guess, there must have been about twenty hutches in each row. The remaining width of the garden was allocated to the aviary area where he kept his prize 'budgies'.

When referring to his rabbits, Grandad spoke of 'bucks and does' and 'blues and greys'.

He showed me how to recognise a quality fur and his breeding techniques. He stopped at one hutch, undone the catch, put his hand in

168

and firmly held the rabbit inside by the lose fur at the back of it's neck and brought it out. It was enormous! He held it in cradled arms and I followed him as he walked to the door, he then placed it on a small table in the garden and released it from his hold. The rabbit remained motionless.

"What do you think of that one Ron?" he asked.

It was a beautiful steel blue. "It's very big Grandad and the colour is different to wild ones".

"That's what makes it special Ron, that's a Blue Chinchilla", he said.

From then on, after my first 'get to know your Grandad period' we had, not a close friendship but it was at least a pleasant rapport. It was not close because when he was not at work he would be either at a rabbit or bird show or preparing for one. Unfortunately, I saw very little of him. Maybe it was the shock of the loss of his youngest Granddaughter, a few months earlier, that encouraged him to 'open up'. Where as in the past he appeared to me as being a hard man with no emotion I now saw him as a caring man.

Pat and I were his only two Grandchildren.

He was physically strong and a heavily built short man. He was 'tea total' but smoked the strongest black and foulest smelling tobacco that could be purchased. He bought loose tobacco and rolled it to make his own cigarettes. He only smoked one brand: 'Boars Head'.

Once, testing my mother if I could get away with swearing, I called it 'Boars Shit' in her company. I was promptly told not to say it again but my private name for it remained with me.

The danger of the poisonous black manure, called tobacco he smoked was most probably, the cause of his death.

He never owned a motor vehicle. I don't believe he knew how to drive one. His only means of private transport was a heavy old bicycle. He made a large wooden box that he attached to a carrier frame and made secure behind the saddle and above the mudguard. The box catered for his living animals. He made all of his rabbit hutches and aviaries, which called for a constant supply of clean timber, which he always brought home tied to his bicycle. The larger pieces of timber, he brought home by tying them to the bicycle crossbar.

During and after the 1939-1945 war until his death, he worked for the Southern Railway at the Nine Elm Yard depot, Wandsworth.

I believe he was able to get all of the timber to meet his requirements from used large packing crates that were broken up at the yard.

Because of the weight he carried, he regularly wore out the bicycle tyres and more often still he would be mending punctures. He once arrived home with so much timber tied to his cycle; he was unable to ride it. He had used his two wheeled transport as a wheelbarrow and pushed it all the way from his place of work, something like five or six miles away.

He also kept chickens in another open area of the garden: On one occasion he was having a problem with his chickens not producing a shell around the egg. While Pat and I were in Mum's company, we overheard Mum ask Grandad if the chickens were better and laying eggs again.

"No" Grandad replied, "They are only laying soft ones": The chickens diet was not balanced properly causing them to lay eggs without a firm shell. A day or two passed and Grandma' asked Pat to look in the chicken run to see if there were any eggs. Pat returned with a handful of chicken shit. She held the contents of her hand out and said "They're still laying soft ones".

I attended a boys' only school in Gaskell Street. Pat attended a girls' only school ten minutes walk away in Priory Grove. Like most other children during the war both Pat and I had our main meal of the day at school. I believe the cost was five pennies a week.

My school did not have the facilities for supplying meals so I, with the rest of my fraternity, had to travel to the nearest school that did. The school that supplied the catering was the one my Sister Pat attended.

To reach Pat's school from Gaskell Street was a short walk along Larkhall Lane, although I say a 'short walk' the distance was nearly always covered by running. The run was necessary to beat the rest of the school. Failing to do so meant most of the midday break would be wasted waiting in a queue to get served.

There was a baker's shop on the route between the two schools where, with some of my school friends, I would stop and buy a bread roll to have with our dinner.

While in the baker's, a day or two after my first visit, I noticed that a lady in front of me had bought five rolls and was only charged one penny. The cost of one roll was a farthing, a quarter of a penny: A large number of children would, like myself, go into the bakers for one roll. Like the previous customer, I also asked for five rolls for a penny.

My speculation paid off. Once outside the shop I sold four of my five rolls for a farthing each to four of my classmates and saved them wasting time waiting in the queue to be served in the baker's.

I offered to buy their rolls each day if they would save my place in the meal queue. They were happy to agree, so every morning thereafter I collected their farthing and at lunchtime I bought their rolls and got my one free.

I don't know if they though I was 'soft in the head' to 'line up' to buy their rolls but I did not let it be known to them of my 'bulk buy' deal.

This was my first experience at 'private enterprise' where I paid for something to pass on at a higher price. I continued with deals with various commodities for the rest of my school days.

Other money making ideas followed in easy succession, not all of them novel, but all small time in their schoolboy conception and not always painless.

Next door to the baker's was a shop that recharged wireless batteries: Wireless sets used power from either the main household electric circuit or portable batteries. I believe a mains operated wireless was more expensive to buy than a battery run version which would be an excellent reason for the one we had at home being run by portable wet cells. The batteries, or accumulators were made of a heavy-duty transparent glass the contents were lead plates and sulphuric acid. The design was on the same principle as today's motorcar battery but less than a quarter of the size and weight. With normal usage the battery would last about a week before it needed to be recharged.

It was normal practice in our house, like most other wireless owners, to have two batteries. One battery would be in the shop being charged while the other was in use.

Unlike today, shops of that period had a tendency to specialised in one product and was not involved in any other line of business. The content of the batteries were sulphuric acid, H_2SO_4, and very corrosive and dangerous if they got broken. Spillage was a hazard and as a precaution against being burnt by the acid they were carried in tailor made wooden boxes.

Reading books, playing board games and music was a popular pastime but radio had become, by far the most the popular source of home entertainment. Family home comedy shows on the radio were listened to as television is watched today. I played in the street or in bombed houses every day of the week with my two regular pals but I always made time to be at home when my favourite radio shows were 'on the air'.

Radio was the only home entertainment where we did nothing but sit and listen. 'Monday night at Eight' and 'Penny on the Drum' were two titles of my favourite programmes. There were others, but my most favoured programme was on a Thursday night. Thursday Night was 'ITMA' night. ITMA was probably the most successful and most listened to radio show during the war. The star was Tommy Handly. He introduced the idea, on radio, of using only the initial letter of each word in a sentence. TTFN became an everyday word that substituted Tat Tar For Now'. TTFN must be the nearest the English language ever got to an equivalent of the German auf wiedersehen or the French au revoir. The ITMA show was on the air all through the war years and continued until Tommy Handley's death in 1949.

Motorised traffic was so limited that it was normal to see children play in the main roads.

It would have been more likely to have an accident slipping in horse dung or dogs droppings than through colliding with a motor vehicle. Rounders, Marbles, Cricket, Football, Flicking cigarette cards and Cannon were some of the favoured street games:

Cannon is a game that I have not seen played for many years, it is, or was, a ball game, with a mix of cricket and rounders with something added; The game could be played by two or more and required four stick of woods, about six inches long, and one tennis ball. The sticks were placed against a wall three upright and one across the top like the stumps in cricket. The bowler aimed for the stumps, as in cricket but there was no batsman. The scoring was achieved by the bowler aiming to hit the stumps, on doing so he would run to reassemble the stumps before he was touched by the ball he had thrown.

The person attempting to score did so alone while the remainder of the players joined forces to stop a point being scored. The ball was passed to each other to get near enough to the bowler to be able to safely throw the ball and hit the bowler before he could reassemble the stumps. Playing 'marbles' and 'flicking cigarette cards' also used a lot of my playtime activities.

The ten minutes walk home from school usually took about an hour due to playing marbles that now replaced searching for shrapnel.

The method of playing marbles was; the first player rolled a marbles along the edge of the road in the gutter. The second player would then roll his marble with the objective of hitting the first marble. If the second thrown marble hit the stationary marble the owner of the second marble won the first. So the game continued with each player taking it in turn, one attempt at a time to win the other player, or players, marbles. Playing marbles, in addition to being a game was also a source of income.

For those inclined towards 'commerce' there was always a lively market at school.

I usually had a quantity of marbles for sale. The most valuable marbles were those of pure deep red called 'Bloods'. Pure black were called "Jets". I believe 'jet' came from jet black ink for these two colours it was common practice to hit them twice before they could be won. As a result they were worth two of any others that made them twice the price to purchase.

I learnt very little English, Poetry or Religious Education but trading was a very natural and important part of my school life, it most certainly exercised my knowledge of arithmetic.

The demand for glass marbles and cigarette cards always appeared to exceed supply. Marbles could change hands many times in the course of a day. The trade was made up of losers that wanted to buy and winners that wanted to sell. Boys wishing to buy one day could be the same boys wishing to sell the next. New marbles came on the scene from time to time by means of boys receiving birthday presents but generally the same items kept circulating.

I gained the reputation of being, although we didn't have a name for it, what would be known in present day terms 'a broker'. I was always willing to buy regardless of how many I had. I would buy them at the rate of 'six for a penny' and sell at 'five for one penny'. Not exactly big time but I only thought in pennies.

The simple piece of selling logic came very natural to me. I met no resistance from other boys and I continued trading new commodities throughout my school days. There were, of course, other school colleagues that sold commodities in the same manner but competition was never a problem. Selling and exchanging cigarette cards went on at the same time at a similar rate of exchange but plummeted during late Autumn and winter when the enthusiasm for playing 'conkers' exceeded all other activities.

The abundance of the fruit from the Horse Chestnut Tree was plentiful and left little room for me to 'corner the market'.

Of my buying and selling business, I never aimed to make a profit from the purchase of foreign postage stamps. I never sold or swapped a stamp unless it was a duplicate.

Because the war was still in progress there were soldiers, of many nationalities, living in Great Britain and as a result discarded foreign cigarette packets and matchboxes littered the streets in abundance.

Matchboxes, in particular, carried some very attractive designs. When I commenced collecting, I kept the complete box but within a short time my hoard grew so large it occupied too much space in my bedroom.

To overcome the storage problem, I cut the top of the box and discarded the remainder. The tops I stuck in scrapbooks. Before my interest collecting match box tops ceased I had collected over a thousand.

My collection of cigarette packets were also placed in scrapbooks and exceeded a hundred. I even started to collect chewing gum wrappers, but Philately, was a hobby that captured my imagination.

My interest in postage stamps began during a rummaging session in one of the many nearby large grand house that had been bombed.

The elegant Victorian houses that had once been occupied by wealthy people were now bombed and exposed to the elements and ruined beyond repair. For my friends and I these ruins were playgrounds.

I got a great thrill in entering a deserted bombed building that I had not set foot in before and not knowing what I was about to find.

My awareness to take care and not be discovered was not because I feared being accused of stealing. My caution was mainly based on the notion that if I was observed and challenged I would be obliged to surrender my spoils to my observer.

In one room on the first floor of the house I was in had obviously once been a library, there was no roof nor ceiling to the house but the study still had the four walls and shelves around the room. Only a few books still remained resting on their shelves, the remainder were scattered across the floor. The subjects covered by the books were numerous, but I remember looking through some of them. There were books on History, Natural History, Geography, Science etc and many had the familiar large coloured scrollwork on the capital letter of each new chapter that suggested to me they could be over two hundred years old. There were also old looking maps in broken frames and stuffed animals that had been covered in domes of glass that now lay ruined on a Persian style carpet.

While I was looking through the large collection of books lying scattered across the floor I noticed a very fat costly looking leather covered book. I opened it and as I quickly examined the contents I was astonished to see it was a collection of postage stamps from all over the world.

My heart thumped furiously. I was so excited with my find, even though I knew I was alone, I looked around as I squatted to ensure I was not being watched. As I hid the large book inside my jumper I looked left and right over my shoulder before standing up. This elegant stamp album had been waiting for a new owner. I was now that new owner.

I was constantly told not to play in bombed houses by my mother. I believe she was concerned I could fall through damaged floorboards or down an unstable staircase more than the legal aspect of trespass. But I paid little attention to her warnings.

I reflect upon my activities during this period with no pride but not to record my adventure in its entirety would be tantamount to an untruthful account of myself. In addition to my foraging, I was also guilty of stupidity and total ignorance not only of beautiful objects but also things of value.

The house I lived in was like all of the other houses in Studley Road, there were built in the early part of the twentieth century and occupied by wealthy people that were affluent enough to employ servants.

Most of the houses became empty at the outbreak of the war but a small number of wealthy residence remained after the declaration of war until the bombing commenced.

The semi basement floors of these houses bore all the signs of servant quarters with the contrast to the remainder of the houses that bore hallmark of master status.

Attached to the wall, on a wooden board, in the downstairs kitchen were a number of small brass bells. They were numbered from one to six, and represented a bell for each room. A silk bell cord with a tassel left an upstairs room and entered the kitchen as a wire cable.

It was usual to find a basement cupboard that contained medicines, oils, powders and herbs ranging from the sweet aromatic to foul smelling concoctions.

My friends and I had great fun and spent many hours mixing up contents of bottles, packets, boxes and jars. We had no idea of the value of the compounds in terms of healing or damaging nor were we, in any way, concerned. Powders, granules, liquids and oils would be mixed together and hit with a heavy objects or we would try to ignite with a match. We were seeking a formula by combining the mixtures, to make an explosion. Luck was on our side we never found one.

One of the many decorative features these grand houses had in common were the magnificent moulded plaster covings. That is where walls and ceilings remained. The designs varied from house to house, but were mainly of flowers, birds and cherubs. But the most striking feature of most of the premises was the large crystal chandeliers.

As a result of the bombing, some of the houses were subjected to fire damage only, while others, where they had been hit by high explosive bombs crashed through roofs and blew out walls. Many chandeliers had broken from their ceiling clamps and had smashed, on impact, on the floors below. Others proudly remained suspended from bare floor joists, like skeletons wearing expensive jewellery. When the sunlight caught them they glittered, still proud and defiant in the midst of the rubble.

Like morons, my friends and I finished off what the enemy's bombing had failed to do. We used them as targets, like that at a fairground trying to hit a coconut by catapult or throwing parts of broken bricks at them. We made it a competition by scoring for every piece of crystal we knocked off.

It was, of course, a serious criminal offence to loot bombed and deserted houses but for most semi-literate schoolboys like me, it was just an adventure. The illegality and keeping out of sight from the police just added to the fun.

My friends and I chose an old coal cellar for our gang den. The cellar was in the front garden of a badly bombed and deserted house in Studley Road. In the front garden stood a magnificent Mulberry tree:

During Queen Victoria's reign the Mulberry tree was as common in a gardens as Apple and Pear trees are today. Their leaves are a food source for silkworms

I believe the Mulberry trees, in England, must be on the threshold of becoming an endangered species, I have not seen one for years. Their numbers were greatly reduced when they were uprooted as the city houses with large gardens were demolished to make way for the new homes building programme after the war. The fruit of the Mulberry tree is very similar to a large loganberry. From the limited choice available it was one of my favourite fruits.

Before the house had been destroyed by bombing it was a mirror image of the houses that Benny and I lived in so we were familiar with our surroundings but now only a portion of the outside walls remained upright.

By removing timbers and bricks at the front of the house we discovered we were able to gain entrance into the servants entrance through the basement flat door. Once we had cleared enough rubble to enable us to open the door, we made our way inside. Only the ceiling of the basement flat, now underneath the bricks of the demolished house, supported the roof of our cave. The narrow passage facing us would have led us, had it have been there, to the kitchen door, and on our left was the route to a coal cellar.

The door was held shut by a simple latch which offered no resistance: The ceiling of the cellar was the underside of the main outside steps that lead from the front garden up to the main door of the house. As we groped in the dark below ground level, we entered the coalbunker that we calculated the coalhole cover was above our heads. We found it and with little effort I was able to poke the cover from its resting position that upon removal, allowed us some daylight. We expected to see remnants of coal, but as our eyes grew accustomed to the darkness, we noticed the walls had been whitewashed and wooden wine racks were attached to one of the sidewalls. We joked about our disappointment that the cellar had been 'cleaned out' and the racks were empty but decided it was a perfect location for our gang den.

In one house, we found a dining room table and in another house we collected some chairs. We also found a quantity of candles and in another derelict house we found a cupboard that contained linen. Sorting through some of the dusty, but preserved, contents we found a tablecloth. We recovered a radio from an old dilapidated garden shed and placed it in a corner on a table. The radio had no batteries but the fact that it did not work made no difference. We were pleased with our acquired furniture and fittings and moved into our new meeting place. We also modified the wine racks and stacked books and magazines on it. We used our new meeting place daily during our school summer holiday.

In the space of little more than two years, since the war had begun, the civilised world was at the edge of a 'precipice': The Axis forces, Germany, Japan had almost complete command of the Atlantic and Pacific Oceans and German troops came within a 'whisker' of controlling the oilfields in the Middle East.

Almost half of the world was now ruled by two ruthless military systems and Great Britain ruler of the greatest empire history had known was bankrupt.

True to the saying 'it is always darkest just before dawn'. It was, paradoxically, the result of a disaster that made things better. I refer to the infamous attack, by the Japanese, on the American Pacific Fleet Naval Base at Pearl Harbour before a war had been declared.

The bombing of American soil brought the USA into the war. The action of the Japanese must have been the most significant factor of turning the war in Briton's favour. The consequence of the bombing of Pearl Harbour was not immediately obvious and the Japanese action did not suddenly 'turn the tide', but it did force America out of her isolation policy.

On15th January 1942, less than a month after 'Pearl Harbour', an Inter-American Conference took place in Rio de Janeiro. Led by Britain, America and The Soviet Union, the conference concluded with a pledge: To ensure life, liberty, Independence of religious freedom and to preserve the rights of man and justice. It was signed by twenty-six nations and marked the beginning of the United Nations Organisation, UNO.

As the end of 1942 drew near the areas that became occupied by enemy forces reached their zenith. The pendulum of war was about to swing back.

As part of a wartime measure, the government announced it was withdrawing pencil sharpeners from civil servants to economise on pencils. Wow!

Rear: Mum at the age of 18 in the garden of Milwood Road, Balham. Mum and Dad had rented a room from his Uncle Ted Woodhall. Front row left to right: Ted's wife with Mum's eldest Sister Lou.

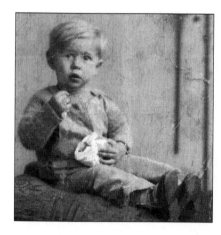

I stayed with my Aunt Lou from the summer of 1935 until November during Mum's pregnancy. Aunt Lou took me to a photography studio in Brixton and bought me a bag of sweets as a persuader to keep still while this photograph was being taken.

My Sister Pat on Dad's shoulders with Uncle Bill, 1937.

Mum holding my youngest Sister, Bebe in the garden of Studley Road.
Bebe of pneumonia in 1943.

The end of a 70 mile solo cycle ride from south London to
The isle of Wight, 1947.

Mum, Pat and I on the beach at Littlehampton, 1946.

Mum astride the Triumph combination outside our bungalow in Buckinghamshire, 1937.

Dad is wearing his ExWd fighter pilot's kapok filled flying suit. Circa 1953.

SEVEN

"THE BEGINNING OF THE END"

The tragic ground losses and 'see-saw' battles were no longer disadvantages to Britain and her allies. One victory after another was reported in our favour and negative speculation about the outcome had now changed into positive thoughts. No more thoughts about fighting the Germans on our beaches. We were going to win. It was just a matter of time.

On January 23rd 1943, the British 8th Army entered Tripoli.

By February 4th, advance units of the 8th Army crossed the border into the French colony of Tunisia. The good news regarding the progress in North Africa continued to be reported and I eagerly registered the progress on my war maps.

During the second week in May the entire German army in Tunisia surrendered and thus ended The Desert War. The North Africa Campaign was over. Two months later, in July 1943, British and American paratroopers landed in Sicily.

Away from the Mediterranean, on the Eastern front at Kursk, to the South of Moscow, a battle between six thousand tanks took place: It was the biggest tank battle of all time.

In the two years of fighting the Russians, the German army lost over half a million men. In the same month, American aircraft bombed Rome. In spite of the fact the allies were now solidly winning the war on land, the war at sea was still perilous. Many merchant ships carrying vital food and other supplies were being sunk by German wolf packs of U boats.

Our gains on land made little difference to our meagre food rations.

Our ration books had to be shown and the coupons either deleted with a cross or cut out every time a particular rationed item was purchased.

All commodities other than food, in addition to displaying the price showed the number of dockets or coupons needed before making a purchase.

Young couples, on proving they were, or had just got married were issued with an extra allocation of dockets to buy utility furniture and other commodities needed to set up a home. There was also a supplementary section at the back of each ration book that allowed for luxury items to be purchased that were not available as a regular item to be rationed. In the stricter sense, sausages were not rationed and were sold to regular or customers in favour with the butcher. Items such as these were 'marked off' at the back of the book on the supplementary page.

A 'save waste paper and scrap metal' campaign had been introduced a couple of years back, a result of which allowed me to enjoy a new interest:

Iron railings from gardens and parks had been removed but for some odd reason the lead that fixed the railings to the concrete plinths, had not been collected.

It was odd because lead was a valuable commodity and more costly than the cast iron that was being taken away: The part of the bullet that left the cartridge behind after being fired from a gun were made of lead.

From the earliest days I can remember, I had an interest in making things by carving pieces of timber with a penknife or sawing and joining with glue or nails.

While having breakfast one morning, I looked out from the kitchen window, into the rear garden, and noticed John sawing a piece of timber. I finished eating and went downstairs. As I stood by his side I asked what was he was doing. His immediate reaction was secretive and tried to hide the objects around him from my view. He told me to go away and to be careful not to knock over the metal pot at his side: The small pot was suspended over a fire and held by a rod through its wire handle. I remained motionless and after a while John must have realised I was not going to go away. He told me I could watch for as long as I didn't touch anything. He showed me a how to make a toy soldier from pieces of scrap lead, a couple of handfuls of sand, a few pieces of timber and model toy soldiers:

From two pieces of hollowed out timber, about three by four inches and about two inches deep, he packed damp sand into the hollowed out area, pressed a lead toy soldier in one box and then used the second box as a lid for the first. He then pressed them together and carefully removed the lid and the toy soldier. Left in the sand was a perfect impression of the soldier he had taken out. All he had made, of course, was a mould but I squatted at his side fascinated. He then replaced the lid on the box, stood the mould upright between two house bricks and through a previously made hole in the top of the box, he poured in the boiling lead. Within less than a minute he separated the box and to my astonishment, there lying in the small bed of sand was a perfect replica of the original soldier. To me, it was like he had performed magic. I had never seen anything made from a mould before. John allowed me to make the second one and that came out as good as the original.

I remember his warning of the danger of pouring boiling lead on my fingers and his instruction never to hold the box while pouring the lead into the mould.

Over the next few months making soldiers occupied all of my spare time. I was careful never to be seen by my mother, for she would most certainly have put a stop to my fun.

I also heeded my uncle John's words of caution. I never had an accident. I was able to keep my dangerous toy soldier activity a secret from my mother although she did, on one occasion, ask why I had such a lot of small pieces of lead in my bedroom. Lead, being the raw material for my production, necessitated me going out with a small hammer and chisel and knock out my requirement from the base of removed railings from front gardens of deserted houses. To complete the product they needed painting. The paint came from garden sheds and garages of vacated premises that were also subject to my scavenging.

Dad's enthusiasm for making our toys and other household items must have 'rubbed off' on me, I also had the advantage of having his tools; saw, pliers, hammer and nails etc. available at my disposal anytime I needed them. Dad drew no boundary line around his 'talent'. If anything got broken or something new was needed his instinct was could he mend it? Or could he make it?

Dad never wore a belt but the braces he wore to hold his trousers up were hand made: He made them from motor car rubber inner tubes, this was in the days before tubeless tyres were introduced. He once made me a pair and I watched as he did so: His first action was to cut across the tube to make one length rather than circular. He then cut along the length that then gave him a long flat piece of rubber. 'Measuring me up', he cut the rubber to the correct length to fit me, from front to back and then cut out a shape and the holes for the buttons on the trousers to go through, I then had a pair of braces just like Dad's. I displayed them at every opportunity. I was not so proud, however, of the home made footwear that Pat and I had to wear.

The idea came to Dad from a Ministry propaganda advertisement to wear clogs, made from wood.

Clogs were a normal part of the dress code for people earning their living in the mills in the North of England and had been so for many years long before the war. The government's campaign to encourage the use of clogs in the south of England for other workers coincided with the appearance of clogs in the shops.

From a block of timber and tools, Dad decided to make Pat and I a pair each. A saw, a chisel and sandpaper were all that was needed to produce the sole. For the part that came across the top to hold the clog to the foot, a discarded rubber inner tube again came into use.

Wearing the clogs was not uncomfortable, but the noise was something to hear to be believed.

My clogs wore much quicker than Dad had expected, so Dad nailed a strip of old cycle tyre on the bottom of each sole to make them last longer. It 'done the trick', the rubber lasted much longer than wood but the advantage was twofold, it also made them quieter. There was one disadvantage however: the added weight.

The introduction of the clog could be considered as a forerunner of Dr Martin Scholes footwear.

Attached to the rear of the church in Stanley Villas was a small drill hall that catered for the Girl Guides, Boy Scouts and the Cubs plus a number of other pastimes and activities.

The scouting movement was the brainchild of Lord Baden-Powell, of Boer War fame. Baden-Powell was reputed to have been a friend of Rudyard Kipling (1865-1936) and inspired to form the 'Scouting Movement' by the characters in Kipling's Jungle Book.

I was encouraged by Mum and Dad to limit my playing in bombed houses and I responded to a suggestion to join the local cub troop. The Cubs were a junior section of the Boy Scouts.

I made some enquiries and found the minimum age to join was ten. Being ten years old was the only qualification I needed to join which was certificated by a letter supplied by Mum. My initiation pledge was to obey the Scouting code of honour while pointing my first and middle finger of my right hand at my temple like imitating an attempt to commit suicide with an imaginary gun.

'I promised to do my duty to God and the King

I promised to be clean and tidy,

I promised to be polite and to help others at all times', etc, etc.

As I repeated the oath at my initiation, behind my back I crossed the fingers of my left hand in my childish belief that this action would release me from any promise I was making. I did not want to make a pledge that would not allow me to continue to enjoy myself.

My weekly subscription included a small percentage of money to be set aside to buy my uniform. The uniform consisted of:

A green cap with a silver wolf's head badge, a green shirt, a green woollen jumper for use during the winter, grey socks and black shoes, a yellow cotton tie held together around the neck by a leather toggle and grey short trousers. I was given four strips with 22nd Clapham embroidered on them to be stitched on the sleeves of my jumper and shirt.

I considered and chose not to wear my splendid hand crafted black inner tube braces.

I had a certain amount of pride for the badges I wore on the sleeve of my cub jumper. I passed the tests and wore a badge for tying knots, good housekeeping, drawing and painting. I was the only cub in my troop to have passed the test in flag semaphore, which qualified me to wear the badge of two crossed flags. Good housekeeping was the easiest badge to earn. I only had to get a letter from Mum to prove I kept my room tidy.

The only part of being a member of the cubs that I really disliked was the church parades. The idea that a person could only be good if he or she attended church goes back many centuries and in some lesser degree still prevails today. Religion still remains a solid plank of the scouting movement.

Church parade meant assembling outside the church on the first Sunday of every month.

In full uniform we would wait in an orderly line until the cub leader gave the word of command to march into church. During this period I always thought of going to church as a waste of time. We had to keep getting up and down, sitting and standing for reasons that seemed to have no logic.

I did 'figure out' a simple rule that we 'stood to sing' and 'sat to chat' but it didn't always work out that way.

I had no real anti Christian feelings but in spite of always having better things to do I did go to church.

Every first Sunday in the month, before leaving the house in my uniform for church parade, Mum ensured I had a penny or two to put in the collecting tray. To be precise it wasn't a tray at all, it was, in fact, a deep cloth sock, surrounded at the top by a silver handle like a long tea strainer.

During the service the collecting pocket was passed along by one of the female adult cub leaders: Arkela or Baloo. (Arkela and Baloo were two characters in Rudyard Kipling's novel; Jungle Books).

Each time the sock passed along the line and changed hands we would be watched by Arkela, as a hawk watches its prey.

When the sock reached me, I took the handle in one hand while in the other hand I proudly displayed my donation. By holding my penny between forefinger and thumb, as we exchanged smiles, I dropped the coin in. My unseen 'inner smile' was so much greater it was almost a laugh. I deceived Arkela by my 'slight of hand'. A slow motion camera would have detected the penny had not gone down into the 'sacred sock' but went up into the palm of my hand and held there by my third ring finger. 'Palming', was just one of many 'dodgy' tricks that Uncle John had taught me.

I regularly attending the cubs and not long after I joined, a scheme was launched from the movement's Headquarters, in Buckingham Palace Road, London, to raise money for charity.

The idea, called 'Bob a Job Week', was for every scout or cub to ask a neighbour or local trader if they had any small tasks that needed to be done. A completed task would earn one shilling. It was a nationally recognised scheme and received publicity from the radio, newspapers and church organisations throughout the country and as the title suggested it was to last a week. 'Bob a Job' must have been very successful for 'the week' was extended to another week and then a month and ran on well into the following year until it eventually 'ran out of steam'.

As a direct result of my participation in the 'Bob a Job' campaign I got a Saturday morning job helping to deliver milk for the 'Co-Operative Society': Bottled milk was transported by horse and cart and delivered daily to almost every house in the country. In some country areas, however, milk was still being supplied from the urn, via a measuring ladle, directly into the customers own milk jug, eliminating the need of a milk bottle.

A rather fattish jovial lady delivered the milk in my area and after Mum asked if she needed any weekend help, I began assisting her every Saturdays. She paid me a good wage for my day's effort. Had I have realised the effort required to put a bottle or two of milk outside someone's door, I would not have agreed to start. It was a long hard day but in addition to my wage it did have a perk:

I noticed, how could I not have, the horse was not only a means of power for pulling a cart, it was also a very prolific manufacturer of manure. A perfect food source for tomato plants!

Our milk lady called at our house daily and before the next Saturday arrived, I asked her if she had any objection if I kept a bucket under the axle of the cart and collected the horse's droppings. She had no objection. Another new avenue for an income was in the making.

While the four of us, Mum, Dad Pat and I were eating at the table one evening, as a passing remark, Dad casually asked me if I liked my new job of helping the milk lady.

I told him the pay was better than I was at first told and I also had some gardeners that wanted the droppings from the horse that pulled the milk cart.

Before I could finish telling Dad I already had two likely customers at sixpence a bucket, he burst out laughing. With his teacup still in his hand and the contents in his mouth, his cheeks bulged in an attempt to contain the tea and restrain his laughter. He failed on both counts and exploded a mouthful of tea most of it went back into his cup and some went on the table.

He coughed and spluttered and with a great effort he was able to stop himself from choking but unable to control a spasm of laughter, tears rolled down his face and tea came out of his nose. I couldn't understand why Dad thought selling horse droppings was funny but his laughter was contagious and we all laughed.

I had not seen anything funny in what I had said, but after we had all settled down again and resumed eating I asked: "what did you laugh at Dad?"

My simple question wasn't funny and it wasn't meant to be but it caused Dad to start laughing again but this time he really was choking. He rushed to the sink in an attempt to cough up a lump of jam sandwich that had got stuck in his throat. Mum rushed to his aid by thumping him in the back to clear the blockage. After a minute or two had elapsed, Dad wiped his eyes, regained a little of his composure, faced Mum and said: "Do you remember what I said last week Mam? Didn't I say that cheeky little bugger could sell shit to a sewerage worker?"

Mum saw no humour in his words but reprimanded him for using nasty words at the meal table. 'Shit' *was* the nasty word. In the house, bloody and sod were Dad's normal swear words.

I was not aware until that moment that my small time commercial activities in, or out of school for that matter, had been a topic of anyone's conversation and had been made known to my parents.

I later discovered the school authorities, disapproved of an extra out-of-school education if it did not fall within their curriculum. I could not understand the authority's lack of imagination. All of my little 'earners', were commercially sound and legal, or very nearly and should have been seen as a good education in preparation for adulthood. I believe, my Father was proud of my antics not that I recall ever receiving a compliment from him but nor was I ever reprimanded.

My Saturday milk round lasted all through the summer and although I found it hard work it was most enjoyable. I cannot remember how it came to an end.

I regarded the charity business of doing additional odd jobs serious and went about collecting money as it was intended but I did have a weakness. I was less enthusiastic to participate at the donating end. A problem, regarding my arithmetic, regarding the ratio of distribution arose a little later.

Although the term 'A bob', slang word for a shilling, was used as the reward for doing a job, it was recognised that some people who received a service or had a job done would pay more than just one shilling. The slogan actually meant 'earnings' and not a precise shilling, as it suggested. I really did not regard it being dishonest if I kept the difference between what someone had given me to do a job and what the movement expected to receive.

The procedure the cubs and scouts were instructed to adopt was, while dressed in uniform, knock on doors, show the 'Bob a Job' charity card and ask the residents if they had any simple household jobs they required to be done. Upon completing a small task, we were then given a payment.

Some people gave money without a job having been done but there were others, however that took advantage of once having had a small task completed would not want to pay anything believing the charity was for *them*.

I took a cut from any money I received for a job I got paid for and handed in a smaller token amount to the scouting organisation.

In more recent times, like during the 'Prime Minister Thatcher years' I guess my commission would be called 'paying for expenses'. Although I kept most of my earnings for myself, I still handed in more money than anyone else in my group. Some cubs and scouts did not bother to join the scheme and therefore subscribed nothing.

In addition to selling horse manure from which I now had regular customers and helping the milk-lady on Saturdays, I chopped up logs and tar blocks into sticks and bundled up to sell for kindling wood:

Wooden blocks were sunk and levelled in the road along the outside and in between the tramlines. After they were placed in position in the road hot liquid tar was poured over them. The tar served as an excellent adhesive and a preservative against weather conditions and sealed them against wood rot and expansion through getting wet. They were the 'Rolls Royce' of firelighters.

When Dad inquired what was I doing with all of the money I was earning, I told him that some of it was going towards 'Bob a Job' that I handed to the Scouting Movement each week. Dishonestly, I implied I got little in return for my effort.

Dad, believing that I was handing over too much of my earnings, wrote a letter of complaint to my group cub leader without me knowing the contents, I delivered the letter at the next weekly cub meeting. After some to and fro' communication the agitation was defused by a compromise.

A problem that could have resulted into something more serious was resolved by a simple reinstatement of the agreement. Any future money I collected for jobs I performed while not wearing my cubs uniform would not be subject to the fund raising campaign and I would therefore keep all of the earnings.

My new understanding was to my benefit for my firewood business, my horse manure deliveries plus my milk round money was conducted without wearing my uniform. But for all the effort I put into my schemes, I only thought small time, in 'pennies'.

My weekly income allowed me only a little more than the cost of my extravagant supply of comics.

One evening after selling a pram load of chopped firewood, I stopped at a small newsagent, tobacconist and general store in Larkhall Lane for a penny fizzy drink.

The shopkeeper remained on his side of the counter as I drank. He had sensibly stayed watching me because he didn't want me taking anything I hadn't paid for. While still drinking and looking around the interior of the small shop I noticed stacked up under the counter, on my side, bundles of firewood. The bundles were smaller and more expensive than I was selling.

To break the silence and in a cocky manner, I mentioned to the shopkeeper, I was selling larger and cheaper bundles of firewood than he was. I did not expect him to react to my cheeky statement but his reply was a request to have a look.

I cannot recall the actual conversation that followed but I came out of the shop with an agreement to supply the shop keeper with a pram load of cut and bundled fire wood each week at the same price per bundle I had been asking for on my round.

At any one time in London the seemingly endless miles of tramway lines were always being repaired somewhere. Repairs had increased from the normal, peacetime, level due to damage by bombing. Knowing where the old damaged blocks were stacked during the hours of darkness, even the new ones, was the key to success or failure to a schoolboy penny entrepreneur.

Two or three 'visits', after working hours, to a stretch of tramline that was being relayed allowed me to collect a reasonable stock that could keep 'my business' going for a couple of months. Unfortunately, tar blocks were not always available within a reasonable walking distance. On these occasions I had to resort to hand sawing floorboards collected from vacated bombed houses.

When I made my agreement with the shopkeeper he did stipulate, however, that I stopped selling privately. I agreed and had the forethought to mention the sticks would not always be cut from tar blocks. It was a good deal. It saved me spending a lot of time walking the streets and knocking on doors. From then on I delivered bulk, per pram load, to the retailer. I suppose that made me a wholesaler:

The electric powered trams were still running long after the war had finished. The last London tram ran in 1952.

School commenced each morning with an assembly of all of the school's pupils in the main hall. The purpose for the gathering was to listen to the headmaster as he read a sermon from the bible. On completion, he would compare the message to present day conditions.

It would have been too much for the Headmaster to have hoped the children had been listening but when the Headmaster was satisfied that the staff, at least, were fortified we would leave the hall.

Out of step, we would all march out of the hall to music played on the piano. As we vacated the hall, some of my classmates and I would imitate the rolling gait of chimpanzees while we quietly sang to our own stupid lyrics. One regular piece of music was: 'The march of the Toreadors'.

Monday was School Dinners Day. Immediately after assembly all children requiring a daily meal for the week would have to queue to pay their School Dinner money of 5d (2pence) towards the cost.

After the Monday morning administration was settled, school life went down hill until Thursday; Thursday was sports day, it was the only day that I volunteered for anything.

Our Tarmac playground substituted for a grass sports field but as I played more in the streets and concrete than playing on grass it was never a problem. I had a preference for football, running and cricket. I didn't like basketball because it looked too much like the girls game of netball.

Thursday wasn't bad but Friday was my favourite day. It was hobbies day. All Friday morning was allocated to watercolour painting, the afternoon was stamp collecting.

Pat and I like most other children when to school on Friday with a silver sixpenny piece to buy a saving's stamp. Hobbies day, for the school, meant 'business day' for me.

I took my foreign postage stamps into school, officially for discussing and swapping. In my case I was more interested in selling or swapping my duplicates. In the classroom, the acceptable going rate for postage stamps of any category or value was a penny each.

In addition to postage stamps, marbles and cigarette card trading was conducted during playtime in the playground. Friday also had that extra bonus that it preceded the two days that I could plan my own activities.

Two of my favourite lessons were drawing and painting. I favoured art because it was the only lesson I received a good result. My school reports were never complimentary but there was one occasion I received a report from my english teacher I regarded as a compliment, she wrote: He could do better.

Once a week, each class had a singing lesson. The singing periods were taken by two teachers, one played the piano while the other stood in front of the class waving a baton about.

Singing and Poetry were even worse than English, they were all 'sissy lessons':

The music teacher's actions were a well rehearsed ritual: Each time she was about to instruct the singing to commence, she would tap her 'stick' on the top of the piano and then sharply bring it up horizontally in unison with her free arm and then pause. The downward movement was the signal for singing to commence. At the sound of the first note of the cacophony, she would put one finger of each hand to her forehead and for a few seconds she appeared to be enduring a terrible pain. Her eyes would close and her lips would purse as though she was reminiscing how she had once sucked a lemon.

On one singing lesson in particular, as it was about to commence, a fellow classmate standing next to me suggested that somewhere inside her body, her eyelids were attached to her arms: Not until she lowered her baton again did her eyes open.

It was normal for the teacher to accuse somebody or anybody of wrongful singing but during this period she was more vociferous than usual.

"Stop! Stop!" she shouted with the authority of a policeman on point duty. "Someone is singing flat. Who is it?"

I wasn't a gambler but I would have bet all of my conkers and marbles I knew the answer.

For the teacher's answer she heard no words, just an uncomfortable shuffling of feet.

"Then we shall try again children".

Again, she flicked her baton on the side of the piano, 'Tap' 'Tap' for everyone to pay attention. She then brought it up to her face, level with her forehead, signalling to the pianist to again prepare to commence. She gave her normal signal to resume singing.

With three fingers pointing straight out and her first finger and thumb holding her 'stick'; as though she wanted as little finger contact as possible, she brought it down with a jerk and we all started singing again. Slowly, with stick still going up and down as though a yo-yo was on the end of it, she stalked, as though walking on glass.

Along the line of singers, from the end furthest from me, she slowly walked nearer. I dare not look anywhere but straight ahead but by taking a sidelong glance I noticed she was smiling but it was not a kindly smile.

She was poised ready to pounce. I felt, even with a distance between us she knew the culprit and she was just going through a dramatic act to prolong my agony.

Occasionally she would stop and repetitively push her head forward and nod her approval like an old chicken in a farmyard looking for worms. With only four singers between damnation and me she stopped. Her wicked smile suddenly left her face. It was replaced by a snarl.

At four paces away she 'speared' me with her eyes. Only seen by me she transformed herself into a witch, she looked as though she was about to do an autopsy on a skunk.

She was suddenly at my side it seemed, without even touching the floor and for all of the assembled class to hear; "It's you! It is you! Isn't it?" she screeched.

Her verbal assault was with such ferocity it would have appeared that it was on her personal list of worst crimes my wrong doing was only second to murder.

"I don't think so Miss", I said.

" I don't think so miss!" she foolishly mimicked. "What do you mean, I don't think so miss? Don't pretend you can't sing boy!"

"I'm not Miss"

"What do you think you are doing then? Do you think you can

sing and you are pretending you can't, or do you believe you can't sing and pretending you can?"

"I don't know miss".

The question was too complicated. I needed more time to think about it. I lost track of what answer would satisfy her. While I was still searching for an answer, her patience failed her and solved my predicament. She let out a loud puff. I was disappointed that flames didn't follow. I wished I could have turned into a turtle so I could have withdrawn my head inside my shirt collar.

"Go to the headmaster's office at once and tell him you can't sing".

I had no misgiving about reporting myself to the headmaster I had been there before. But this occasion would be the first time that it was due to schoolwork.

The previous two occasions were because someone had reported me for performing a small time commercial activity.

My delight was greater than the disgrace. I left the 'hall of music' and walked along the corridor and made my way towards the headmaster's office. I knocked on his door.

While waiting for an invitation to enter I thought if 'I play my cards right' I could get barred from all future music and singing lessons.

I responded to that what sounded like a bored groan but I guessed it was "come in".

I partly opened the door and squeezed in the smallest possible gap between the doorframe and the door handle.

"Come in boy" he said, as though I had just compounded all of the troubles that rested on his shoulders, and I was the last straw. "Close the door behind you and come nearer to my desk. Pross is it?"

"Yes sir, I've been told to report to you sir".

"Oh! Have you! Have you blown up a fellow classmate? Been caught selling incendiary bombs or is it something more important?"

"No sir, the music teacher told me to tell you she thinks I can't sing".

"Did she now?" he said, unsuccessfully trying to hide a smile "and what do you think?"

I got the feeling he thought the music teacher could be right and now only wanted a little amusement.

"I don't know sir", I said as I shrugged my shoulders.

"Well I know what I think" he said pulling at his ear lobe, "I think there is just a slight chance she may be a better judge than you, so I want you to go back to your class room, find a book to read until the music lesson is finished".

Pleased with myself that I didn't have to go back to the music class I left his office and returned to my empty classroom. I sat at my desk and started to read a book. Before the music session was over the headmaster came in.

"I am told you like drawing and painting Pross" he said.

"Yes sir"

"Would you like to do a little job for me? It would entail some drawing and painting each week and I would expect you to do it while the rest of the class are at music study".

He told me what he had in mind and suggested I report to the art teacher for the necessary equipment:

When I got to the art department, the art teacher was waiting for me and confirmed she was aware of the headmaster instruction. She told me the headmaster wanted me to design and paint a large poster for the forthcoming Schools National Savings Campaign:

The poster was to reflect the total value of the sixpenny saving stamps that children purchased once a week in the classroom. I was told I had a week to think about the composition and I could do the drawing and painting, starting next week, during the music lesson.

To relate I was thrilled with the idea would be an understatement, when school finished I lost no time getting home to tell Mum.

During that evening I got some guidance from Mum and Dad and drew out a rough draft.

The following week I explained my thoughts to the art teacher.

"That is an excellent idea", she said. "We want it to go from the bottom to the top of the wall in the Assembly Hall".

From floor to ceiling was about fifteen feet, roughly four and a half metres. The poster was to be so large the teacher was unable to get one piece of cardboard long enough. It was decided I should use a roll of wallpaper and stick it to sections of cardboard.

The art teacher told me I was not to tell any of the other school children what I was doing. As the class went out to the hall for the once a week music lesson I left with them but went into the art room. The teacher unlocked the art cupboard that held the paints and brushes, put all of the necessary items in front of me and left me to it. On her way out of the classroom, she hung an 'OUT OF BOUNDS' notice on the outside of the door and told me she would return when the singing lesson was over. She then left.

My theme for the poster was a character like Charlie Chaplin as a window cleaner climbing a ladder. Each run of the ladder represented a value in £s that was collected by the school each week. At the top of the ladder I painted a window in which the target figure was displayed. Over the coming weeks her part in ' looking in' on my clandestine activity became routine. In great secrecy, the poster began to take shape.

The headmaster would come in from time to time and make an encouraging comment and complimented me on my progress. I cannot remember any other time my school life was so pleasant. I was doing something I liked doing. It was also my only time at school that I felt proud and I was achieving something worthwhile.

But I didn't let it go to my head I knew my pleasure would be short lived. Teachers were trained only to make school life miserable. Once it was noticed I was enjoying myself any observing teacher worth their title would realise they were failing. I knew I was being used on two counts:

One, I was doing something the headmaster wanted. Two, by being absent from the music class was something the singing teacher wanted. I realised my poster would be finished too soon. Being happy at school was not going to last. As the weeks went by and the poster got nearer completion, while in the art room, I began wasting time on my official project and studied other objects.

During one lesson, to 'slow down' my progress, I started reading a textbook on art describing 'vanishing points' and 'perspective'. The book impressed me so much, after I had read it, I took it home and read it again. I had not previously realised and I had not been taught at school that all things appeared smaller as they became more distant.

I practiced, by copying some of the illustrations, on paper and proving the information to be correct by my own observations of real objects.

The day eventually came when I had to report that I had completed the poster and I reported the fact to the headmaster. He then organised, with me in attendance, a private viewing for all of the teachers. I wallowed in their compliments. Never before had I, as a result of schoolwork, experienced such complimentary attention. I thought it would be a pleasant change if all of my remaining school days could be as pleasant as this day. The following week all of the children at school took a letter home with the instruction that the envelope was to be opened only by our parents.

Many months had now passed since my start date for the project and I guess my Mother and Father, after their initial input had thought no more of the saving campaign,

As they were also subject to my singing at home, I can't blame them if they thought my poster idea was just a ploy, by the teacher, to 'eradicate' me from the singing class.

My Mother opened the envelope that gave notice of the unveiling of the school's savings poster would take place on the following Friday. The letter made no mention of the owner's name so Mum was still not aware that the poster, about to be displayed was the one that I alone had been working on.

On Thursday evening, the day before the event, I asked Mum if she was coming tomorrow to see my painting.

Frowning Mum asked: "What painting?"

"You know! My savings painting, the one I have been doing at school".

"How many paintings are there then, beside yours?"

"There isn't anymore. There's only one and it's mine. It's the one I have been painting instead of doing singing ".

"Why didn't you tell me? Does your Father know? The letter doesn't say it's yours!"

Mum wasn't expecting answers, she was thinking aloud but I replied to her last statement.

"The letter doesn't have to say it's mine Mum! I am the only one that done a painting. I know it is mine", I said proudly.

"You could be called to stand on the stage next to the headmaster tomorrow so just make sure you wash your neck and ears properly" Mum said.

On the day of the presentation I had a nice feeling, not for myself for I knew my being in favour with the teachers would not last but I was pleased that my Mother looked proud of me.

By the side of the headmaster, I stood on the stage, facing the whole school the first time for a reason other than a misdemeanour. I had stood there before, in almost the same spot, on two previous occasions but this time it wasn't to be humiliated with a public caning. Instead of ridicule and abuse, I was being attributed to something that was worthwhile.

The headmaster made a brief speech, praising the virtue of saving and although he did mention my name, it was clear, even to me, he had no intention of elevating my status to that of a new cult leader.

The art teacher then gave a tug on a piece of old bleached white sacking that covered an area on the wall and unveiled my cardboard cut-out masterpiece which was followed by a shy but polite and maybe sympathetic round of applause from the teachers and invited parents to do the same. I was then presented with a book.

Had the book been about music or drawing or painting or even like the one I had 'pinched' from the art room it would not have surprised me.

I looked down and read the title; it was 'Treasure Island' by Robert Louis Stevenson. It may have been a 'Freudian slip' on the headmaster's part subconsciously hoping that I would go on a long sea journey like young Jim Hawkins. But if there was a connection between 'national savings' and being 'kidnapped' it was too clever for me to work out.

To the headmaster's credit he made no mention that my single item on exhibition was born as a result of me being a rotten singer! The book was not a possession that I was most pleased about but I was happy that the headmaster remained complimentary and did not spoil my day. The ownership of my prize had little impact upon me for I had previously read the story. Nor did it gain a place in my treasure chest. I soon misplaced it.

The reciprocal bombing raids over England and mainland Europe continued.

One particular raid on Hamburg on July 28 lasted forty-three minutes during that time forty two thousand civilians died. The casualty rate was greater than the total British civilian death rate during the whole period of the blitz.

Throughout July, the fighting continued in Sicily, axis soldiers defended the Mediterranean island strongly and loss of life was high on both sides but the American casualties were horrific.

During September, the remnants of the defending German and Italian army either surrendered or escaped across the Straits of Messina to the Mainland of Italy. After thirty-nine days of bitter fighting, Sicily was under allied control.

Rome was bombed on 19th July and a week later Mussolini, Italy's dictator and Hitler's ally, transferred his power to Marshall Badoglio.

Three weeks after the bombing of Rome, I was playing in the rear garden when I found, covered by a cardboard box, a lorry battery belonging to Dad:

I was soon to be tested for my Scouts Morse-Code Operators Badge so I thought with the battery at hand it was a good opportunity to put in some practise. I went upstairs to my bedroom and from under the bed I pulled out my 'collecting and tool box'.

I lifted the lid and looked in and found what I was looking for.

The contents of my box contained a number of books and comics. In addition to the paper objects there were glass marbles, steel bearings and nuts and bolts for scooter repairs, a catapult, elastic bands, lengths of string, last years conkers, lead soldiers, a mouth organ, tin boxes of cigarette cards, a penknife and some of Dad's 'old razor blades' for wood carving. There were also pieces of war souvenirs of shrapnel from shells and bombs, spent bullet cases, army cap badges and many more exciting items all of unbelievable value. It was a big box. I took my pieces of 'wizardry' downstairs to the first floor and went out through the door and walked down the steps that led into the rear garden. I sat on the bottom of the garden steps and connected the apparatus to the battery and went through the alphabet.

As I was seated at a level not much higher than my grandmother's sub-basement kitchen window, I could hear music coming from the wireless in her kitchen.

I went through the Morse code alphabet a number of times, using the flashing light to represent dots and dashes. While I was sending out an imaginary message, I was distracted when the music on Gran's radio was interrupted by a news bulletin. for what I had heard on the radio I was overjoyed. I ran up the garden steps and continued running up the stairs indoors until I reached my mother in the kitchen on the top floor. Mum was preparing the vegetables for our midday meal.

"Mum, I've just heard on Gran's radio that Hitler has surrendered".

"Are you sure? Is Gran' downstairs?" Mum asked,

"Yes, come down and ask her for yourself".

Mum gathered up her potato peelings and other vegetable scraps;

saving peeling and putting them in a special container outside Gran's kitchen was one of Mum's daily tasks. It was the source of Grandad's food recipe for his rabbits and chickens.

I took the peelings from Mum and followed her as she excitedly ran downstairs. As I was placing the scraps in the rabbit's bin, Mum walked into Gran's kitchen.

"Ron has told me, he has just heard on the news, that Hitler has surrendered"

"No, he's got it wrong, Hitler hasn't surrendered" Gran' said. "The news, a few minutes ago, said that Italy had surrendered".

I was disappointed but it was still very good news.

I had been distracted from my activity and forgetting about the equipment on the steps, I left the wires connected to the battery.

On most occasions, on entering the house, we would use the rear garden gate situated in Stanley Villas. Dad came home from work that evening, entered through the side gate as normal and noticed on the steps the battery still wired to my Morse key and a dimly lit bulb.

Dad was still delivering food over long distances and did not always get home every night, so it was always cause for a little excitement to see him. Happy hugs for Pat and I were always forthcoming but this evening, before I could greet him in the normal way Dad showed he was grumpy. Mum asked him what was wrong. Without answering Mum, he looked at me and said "Ron, next time you use a battery, make sure you turn it off or disconnect it when you have finished with it".

It was a stern command without an invitation for me to make an excuse.

"I charged that battery up because I needed that for work tomorrow, it's flat now and I shall have to put it on charge again".

No more was said and I ate my tea in silence. By the time we had finished eating Dad had got over the 'telling off' and I went to bed with the customary happy loving hug and the hot pillow.

As Summer gave way to Autumn, the fruit on the trees of the

unattended gardens of the bombed houses became ready for picking. Beechy, Benny and I decided to have a gang feast in our new gang premises.

As the year progressed, I sported a complete uniform and I went to the drill hall, once a week, for each cub meeting. I attended regularly for about a year but the regularity of playing the same silly children's indoor games week after week became boring. The 'call of adventure was strong in my ears' and I could not resist returning to my non-Christian ways of scavenging my jungle that was the ruins of bombed houses.

The fruits from the Mulberry tree, now rarely seen, are large and soft, similar in appearance to the raspberry and blackberry. The colour of the juice, like the fruit, is a powerful mauve and will stain clothing and skin on contact.

Within a short time our hands looked as though we were wearing mauve gloves and our clothing had varying sizes of polka dot splashes of mauve. We decided, for our next gang feast, we would only pick the apples and pears. We bought five rolls for a penny and made fruit rolls: Bread, was one of the few food commodities that was not rationed during the war.

During periods of rain we would remain in our den and just read from the wealth of information we had collected for our gang library shelves.

During the Summer school holiday, we frequented our 'hideaway' less often and sometimes we would not make a visit from one Saturday to the next.

One weekend, while playing in the rear garden of one of the empty houses, it began to rain so we made a 'dash' to our refuge. It was our first visit for over a week. When we opened the cellar door and walked in we were surprised to see an additional piece of furniture. It was a mattress.

I realised that someone other than us must have been in there but thought no more about it. As it was never our intention to sleep there we didn't need the facilities. Upon my suggestion, the three of us struggled with the cumbersome thing and after a lot of effort managed to get it outside. Some time had elapsed when we realised it had stopped raining, we left our hideout and scrambling over the now sodden bedding and continued with our play. At the end of the day, we scootered off to our respective homes with no more thought of how the mattress happened to get into our den. The following Saturday it rained most of the day and large puddles filled the breaks in the paving stones. After the three of us had given up on waiting for the rain to cease, we decided to return to the den. On our arrival we left our scooters in the front garden. As gang leaders do, I took the lead. I walked over broken bricks and rubble to the bottom of the concrete steps to reach the sub basement. Because of the uneven ground, I slowly opened the cellar door and walked down inside. As my eyes became adjusted to the gloom, I froze at what I saw. I wanted to turn but for a second or two I was fixed to the spot. I wanted to turn around and run but my legs wouldn't move. My two mates, directly behind me, unaware what was inside, were 'shunting' me more into the cellar. I tried to shout a warning but no words came out. I turned to run but my two friends obstructed my path, I lost my balance and stumbled. As my voice returned I only managed a gargled scream.

"Get out! Get out!" I shouted in a panic as I tried to reach the daylight coming through the partly open doorframe. My slip allowed my companions a clearer vision of the far end of the cellar that allowed them to see what I had seen.

No more than ten foot away was an old man.

When I had first seen him, his back was towards me. When he turned his head and looked in my direction it confirmed my first guess about his age. But not only was he old he also looked dirty and evil.

He must have been as startled as I but his reaction was much quicker than mine. Before my two friends came to their senses, to begin their retreat, the old man had already covered half of the distance between us. I couldn't understand the words he was shouting but he was frightening and his manner was violent. My two friends turned and scrambled up the steps that allowed me some free space to do the same. I stumbled and reached the door in total panic. My only thought was to get out and escape. As I was about to pass the door I grabbed the handle in an attempt to close it to make a barrier between us, but the sliding rubble restricted the door from completely closing. For an old man he moved fast. With my back to him, I tried to make progress upwards but I felt his hand fall heavily upon my left shoulder. The feel of his grasp and the rancid smell of his breathe caused an unsocial reaction in the department of my underpants.

Good fortune, however, was on my side; part of the door was now between us. As my pursuer moved forward, due to the moving rubble, he also slipped and with the full impact of his fall he hit his forehead on the edge of the door. He let out a curse as he released his hold on my shoulder. His fall gave me a few vital seconds to increase the distance between us. Terrified, I continued my escape and ran up the littered steps. I slipped and slid as though I was running up a landslide. I had to overcome a miniature avalanche of bricks and other building rubble in front of me that was cascading down in the wake of my escaping colleagues. Without stopping I managed to clear the heap of broken bricks and plaster and reached ground level. I made a half turn and continued to stumble trying to clear the garden. I reached the pavement and turned to run down the road but before doing so I gave a sidelong glance to gauge the distance between my pursuer and me. The tramp had cleared the cellar but he was still on all fores and scrambling up the slope and had just reached the top of the steps. This gave me a lead of about twenty feet. In the time of 'a blink of an eye', I noticed that his dirty face except for the area above his nose and eyes was covered in dark hair. During that quick glance, I also noticed a trickle of blood coming from his forehead and down his cheek. He wore a large ill-fitting overcoat that came below his knees that made his movement cumbersome.

As our eyes met, he let out a terrifying roar which encouraged another surge of warm moisture to have a free run down the back of my legs. Still running, looking ahead, I saw my friends about the same distance from me as I was from the 'angry tramp'. I screamed as I ran. We ran passed the house I lived in, on the opposite side of the road but nobody was there to see or hear the danger I was in. It took me about half the length of the road at full speed to get shoulder to shoulder with my friends. I could also hear my friend's screams and I felt some consolation that I was no longer alone. I eased my pace a little to glance over my shoulder to make sure we had lost him. As I turned my head, to my horror, I saw he was only about six feet behind. I could not run any faster yet he had still made up the distance that had been between us when we had started running. As I turned my head, he raised both of his arms to make a grab for me.

"Oh please god, make him die," I mumbled to myself.

I shouted to my two pals "run faster".

We used every ounce of our strength in an attempt to gain more ground.

We reached the end of the Studley Road, unable to suck any more air into our lungs. Our energy was totally spent. As I turned the corner, I dared to take another look over my shoulder. To my indescribable relief, he had stopped where he had made his last attempt to grab me.

He was a hundred yards, or more, away from where we now stood panting and gasping for our next breathe.

He appeared to be in the same discomfort as my friends and I. He was doubled over with one hand across his chest. His other hand was clinging to a lamppost to steady himself.

Even in my worst nightmare I don't think I have ever been more frightened. My knowledge of words is inadequate to explain the extent of my joy and the relief I felt to see he was stationary. Our terrifying few minutes ordeal had come to an end. The chase was over.

As the three of us stood watching our pursuer, also struggling to draw his next breath, I cast an inconspicuous glance down at the backs of my legs for signs that the extent of my fear may be on display. I was delighted to see that both legs were clean. This time I had misjudged the quantity of my discharge. Although the seat of my pants was moist, my bowels had not totally betrayed me.

During the chase my heart had felt as though it had parted company with the inside of my rib cage and had been pumping madly somewhere in my throat.

As we watched the tramp gradually recover his breathe, he stood upright and discarded his heavy army overcoat, we saw the top of his body was bare. He looked again in our direction, shook a menacing clenched fist at us, turned around and with his overcoat under his arm, walked off in the direction of our ex gang den. Still breathing heavily, the three of us walked across Larkhall Lane into the general store where I sold my firewood.

From inside the shop, we were able to look through the window down the length of Studley Road and kept the tramp in sight as he slowly continued to increase the space between us.

We purchased a penny 'fizzy drink' each and drank while we recovered our composure and excitedly laughed as we retold our story to each other as though we had each enjoyed a lone experience.

Contrary to my first thought, I observed during my last glance back, he was certainly not the old man he, at first, appeared to be. Even accepting he was much younger than I had at first imagined, he must have also been a fit man. He ran with the handicap of a heavy overcoat and being stunned by running into the door: His collision with the edge of the door could have given us the precious head start that was critical in our escape.

My running observation of our would be attacker was only a 'snapshot' that lasted no more in time than to blink but the event was terrifyingly and clear enough for the picture to remain with me during my schooldays.

Whenever my thoughts returned to the scene, I am sure my pulse rate also increased.

I wondered if he ever intended to catch me, or us. Was he really as crazy as he appeared to be? Or was his anger just a big bluff to keep us away from his new abode? If it was his intention to only frighten us, to keep way from his new home, he had surely done a very good job. Not only did we never venture inside our den again, we thereafter always passed on the other side of the road, we did not even risk a commando raid to retrieve our scooters. Because he was obviously young, rather than old man, I do wonder if our pursuer had deserted from the armed forces.

For many months, since the enemy had been driven out of North Africa, my largest war map had been that of Eastern Europe but in September the Allies landed in Italy.

All of the newspapers made headlines of the fact that for the first time since Dunkirk forces representing democracy were once again on mainland Europe.

On my bedroom wall, I replaced the map of Sicily with one of Italy.

I can remember only one occasion when I had a stand up fistfight in the street. I got involved with plenty of playground skirmishes, pushing, shoving and wrestling during my junior school days but standing up and trading blow for blow was a far more risky and painful business.

I made the mistake that all bullies, or acts of bullying, encounter sooner or later, I picked on the wrong person. By good fortune I learnt my lesson early in life:

I picked on a boy in my class that was about my build but rather timid. He didn't mix with the other lads and was a prime target for getting 'pushed around'. He came from Cyprus, had black hair and very obvious tanned Mediterranean features. He was the only boy in my school that was not white English. On this one and only act of bullying on my part, I shouted some term of abuse at him. I was with my two friends, outside of school hours on our scooters when the encounter took place.

I was surprised when, not only did he return a similar unpleasant remark, he started walking towards me. As he approached, in a confident challenging manner, I thought he looked taller now than he did at school.

As I was with my friends, I had little choice but to respond to his obvious bravado. I stepped from my scooter and as we got closer to each other within striking distance, I pushed him backwards with both hands. It was at this point of my attack that I became aware I had picked on the wrong person. I knew immediately I had made a mistake because he responded to my push not with another push as I had expected, but with a clenched fist to my face. He really was not the person I thought him to be. His punch landed on my nose and made my eyes water. I swung out to return his blow but it was not well placed, it landed on his chest. With my second punch I incorporated with his Christian name more unpleasant words which accused him of being an illegitimate Cypriot. As he ducked to avoid my punch, he told me I had mistaken him for his younger brother. My new assessment of his height told me my error was obvious. In my haste to show off in front of my friends I had made the classic mistake that all bullies make, I had picked on someone I thought would not defend himself, I was careless. He swung a second punch to my face. As I stepped back to dodge the blow, I trod on my scooter, I lost my balance and fell backwards. I felt foolish and helpless, my two friends looked down at me, their gang leader, spread eagled on the pavement but as I was down, I thought it wise to stay down and accept defeat. My adversary, I am pleased to relate, did not have the aggression that I had displayed but had the wisdom, to consider I may have been taught a lesson.

Before he left the scene, he warned me not to think about getting even by hitting his smaller brother.

I learnt that day, not only the obvious lesson from my act of bullying but also a golden rule of bare knuckle boxing; when hitting with a clenched fist don't tuck the thumb in under the fingers. I had done just that. With my one punch, I put my thumb out of joint and gave myself an extremely painful hand that lasted a number of weeks, much longer than the painful nose and the hurt pride. When I got home I could do nothing to hide my bloody nose and swollen bruised lips from my mother. Mum may have been a little relaxed regarding the knowledge of my whereabouts and behaviour but she was always over protective towards me in the 'rough and tumble department' and, on this occasion, got herself into a bit of a panic when she saw the condition of my face.

When Dad came home, Mum argued that he should go to my sparring opponent's home to complain to his father. I had modified the event by leaving out the vital fact that I had started the fight. Dad was impressed by my attitude, albeit a lie, that I was beaten 'fair and square'. Under those circumstances, the three of us agreed that Mum's instruction was not a good idea and the matter was best forgotten about.

It didn't help matters, however, when on the same night, Dad told her, "I think it a good idea for Ron to enrol at John's boxing club for lessons".

It was not a solution that Mum found easy to agree with and the episode concluded with a compromise. I did not join a boxing club because the nearest was too far so Uncle John would teach me.

John's club, the 'club too far', was The De Vass Boxing Club, Battersea. Uncle John had joined a few months earlier and attended weekly.

John, now fifteen years old was happy to agree to pass on and 'show off' with, the instruction he was himself receiving.

From his club, John acquired an old pair of 'cast off' boxing gloves for me and with nothing else, other than enthusiasm, I was ready to learn 'The Queensbury Rules' on the noble art of boxing.

With John officially appointed as my instructor, he felt he was entitled to turn my attic bedroom into a gymnasium. His first task was to find a home for a punch-bag. After leaving many holes in the plaster on the ceiling John eventually found a firm joist. With

214

lumps of plaster over the floor and an exposed piece of timber in the ceiling John installed a large hook and hung a heavy punch bag from it which, due to my sore thumb, I refrained to use for some time

After a few weeks had elapsed and the bruising on my hand receded, I began to start 'jabbing' the bag, but I could not understand the logic of learning to hit a defenceless canvas bag that was not likely to strike back. When I questioned John on the value of the punch bag, he confidently gave a reply that to me was not an answer at all.

The following week, after returning from the boys club, John brought up the subject of punch bags. This time he supplied an answer to my week old question that made more sense.

"It is to build up the power behind the punch" he informed me.

I realised he had not known the answer when I had asked but to his credit, he had bothered to find out. I continued receiving the lessons and absorbed all the instruction that John was capable of giving and together, we shared many sessions of shadow boxing, sparring and practiced riding punches and counter punching.

During the wetter months of Autumn playing marbles and 'flicking' cigarette cards were not so popular which slowed the 'swapping' and selling market down, but I was still earning some useful 'pocket money' with the milk round, selling chopped fire wood, lead soldiers and a 'trickle' of trade in postage stamps from my swaps or sell album.

The most precious commodity at this time of year was having a pocket full of 'conkers':

I have read that conkers, in some regions North of England, are also called 'a Strung Snail Shell'. I can believe it because there is some resemblance but I have never heard the term used in the South. The Horse Chestnut Trees would get 'raped' daily, after school hours, for their fruit. Climbing the trees was one method of collection but not so productive as a well aimed throw, one lucky strike with a large stick thrown like a boomerang into the branches could bring down three or four.

I don't know how popular playing conkers is today or even if it is played at all. But for all the unfortunate younger people that are growing up believing that a computer game is the only toy to play with I find very sad. I will describe the manner in which it was played when I was a boy:

It is necessary to make a hole through the centre of the nut to thread a piece of string.

There was a belief, by some of my school friends, that a hole made with a hot poker as opposed to being drilled out, gave the conker more strength. A length of string was then threaded through the hole. The game was normally played with two players. Each player took one turn each at swinging his conker to hit the other. The game would be over when one knock from a conker succeeded in breaking or splitting the opponents 'conker' free from the string. If neither conker had been played with previously, the surviving conker was called 'a oner' because it had beaten only one conker with no previous wins. If one conker with a previous record of beating say five others won against another with a record of beating, say, six conkers it was deemed to be an elevener. (Five plus six). That is to say a winning conker always added to his own, the number of wins the losing conker held. There were a number of theories of how a conker could be made strong enough to reach the status of a champion; Baking in an oven was a popular notion. Storing them from one year to the next, thereby only using the previous year's crop, or to soak them in vinegar or salty water. Conkers was an unusual commodity, in my way of thinking, for they were not regarded to be in the 'buying or selling' category. Because they grew on trees they were termed 'natural' and anyone should get them for nothing. Being a collector by instinct, I would amass large quantities of the nut and give some away.

To 'give them away' may sound rather generous and out of character to that which I have portrayed myself. But the conkers I gave were unprepared with no holes, straight from the shell. Even then, I only gave to my customers, in keeping with the old Yorkshire saying; 'Thar gets ought fer nought'.

I gave only to those that bought my home made lead soldiers or

216

bought or swapped my postage stamps.

Dad had a mastoid operation in 1931 but he continued to suffer on and off with ear pain for the rest of his life. He caught an infection while he was a teenager that left him with a perforated eardrum and partial deafness in one ear.

During the summer Dad had an operation on his inner ear. I cannot recall how long he was in hospital for, but I was aware the problem was related to his continuing mastoid pain.

The day that Dad was discharged, Mum took Pat and I to the hospital and the four of us travelled back together by the underground railway. As we came out of the station at Stockwell we turned right and walked along the Clapham Road towards our home in Studley Road Dad said: "Have Pat and Ron been behaving themselves while I've been in hospital Mam": Dad converted his 'u' to sound like the 'a' in alley.

Mum looked at us both, while hidden from Dad, gave us a wink and said: "Yes they've been doing as they were told, they've been as good as gold".

"Good enough for a surprise d'you think?"

"I think so Bill".

It was a little game that Mum and Dad were playing to built up our excitement. We all held hands as Dad led us casually over the tramlines across the Clapham Road. We stopped outside a toyshop on the other side of the road and almost opposite our side turning of Studley Road. We had a brief look in the shop window and followed Dad as he walked inside.

I can't remember Pat's choice but I came out with a folding tin of Reeves watercolour paints. I can't begin to imagine how Mum or Dad could have afforded to be so reckless. But such was Dad's need to reflect his pleasure at being discharged from hospital.

As an item the paint box was small in physical terms but it was a valuable and cherished possession to me. I kept the box long after I had used all of the small solid squares of paint inside it. I kept it for it was a symbol of Dad's affection. I never threw it away.

Dad's paint box gift to me was one of the very few items I

possessed from him that he had not made himself. It remained with me until I was eighteen years old and I went into the army. Because it was empty it must have then been thrown away.

A month or two before the Christmas of 1943, John and I were moved from our attic bedroom. My designated sleeping area was little more than a six feet square box with a window. The room was too small to accommodate anything larger than a single bed which I regarded as good fortune for it was the first time since leaving Devon I had a room to myself and not big enough for any one to move in with me. My new room was in the front of the house and looked out into Studley Road but still only one floor down from the attic.

John was moved to the next floor down from me, on the first floor. I was never told the reason for the change but I now had two lengths of uninterrupted wall space for my war maps. Had I remained in the attic, I daresay I could have either been bitten by bedbugs or bombed out by the doodlebugs which referring to the later was to commence in the coming summer.

Every morning Dad would purchase 'The Daily Mirror'. On Sundays he always bought 'The Sunday Pictorial'. One Sunday, just before the Christmas holiday period began in addition to the newspaper, Dad bought a 'Hobbies' magazine.

The periodical was, most probably, the original handyman magazine and forerunner to the popular 'do it yourself' publications. Each month's issue contained a supplement containing plans and suggestions for making toys and furniture. This particular Christmas edition had a special pullout section that had a very good detailed plan of a 17th century sailing ship.

I must have shown some interest in the drawings for Dad asked me if I would like him to make it. My reaction was obvious and he agreed to commence the construction

EIGHT

D DAY AND DOODLEBUGS

Early in the new-year of 1944, the enemy night bombing campaign on London and the Home Counties intensified with devastating results. The air raids increased enough to be termed, by one newspaper, The Baby Blitz.

When I was eleven years old and after the Easter holiday period, I had reached the age when I had to move to a senior school; I was transferred to Haselrigge Road Secondary School.

My new school was sited between Clapham Park Road and Bedford Road, Clapham. The nearest underground station was Clapham North, one stop on from Stockwell.

The school had at least one thing in common with all other schools; it had been built in the previous century, during the reign of Queen Victoria (1837-1910). My two friends, Benny and Beechy, being the same age as me, changed to different schools at the same time.

John Bennett, Benny, being the brightest of the three of us passed his 'eleven plus' examination and was accepted at Henry Thornton Grammar School, Clapham Common.

Pat Beauchamp, Beechy, not far behind Benny in education went to a technical school; The Brixton School of Building:

Before Beechy's father was 'called up' at the outbreak of the war, he was in the building trade. It was his plan to start his own business in the building trade when the war was over and wanted his son, Beechy, to be a part of it.

By the time early summer arrived, I had forgotten about Dad's project of making the model galleon. By accident, I found Dad's hiding place in a cupboard. The ship's hull and top deck had been completed but owing to Dad's resumption of long distance driving, work on the vessel had come to a halt. I was delighted with what I had seen and when Dad returned from one of his deliveries, a day or so later, I told him I had accidentally discovered it and how pleased I was.

My pleasure must have spurred Dad into resuming his handiwork, for a few weeks later he presented me with the completed object.

Each Friday was hobbies day so the first Friday after Dad presented me with my galleon; I took it to school to show my classmates. The teacher also showed an interest in my model and held the vessel aloft for all of the class to see and said it was a very good example of the type of craft in use in the British navy during the reign of Queen Elizabeth 1.

The teacher's endorsement of Dad's craftsmanship must have influenced a boy in the class to ask me if I wanted to sell it. Had the offer not have coincided with me overhearing Mum and Dad talking about a shortage of money during that same week I would have said no! As it happened, I asked him how much would he give me for it.

The boy then asked if I would let his father see it first. I went home with him from school that afternoon and met his father as he opened the door. After a short inspection the boy's father offered me two shillings and sixpence (12 1/2 new pence). I accepted the half a crown piece and continued my journey home with the coin in my pocket. Thinking the half crown would solve the family's financial crisis I was pleased to present Dad with the coin. My pleasure turned to regret when Dad told me how many hours he had spent making the galleon and said I should have asked him before making the sale. It was not Dad's words of reprimand alone that upset me. My regret was, I had sacrificed something I would rather have kept. I don't think I convinced Dad I had sold it for an unselfish reason. Dad believed I sold it because I didn't like it:

Until circa1946, Silver coins contained real silver. They remained in circulation after 1946 but without the silver. The value of the silver content of the pre 1946 became greater than the purchasing power of the coin itself which caused many of the coins to be melted down by jewellers before they were all 'called in' by the Royal Mint. The value of the silver has given pre1946 coins a greater scarcity value than there would have otherwise have been.

One of Grandad Bridger's rare conversations with me occurred when he complimented me on my selection to design the school's savings poster:

Grandad must have heard the news of the making and selling of the galleon and the national savings poster through the family grapevine.

As I was tending some bedding plants around the air-raid shelter end of the garden, Grandad approached me, and congratulated me on my school painting. He continued talking and eventually asked me if I would like to paint some rabbit hutch labels for him.

After I had agreed, he told me he wanted me to cut out some stiff cardboard tags and paint on them the names of famous sailing ships to place on each of his rabbit hutches: He gave me the task to think of, or find out, as many famous historical ships names as he had hutches.

I started enthusiastically and as I finished each label Grandad and I selected one particular rabbit hutch for the ship's nametag to be pinned to. I remember some of the names on the labels that I completed; 'Mayflower', 'Santa Maria', 'Royal Oak', 'Golden Hind' etc, but within a few weeks of my starting, the war took control of my activity and brought the project to an abrupt halt:

For many weeks prior to the rabbit hutch labelling, there had been a lot of newspaper speculation that the allied invasion of Europe was imminent.

School had become a regular daily event again with little interference from aerial activity. I believe this must have been the quietest period, in the bombing, since air raids began for it was no longer a worthwhile pastime searching the streets for spent aircraft ammunition shells and bomb shrapnel, for there was none. Shrapnel had become semi-precious.

I went to bed, on the night of 5th June with no idea that the next day would change the course of history. While I had been sleeping the beginning of the biggest invasion the world had known had begun. My daily update, on my wall war map, on the Allies achievements had continued showing the enemy retreating on all fronts:

In Southern Europe, Allied forces fighting in Italy were at the doors of Rome.

On the Eastern front, The Russians had recovered their lost territory and were fiercely determined to redress their staggering losses upon their German foe. The Russian army was rapidly advancing towards Berlin in trucks and tanks, many of which were supplied by Britain and America.

In a blind attempt to halt the soviet attack, Hitler had committed 60% of his fighting men, approximately 4.300.000 troops.

In the Pacific area the Japanese were retreating in Asia and vacating the Pacific Islands.

On 6th of June, I awoke early to hear the droning of aircraft engines that was so prolonged it was impossible to ignore. It would be untrue to say the noise of the aircraft was deafening and disrupted my sleep for the sound was muffled due to the high altitude the aircraft were flying. Nevertheless, it was loud enough for me to get me out of my bed and look out of the window.

For a summer morning, the weather was poor; it was cold with drizzling rain. As I looked up at the sky, I saw aircraft, filling the gaps in the clouds. The sight in front of me was on such a massive scale I sensed, even at my young age; I would never witness such a spectacle again. There was an assortment of heavy bombers, light bombers and fighters, a complete mix of types. The aerial armada appeared to be unreal. It was as though a roller blind, with the same pictures of aircraft, had been attached to the outside of my window and was being slowly unrolled for a theatrical production.

The aircraft travelled across my North facing, bedroom window from my left to right which told me they were all heading Eastward and going out towards the mainland of Europe rather than coming back. I hurried from my bedroom to the kitchen and told my Mother what I had seen.

She was sitting at the table, pouring out a cup of tea, with no apparent concern, as though the event I had just witnessed was an every day occurrence. She did not appear to be even a little excited.

"They were going over when I got up this morning", she said.

Although the quantity of aircraft was vast, I didn't realise that this was not just another big daylight bombing raid on Germany. Not until I began to listen to the radio that I learnt the long awaited liberation of Europe had begun.

'D Day 6th June' became a phrase as popular as well known sayings as 'needle and cotton' or 'knife and fork':

The historic invasion on the beeches of France, from Cherbourg to Le Havre, commenced in the early hours in cold and rainy conditions the hundred miles of the Normandy coast was divided on paper into five sections; Utah, Omaha, Gold, Juno and Sword.

Three million men and two million tons of weapons and ammunition had been assembled all over the South of England in readiness for the assault.

The long days of bad weather leading up to the invasion came as good fortune. The thick cloud kept the Luftwaffe from flying reconnaissance aircraft that would have enabled them to observe the large build up of ships in the harbours along the coast of England.

On the early morning of June 5, 1944, it was raining heavily. The waves in the channel were five foot high and the thousands of men that had crammed into assault ships were wet and many were suffering from seasickness. The invasion had already been postponed twenty-four hours when General Eisenhower, Supreme Allied Commander, gave the order to go. It took another twenty hours for the first fighting men to be on their way.

During the first day the Allies landed 154,000 men, many were killed by rifle and machine gun fire as they leapt into the water. Others drowned as their landing craft ran into underwater defences placed on the seabed.

The first troops to land on the beeches of France were the men of the U.S 4th Infantry Division at 06.30. 6 June

On paper the German Supreme Command should have had no problem in repelling the invasion force. Eight Allied Divisions had landed on the beeches of Normandy. The Germans, by contrast, had fifty infantry divisions and eight Panzer divisions in France. Fortunately, for the Allied forces, most of them were in the wrong place: Over a period of many months a most incredible web of deception had been spun and leaked by Allied Intelligence to make the German High Command believe the invasion proper was to take place elsewhere. I do not mean to imply that the allied forces had an easy time, quite the contrary: When the German army conquered France in 1940 it took them just four weeks. It took the allies six months to get it back. By the close of the first day, 154,000 Allied soldiers had been put ashore, 12.000 of them had been killed or missing. German troops suffered similar casualties.

My war map of Italy was relegated to the inside of my bedroom door to make some space for my fresh drawn, much larger, map of the West coast of France.

On D-Day, 6th June 1944 MP's in the House of Commons debated:

1. How many children should a teacher have in the classroom?

2. Raising the national school leaving age.

3. Equal pay for women and whether government Tea-Ladies should be called 'office cleaners' or 'chars': Char is cockney slang from the Chinese word for tea.

I wonder did parliament not know the biggest army the world had ever seen had that day landed in France?

Each morning, after the eight am news, on the radio, The Ministry of Food had a five-minute 'slot' called 'Kitchen Fronts' which informed the nation how to remain fit and healthy on the meagre rations that were available. One week's shopping list of rationed food for an adult included;

Eight ounces of sugar,

Two and half ounces of tea,

Two and half-pints of milk,

Four ounces of butter,

Two ounces of cheese,

Two ounces of margarine,

Four ounces of bacon. The Meat ration was a quantity to the value of one shilling.

Each person was also allowed thirty-one eggs, not for a month, but for a year. But things were getting better, it was announced on the radio that the cheese ration was to be increased from two to three ounces per week. (Three ounces =eighty-five grams).

Even the sun rejoiced, some areas in England the temperature on Whit Sunday reached 87 degrees.

The average male earnings at this time were £4.13shillings (£4.65p).

One of the cheapest cigarettes on the market was a packet of 'Woodbines' and cost 1p for five.

The fear of enemy forces invading our country were now only a nasty memory and in some cases appeared to have been forgotten and now the 'tables had been turned'.

There was some newspaper speculation the war would be over by Christmas but after the rejoicing of the successful invasion had cooled down, the cinema attending public were jolted back to reality: The sea and airborne landings in Normandy were shown on newsreels throughout the country the following week.

The casualty rate had been very high and on one of the American landing areas, the German defenders put up such a strong resistance there were fears that the allied troops would be slaughtered while still trying to advance from the beach. The war was far from being nearly over.

A week after the Normandy landings, Hitler launched the first of his revenge weapons *'Vergeltungswaffe'*. The flying bomb, the V1, was the 'fruit' of the seed that had been planted in 1937 when the first rocket test centre was opened.

Information of the development of a new breed of weapons had been passed on to military intelligence by the French underground resistance long before their launching had been perfected. The construction of 'ski jump' type ramps, used for the V1 launching, at Peenemunde had been observed by aerial photographic reconnaissance taken by the RAF in June 1943. The launch pads were bombed two months later but the damage was minor and by the spring of 1944 the factory went into production. The V1 was the beginning of Hitler's last desperate offensive in an attempt to change the course of the war.

On 15th June, 244 flying bombs were targeted against London:

In the first 36 days of the new phase of air raids, 5,000 flying bombs had been launched. A second 'blitz' had begun and London was in the 'front line' again. The pilotless bomb had a simple jet engine at the tail end of the fuselage. In the nose there was about a ton of high explosive. It flew low, at 3,000 feet at a speed of 400mph. The noise of the V1, Doodlebug, in flight was like the sound of an engine of a 'Volkswagen Beetle' without a silencer. Although there had still been the occasional bombing raids and the 'blackout' and 'fire-watching' were still maintained it was nothing like the night and day bombing of the past.

Three weeks later another evacuation plan, from the capital, was put into operation.

I had been going to school each morning not even expecting to find shrapnel. But about a week after 'D Day'' with the news reports, on the radio, there were warnings that a new type of bombing raid had started.

226

It had become normal for me to be operating one or two, small time and legal, money making schemes; gathering glass jam jars and beer bottles and returning them to provisions merchant or the Off license respectively. The proceeds always allowed me to have some pocket money which allowed me to afford, during my journey to school each morning, to purchase a daily 'paper: After returning home, on completion of each day's schooling, I traced or copied maps and transferred all of the information from the newspaper to my wall war charts to keep them up to date.

One morning, while on my way to school, I heard a very unusual muted engine noise. It sounded very distant and was out of sight so I thought little more of it. I bought my paper from the vendor outside Stockwell Underground Station and my attention was immediately rooted to an unclear photograph on the front page and some technical drawings of a strange new bomber. I was still looking at the front page of the newspaper while walking towards the tram stop when I was distracted by the same unfamiliar aircraft noise that had now got much louder. I looked Southward along the Clapham Road and about half a mile in front of me, above the houses; I saw this V1 pilotless flying bomb. It was the same as that described in the newspaper I was holding. The aircraft or projectile, now nicknamed by the newspapers 'Doodlebug' passed quickly from East to West but I was still able to get a good look at it. The engine noise droned as it continued its flight out of my line of sight and became hidden by trees and buildings. Just as it went out of my view the engine noise stopped and within seconds there was an enormous explosion. The ground trembled.

I read later in the newspaper that when all of the fuel had expired the missile glided to ground. The glide time lasted approximately twelve seconds and exploded on impact. The first V1 had landed in Swanscombe, Kent. Another landed on top of a railway bridge in Bethnal Green, in London's East End, and killed six people.

By the middle of June the bombardment of the new weapon began in earnest.

On the 16th and 17th they were launched with unremitting frequency. On 18th, 121 people were killed while attending a Sunday church service in Wellington Barracks, London.

Early in July, yet another evacuation programme of London was put into action. Our family, that is to say, Mum, Pat and I moved out of the capital, on this occasion without being organised by the authorities.

Before we vacated our house in Studley Road, I took my maps down from my bedroom wall, rolled them and slipped them into a case that accompanied me to our next 'port of call'. We stayed with my Aunt Dot' and Uncle George to return to my early schooldays county of Buckinghamshire.

My Uncle George was, in fact, my great Uncle: George was the younger Brother of my Father's Mother, Beatrice Bonny.

Aunt Dorothy, Dot, was the Sister of Ted Woodhall, the author. They lived near High Wycombe at 26 Sawpit Hill, Holmer Green.

For the short time, while we lived there, Pat and I both went to the same school: Holmer Green Upper school, Watchet Lane. Parish Piece, Holmer Green. The school could be approached from more than one direction. Pat and I used a public footpath from Wycombe Road end. On each side of the narrow footpath honeysuckle and wild roses grew in abundance. Even now, nearly sixty years later, I am unable to pass honeysuckle and roses without being mentally transported back to Holmer Green School.

Uncle George Coverdale was not many months older than my Father, they shared the same light-hearted approach to life and also like Dad he was a natural comedian.

I could never be sure anything Uncle George said was truthful. He would start a conversation by describing a normal every day event but just to make it more interesting he would gradually 'spoon feed' little exaggerations whereupon on its conclusion make the whole event sound like a script from a pantomime.

Each weekend, while we stayed at Holmer Green, Dad cycled from Stockwell and slept with us over Saturday night and cycled back to London on Sunday afternoon.

228

On one of Dad's weekend visits he told me, with a similar solemn 'I wish I didn't have to do this' manner that he had when he told me my baby Sister was dead.

"I'm sorry Ron but I had to give Jumbo away this week".

Dad must have seen my face drop, he wisely continued before I could say a word.

"The house is a wreck. We won't be able to live there anymore and there was nowhere for Jumbo to stay, so I gave him to one of my friends at work".

I was shocked and saddened by what Dad had told me but he reminded me that it would have been selfish of me to want the dog to stay in those conditions with no one to care for him. I knew the man that Dad had given my dog to. I had met him on a couple of occasions when Dad had taken me to his place of work. His name was Fred Bell:

I cannot remember names of many people during my school days but this name I remember because his work mates knew him as 'Ding Dong'.

Dad went on to tell me during some of the nights, while he was away from home; there had been more V1 air attacks.

On one of the raids, the roof had been blown off and the rooms at the rear of the house were very badly damaged. All of our windows had been blown out and broken glass littered the floors. The room on the second floor, at the rear of the house, was used as a kitchen, dining and sitting room. A couch that was placed beneath the window, on which Jumbo always slept, was also covered in glass.

Jumbo had the freedom to roam the house and garden and on hearing the air raid warning to take cover, would run to the air raid shelter. It was fortunate that he continued with this routine, he would have been, at least, badly cut if he had not.

After being away from home for three days and nights Dad saw Jumbo in the garden, his fur, was splashed with red. From a distance Dad thought it was blood but on a closer inspection he discovered it was the contents of a broken bottle of tomato sauce.

Our stay in one place, again, was short and uneventful. We could not have been with my Aunt and Uncle at Holmer Green for more than three months. But in that short time I do recall making friends with a couple of lads of my age that attended the same school.

One of the boys lived beyond the crossroads at the top of Sawpit Hill, in an old farm labourer's cottage. There was no lavatory inside the dwelling, all body functions had to be controlled until a long walk to the far end of the garden had been accomplished.

The toilet was surrounded by a number of apple trees and looked like a small inoffensive garden shed. As I walked along the path and got nearer I realised my nose was more reliable than my eyes.

It is likely that during the colder days of winter the smell was less intruding, but my observation was during the heat of summer and the aroma, which greeted me, was not compatible with my thought association of countryside and sweet fragrance. I must add, however, before we moved back to London, I discovered the apples were delicious. I only used the toilet once and on that one occasion I noted there was no water cistern and no pipe work. There was only a large wooden box to sit on, with a hole in the middle, which covered a very deep circular hole in the ground. It was the first time I had seen a cesspit. The danger surprised me more than the primitiveness.

Looking down into the hole, nothing could be seen because it was so deep, just total darkness. When the wooden frame around the seat was lifted, the hole was large enough to accommodate an average size human body. A child of my size could have fallen into it even with the seat down. Anyone careless enough to fall into it would, I am sure, have disappeared never to be seen again. But then considering what the unfortunate victim would have fallen into, nobody would have wanted to have seen the person again anyway.

The boy that lived in the cottage suffered from epileptic fits but I will make no joke of the probable cause.

Once, when I was playing with them, the one that suffered from fits had a convulsive seizure. The other local boy recognised the signs that he was about to go into a fit and supported him before he collapsed. He eased him to the ground by the side of the road as though he had gone through the same procedure many times before. The confident professional manner in which he handled the situation made a lasting impression on me.

Had the same situation occurred in my previous school in London, he would have been allowed to fall and be laughed at. Ignorance is not always bliss.

The subject of lavatories and Holmer Green reminds me of another occasion of my stupidness: While we were still at Holmer Green, Mum had got a herself a daily job in a small factory making 'Bonamint'. The factory was at Gerrards Cross only a few miles from Holmer Green.

The manufacturer produced chewing gum and chocolate. The fact that sweets and chocolates were rationed made it easy for some of the chocolates to fall into Mum's handbag and she accidentally brought them home, she told me.

Once, and only once, I helped myself to a packet without asking. I finished off the pack of six strips. In almost as many minutes later, I had a severe bout of diarrhoea. Not being able to keep it a secret, I informed Mum of my predicament where upon she checked her handbag and immediately realised I was not suffering from food poisoning. She had no need for a doctor's qualification or to give me an examination to guess what was wrong with me. There was no need either for me to be harshly disciplined. I had inflicted punishment and educated myself at the same time. The sticks of chewing gum were laxatives.

After our short stay with Dot and George, we returned to our house in Studley Road but only to cook a mid-day meal and tea making in Gran's basement flat:

I do not know the reason nor can I understand the logic of our move from safety. Again, we had moved back into the danger zone of the air raids.

The missile launches still persisted and the house we had lived in was in a worse condition on our return than before we had vacated it. Dad had not exaggerated, it was in fact, worse than I had expected: The room that had once been my bedroom, for less than eleven months, no longer existed. The roof and all of the rooms on the third floor were gone. All but for a few bricks that clung to the window frame that had once been the second floor was also missing. The top of the house that had been blown off was scattered all over the back garden.

In defiance, as though wanting to hang on to the last remnants of respectability, the curtains, although shredded and ripped into strips, still hung in the solitary window frames like long forgotten bunting. A few remaining burnt roof timbers, defiantly pointed upwards, like ugly charred fingers as though accusing the culprit.

A lot of action had taken place in the Pacific and in Europe while we had been away. Allied gains were now taking place more rapidly than any other time of the war.

I was excited at the Allies advances but disappointed that I had nowhere to hang my war maps. They had remained in my small brown battered suitcase all of the time we were at Holmer Green. When we came home they were all out of date: American marines had taken Saipan, in the Pacific Ocean in the Marianas Islands group.

The distance between Saipan and Japan was short enough to enable American bombers to bomb Tokyo. This was another big stepping stone forward towards ending the war with the Japanese.

American troops had opened a new front by landing troops in Southern France. Paris, Antwerp and Brussels had also been liberated.

I read the headlines on the front page of my newspaper Adolf Hitler survives another assassination attempt'.

Tucked away on another page I read an article that created very little attention; Iceland had gained its independence from Denmark.

Most of the houses in Studley Road were now reduced to heaps of bricks and rubble.

Of the houses that remained standing, most were without their roofs and the second floors walls had been blown out. A satirist could have got the impression of angry tenants getting together with a crude plan to convert their houses into bungalows. The road and the surrounding area was a mass of ruined houses. Some people, as we did, remained with their humble possessions and lived like moles in their basement. Only Gran' and Grandad's living area in the semi-basement was in any state of reasonable safety. It could best be described as looking into a cave in a mountain of bricks and rubble. Due to the near miss and the upstairs of the house collapsing, we no longer felt safe sleeping in the garden shelter. We joined a growing number of people that slept at night on the platform of Stockwell underground station:

I do not suggest the movement began in Stockwell. I don't know how the idea developed but Londoners used this form of shelter widely during the war throughout the underground rail network.

The Royal Mail, then a department of the General Post Office, GPO still operated and unless the premises addressed on the envelope was totally flattened letters were still delivered. In the worse cases addressees made their collection from the sorting office.

From as early as the beginning of the bombing in 1940 some homeless people spent most of the day and all night underground on the platform, while others would get up out of their sleeping position in the morning get on a underground train and go straight to work.

The authorities recognised the potential in this temporary form of shelter and overnight sleeping in the underground became official. Metal-framed bunks, to sleep three high, were erected along the platform wall. By the end of July more than 70,000 people were sleeping in London's underground. Fortunately, during the early years, our family was not included in that number. But now, nearly four years on, we were. But again, good fortune stayed with us.

We did however have the handicap of having to carry our humble role of bedding each day from the basement of our bombed house to the station which was about a mile round trip.

One evening, while I was walking along the underground platform to bed-down for the night, I noticed a few children of my age group assembling jigsaw puzzles. I thought I wouldn't mind doing the same thing myself: I was aware of a jig-saw puzzle shop in South Lambeth Road, just a couple of minutes walk from my house. When I went into the shop I was surprised to be informed I didn't have to buy, I could hire at a fraction of the retail price.

To loan a puzzle I first had to become a member, free of charge, of the library club. The cost of hiring was cheap and calculated on a daily rate.

I joined the club and hired the puzzles frequently for a couple of weeks until the idea of putting broken pieces of card board together, only to take them apart as soon as the puzzle was completed, seemed pointless. The last puzzle I hired I completed in one evening while in the underground. I dismantled it, returned it to the box and forgot about it. Enough time elapsed for the shop to send me a reminder that I still had the puzzle and I now owed as much in the rental charge as it would cost to have bought it. I had the money to pay the financial penalty but not the will.

I mentioned the situation to Dad but got little sympathy. He told me to return the puzzle straight away and pay the bill before the cost got greater. I decided to return the goods and pay-up the next day. I went to the underground shelter that night, with Mum and Pat, and every intention of discharging my debt the next day.

We returned home the next morning and as I came out of the underground station, immediately in front of me, on the opposite side of the road, the first shop in the parade of shops, of which the puzzle shop was a part, was a burnt out shell. I got indoors thinking how unlucky it was that the bomb had not dropped just twelve yards further north and demolished my puzzle shop.

After I had finished my breakfast, I prepared myself to pay my debt. With the puzzle in my hand I passed the bombed shop on my left and turned into the main road. I paid little attention to the now common acrid smell of burnt and water soaked timber. To my surprise and unbelievable delight, the second, third, fourth and fifth, the whole block of shops was totally destroyed. I had a free puzzle and didn't have to pay the bill. At the first opportunity I told Dad of my good fortune. I couldn't believe that Dad wasn't happy for me. He must have had something on his mind other than last night's bombing that made him so stern and out of character, he told me off for being pleased.

"Don't think you will always be saved from paying a debt. Bombs won't always just drop out of the sky on shops just because you owe them money".

Had Dad not have been in a grumpy mood, I am confident he would have seen the funny side of the event and we would have both had a good laugh.

A few days after the puzzle shop had been bombed Mum was issued with permanent numbered pass tickets for the underground shelter. The pass number was that of our bunk numbers, which then allowed us, like all ticket holders to leave their bedding and possessions rolled up on the bunk all day. Although items of bedding, personal washing equipment and tea making utensils remained unattended all day, I never heard of any items being stolen.

Prior to the introduction of a ticket system, getting a space to sleep was on a 'first come first served' basis. I cannot recall there being any toilet facilities and there were certainly no provision made for undressing. Many people slept in their day clothing other manoeuvred themselves into nightwear like changing into a swimming costume while on the beach. But for the newly made homeless, it was a small inconvenience to pay for being able to take shelter all night. The underground was a blessing:

The deep shelter at Stockwell, not to be confused with the underground railway platform shelter, was built on part of a grassed area that was a local war memorial for the people that had died fighting in the

Great War. Both memorial and shelter still exists today at the junction of Clapham Road, Stockwell Terrace and South Lambeth Road.

I have knowledge of two additional shelters, one at Clapham South and another at Goodge Street in North London. But I am sure there must have been many more.

From the 1950's the Stockwell shelter was used for storing archives. Deep shelters were then maintained by the MOD, Ministry of Defence.

The advantage of having good night's sleep after the trains stopped running outweighed the disadvantages. The nearest toilets to Stockwell station were the public conveniences outside on ground level in Binfield Road. Obviously, from the sanitation point of view alone, with that many people in one bedroom, the arrangement could only be regarded as a temporary one.

As a result of being classified officially homeless and using the underground railway platform as a bedroom, our family, like thousands of others, was offered a more secure sleeping arrangement and issued with a pass that allowed us to use the deep, purpose built, underground shelter. Being able to use our new pass was, however, subject to rules:

To ensure the pass holders did not remain underground all day we had to be out in the morning by eleven am and were not allowed to 'check in' again before a specified time in the evening. At street level the reinforced concrete structure had a heavy secure entrance and exit door and an air purification plant on ground level alongside the top of the lift shafts.

We arrived at our new sleeping quarters during the early evening at Stockwell in good time to get settled into our allocated bunks only to be informed that we were at the wrong shelter. We had been allocated bunks in the deep shelter at Clapham South. I think Mum must have assumed we had been allowed an allocation in our nearest shelter and had not read the pass. We were, however, permitted to stay and given a pass for that night:

We got into a large lift with a few other people that took us, what felt like to the bowels of the earth, the lift was big enough to get two motorcars in side by side. When the lift stopped and the doors opened I was amazed to see a vast network of tunnels. They were as wide as the tunnels in the underground railway. What distance could be covered, to walk from one to the other, I don't know. One person got out of the lift with us, mounted a bicycle and peddled away.

Directly in front of the lift area was a small reception desk, which was manned by an ARP warden. From this area we were directed to our sleeping quarters.

At the age of eleven, I had not experienced the procedure for booking into a hotel nor been in one but I can now see the similarity. The following evening Mum, Pat and I travelled, by underground, to our new bedroom. We got off the train at Clapham South, three stations on from Stockwell travelling South. As we walked along the platform, I noticed a large sign with arrow and the words 'Deep Shelter'. We followed the sign that led us to a smaller connecting tunnel. This allowed people that had travelled by train to enter the shelter without having first to return the entrance at street level.

The administration procedure was the same as the previous night. As our passes were new and the ARP man had not seen us before we were politely given a quick scrutiny. Mum was then given a small book of rules and regulations before being shown to our sleeping quarters. We were instructed to follow a man waiting behind us with a trolley. On the trolley I saw there were new mattresses, pillows, blankets and starch stiff white linen sheets. Real sheets! Real blankets! Pillows with pillow cases! What luxury!

I knew I was going to enjoy our new sleeping arrangements: The bed covers we had at home consisted of bleached sacks, overcoats and the clothing we wore. Good fortune was on our sides. We were now living like posh people.

Tunnels spread out from the lifts and reception point, to the four points of a compass, like spokes from the hub of a wheel. As we walked and passed other tunnels, I noticed they were all named differently after a famous people. The trolley man stopped at the first three spaces without bedding on and placed the mattresses on each of the metal springs. After he unloaded and allocated the remaining bedding onto each bunk he informed Mum that it was time for the tea lady to arrive. With that short conversation and his trolley behind him he then walked off.

After Mum had put the sheets and blankets on two of the beds and was about to finish the third, I saw the tea lady. She was dressed in Women's Voluntary Service, WVS, uniform walking along the tunnel pushing her trolley with tea and other refreshments. As it was still quite early in the evening very few people had occupied their bed space and the tea lady was soon offering us tea. It must have been free for we had a cupful each. Unlike being at home, none of the cups we were offered were chipped. Not only were the cups undamaged we were also given saucers.

Before I got undressed I wandered off to the toilet and to explore the surrounding area. I had no idea how many nights, weeks or months we would spend sleeping so deep below the ground and felt a spasm of excitement at the prospect of enjoying a new and such a luxurious experience.

I walked back along the route we had taken from the lift area. At the reception area I began to read, from a notice board we had earlier passed, some of the hand printed posters and advertisements. There were numerous activities with hobbies and competitions going on at night.

Bingo was played every Thursday night; it was then called 'Lotto' or 'Housey Housey'. Every Friday night there was an amateur talent competition.

Card games, chess and draughts were played every night. Even Ludo and Tiddly Winks.

All but one of the board games listed, I had played before but my attention was drawn to one I had neither seen nor heard of. When I returned to my bunk, I told Mum of all the activities that were going on. I asked her if she had heard of the new board game, I had seen advertised, called 'Monopoly'. Mum said she had not but a lad

238

about my age, now occupying the bunk next to mine, overheard me. He told me he had the game at home and promised to bring it with him the next day to show me how it was played. True to his word, the next evening he arrived with the game in a box inside a brown paper carrier bag. After playing under instruction once around the board, I decided it was the best board game ever invented. From that first day, we played Monopoly every night. Sometimes lack of time did not allow us to complete a game before going to sleep, in these cases it was carefully placed under the lowest bunk and left there, to be continued the following night.

The game became so popular, not just with me; adults also participated in on going knockout competitions, which could last for months. Each event was organised by tunnel groups. The winner of one tunnel would then play the winner of another, which went on to a grand final.

Each tunnel also had their darts team and solo champion. Snooker and billiards champions were found in the same manner.

Although it was new to me, in fact 'Monopoly' had been invented by Charles Darrow in 1933 and patented in America in 1935.

Within a few days after settling in to our new sleeping quarters at Clapham South, early in September, a mysterious explosion killed three people in Chiswick. There had been no aircraft nor Doodlebug reported in the area, the immediate and most obvious explanation was a ruptured gas pipe had leaked and exploded. It was very soon discovered that was not the case.

'The silent killer', as one newspaper headline called it, was a rocket, Hitler's Revenge Weapon No 2. A new type of warfare had been launched and a new era had begun.

As the V1s and V2s continued to fall on London and South East England, more and more people began to rely on deep shelters and the underground to sleep in.

In addition to the nightly underground sporting activities there was also, once a week, stage entertainment.

One night Dad, resting from driving his lorry, came to the shelter with us and surprised me with an appearance on stage. He played his ukulele and included in his performance many of the songs made famous by 'George Formby'. He also gave a good account of himself with an impersonation of 'Rob Wilton': George Formby was a very popular wartime variety artist and appeared in many morale boosting comedy propaganda films.

'Robb Wilton' was one of my favourite comics. He commenced his act by saying; "The day war broke out my wife said to me". He would give the appearance of a timid old man. He sucked his thumb and fumbled his words while he explained how he planned to beat the enemy single-handed and maybe with a few of his friends in the dart team at the pub.

While travelling home one morning, after having slept in the deep shelter, I observed what I considered to be a 'loophole' to be tested to enable me to travel free on the underground railway system

As we reached the top of the escalator, I noticed, in the exit lane, there was no ticket collector in the office. On this morning, each passenger, as they passed the exit side of the office, placed their expired ticket on the unattended counter. I cannot be sure if we actually purchased tickets for our nightly journey or we were issued with a free family pass but that made little difference to my proposed course of action.

I positioned myself to be behind Mum and Pat as we alighted from the escalator. By the time we reached the unattended ticket office many passengers had passed through in front of us and made an attractive pile of used tickets. Like the bottle of pills in 'Alice in Wonderland' with the label 'Please take me', they were waiting there for me. As Mum and Pat went on, I pretended my shoelaces had become untied. I stopped, dropped onto one knee and went through the process of retying a bow. As I did so, I quickly glanced around to check that nobody was behind me. Satisfied I was not being observed, as I walked passed the counter, I snatched a handful of the tickets and rapidly put them in my pocket. My action was smooth and confident and I was sure I had not been observed.

My logic should be questioned at this point: If the tickets had been used, how could they be used again? The answer was simple. They were not always date stamped. If they were not handed in they could be used time and time again. I had observed tickets on previous journeys, on the underground and came to the conclusion it was only the tickets that were dispensed from the ticket machines that were not date stamped. Only the ticket purchased at the office were manually date stamped at the time of issue. Later, the day that I had 'snatched a handful', upon inspection, I found that from about the forty or fifty tickets I had stolen, something like only half a dozen were undated and of any use to me. I disposed of the bundle of unwanted date stamped tickets by secretly burning them in the back garden.

I introduced Benny to the swindle and, when on days when the weather did not permit cycling, every spare Saturday or Sunday we explored the London underground rail network with 'dodgy' tickets.

During our underground travelling, we always kept a sharp lookout for further tickets that would suit our future needs.

The 'used ticket fiddle' was a great success and I believe the reason I was never caught was because I was cautious. More often than not, the ticket collectors would be at their posts', which meant I had to hand my ticket in, as expected. On occasions when there was no collector, my ticket would be used again, but as soon as I thought the tickets looked a little worn and shabby I discarded them and used a newer one from my stock.

I continued my fraud with confidence long after I left school. In fact I did not cease completely until the summer of 1951, three months after I was eighteen: The significance of my age was due to my 'call up' to do National Service.

There is a quotation that suggests; 'success breeds success', this was very true in my case. Had my 'used ticket' scheme not succeeded, although I do not know how it could have been challenged, it is most probable I would not have progressed to a better and, by far, more profitable method of free travel and not yet but later, an income.

Allied forces, now confidently moved inland through Europe, fought desperately to reach the launch sites to put them out of action but by the end of the year the missiles were still coming.

During November, the biggest civilian fatality inflicted by a German air raid on the United Kingdom occurred when a V1 came down on a Woolworth's shop in West Ham, London. The bomb fell into a Saturday afternoon shopping crowd killing an estimated 160 people:

Before the war commenced in 1939, there were thirteen million houses in the United Kingdom. In the 4 years before 'D Day' four million of those houses had been destroyed or damaged by enemy action. Within the first three months of the German's flying bombs campaign another half million were added to the total.

The difference between the V1 and the V2 was: the V1 had a noisy jet engine. The VII was a rocket.

The VI was launched from a ramp. When it reached its flying height, it travelled horizontally and fell to ground when it ran out of fuel. It exploded on impact.

The German intelligence gatherers informed Hitler there were no British aircraft that were capable of flying fast enough to catch a V1. They were wrong. A 'Tempest' could reach a speed of 416 miles per hour. Some Royal Air Force fighter pilots developed a technique of shooting the V1 down before they reached the South East Coast; They would patrol the English Channel higher than the V1's normal flight path and as soon as one was seen it was attacked from our diving fighters.

The V2 had its first successful test flight November 1942. It was propelled by liquid oxygen and alcohol, which allowed it to travel almost silently, it was forty-six foot long and travelled at 3,600 mph. It was launched from a gantry but unlike the V1 it did not level out, it travelled in an arc. It too exploded on impact.

When the garage/work shop in Paradise Road where Dad parked his lorry was bombed, his employers leased another garage under one of the railway arches in Queenstown Road, Battersea.

Using the term 'we moved' may give a mental picture of what could be considered normal today; a large furniture removal lorry being loaded from one house and then being unloaded at another, plus the administration of the change of address letters that would have to be dealt with. That was nothing like the scene at all. At no time, war or no war, had we ever enjoyed the cumbersome luxury of an adequate amount of furniture but we must have now been at an all time low.

The bombing had reduced the humble amount we did have to little more than a bed, a table and four chairs. All other items were small enough to be transported by hand in a paper carrier bag. Our possessions were unceremonially loaded onto a costermonger's barrow and pushed to the next street to take up our new residence. The house that Dad and Grandad had chosen had been empty since before the outbreak of war which was the most likely reason for there being no air raid shelter in the back garden.

Like nomadic Bedouins, without seeking permission from the owner, whoever they may have been, or local council, we moved in, our new address was 4 Binfield Road, Clapham S.W. 4.

During the first few days, to establish residency, we just sat on the dusty floor in the downstairs rooms and drank tea. No one challenged our trespass and to my knowledge nor was anyone aware we were there. We had no neighbours. All of the houses in the road were in a similar state as the house we had just moved from. They were either in ruins or just abandoned, I believe we went through this ritual to comply with some advice that Dad had received from a 'barrack room lawyer' at his place of work. It was my parents hope, by this action of just sitting in the house for a few days, we could claim our tenancy by using a centuries old, and little known, law called 'squatters rights'.

An incendiary bomb during the blitz had hit the house but other than having a large hole in the roof and no windows the task of repair was a modest one. The incendiary bomb had travelled through the roof and came to rest in a ground floor room.

Most bombs of this type would normally have caused the house to 'go up in flames'. I did not know why that had not happened in this case but the evidence of the attack was plain to see. By looking up at the ceiling, it was possible to see daylight coming in from the roof through three floors above the basement.

On the second day Grandad, went up on the roof and covered the hole. Apart from the lack of windows, we now had good protection from wet weather.

Once the roof had been repaired, Grandad acquired a stopcock tool and covertly reconnected the water supply in the street:

This was technically an illegal action for only a person employed by the Water Board was permitted to turn water on or off from the mains outside the house. Had we waited for an official response, we could possible have stayed 'dry' until the war was over. For expediency, combined with not knowing if we would survive the next air raid, this small infringement of the law was of little consequence it was therefore ignored.

Our occupation soon became known to the landowner and to encourage us to leave the house, the landowner refused to reconnect the mains services of water, gas and electricity. He was unaware that during the short space of time between our moving in and he being informed of the fact, all of the vital services had been illegally tapped into and we were well established. We also enjoyed the service without being charged for that which we used. The house, having been subject to the elements with rain coming in through the roof and no glass in some of the windows for four years, was in a miserably poor state of decoration. That little detail had never been a concern before the war, so it did not cause the adults any loss of sleep now:

We had been living in the house for a number of years after the war but the owners of the property had still not officially recognised we were in the house and had not issued with a rent book. Collecting rent from the property would have committed the owners to make costly improvements so we remained listed as squatters: It was not until the first post war Labour Government Slum Clearance Plan and the London County Council Redevelopment Plan was announced that the property acquired value, almost overnight: If the house was registered as having tenants and habitable, the house was worth much more than if unoccupied.

At this juncture 'Cluttons', the owners of the property, generously supplied my Gran' and Grandad with a rent book. Mum and Dad became sub tenants.

Dad continued driving a lorry and on one of his journeys to the North of England he purchased a 1932 Wolseley, 'Hornet' open touring car.

It had been registered and owned by the Lancashire Police from new and then sold privately in 1935. The owner had told Dad, the car had not been used since 1936 and when Dad saw the car, it was in the same garage in Warrington that it had been stored in all through the war years. Dad bought the car, knowing it was in need of restoration and brought it home on his return journey, in the back of his lorry and stored it at his employer's lock-up in Queens Town Road, Battersea.

One Saturday, a few weeks after we had moved our meagre belongings from Studley to Binfield Road, I went with Dad to assist him in loading the Wolseley into the back of his employers lorry to get the car home. The engine was not in working condition so I sat in the driving seat and with the aid of ropes and a pulley block I steered while Dad gradually pulled the car into the back of the lorry. There were no mishaps during the transporting and with little effort we reversed the procedure to unload the car in the road outside our front garden:

I found a photograph taken at the time. Dad wrote on the back of it that he had purchased the vehicle for £2. On a closer inspection, Dad discovered the car was in a worse condition than he had at first envisaged for when we got it into the back garden Dad seemed disappointed that all of the body was rotten. The coachwork, from the drivers seat back to the rear bumper was so badly rusted that Dad had to strip it all off and rebuild it. Had Dad know the car's true condition, I wonder if he would have offered less than £2. Before the following week-end all that remained of the Wolseley was the engine on the chassis and four wheels.

Dad's workshop was not equipped to mould the discarded metal side panels to its original condition so he rebuilt the sides with sheets of aluminium framed and supported with timber in the style of an American station wagon. All the flooring consisted of timber, with boards similar to that of house floorboards. As all pre-war vehicles were built with a chassis as opposed to a sub frame, it was a carpentry job and did not call for welding. It was possible with all cars manufactured before 1947 to be able to place a seat on the chassis, between the four wheels, and drive the vehicle with neither sides nor top. Unlike today's vehicles where sections of the body panels are welded together to form a pseudo chassis, it is not possible, for instance, to remove the whole middle section of the bodywork and still have the four wheels connected.

From Nine Elms railway goods yard in Wandsworth, one by one, Grandad brought home wooden railway track sleepers, on his bicycle.

Each railway sleeper must have weighed in excess of one hundredweight (112 pounds) equal to approximately 50kgs. Together, Dad and Grandad used them, like pit props, to support the ceilings in the two ground floor rooms. The condition of the ceilings, apart from the cosmetic aspect, was good. In normal, peace-time it would have been unnecessary to take such drastic action to reinforce the ceiling but due to the V1 and V2 missiles still being launched on London, Kent, and the Home Counties the props increased the room's safety factor a great deal.

Although we now had one room in the house that was as safe as a garden air raid shelter Mum, Pat and I still made the journey to Clapham South deep shelter nearly every night to sleep.

Buildings of all types, in the cities, were destroyed quicker than they could have been rebuilt in addition to the fact resources in materials and manpower were very limited. A rebuilding programme was not attempted until hostilities ceased.

The council's priority was to keep the streets free of rubble to give ambulances, fire engines and other emergency vehicles a clear passage. All of the debris that fell in the roads, when houses were bombed, was returned onto the site where a house had once stood.

This abundance of timber and bricks gave an amateur builder a plentiful supply of raw materials. Dad and Grandad were just two of this type of freelance builder: They would wait until nightfall to gather in undamaged joists and floor board to enable their flow of building work, inside the house, to continue.

Apart from the very heavy railway sleepers, all of their requirements would be near at hand.

Grandad would use nothing more than his own strength for carrying his needs. He would carry a length of twenty feet long piece of timber, approximately six metres, on each shoulder:

Dad having recently purchased a 1932 BSA, Birmingham Small Arms, (BSA also made pistols and rifles),'Gold Star' motorcycle and sidecar removed the sidecar from the chassis and placed the timber, he collected, along its length.

After working hours, Grandad set to work in building a new bank of timber rabbit hutches and an avery. A chicken run, having the least priority, followed.

Accommodation for Grandad's animals was built at the end of our newly acquired and very long rear garden. Along each side, for the whole length, of the garden in Binfield Road, a six feet high brick wall separated our garden from the gardens on each side at number two and number six. Some of the walls in the road had been destroyed, others, including those on each side of our garden remained almost undamaged.

Dad's building handiwork amounted to a twenty foot by ten feet garage and workshop in the back garden. He utilised the garden brick wall for one side of his garage. The three remaining sides were constructed of sheets of corrugated iron bolted together and screwed to a timber frame.

The passageway between our garden wall and the side of the house was just wide enough to allow a car to pass. The semi-basement entrance to the house from the side door was gained by walking along the side path, in the garden, and down four concrete steps that occupied half of the width of the passageway. It was the half of the pathway with the steps that led to the basement that restricted vehicle access from front to back garden.

Dad got over the obstacle by making a portable wooden bridge from two cut down scaffold boards. The wooden bridge was only placed over the steps when movement to and from the rear garden garage, for either a car or a motorcycle and sidecar combination, was required. When the garage was completed, the bridge was first tested with the motorcycle and sidecar. Going into the rear garden, the motorcycle remained on the solid footpath while the home made wooden bridge only took the lighter weight of the sidecar.

The board got a greater test when Dad drove from the back garden to the front of the house: The bridge had not only to take the heavier weight of the motorcycle but also Dad's weight. The temporary bridge stood the test, but Dad kept up the suspense by letting us know of his concern that the next operation was going to be the major test, by driving a car over it.

Since Dad had brought the 'Wolseley' home it had remained parked with a heavy tarpaulin sheet over it on the higher ground of the front garden. But the time had now come to get the car to the rear of the house.

After a lot of effort of pushing and pulling was used, the engine was not working, manoeuvring the car to point in the correct direction we eventually got it lined up between the garden wall and the side wall of the house.

Dad sat in the driver's seat and inch-by-inch controlled the car's progress down the slope by releasing and applying the handbrake. Dad gingerly steered the car down the slope between the garden wall and the brick wall of the house.

Not knowing the maximum load the boards would take, we all 'held our breath' as the car approached the point of no return. Because of the tight squeeze between the two walls, Dad was unable to open the doors of the car which, of course, meant he was not able to get out until we cleared the house wall and got into the back garden.

I think Dad must have tested the strength of the board and done his homework before commencing. He would not have left the outcome to chance but he let us all believe it was a risky operation and built up what I believe a false anxiety just for a bit of fun.

Slowly Dad progressed until the car stopped as the near side front wheel came into contact with protruding edge of the ramp over the steps.

Mum, Pat, John and I were all behind the car and on the word 'go' we gave a push to ease it over the lip of the board. The wheel rolled onto the board and we excitedly kept on pushing until it cleared the hole and reached the other side. The heaviest part of the vehicle was across. All that remained was just to push the rear end across the board and into the rear garden. The suspense was over. The doors of the garage lined up with the side entrance passageway and we continued pushing while Dad steered the car into the back garden, straight into the garage and under cover.

The need for the vehicle to be inside the garage was not a safeguard against further deterioration. The badly rusted coachwork was beyond saving but it did allow Dad to work on it in bad weather.

Dad had already stripped off the doors and side panels when he told me of his intention to rebuild it as a station wagon. Which meant using a large proportion of exposed timber.

A week or two later while Dad was still working on the engine by a lucky coincidence, I discovered a stock of the quality of off cuts of timber that I reasoned could be very useful for making the frame work of the car body.

The source of supply was a shop in Wandsworth Road and displayed the sign Ashtons Funeral Parlour. The office was a corner site and adjoining a carpentry shop at the rear where the coffins were made. In the yard there were two large gates that opened into the side turning of Lansdowne Way.

One day, both of the side gates had been left open and as I passed on my bicycle I noticed, just inside the yard, a pile of off cuts of oak and beech timber.

I walked into the yard and to make sure there was nobody watching before I picked a piece, I walked into the carpentry shop to check. Somebody was there, so I asked if I could take a small lump of hard wood to make a toy.

"Help yourself son, it's free, take as much as you like, it's all scrap. Tell anyone else you know that may want some"

I responded quickly to the invitation; "My Dad's making a car, can he have some?"

One would think, the response would have been; "how is he going to make a car out of wood?" but he asked no such questions.

"Yes!" he said. "Tell him the gate is always unlocked during working hours he can help himself".

Honesty, in this case, had most certainly, been the best policy!

I sorted out a small piece of oak with a beautiful designed grain for myself and a long piece that I thought could be useful, as a sample, to show Dad.

Pleased with myself, I continued on my journey home and anxiously waited to tell Dad, when he came home from work that evening, I showed him the piece of timber. He could not believe that such quality timber would be given away free of charge. I tried to assure him I had got the message correct but he treated my news with only lukewarm enthusiasm.

A day or two later, still in some doubt but not wanting to miss a good opportunity, Dad, confirmed my hearing as being correct by coming home with his sidecar overloaded with large pieces of quality hardwood.

I was pleased to see the load he was able to collect but I got an extra thrill to see him so happy at getting it at no expense from information that I was responsible for. During this time, with the aid of rope and pulley, Dad had lifted the engine from the car and had left it positioned on the bench. He was in the process of dismantling the engine when he brought the timber home for the bodywork.

Over the following months, as the restoration work progressed, I willingly gave Dad a hand each evening although the job was a lengthy process. As each part of the engine was removed and inspected and sometimes replaced Dad told me the function it performed and the need for precision in reassembling. I used a torque wrench and a micrometer for the first time. Dad recognised my genuine interest and inspired by my eagerness to use the tools he taught me the theory as well as the practical aspects of mechanical engineering. After we had 'washed up' each night and sat indoors, I enjoyed our conversations as Dad talked about his concern or pleasure regarding the night's work we had done.

He told me he was concerned that the four cylinders really needed a rebore. As he did not have the expensive machinery to do it, the engine should have been taken to a specialist but it was too costly for him. He was unhappy that he had to settle for just replacing the piston rings.

Although Dad had a low opinion of his own school education he had a very good understanding of anything electrical or mechanical. He was a practical man and a good tutor. I 'soaked up' all of the instruction he gave.

The day eventually came when the reconditioned engine was completed and returned from the bench to the chassis and ready to be tested. So as not to be engulfed in carbon monoxide fumes we pushed the vehicle out of the garage to start it up. Dad sat in the driver's seat and after a few pushes on the starter button the engine came to life. He got down and gave me instructions to follow, I eagerly responded to his invitation to sit in the driver's seat. He then walked to the front of the car and explained to me what he was doing while he made a small adjustment to the micrometer setting on the distributor's advance and retard screw. He also adjusted the carburettor until he was satisfied the engine had a nice 'tick over'. He then walked to the rear of the car and told me to give a sharp jab at the accelerator pedal, as I did so a cloud of dirty blue/black smoke emitted from the exhaust pipe.

"Oh, bugger it"! I heard Dad exclaim from behind me. "I thought that might happen, can't do anything about it now though".

Dad walked back to the side of the car where I was sitting.

"That smoke coming from the exhaust pipe is the engine oil burning. Can you smell it?" he said.

I could see it. I could also see he was clearly disappointed and I felt sorry for him because while he was rebuilding the engine, he had taught me so much. I wanted him to be satisfied with the result of his labour.

"Let that be a lesson to you Ron. You can't repair an engine on the cheap".

The advice was unquestionably true but to be honest and with loving affection, I have to report; where money was concerned, Dad did not practice what he preached.

I recognise I also have 'followed in my father's footsteps' in this respect. Making something out of scraps and improvising is an integral part of my upbringing.

"Well! It's not as good as I was hoping for but I am not going to strip it down again. We'll leave it at that for today, tomorrow we'll start on the woodwork"

Dad showed me how to shape the pieces of timber to go over the rear mudguards: By making a series of shallow cross cuts, where the inside of the bend in the timber was needed and then tying with string and leaving to soak in water the wood could be moulded to the desired shape. We were well into restoring the flooring and replacing the rotten wooden bottom runs of the body frame when a man in an army uniform called out to Dad from the side steps.

Dad told me to carry on with what I was doing and they both walked out to the front garden together as I continued painting some red primer paint on the chassis. When I had finished my painting and Dad had not returned, I put the brush in a jar of water and went to see what he was doing.

They were in a friendly conversation talking about the motorcycle at the kerbside. The machine was an Ariel 600cc 'Square four'.

I returned to the garage and a short time later Dad followed. "Ron!" he said, with a clap of his hands, "WP Motors have just started in business. We have got our first repair job".

That was the beginning of a long and friendly relationship with 'Taffy'.

Other motorcycle and car enthusiasts, needing repair jobs to be done, began to call on Dad. Many of the car repairs customers were 'one offs' and did not return but all the motorcyclists became regular visitors, almost like a club. Dad never mentioned how he became known for being available for vehicle repairs and it never occurred to me to ask. I can only guess that he started off by placing an advertisement somewhere.

Within a few months of Dad having completed Taffy's repair job, he had enough work to keep him busy every day. Complete strangers would arrive at the house wanting some work done after being recommended by one of Dad's, now growing list, of satisfied customers:

Dad started his motor repair business by doing the work after he finished his normal day's work but he became so popular he was refusing work because he could not fit everyone in. On a number of evenings over many weeks, I heard Dad resisting Mum's argument that he should stop working for someone else and become full time self-employed.

One evening, I went out to the garage. Dad was there with a board and a fine paintbrush, putting the finishing touches to a sign

WP Motors. Sales and Repairs.

He wiggled the brush in a small jar of petrol and as he wiped it clean he looked back at me with a smile and, as though it was his idea, said excitedly; "What do you think Ron? We are going into full time business for ourselves".

Although he asked "'what do you think?"

He wasn't seeking an answer. He was making a statement. In return I just said, "That's good Dad".

I didn't tell him I knew it was Mum's idea.

Another man, that became a regular, was the owner of a pre war 'V' engine 1,000cc Matchless. He was proud of his big machine but almost paranoid about a rather weak sounding horn that was not befitting the size of the monstrous piece of machinery. He was heavy man with a strong Birmingham accent. On his first visit to the garage, he introduced himself as Bert. He wanted Dad to adjust the horn that was situated under the saddle. He pressed the horn button to show Dad how feeble the hooter sounded. It was an anaemic sounding thing like that of a squeak from a baby's toy. Dad did something, which made a slight improvement, and after some idle talk about motorcycling in general he went away. A week later he returned:

"Bill, will you have another look at my hooter. I would like you to increase the volume to be robust and have more aggression. It sounds as though it belongs on a bloody bicycle".

He then made a 'honk' noise that came from his throat of how he would like it to sound

"It doesn't alert anyone. It sounds like a bloody bee and all it does is tickle my arse."

By pursing his lips and wrinkling his nose, as though he was about to sneeze, he made a buzzing noise. This comic act came in his Birmingham dialect and sounded very funny. From then on Dad and I referred to him as 'Birmingham Bertie and his motorcycle we nicknamed 'Buzz Buzz'.

Another character that became a regular customer was a market trader. I cannot recall his name, but I remember he lived at Camberwell Green.

He manufactured and retailed is own products. He made plaster models of animals and decorative objects to hang on lounge walls. Animal faces and flying birds were his most popular commodity: During the 1950's, these flying ducks became a very popular wall ornament but went out of fashion in the 1960's to become a collectors item in the 1990's.

He sold them in market places, fair grounds and garden fetes. He also supplied stallholders. His delivery vehicle was a motorcycle with a sidecar.

Between slack periods and fresh work coming in Dad slowly progressed with rebuilding the Wolseley.

When the newly shaped Ashtons oak wooden struts and aluminium panels were put in place and the job got nearer to completion, it was unrecognisable as the rusty old metal wreck that Dad had brought home. It now looked more like a *modern* wooden wreck.

On another day's visit from The Camberwell man, Dad was asked if he wanted to sell the nearly finished station wagon.

At the time Dad did not want to dispose of the vehicle and postponed an agreement but not wanting to lose out on a 'bit of trade, promised when he decided to sell, he would be given the first offer.

Benny lived in Studley Road, about six houses away from where I lived; his house was also damaged beyond repair. His family moved to Grove Way, a turning off Brixton Road, about the same time as our family move to Binfield Road. Grove Way was one of the roads that made up part of the paper round I had. Due to the pressure of homework, more on the part of my two friends than me, we saw less of Beechy during the evenings of school days.

Just before our move while rummaging through a fresh area of damaged buildings, Benny and I found, in a garden shed, two old bicycles and some spare parts. We took the bicycles and the spare parts home and made both cycles roadworthy. Our noisy scooters were then replaced for bicycles and because they were much quieter they were more socially acceptable. We overcame the obstacle of distance between our new addresses by cycling.

The first weekend, Benny and I had our new toys we both cycled to Beechy's house.

Seeing us on our cycles must have encouraged Beechy to clean up an old machine in his back yard that belonged to his father.

In a short while, before the summer came to an end, the three of us were exploring new areas outside our normal 'patch'. At weekends we cycled to places like Kingston, Hampton Court, Walton -on- Thames and Richmond Common. Cycling on the footpaths along the River Thames became our favoured recreation.

After the allied invasion of Europe, during the summer of 1944, there had been a lot of speculation that the war would be over by the following Christmas. Now that autumn was giving way to early winter it had become painfully clear it was not to be.

The allied advance into the mainland of Europe had still not yet put a stop the to Doodlebugs and Rockets being launched and landing on London and South East England.

We still slept in the deep shelter at night but in spite of the constant threat of enemy missiles, day or night, schooling, unfortunately, was no longer being interrupted.

One Saturday morning, Benny and I were playing marbles along the gutter in Binfield Road when a couple of local lads that we knew ran up to us. Excitedly, they informed us there was a soldier and a lady having a 'bunk up' in, what used to be, Benny's back garden. As this would have been my first 'eye witness account' of a couple in the act of love making, I rushed eagerly with the other three to observe the action.

It was unnecessary to run the whole length of one road to get to the next; we went through the remains of buildings and gardens and reached the activity area in a few minutes. One of our informants then pointed out a distant bush where the sport was taking place. As we got nearer and quietly made our approach we stopped at a low thick bush where our colleague indicated the couple were laying on the other side. We had rushed to see the rude events, but now we had reached the spot, we did nothing more than crouch down to keep out of sight, stifled our giggles and listened for the sound of any movement.

After a few moments, I cautiously peered over the top of the shrub to see why they were so quiet. It was quiet because nobody was there. Only some pages of a newspaper had been spread out and remained as evidence. We had got there quick, but not quick enough. The lovebirds had flown. The four of us got up and walked around to the other side of the bush and stood there as though we were inspecting the paper. It was a disappointment but only because we had missed a bit of fun, sexual fantasies were not yet on my entertainment list.

One evening, while playing 'Monopoly', I asked my deep shelter friend if I could borrow his board game for a weekend. He agreed and I took it home on a Friday morning. When I showed the game to Benny that evening after school, he was as enthusiastic about it as I was. We had no time to waste to copy all of the details. We duplicated all of the 'Chance' and 'Community Chest' cards, the money, the board and the player's markers. We cut out small blocks of wood for houses and painted them green, the hotels we painted red. It was a tedious job but before I returned the original game to its owner, on the following Monday night, we had made our own game of Monopoly. Playing 'Monopoly' was not just 'playing a game', it was an education; buying and selling property, raising money by mortgaging, and building houses and charging rent is consistent with modern day life. The game progresses with the rolling of dice and therefore is dependent upon luck but then so is business in real life.

'Monopoly' accounted for a large percentage of my time spent indoors. It placed, my hitherto recording the war from first to number two position. Collecting postage stamps still remained a popular interest to me in my list of pastime but most of the daylight hours during the weekend were spent out of doors on a bicycle, which revived my attention to the pastime of train spotting.

As the threat of the Doodlebugs and the Rockets decreased, so Mum relaxed on our urgency to travel to the Clapham South deep shelter to sleep each night. On these occasions, we slept at home in the one room downstairs. It was not a good idea. During one such morning just before we were about to get out of bed, without warning, there was an enormous explosion that sounded very close. We all got out of bed and after I had a wash and a quick breakfast, I rushed out into the road to see the damage. I was very surprised to see there was no evidence that anything had happened. I briskly walked the two hundred yards to Stockwell underground station and stood at the carfax of Clapham Road, Stockwell Road, South Lambeth Road and Binfield Road to view a wider area.

I looked along Clapham Road going South towards Clapham Common, and saw the area in which the missile must have dropped for I could see smoke and a number of fire engines parked in an haphazard manner in the main road. I did not want to be beaten to any collectable pieces of shrapnel that could be lying about so my walking turned into an excited run to get there as quick as possible.

The rescue service was in much evidence: Ambulances were coming and going with the injured. ARP men were moving piles of bricks, searching for anyone that may be buried under the houses they had been living in.

The acrid smell of charcoaled house timbers and paper and the dust of century old plaster and cement filled the air. But for small clusters of burning embers the fires had all been extinguished. The fire hoses remained twisted across the streets still spewing out gallons of water. The heavy canvas water pipes obstructed the footpath and roads like an invasion of giant anacondas.

As I stood looking, almost mesmerised, I saw two old ladies being helped out from under a pile of rubble. They were both able to walk unaided.

A path in the road with bricks and rubble piled high each side had been cleared to allow free movement for fire engines and ambulances. This was my first and only experience of witnessing the result of a bombing raid so soon after the event and the impact it had on the inhabitants:

Being so near to the scene, when our family survived our two near misses, did not allow me to see it as an outsider. On the occasion the land mine was dropped very close, my immediate impression was that of disappointment. At first I thought it would have been more thrilling to observe the chaos with motionless injured, maybe dead, bodies scattered across the street. But that was not the case. Paradoxically, in the midst of the aggression of war, the street looked peaceful. During my few minutes observation I like to think I grew a little wiser. I didn't like what I was looking at:

People were calmly but sad looking and almost trance like, walking in and out their ruined houses to collect small items of value and returning to put them in boxes and suitcases outside on the pavement. They went about their industry neither at speed nor panic but more like a state of bored disbelief.

I saw a number of firemen, with dirty faces and civilians standing in groups and talking while drinking tea at a mobile stall. A policeman walked up and down the street letting his presence be seen to deter looting. He stopped and joined the tired looking rescue workers and ordered a cup of tea for himself. The excitement I felt while rushing to reach what I imagined a scene of carnage had changed to that of melancholy. I felt sad for those that had been made homeless. It was more of an injustice because the mood of the nation was elevated by the belief the war was nearly over. I believe this was my first visual experience of feeling sympathetic for people I did not know. I slowly walked home with a different attitude towards air raids than I had ten minutes earlier. I decided I didn't even enjoy the war anymore.

All of my maps were still either folded or rolled in the old suitcase somewhere in the house. There they remained until, I can only guess, they were thrown away when I joined the army.

I have nine scars on my body, which are now hardly visible but upon close inspection can still be seen. One of those scars is across the bridge of my nose, two are on my left leg, and one is on my second toe of my right foot. Five scars are on my right hand.

The scar across the bridge on my nose is the result of a street gang fight. On this particular skirmish, a day after an air raid many roofs had been blown from their houses. The damage caused slate roofing tiles to be scattered in abundance in the streets and gardens. They were the most obvious weapons for they were easily at hand. Slate tiles, being thin, if thrown correctly, could be made to spin and glide over a greater distance than throwing stones. These made ideal weapons for schoolboy's street warfare. It also gave each side a wide distance of no-mans-land and a good head start, to make a hasty retreat, if required.

Each battle plan, be it with stones, bricks, bottles, slates or catapults was based on a simple strategy; throw and duck, throw and duck. Each fight terminated with someone getting hurt or cut. The winning side would then run away before getting the wrath of the injured boys parents. My first scar is due to my nose getting in the way of a high-speed slate. I should have been ducking instead of standing and throwing.

Another nasty injury I received was not through aggressive behaviour but during the process of redistributing rubbish in the rear garden:

I was being assisted by Benny to carry a heavy length of broken cast iron drainpipe. We were both drawn to this length of pipe because it resembled the barrel of an artillery field gun. We were moving it to an area where we had simulated a mounting to place the pipe to improve the illusion of it being a gun. To enable me to walk in a forward direction, I lifted the pipe with both hands behind my back. My friend then lifted the other end in front of him and we started walking. After taking only a few steps my friend complained the pipe was cutting his hands. Without further warning he dropped his end of the pipe causing my end to slip from my grasp. The jagged end of the pipe cut deeply into my leg at the back of the knee joint and cut into the fleshy area of the crease. The wound bled heavily but by good fortune, the tendon was not severed. A visit to the hospital rewarded me with a few painful stitches and a stiff leg that lasted longer than I would have preferred.

During the later part of the war Grandad, 'Stylo', was an auxiliary policeman, stationed at Brixton and had no such thing as a vehicle to do their rounds. Policeman had a beat that they had to walk. The boundary between the Brixton Division and The Clapham Division was the Clapham Road; neither crossed into each other's territory. Binfield Road was just on the wrong side of Grandad's beat but that did not stop him from regularly popping in for a quick cuppa. One night, a few weeks before Christmas while drinking his usual cup of tea, he asked Mum if Pat and I would like to go to the policemen's children's Christmas party. We both, eagerly, said yes.

The bombing had taken its toll on cinemas and theatres and many were totally destroyed. In addition to those bombed but remained standing many were beyond repair. Many theatres just closed down due to the lack of production staff and stagehands. Stylo's professional activity, as a variety artist, came almost to a 'standstill'. His age was most likely to have been an influence.

Very often his evening visits coincided with an event that would be taking place at the deep shelter. When there was something, like a competition or an amateur talent night taking place, I tried to urge Mum to leave the house early before Grandad knocked on the door for his usual cup of tea. One evening, when a special event was on that I particularly wanted to see, we were just about to leave the house when Stylo knocked on the door. Because Grandad's stay was never for just five minutes, it seemed like hours; I knew we were not going to get to the shelter before the entertainment was over. I put on a big act that I was frightened of the air raids and I wanted us all to go to the shelter quickly.

My unruly show of bad behaviour made no difference. Grandad stayed long enough for us to miss the show. I had fooled nobody. Stylo did compensate for being the cause of our late arrival at the shelter however. He gave Mum the tickets for Pat and I to attend the forthcoming Brixton Policemen's children's Christmas party.

When the big day came Pat and I travelled by tram from Stockwell to Gresham Road, Brixton and alighted opposite the police station at the Odeon Astoria.

We had sandwiches, pies, fruit jelly and custard. We saw the usual circus type clown, a ventriloquist and a small orchestra playing popular patriotic music.

Vivid in my mind is a competition that was held to test each of the children in their ability to conduct an orchestra. One little 'clever dick', being me, knew it all and was silently critical of all of the contestants before me. Most of the competitors were just walking onto the stage and swinging their arms up and down not knowing what was expected of them. I was eager to get on the stage to show off my knowledge and win my prize. I knew I was going to win because I had taken notice how conductors used their baton and hands to instruct different sections of instruments in the orchestra. I waited anxiously until my turn arrived. When my turn eventually came, I was handed a baton and took my place on the rostrum. I confidently positioned myself in the centre of the stage in front of the musicians, raised both hands and brought them down together and the music started. The first downbeat was music, the remainder, of my orchestral debut, was a terrible cacophony. I believed I was using the hand movements of a bandleader correctly, that is to say I would point at one particular player to enforce Andante, Moderato or Allegro, which I understood. I failed because of an inability to keep the whole tempo at an even pace.

Because of my erratic hand movements, the section controlled by my left hand would be playing something like an adulterated version of Brahms Lullaby while the section to my right was

262

racing away with something that would have beaten The Post Horn Gallop. Because of my cockiness, the musicians acted very precisely to my instructions. If I proved anything, it was how much influence a conductor had. I am sure it was very enjoyable and funny to everyone except me. There were no prizes for the worst display, so I received nothing for my effort other than a few more words to fill my book of experiences.

"A week before Christmas, 1944, the Germans launched a massive counter attack in the Ardennes. The allies dubbed it 'the Battle of the Bulge'. The surprise German counter offensive was successful and the American forces could not hold their line of defence and suffered heavy casualties. At the time, it was considered that the German plan was just to regain Antwerp and cut the Allies main port for supplying the army. But mainly due to the lack of their own supplies, petrol and diesel, the German attack eventually came to a standstill. It was to be the last German offensive of the war. That event of the war could have ended there but for an almost unbelievable story that through the fifty years rule governing military records, was kept secret until 1994.

Despite the wartime myth that no German prisoners of war, POW's escaped captivity while in Britain, breakouts were rife. It is true, however, that they seldom got very far which was probably due to inadequate escape briefings and an alert local population.

Maybe the following story does not belong in my autobiography but I make the excuse for including it because it must rank as one of the most extraordinary stories of the war. It is one that I had not heard of before reading the book 'For Fuhrer and Fatherland' written by Roderick de Normann and published in 1997. It was written as a factual account but I cannot vouch for its authenticity. I quote: The story begins at a German prisoner of war camp near Devizes, Wiltshire. It was late November 1944 when ten Germans, POWs, escaped. It was considered just another routine escape when they were recaptured; two trainee intelligence officers interrogated them.

While being questioned, one of the German soldiers mentioned an eleventh man, Herman Storch.

Storch, who had escaped twice before, claimed, when interviewed, he had not been involved in the latest breakout but revealed a story that left them speechless.

He said that there was a plan afoot within the Devizes camp for a mass breakout of 7,500 prisoners on Christmas Eve, which would be led by SS officers. They would seize transport and tanks reconnoitred on previous escapes. The hijacked armour would sweep across southern England liberating fellow Germans from other POW camps and then head for East Anglia.

They would then hold the Norfolk coast along the Wash for German ships to bring reinforcements or assist an evacuation if the plan went wrong.

The whole amazing plot was, code name, "The Third Front" The story was barely credible. Herman Storch was at first judged to be a weasel that would say anything to ingratiate himself with his interrogators. The British Enigma code breaking equipment, however, picked up a message from German High Command that gave credence to Storch's tale. Soldiers were being recruited from within German regiments to form two new battalions, the prime qualifications for membership was knowledge of English with American accents.

They were to be led by Otto Skorzeny, the SS hero who, in 1943, had rescued Mussolini from his Alpine mountain prison.

Skorzeny's battalions were to be ready for 'behind the lines offensives' in December 1944. The Allies, at the time, were not aware that this would have coincided with the Germans last-ditch Ardennes offensive launched on December 16.Although the two American interrogators still doubted the story told by Storch, they soon learned to respect his ingenuity. For during the time of his being questioned, he had also organised another mass break out of 700 men. When another German POW gave information that orders had been issued, in the Devizes camp for the escape, the two young American trainee interrogators were replaced.

On December 14, battle experienced paratroopers crept into the Devizes camp and seized twenty-eight prisoners from their beds. They were taken under heavy guard to London and put in, what was called, The London Cage, the headquarters of M19 what is now known as 8 Kensington Palace Gardens. After a week in London, the tight-lipped prisoners were delivered to a much tougher POW camp in Comrie, Perthshire, reserved for hard-line Nazis. The camp was tightly guarded outside but inside the Nazis ran the prison with iron rule.

When the would-be escapers, including Storch, arrived from the London Cage, the hunt for the traitors started. A Nazi court of honour, *Ehrenrst*, found Wolfgang Rosterg to be the traitor. Rosterg had been used as an interpreter at Devizes and had been cleared by the British interrogators of having any part of the escape plot. Why he was included in the group of prisoners sent to Comrie is unknown but it was to be his death sentence.

The Ehrenrst met on December 23 the result ordered Rosterg to "Redeem your honour. Hang yourself". He was found at 6am on Christmas Eve, the day scheduled for the mass break out at Devizes, hanging from a water pipe in the washroom. A post mortem, however, revealed that Rosterg had been strangled and was dead before he was strung up. Twelve Nazis suspected of being the ringleaders were arrested but only eight were eventually put on trial. Five of them were sentenced to death for murder.

The executions took place at Pentonville Prison on October 6, 1945. They were the last multiple hangings to take place in Britain.

The German POW's made their mark in history by being the subjects of the largest multiple hangings since the Dublin Phoenix Park murders of 1883 when four people were executed. It has not been given any officially recognition whether Herman Storch had exaggerated the plot or whether the daring escape plan really did exist. If it did and it had succeeded, it would have most certainly changed the manner in which the war ended in Europe".

NINE

VICTORY!

One Saturday morning during the January of 1945, Pat and I walked to 'Stanley's', the bakers, to get a penny's worth of stale cakes; one penny's worth of yesterday's cakes filled a 12inch square paper bag. I used Stanley's regularly, sometimes more than once a day, not only did I get the bread for Mum I also got bread for Granma and less frequently for my Aunt Rose.

Because of my regular patronage, one of the two female shop assistance gave me special preference. When there were not enough old cakes left over from the day before to fill a bag, the counter assistant would make up the shortfall with fresh ones:

Stanley's bakers shop was situated opposite Stockwell Post Office in Clapham Road. As we came out of the shop, a neighbour, about to go into the baker's, stopped Pat to ask how our mother was. She obviously wanted a conversation because my reply of "OK" was not sufficient for her.

"Do you know you are going to have a baby brother or sister soon?" she said looking at Pat.

I believe Pat was more excited about the forthcoming event than I was. "Yes", Pat said.

"Do you want a baby sister?" our neighbour said to Pat.

"Yes I want my baby sister Bebe to come back". She replied.

"I have noticed you have started sleeping at home every night.

Are you not going to use the deep shelter any more?"

She was correct in her observation. We had not been to the shelter to sleep for about three weeks. Our last visit was for the1944 Christmas party but we didn't know the answer to her question. Mrs Busy body must have had plenty of time to spare for she talked on and on and directed all of her questions at Pat. Eventually, she allowed us to continue on our way home.

As soon as Pat and I were alone again, Pat said, "She's a nice lady Ron. She's the lady that lives next door to us, in number six".

"I don't think she's a nice lady. I think she's a nosey old cow". Such was my view of neighbourly friendliness and conversation.

On February 3rd 1945, a thousand American air force bombers raided Berlin. The raids continued on German cities with the Americans bombing at night and British aircraft bombing during the day. The heavy bombing was an attempt to force Hitler to 'throw in the towel' but Germany's surrender was not yet forthcoming.

Ten days later bombers of the Royal Air Force raided Dresden. This particular air raid has since been described as one of the most infamous acts, conducted by the allies, of the war. In that one single air raid estimates ranged between 25,000 and 135,000 civilians were killed and another 30,000 were injured. The duration of the raid lasted approximately 12 hours, the same time as the German air raid on Coventry in 1940. Still no surrender from Hitler was offered.

On March 27th, the Germans launched their last V2 rocket from an area in Europe that was still occupied by German forces. The rocket landed in Orpington and killed a housewife. She was the last British civilian to be killed by enemy action: In London, there had been a total of 1,224 air raid alerts. The last air raid alert was March 28,1945. Two days later the last V1 Doodlebug fell.

The total civilian casualties of the war in the UK, by bombing and long-range bombardment totalled 60,595 killed and 86,182 seriously injured. Approximately half the number killed was in London. The long-range bombardment came from German high powered cross channel guns sited in France and killed 148 people.

During the Spring there was daily speculation that the surrender of the German army could be announced any day.

Since moving into the house in Binfield Road, I had neglected the updating of my war maps. I still listened to the news on the radio and read the newspapers to keep up to date with the allies' progress. But I had lost my appetite for the war and I was now eager for it to finish. I did have another good reason for not keeping my maps up-to-date; I didn't have my own bedroom. I did not have a bedroom of my own again until I went in the services.

While the war continued, we only used one semi basement room in the rear of the house for eating and sleeping. Gran and Grandad use the other room, in the front of the house for cooking and eating. Houses in Binfield Road, with semi-basement rooms, were very similar in design as the Studley Road house we had moved from.

The semi-basement ground floor rooms we now lived in were designed to accommodate living in quarters for servants. On the first floor, Gran and Grandad had a room immediately above, in the front of the house. John had a room on the first floor, above our all-purpose lounge/diner/ bedroom.

Due to the constant fear of air attacks, the top of the house was not used for living in. It would not be true to say, however, the rooms were out of bounds. The kitchen on the second floor had a bath and a large water heater. Although the kitchen was not used Grandad, Gran, Mum and Dad occasionally used the bath.

We still had the railway sleepers propping up the downstairs ceiling. The props remained in that position until the war in Europe was over. Four large and extremely heavy pieces of timber, longer than a steam locomotive is wide, surrounded a double sized bed, one on each corner. Had the rough cut, railway sleepers, posts been made of a respectable timber; such as oak or mahogany veneer and been further decorated with lace work, with a stretch of the imagination, it would have passed as an antique 'four poster' bed, circa early Tudor.

Deprived of furniture and wardrobes, an assortment of clothing such as jackets, topcoats, woollen cardigans and jumpers hung on each of the corner posts from six-inch nails.

Being without wardrobes, the bedposts served a double purpose. But as clothing was rationed and only obtainable with coupons, we did not have a selection of what to wear from one day to the next. Most of the time, however, the clothing that we were not wearing was hung over the backs of chairs. Our dress was dictated by weather conditions rather than fashion, therefore there was less clothing hanging on nails in the winter than summer.

Sometimes Mum had a rare spasm of mustering her energy and tried to make the room look tidy. On these occasions, during warm weather, all of the nails on the bedposts would be utilised. At the foot of the bed we had two easy chairs, a dinning table with four dining chairs between the fireplace and a table. The table was the same one that Dad cut the corners off of when we lived in Buckinghamshire before the war.

The room had no windows but did have a large pair of half glazed French doors that led to the garden, in our case it was also the main route to the garage. There was also a kitchen, about 6ft x 10ft which had a very old gas cooker. There was one tap only, which contained cold water; there was no hot water, above a large white and brown polka dot heavy square sink. The intermittent patterns of brown were where the white enamel had been chipped.

At the far end, a door separated the kitchen from a coal cellar. The ceiling of the cellar was directly below the steps, outside the house, leading to the first floor front door.

February 10th 1945 Mum had her fifth child, in the back downstairs room, in the 'four poster'. Our newest member of the family was a boy. Mum told me his name was Rex.

"Rex! That's a name for a dog?" I said.

Maybe that is what she would have preferred. I thought it was funny and made the comment as a joke but Dad didn't appreciate my humour. He told me Rex was a Latin word for King. I was surprised Dad knew any Latin words. Later, I looked the word up in a dictionary at school just to make sure he had got it right. The dictionary confirmed what Dad had told me was correct but it also stated that Rex was a type of cat of two varieties. a Devon Rex and a Cornish Rex. There is also a Rex Rabbit. Within seconds I came to the conclusion that the odds were three to one against Dad's information. I concluded Mum's preference must have been for a furry animal. My humour was in bad taste, however, I was not to know the fate of my Brother Rex.

From the time Rex was born he struggled to survive. He died four months later from pneumonia. I regret, apart from his name, I can only think of one incident that allows me to remember him:

Dad purchased from 'The Swan' a small quantity of brandy to give Rex as a medicine, in a vain attempt to keep him alive.

The completed 'Wolseley' was now parked in the front garden. Had the vehicle not have had windows, like a car should have, it could have passed for a small version of a van. But the style was an acceptable one, the new exposed varnished wood and painted aluminium coachwork was taken from a popular design imported from America. This style of bodywork in America, although a poor copy, was called a 'Shooting Brake, In England it was called 'Utility'. Dad was reasonably happy with the result of the car's appearance and it was ready to try it out on the road.

Petrol was still rationed so every drop was used sparingly. Dad didn't take it out for a test run only. The test was incorporated with another necessary journey.

One of the major aspects of Dad's skill at car maintenance was being able to adapt a vehicle to use as little petrol as possible. Dad would make unimaginable modifications to improve the petrol consumption. I affectionately recall Dad jokingly refer to his own miserliness with petrol. Sometimes he would only change a jet or two in the carburettor, other times he would strip all the worn parts and replace them.

A good 'tick over', on an engine, was a quick test that petrol was being used efficiently. Dad's economy tests were not measured by the gallon but by cupfuls. Often, while on a journey after taking the car out of gear and cruising downhill in neutral, Dad would playfully suggest how many spoonfuls of 'juice' he had saved. So to 'kill two birds with one stone' our test run, in this case, was incorporated with a journey to collect another consignment of timber, with the compliments of Ashtons.

I accompanied Dad as he drove the car to the back of the carpentry shop of the funeral parlour in Lansdowne Way and loaded the back with off cuts of hard wood and took all of the timber that was in the yard. When fully loaded, the tyres on the rear wheels looked dangerously close to the mudguards.

"Not only are we testing the engine, we are now about to test the suspension" Dad said with a smile. With the exception of the clouds of burning oil coming out of the exhaust pipe Dad was reasonably happy. It was good enough to eventually sell to 'Camberwell Man'.

There were occasions when Dad had a second vehicle 'stripped down' in the garage. At this period, however, with the exception of the 'smoky' Triumph, the garage was now empty, with no work in the 'coming in diary'.

Dad's idea of running his one-man business, up to this time, had been to 'buy a vehicle, make it presentable and then sell it before he would buy another. Dad thought it was neither practical nor good business practice to have money, which he had very little of, invested in something that was doing nothing. He did not believe in idle capital. That is to say, Dad's daily transport was the vehicle that was for sale. Not until it was sold would Dad buy another. With a persuasive argument from Mum, Dad changed his business strategy.

Dad was an avid reader of 'The Exchange and Mart' and most of the vehicles he bought for selling came from this publication. He visited the newspaper stand as soon as it opened every Thursday morning when each weekly edition of the E&M went on sale.

One Thursday morning Dad returned with the Daily Mirror and the E&M, sat down at the table and while reading the motorcycles for sale section, had his breakfast.

"There's a super bargain we're going to miss", Dad said. "A 1937, 600 Panther. That's a lovely bike! We really ought to buy this one Ann".

"Well don't mope about it. If you want it break a bad habit of a lifetime. Go and get it. Have two bikes in the garage. We've got the money", Mum said.

"I'll bet it's already sold!"

Dad needed extra pressure put on him because of his concern about his own reckless thoughts of spending money. Dad made an argument defending what, to him, was prudent but Mum knew Dad well enough to know he was only seeking a little more encouragement. By the time Dad had finished his breakfast, Mum had convinced him he should at least go and have a look at it. Dad asked me if I would like to join him and we were soon on our way.

We went on Dad's 'BSA' with a specially adapted sidecar chassis: In place of a sidecar were two, bolted down, builder scaffold boards. Dad drove us off in the direction of Camberwell Green. Very few people had a telephone, so we left our house without appointment not knowing if the vehicle had already been sold. In less than fifteen minutes we arrived at the advertised address in a scruffy area and within throwing distance from railway arches off the Walworth Road.

The exterior of the house was in an ill state of repair, but blended very well with it's surroundings and was very similar state of disrepair to the house I lived in.

Dad walked down the short path and knocked on the front door while I remained sitting on the pillion seat. An older man answered Dad's knock. Dad's back was towards me so I could not hear what he said but I heard the other person tell Dad to follow him. I rushed to join them and fell in behind to overhear Dad saying the BSA he had was too small for his growing family.

The machine for sale was leaning against the garden wall with a tarpaulin sheet covering it. The seller pulled the cover away, as he did so he must have filled his shoe with rain water from a puddle that had collected in a crease. He swore and danced away on one leg while Dad gave the motorcycle a quick inspection.

Characteristically, acting as he always did before making a decision; Dad thrust his lower lip over his upper one, frowned and, as though checking if he needed a shave, rubbed his hand several times around his chin. Words were not necessary, Dad's face said it all, and it was an expression of woe.

This was not always an indication that Dad did not like what he saw, however, it could have meant he liked what he saw but did not like the idea that he was about to part with his money. Dad never gambled by betting on the outcome of horse racing, dice or playing cards, he did sometimes assist Mum in filling in her football pools coupon. I have no doubt that was the extent of Dad's gambling habits. However, my judgement, after watching Dad perform in buying and selling, he could have been a good poker player. Dad gave the motorcycle a shake a couple of times, by pulling on the handlebar. The splashing noise told Dad there was petrol inside the tank.

He turned the petrol tap on, primed the carburettor and gave it a few sharp treads down on the foot start. The engine came to life but stalled as soon as Dad increased the revs'.

"Mmmm, not as good as I imagined it would be" was Dad's first comment.

"There's nothing wrong with it mate. It's in good working order!"

"That's as may be but I didn't want to spend a lot of time and money on it. It's a bit too scruffy for me", Dad replied.

"Well, it's my son's bike. He's joined the army. He wants it to be out of the way. He asked me to get what I can for it. Would you like to make me an offer then?"

That was music to Dad's ears. The seller had made two statements a seller should never say:

'He wants it out of the way' and 'Get what you can'

In Dad's view, it was invitation from a 'sucker' and an invitation for a very low price to be offered. I looked up at Dad, but he disguised his pleasure very well. He could have passed a theatrical acting audition for someone that was being tortured and suffering from a terrible pain. After some consideration, helped by pulling on his nose Dad was about to make his agonising offer.

"Well", Dad said after a long sigh, as thought he had been placed in tight corner with no way of getting out of it.

"I don't really want it but if you want it out of your way, I suppose it could be useful to break down and use for spares. I could take it off your hand". Dad then said a price.

"Oh no! That's much too low. I could never sell it at that price, surely you could make me an offer better than that?"

"Of course I could and if I wanted it bad enough maybe I would, but sorry pal I don't really want it, I was trying to do you a favour. You're asking too much for it. It will take a lot of time and money to get it back into tiptop condition. That's the most I could go to. I've got a busy day in front of me, so we mustn't waste each others time".

That looked like Dad's final words. He turned and faced me. "Come on Ron, we've got work to do" he said.

As the old man recovered the motorcycle with the waterproof sheet, Dad ushered me to the gate towards our transport parked at the kerbside. Dad and I walked ahead of the man selling the motorcycle, when the seller was out of hearing distance; I quietly asked, "Aren't you going to buy it Dad?"

"Yes I think so but you never can tell but he's on the hook, let's just wait a minute and see", Dad said quietly to me and winked.

The seller followed us and stopped at his garden fence. As we reached our motorcycle, parked in the road, he called out "you're not a dealer are you?"

"Do I look like a dealer?" Dad answered his own question. "Of course not. I told you I wanted it for my own use. A dealer wouldn't touch that with a barge pole".

Technically Dad was lying. He was a dealer. He was just not a very successful one.

A little humbled, the vendor asked "Could you pay cash for it now and take it away today?"

Dad exaggerated his movement to turn the petrol tap on under the petrol tank, and while bending down, out of sight of the old man, Dad looked up at me with a playful smile. Without a word being spoken Dad's smile said it all he casually reached for his leather gauntlets and put them on. Dad did not answer until he was sitting on the saddle. Not a trace of his smile remaining he said "I could pay you cash right now and take it out of your way in ten minutes but I don't want you to think you are doing me a favour".

"OK, it's a deal".

From one moment of looking disinterested and ready to leave, Dad's faked unconcerned attitude changed to that of 'action man'.

"Get the rope from the tool box Ron":

There was a toolbox bolted to the chassis boards, where a sidecar would normally be. While Dad was getting his wallet out of his pocket, they both walked into the house. I got the rope out from the toolbox and waited. Within the ten minutes that Dad had suggested, the deal had been completed. Dad walked back to the 'Panther' carefully folded the tarpaulin cover and put it on the saddle. Without asking if the sheet was included in the sale, Dad pushed the 'Panther' from its resting position against the garden wall and out through the gate to the rear of the sidecar chassis. While I steadied the balance of the Panther at the rear, Dad lifted the front of the motorcycle onto the rear of the sidecar chassis frame and let the front wheel drop in the gap between in the two boards. The rear wheel remained on the road and after the machine was secure with the rope, we drove off.

During our journey home, from his normal riding position, Dad half turned his head to me and as though giving me some credit that I had taken part in the buying, he said; "Well, we done alright there Ron! Didn't we?"

The ride home was a short one and as soon as the new acquisition was untied from its cradle on the sidecar chassis it was pushed into the garage and Dad started checking it over.

WP Motors was now in big business. Dad now owned; one car, one motorcycle combination and one solo motorcycle. All stock was for sale with a Total value of approximately £200. Approximately forty weeks wages for an adult male.

I was walking down Lingham Street, returning home from Brixton market one Saturday when I caught sight of a notice, in the window of a newsagents and tobacconist shop. The notice read:

'Boy required for an early morning newspaper delivery round, must be ten years old or over. Apply inside'.

I went into the shop and told the proprietor that I would like to do the paper round that was advertised in the window.

After I had confirmed that I knew the area that the paper round covered, the shop owner told me I could start the following week if I supplied him with a letter of approval from one of my parents.

The job was for nine hours, Monday to Saturday, one hour and a half per day.

Mum had no objections and I started on the next Monday at five shillings a week, (twenty-five pence).

The fear of constant enemy bombing had now passed, giving way to infrequent retaliation raids and there was no apparent danger from any other quarter. From my point of view however, there was a 'built in obstacle' in the job and that was getting up early but I looked forward to a new adventure.

For my first morning, I got out of bed at five thirty and left my house in Binfield Road at six o'clock. I reached the paper shop to find that I was too early; the shop had not yet opened.

Before the first week was through, I was getting out of bed at six fifteen; I washed and dressed, covered the fifteen minutes walk to Lingham Street, off the Clapham Road, with a five minute run and I was at the shop, ready to start, at six thirty.

It was just after my twelfth birthday when I started, it was early Spring and, I believe, there was 'a double summer time' which meant clocks were advanced two hours instead of the now customary one hour.

The sharp nip in the morning air was giving way to a more tolerable light chill and the fresh clean air was invigorating.

Even at that early age my Dad had conditioned me to appreciate fresh air. On the occasions when we went out walking together, he would remind Pat and I to "take a big sniff up and fill your lungs with good fresh air".

In turn, some fifteen and more years later, I passed on the same valuable advise, albeit regarded as a joke, to my nearest and dearest.

After a few weeks, I was thoroughly acquainted with the paper round and getting out of bed early became normal. Being out in almost empty streets, so early in the morning gave me a feeling of freedom and the satisfaction of 'growing up'.

After having just arrived at the shop one morning before commencing my round, I was filling my delivery sack with newspapers, when my employer asked me if I would like to do a Sunday round as well.

"If you do" he said, "I will increase your wage to seven shillings and sixpence a week".

The Spring had now progressed into Summer and the mornings were warm, I said "yes", without hesitation but after agreeing I instantly regretted my haste. I thought the money was not enough.

As I reached the shop door to go out, the shopkeeper added "You had better ask your Mum and Dad if they approve first, let me know what they say tomorrow".

He had negated my acceptance and allowed me some leeway to change my mind.

During my round that morning I had a mental conversation,

playing a dual role, one was the shopkeeper, the other myself; In my imagination I acted out the role of being a tough negotiator seeking a better rate of pay. My big thinking had one flaw; in real life I had neither the courage nor the verbal ability.

The next morning, my concern was short lived, for as soon as I entered the shop, I was asked if I had got approval from my parents to work on the Sunday morning. Taking advantage of him being a pleasant man, in an off hand manner I said, "My Dad said no. It is worth fifteen shillings"(75p).

With an understanding smile he replied; "That's all right then, not to worry, I'll get someone else".

I left the shop with my papers and like the previous day, my mind was again engaged in active conversation but today my cocky ideas were dashed. I was telling myself how stupid I was. I had lost the opportunity of earning an extra two shillings and sixpence a week.

Saturday came and as I was about to leave the shop to commence my round, the shop owner looked up, smiled, and said; "Ask your father if twelve and sixpence is alright. If he agrees, you can start tomorrow. Come back today, when you have finished your round and let me know".

I could hardly contain my joy. The fact that I had cowardly misrepresented my father was far from my mind, for my father knew nothing of my proposition to the shopkeeper. I walked my round in a state of euphoria. I didn't particularly want to work on Sunday morning but I had the glowing feeling of having won something from a 'grown up'.

After I had delivered all the papers, without going home, I went back to the shop and from the open door frame I said; "My Dad said it's OK, I can start tomorrow".

In April delegates from fifty countries met in the USA to draw up a charter for the United Nations Organisation, UNO. The charter was signed on June 26, 1945. But not by the United States wartime leader, President Roosevelt, he had died April 12.

I heard on the radio news on 28th April that Mussolini, the Dictator that took Italy into the war and twelve of his colleagues had been captured by Italian partisans and executed at Lake Como. A day later German troops in Italy surrendered. A day or two after that it was also reported Hitler had committed suicide in his bunker in Berlin. He was 56.

The surrender of the German High Command came on May 7th but it was not announced until 7.40 in the evening. The next day commenced an official two-day national holiday to celebrate 'Victory in Europe Day'.

On VE Day, May 8th, Whitehall and the Mall were packed with happy crowds caught a glimpse of Winston Churchill as he drove from Downing Street to Buckingham Palace for lunch.

Later from the cabinet room, Churchill spoke on the radio and announced that hostilities in Europe would end officially at midnight. He rounded off his speech that had the ring of a Shakespearian actor and said in his unmistakable lisping impediment

"The evil doers now lie prostrate before us. Advance Britannia! Long live the cause of freedom! God save the King!"

The country was in a festive mood, seemingly, forgetting the war was still being ferociously fought against the Japanese in Asia and the Pacific Islands.

Churchill's car was driven to the House of Commons and greeted by flag waving crowds. In a speech, he moved that the 'House' attend St Margaret's, Westminster "To give thanks for our deliverance from the threat of German domination".

He later waved from a balcony in Whitehall to the happy crowd below. He had his, now symbolic, giant cigar between two fingers of one hand and his famous two fingered V for victory salute from the other hand.

"This is your victory," he told the dancing crowd "God bless you all".

Standing at his side was Ernest Bevin, MP, who conducted the streamer-throwing crowd in singing ' For he's a jolly good fellow'.

Although the 'blackout' had been lifted, nearly two months earlier, on 20th April, London was suddenly a city of lights. Singing and dancing filled the streets and total strangers kissed each other. Bonfires, with effigies of Hitler and street parties were the main element of the celebrations. Fireworks exploded and the anti-aircraft searchlights 'danced' across the sky. One pair of searchlights intersected to display the cross on the top of St Paul's Cathedral. I remember watching and joining the festivities in London, but I can no longer remember clearly between what I saw in photographs in the newspapers, the newsreel coverage at the cinema and what I actually saw first hand. Many streets had their own victory parties which residents had been saving money and food from their meagre rations,

Adolf Hitler once said, "When I die, I will leave behind a great and strong Germany that will last a thousand years".

He died by shooting himself. On 30 April 1945. He left a conquered and shattered Germany in ruins. Hitler's legacy was proof that human beings had not changed in their barbarism since recorded history began. He showed that mankind could behave worse than wild beasts in a jungle. But the end of the war in Europe did not bring everything suddenly back to normal.

After the two days of celebrating people returned to their normal place of work but were brought back to reality by realising nothing had changed: While citizens of Western European countries rejoiced, the people in Eastern Europe descended to conditions little different to that of the' dark ages'.

The national press and radio now concentrated on the progress on war against Japan that was expected to carry on for at least another year.

Demobilisation of the armed forces began on 18th June but thousands of 18-year olds were still being 'called up' to fight against the Japanese in the Far East.

Since 'The Battle of Midway', probably the most significant sea battle of the war, the American navy had regained superiority in the Pacific Ocean. The Japanese having lost most of its aircraft carriers adopted new tactics and brought a new word into the English dictionary; *'Kamikaze'* The strict Japanese translation meant 'divine wind'.

It may have been spiritually divine to the Japanese pilot about to join his ancestors, but it meant 'suicide pilot' to the rest of the world. The forces still fighting the war in the Far East gained the title of 'the Forgotten Army'.

They were aptly named, for unless one had a relative still fighting, the war did appear to be over. They were forgotten.

A week after Dad bought the 'Panther' he also bought, via an advertisement from the 'Exchange and Mart', a second-hand sidecar chassis. It took Dad only a little time to bring the most recent purchase 'up to scratch'. Now it only required a sidecar to complete the outfit. Another week elapsed between buying a sidecar chassis and Dad selling the BSA combination that had been in daily use. In the meantime, he had got to work selecting the hardwood for making the first 'WP Motors Ashton's special'.

During one evening Dad had made two drawings of different sidecar styles, one single seater and a two seater. A week elapsed and the skeleton of a two-seater sidecar had been completed.

The 'Wolseley' utility came in useful, for Dad also used it to collect a number of low budget sheets of aluminium and Perspex from a government surplus store at Wimbledon.

When the sidecar was finished and mounted onto the chassis on the motorcycle it looked like a professionally manufactured piece of equipment. Dad was so pleased he set about drawing plans of a variety of models and immediately started on the skeleton of a single seater.

One evening, I overheard Dad telling Mum he intended to frame the plans; he had just drawn, to hang in the garage.

"If you are going to make more than one style, you should give each model a name". Mum suggested.

Dad agreed and said he would have to think of a common theme. Before the drawings were hung in the garage, I gave an input to Dad in offering a list of names for the sidecars.

I suggested Pennine, Mendip and Cheviot etc. I was delighted with Dad's response.

"This is a good idea Mam", Dad said to Mum. "Ron has 'come up' with a clever idea. He thinks we should name our range of sidecars after some well known English hills".

"Yes! That *is* a good idea Ron".

After a short pause and more thought Dad said; "did you think of it while you was doing a school geography lesson?"

"No!" I said, "I thought of it because we got the wood from the coffin makers yard, we could name the sidecars the same names that Ashtons use to name different styles of coffins":

Dad thought that was hilarious and I joined him in his laughter and while still laughing he told Mum. Mum missed the point entirely of what Dad had thought was so funny. Dad had to explain, while still laughing that not only did the sidecars look like coffins they also took the name of the funeral directors favourite range. Mum forced a smile and told me not to take anything other than the timber that I had permission to take.

After Dad's laughter had subsided he told me the names were a great idea but it would not be such a good idea to let a customer or anyone else know the source of the timber, nor why we had decided to name the sidecars as we had.

With the war in Europe, not yet The Pacific, now over Dad spent little time before he began to think of our long awaited, post war summer holiday.

Dad had recently acquired a bell tent. But it was not just any old tent: It was an ex Ministry of Defence Antarctic Expedition with an igloo type entrance. That meant there were no side flaps we had to crawl to gain entrance. Once inside, it was warm and if we had ever planned to spend a future Christmas in the Outer Hebrides, it would have been perfect. But it was not all bad we did, at least, have a holiday.

In most cases, people only travelled by bus or tram or as far as they could walk. Relatively few people owned their own transport and most working class people never had a holiday, nor, if they lived inland would have ever seen the sea. It was unusual for working class people to take a holiday away from home. Dad, being in the minority, owned a motorcycle and a car.

Mum and Dad's favourite pre-war seaside resort had been Camber Sands in East Sussex. Camber was, therefore, a natural choice to be our first post war holiday destination.

Dad had completed all the necessary adjustment to the Panther and with a WP sidecar on a newly acquired sidecar chassis we set out early on a scorching hot Saturday morning for the South East coast.

The twin seater sidecar, with Pat and I inside, was packed to capacity with camping equipment.

In spite of the heat of the day, Dad was dressed in his usual government surplus, ex RAF fighter pilots, kapok filled and silk lined flying suit. Dad also wore ex army celluloid mustard gas eye protective goggles but only to keep the flies out and a cloth cap. Mum had a matching outfit that differed only by wearing a floral headscarf that substituted for a cap.

Between them, Mum's scarf was the only item of clothing that had not been purchased from an ex War Department, WD, surplus store.

Once out of London and in the country, the roads still showed signs of the 1939 preparations that had been taken to obstruct the advance of the expected invasion of the German army. Unrolled lengths of abandoned barbed wire were pilled in readiness to be unrolled at a moment's notice. Concrete 'pill boxes' and anti tank obstructions littered the roadside:

All road signs had been removed at the outbreak of the war and it was too soon for them to have yet been replaced. When we had covered about half of the distance to the coast we stopped for a 'brew up' in a shady lay by. After a brief rest, we set off again but before we reached our holiday destination, the engine gave a few splutters and coughs and then stalled. Dad pulled off from the road and stopped on a wide grassy area between the road and hedgerow to investigate.

As Dad got off the saddle I heard him tell Mum that it sounded as though there was a piece of muck blocking one of the jets in the carburettor but would be no problem to correct.

His first natural reaction, however, was to unscrew the petrol cap on top of tank. He broke off a small twig from a nearby tree to use as a depth gauge and inserted it into the petrol tank to check the level of the petrol. When Dad withdrew the twig the look on his face was that of disbelief. He stood there as though mesmerised.

"No! It can't be", Dad told himself but for us all to hear. Dad returned the twig into the tank to double check and hoping he had been mistaken.

"Nan, I can't believe it! We're out of bloody petrol!'

It took a little while for the significance of our serious situation to register:

Dad had used his monthly ration of petrol and we were now stranded somewhere that could have been in the middle of nowhere. We hadn't seen a sole on the road since we had started off again after our tea break.

"Our only way out of this mess is to hope that we can find a Good Samaritan living not too far away," Dad said.

I had never heard the word 'Samaritan' before. The fact that Dad said he was going to look for one intrigued me: What would a Samaritan look like? How could one be found? I wondered.

"What is a good Samaritan Dad?"

Dad attempted to keep the explanation of a Samaritan brief. "It is someone that is caring and gives help to those in need", he said.

Although, I found later, that was an accurate description that was not enough detail for me. I imagined Dad was about to set off, leaving us at the roadside on a quest to find a man that looked like Jesus.

"What sort of clothes do they wear?" I asked.

Dad, in reply, told me he would explain in more detail some

other time, but added; "They don't dress in any special clothing. They are just ordinary people. You have to ask to find out if they are Samaritan or not".

It sounded daft to me. Surely nobody volunteered to be good!

I was none the wiser from his description and Dad was in no mood for me to pursue my enquiry but I realised, at this moment, my education was not on Dad's list of priorities.

It was about midday when Dad set off, with an empty one gallon ExWD, (approximately 4.5 litres) petrol can for the nearest village. As Dad left, he warned me not to go wandering off to explore the countryside.

It was a scorching hot day. There was not a cloud in the sky and cover or protection to use for shade from the sun. The sweat on my face and arms attracted wasps and other smaller flying insects that stuck like flies to sticky fly papers, The heat of the day dulled my normal sense of adventure so it was not difficult to comply with Dad's instruction. There was no traffic, vehicular or pedestrian.

Paradoxically, Dad was gone for such a long time and nothing happened it was though time had stood still. I wondered if we would ever see him again. When he eventually returned he was carrying, in addition to the can he had taken with him, an American Army five gallons jerry can also full with petrol.

I overheard Dad telling Mum how he managed to obtain our means of getting back home: He had found the local village police station and told the duty sergeant of his plight. Before Dad was loaned the petrol, however, he was warned it was a criminal offence to obtain rationed goods under false pretences. He had first, to put his signature on a statement that the story he had related was true and to pledge the surrender of the equivalent value of future months petrol coupons on our return home.

Before we set off again Dad tried to clarify the definition of Samaritan but only added to my confusion of who, or what, a Good Samaritan was.

"Ron! Today my Good Samaritan was a policeman".

We continued on our journey and eventually arrived at Camber Sands late in the afternoon. It soon became obvious to me that Dad had not informed anyone in the holiday trade that we were coming; there was in fact, no holiday trade.

As we approached the beach road, I saw the first of many warning wartime notices 'Beware Land Mines' and 'Don't drink the water' etc.

Dad stopped the motorcycle, got off and walked over to the side of the road to read the smaller print on one of the signs. Dad had stopped between two large posts, one on each side of the road from which barbed wire was attached. The barbed wire stretched out along each side of the road for as far as I could see.

The road divided the pre war holiday chalets on our left from the sand dunes and the sea on our right. Next to each post was an empty sentry box, which suggested the road ahead had been, until recently restricted entry to army personnel only. There was a single pole barrier, each end of which would normally be at rest on the posts across the road. The barrier pole was now pointing skywards suggesting the road was open allowing us to continue:

Before the war there were very few permanent residence. Camber Sands was no more than a summer holiday town with small wooden chalets.

Except for traders and contractors, to supply army personnel, civilians had not been allowed in the area for five years. The chalets and bungalows were small and only designed for summer holiday occupation but it was evident that these little wooden huts had been commandeered by the military and had been used for billeting soldiers.

Dad returned with Mum still sitting on the motorbike and Pat and I in the sidecar.

"I'm a dopey sod," he said, telling himself off before Mum did.

"The bloody war's only been over for a month and the picture I had in my mind was to see this place as it was when we saw it last, six years ago":

In fact, the war was not over, only the war in Europe had ended.

The war with Japan was still going on.

Mum and Dad must have agreed between themselves to stop for the night because Dad got back on the saddle and drove along the corridor of a spiteful looking hedge of barbed wire. We continually passed signs telling us to 'Keep to the road'.

Dad drove on until the road and the wire came to an end. In some areas of the dunes large patches of course grass grew which enabled Dad to drive the motorcycle on without getting stuck. There was plenty of space to pitch a tent for the night. Dad soon had the tent set up and beds made ready for a night's sleep in the open air:

Camping, as it was then, should not be compared with the luxury of camping as it is today. We had no sleeping bags. No plastic sheeting nor portable camping 'gaz' for lighting or cooking, only a 'Primus' stove: Preparing the 'Primus', paraffin oil stove, could be a very tricky task for someone not experienced. The jet on the stove had to be hot before the oil would vaporise to burn smoothly. This was achieved by pouring a small quantity of methylated spirit into a small tray beneath the jet and lighting it. When the jet was hot enough a fine spray of paraffin would be emitted from a tube in the tank. The spray could then be ignited with a match and the airscrew closed.

If the temperature of the fuel was correct it would burn as good as a kitchen gas stove. If it was not correct, however, a flaming geyser would shoot two or three feet into the air.

To finish the job, air had to be pumped into the paraffin tank to keep a pressure inside to force the vaporised paraffin up. It was a messy job: While the stove was being transported it had to be kept upright, so as not to spill the contents.

A bottle of methylated spirits, a bottle of paraffin, cleaning rag, a box of matches and most important, a 'pricker', for clearing the eye of the jet when it got blocked was always carried. Dad kept all this equipment in a wooden box. It would have been cleaner, quicker, safer and much more comfortable to stop at one of the numerous roadside cafes that existed but that was not a consideration. Getting back to a pre-war life style as soon as possible was Dad's prime objective.

But what used to be was not now. Life is different now. Thank goodness! We say unanimously. But I am not so sure. It was good fun. The little water we had, remaining from making tea on the journey, had to be saved for a cup of tea in the morning. So we went to bed having had nothing to drink since midday.

We awoke early the next morning by the sound of distant singing. It wasn't the voice of just one milkman, it sounded like the whole Welsh rugby team choir. I began to doubt my belief that the dawn chorus only referred to birds.

The day before, we had not seen a person for miles before we reached the beach so where was the singing coming from? Very strange.

It did not take long, however, to solve the puzzle of the mystery choir. In the distance, about two hundred yards away I noticed, coming out from between the huts, a group of men marching towards us. I assessed there were about fifty men dressed in British army style uniforms but not the same colour. Dad said he thought they were German prisoners of war, POWs, being escorted further on along the beach to clear the beach defences. They were, obviously, not singing in English but I recognised the song.

The only German soldiers I had seen before this moment were those on the cinema news after they had been taken prisoner. They had then all looked villainous, miserable and unshaven dirty wretches. Now they looked like British soldiers.

In hindsight, I believe, at that time the POW's were filmed, they must have been specially selected for the camera for propaganda purposes. What a contrast to see them now. They all looked happy, clean and well fed. Many of them waved to us in a joyful manner, maybe they thought they had won the war, or maybe they were glad they hadn't, or perhaps they were only waving at Mum while fantasising.

A British army sergeant was at the rear of the group with the swagger one would expect of a soldier with three stripes. He looked as though he was the senior rank and in charge of escorting the working party. As the group of soldiers marched passed and the sergeant was near to us, he broke away from the group, walked over to Dad and spoke to him. He told Dad that it was not wise to camp anywhere in the area we had chosen. He recommended we moved back inland: The reason for this advice was because mine clearing operations were in progress. Dad agreed with him and told the sergeant we would be leaving within the hour. The prisoners continued singing as they marched and were still singing as they entered the barbed wire area. Stitched on the back of each one of their jackets I noticed a large diamond shaped piece of material.

Before the soldier left, he also advised Dad that it was only safe to walk on previously made footprints. It was sound advise, but as we were on sand, one of us, at least, would have needed the skills of an aborigine or Davy Crockett to have walked about with any confidence of safety.

We had camped at Camber for one night only and with one tank full of petrol in the motorbike, and a cup of tea in each of us, we travelled home by the shortest route.

When we got back home, Dad complied with the condition he had accepted from the 'Samaritan Policeman' and immediately presented himself to our local police station, at Union Grove, Larkhall Lane, Clapham, to surrender his petrol coupon book. The book was returned after the appropriate number of coupons were cancelled.

Having dealt with the concern of owing the police a part of his petrol ration, Dad wasted no time in removing the carburettor from the 'Panther' and investigated the reason for the poor return of miles per gallon. The problem was soon overcome. Dad refitted the same carburettor with a smaller auxiliary and main jet and altered the setting of the float in the chamber. There were a number of widely accepted methods in the trade to botch repairs and Dad, it appeared, knew most of them. One trick to renovate an old carburettor was to run lead solder into the worn part of the main body. It was then smoothed off with the very finest 'wet and dry' abrasive paper: The object was to fill in all of the scratched and scared areas, thus allowing finer tuning and more efficient running.

When all that could be done, in the quest for greater economy, Dad replaced the carburettor and after a few twists and turn of the small screws to adjust the mixture he appeared happy with the result. The real test then was to use the motorcycle on the road. The normal test had to answer the question: How many miles were covered per gallon of petrol? Dad's test was what distance could be travelled per cupful?

Within a week, the fault was corrected Dad was happy that the replacement of spare parts and adjustments he had made were satisfactory.

His joy was compounded by the fact that he had accrued no cost.

With the Panther Motorcycle 'back on the road' Dad's thoughts returned to us having a holiday to replace the one we nearly had at Camber.

There were still a number of weeks, of the school holiday period, of summer remaining, when, by coincidence, Dad received a letter from his Aunt: Dad's Aunt was Olive Coverdale, a Sister of Dad's Mother. They lived at Upton, some distance between Warrington and Liverpool and lived with her family in Lancashire.

I was not made aware of the content of the letter nor the total contents of Dad's reply. But Dad did ask Pat and I if we would like to spend a week not far from where he spent most of his childhood. I then assumed the letter must have been an invitation to visit them. I later learnt the reason for the invitation was to discuss arrangements for one of Dad's distant relations to live with us permanently.

The journey must have been uneventful for I cannot remember travelling there, or the return journey home. I can recall, however, one frightening incident during the week of our stay. I also remember the location and the house we stayed in: Their house was a stereotype

Lancashire terraced one that had the traditional door at the front of the house and a second entrance from the backyard.

The rear door was used from Monday to Saturday while the front door was used only on Sundays. A narrow cobbled public footpath beyond the back yard also served the rear of the, mirror image, houses in the neighbouring street. While we were at the table one morning having breakfast, a woman came into the parlour from the yard. She walked across the room and, as though she lived there, introduced, herself with friendly "hello all".

Mum, Dad, Pat and I, not having seen her before, all looked up and watched her.

"I won't disturb you all while you are having your breakfast Olive. Carry on. I've just come to borrow some sugar".

She walked passed us and opened the door of a food cupboard, helped herself to a cupful of sugar, closed the cupboard door and walked out. Aunt Olive showed not the slightest concern that someone, albeit maybe a long time friend and neighbour had walked into her house uninvited. Between eating a few mouthfuls of toast and marmalade, Aunt Olive told us it was her next-door neighbour. She recognised that we had watched the incident with amusement and commented "we do things like that up here".

During the week, with one of Olive's sons, Dad and I went to the local cinema. I recall the event not for the film we had seen but for our exit before we had seen the whole film.

We had got to the cinema late and went in while the film was in progress. When the film came to an end the cinema was emptied and fresh tickets were sold for the next performance: Which meant, if we wanted to see the beginning of the film we would have to buy more tickets. Dad complained that it was a daft idea not to be able to see the whole film with the same ticket, even if it meant seeing it in the wrong sequence, i.e, the end before the beginning:

That situation has now become standard but that has not always been the case. Cinemas in London and the Suburbs had continual performances. Maybe it was the same in many other cities and towns but not in this part of The North.

While still on our Lancashire holiday, one morning Pat and I went out to explore the local countryside. We only had to walk a short distance to leave houses and people behind us to be walking in fields. We walked along an open public footpath that led us to a riverbank. My passion for water, like streams, rivers and the sea was like metal to a magnet but not so much that I found washing or bathing appealing. Upon seeing a stream, I led the way by following the very shallow but swift flowing clear water along its shingle and cobbled bank towards its source.

The river had a rocky bed with many boulders above the water level that allowed us to cross from one side of the bank to the other with no difficulty.

As we played chasing each other, we zigzagged on stepping-stones across the river many times. As we progressed further along the water's edge, I had not noticed the surrounding scenery had gradually changed from flat level fields and a low bank, on each side of the river, to a high-sided copse. Grass had given way to ferns, small shrubs and trees. The taller trees shaded us from the direct sunlight and we noticed the drop in temperature. We decided to escape the cold by, what we believed to be the quickest route out of the shade and into sunshine. On each side of us, the riverbanks were now as tall as houses. We began to climb.

The sides, at the river level, rose very gradually and we both started our climb with little effort. On the high banks of the ravine, young saplings between more established trees had taken root, which gave us handrails and footholds thus allowing a comfortable accent

Because we started off easily, I failed to plan my path. Consequently, with less than three or four feet from the top, we were suddenly barred from further progress by a block end. We were confronted with overhanging rocks above our heads. Where our feet should have taken the next step, the path had become a victim of a landslip. The accustomed fern, small pieces of rock and soil had given way. Only old tree roots were exposed. Our situation became all the more perilous when, as Pat took a step to get directly behind me, the path behind her crumbled away. I looked to each side of me to plan the best route and then looked down. I was alarmed to see how steep the drop was and how high we had climbed. Our climb, although it had, up to this point, been pleasant and we had reached it with little effort, we were suddenly in a dangerous position. Had it have been as easy to go down as it was to come up we could have returned by treading in our own foot steps and followed the river back along the same route to our starting point. But it took little brainpower for me to realise we were stuck.

We could move neither up nor down. I had mixed feelings about our position but I observed that Pat did not appear to be at all distressed.

She was either not aware of the danger that I had placed us both in or she was braver than I. I chose to believe the former and tried to conceal my fear.

"Which way are we going Ron?" Pat asked, with no more concern than asking what we may be having for tea.

I looked around me for the best next move "I'm just looking for the best way to go" I said.

It had been an easy upward climb to reach our present position. We only had to step onto large pieces of jutting rock like steps. There were no options. I could see the top and I could see the sunlight coming in through the widening gaps in the trees. We had to continue upwards.

I now had to think of a different approach to conclude our climb to the top. I considered the only move that was open to us was to use the exposed tree roots at my shoulder level, as grab rails. I imagined we would have to hang by our arms with legs suspended and swing across the gap, in the same manner monkey bars are used in a children's adventure playground.

I told Pat what I had in mind and suggested she stayed where she was and watched while I tested the idea. The tree roots that protruded from the rocks and soil, like half circular runs in a ladder substituted for handrails. I reached forward to hold the first root above me, which allowed me to lean forward enough to grab the second. My body was now at an angle of forty-five degrees, my hands were half way across the gap but my feet were still on the start side. By good fortune, I noticed, where the soil had eroded, tree roots were jutting out of the bank above and below the side of the drop which gave good foot and hand holds. Our position was not as precarious as I had at first envisaged. By first getting a firm right hand grip, I kicked away a small quantity of soil and stepped into my newly exposed root to make a foothold. Continuing this process of utilising tree roots I managed to cross the gap and safely reach the other side in three steps. I cautiously turned around and reversed the process to get back to my starting point. On the lower side again with Pat, I asked her if she thought she could repeat what I had just done. She wasn't exactly bursting with confidence but she showed no outward signs of fear and was brave enough to say she would give it a try.

As I slowly squeezed myself behind my sister, I looked below at the path we had taken to get this far. I didn't like what I saw. As I helped Pat get a firm hold I told her not to look down and to keep looking straight ahead, just like I had read in my weekly 'Adventure Comic for Boys'. I followed closely as she took her first step out to cross the narrow chasm.

She faltered a little as she reached the middle but continued when I told her to repeat what she had just done. I moved up to have body contact to encourage her to keep going. She did so and we both reached the other side unscathed. We continued the climb on all fores until we reached the top.

During our return fast walk to Aunt Olive's, we joked of our escapade. I made light fun of the adventure in an attempt to convince Pat that at no time had we been in danger. My motive being that I did not want Pat to tell Mum how perilously close I had put ours lives at risk.

I told no one of our secret and I cannot recall Pat ever referring to the event in later years.

While the war had been in progress, the country had a coalition government but two months after the war in Europe came to an end, a general election took place.

The first post war General Election resulted in a massive majority in favour of The Labour Party. The new government, led by Clement Attlee, began a programme of bold social and economic reform, the like of which the world had not seen before:

The Bank of England, Coal Mining, Electricity, Water, Gas, Telephones, Railways and Hospitals etc were all to come under state control.

A free health care service, ' The Welfare State' for everybody was then an unimaginable leap forward in social reformed. No country had ever attempted such an imaginative plan before. Great Britain was the first. It was bloodless revolution. The electorate kicked out the old Conservatives ideas forever. Even the Conservative Party would never be the same again. Or at least that is what was hoped.

This radical thinking was anxiously awaited, but it could not be implemented immediately for Great Britain wasn't great anymore. Due to the enormous cost of the war, Great Britain like the rest of Europe was bankrupt and relied on the Untied States of America for huge loans. The situation was so serious that not only did rationing remain, with some food items it became worse and continued to be rationed until 1954. For reasons that are beyond my comprehension, bread, that was easily obtainable and not rationed during the war years, became rationed in 1946.

The bacon ration was reduced from four to three ounces per person per week. Meat also became scarcer. The clothing allowance was also reduced and remained on ration until 1949.

Petrol became available but only with coupons and was rationed until 1950.

The war in Europe had finished some three months when I returned to school, after the summer holiday period. The interrupted sleep, due to the bombing had been my most reliable excuse for lateness or non-attendance. My old excuse was no longer valid and I began to attend school more regular and take the lessons a little more serious but only a little more.

My most favoured lessons were History, Geography and Chemistry. History appealed to me because I liked the stories. I was attracted to geography and natural history because I liked drawing the maps.

Chemistry has a lot to answer to for in the manner in which it shaped my approach to an argument or discussion in later life. Chemistry impressed me for the way in which, during each experiment, the notes were taken.

I liked the discipline in the layout of the report. Each stage of an experiment was written under defined headings

Experiment: What happens when X is applied to Y?

Utensils: What are you going to use?

Method: How are you going to do it?

Result: =Proof

The research for proof was most important to support the conclusion. It is worth recording at this point, if only for the humour, that my commercial activity did not cease because of my new location. Only the commodity changed. New school. New customers. New merchandise.

During one particular lecture in a chemistry period, the teacher made a brief reference to the manner of lighting on motor vehicles before electric dynamos and batteries were introduced. My interest was particularly aroused because during one of my bombed ruins adventures, during the war, I had found, in a garden shed, an old lamp.

The system the teacher was now describing made me wonder if my lamp could be one of the same types.

The lamp was made of brass and had an old, out of date, peculiar shape. The only thing the lamp had in common with lamps of the present was the manner in which it was made to attach to a cycle. Inside the lamp, there was no provision for a bulb but in its place was mirrored glass on three sides. I did not make my interest known to the lecturer but saved my questions for Dad when we were next together. When I arrived home that afternoon, with a new interest, I inspected and cleaned my mystery item in readiness to show Dad.

When the opportunity was right, an evening or two later, I showed Dad the lamp and asked him if he knew what it was. He was very enthusiastic about the devise and told me a brief of the history of 'carbide lighting'. Although we spoke on the same subject for the remainder of the evening only a very small part of the information was imprinted on my brain; that small part of information was; "If the carbide got wet it gave off a terrible smell. It is critical to keep it dry".

As an after thought, Dad said; "you can still buy packs of carbide crystals. Halfords sell them".

"Can you?" I eagerly replied.

My mind was racing. I could hardly wait for the next day to come. I wanted to see if I could get my lamp to light. But that reason was of a lesser priority. Mostly I wanted to make a stink bomb!

The next day's lessons at school were wasted on me. I could think of nothing other than my lamp. When the midday break came I sacrificed my school dinner for a tube of carbide crystals.

I walked to the Clapham Park Road end of Haselrigge Road and caught a number 37 bus that took me along Acre Lane to Brixton. After I got off the bus at Lambeth Town Hall, I had no more than four paces to walk and I was in Halfords shop. After the counter assistant told me the price of my purchase, I had difficulty in regaining my voice, and when I did I wanted to protest it cost 2/6d. I thought the cost for me to carry out such a simple experiment was exorbitant and asked if it was sold in a smaller quantity. It was not normal for me to carry such a large sum but with fortune as it is, for good or bad, I had the money with me. As no smaller amount was available I purchased the item and left the shop:

The tube was about 12inchs long and about 4inchs diameter and heavier than I had expected it to be. While on the bus, on my return journey to school, I broke the seal around the tube and opened the lid. The cardboard container was full to the brim with small pieces, of what looked like large crystals of soda. It was difficult for me not to tell any of my closer school colleagues of my shopping trip.

My purchase remained in my satchel until I got home. I eagerly awaited the bell that informed everyone school was over for another day. At home, after I had eaten, I went out into the back garden with my lamp, the tube of carbide and a box of matches. I entered Dad's garage and for secrecy closed the door behind me. I opened the front of the lamp, placed it on the bench and inserted some water and the crystal in the space provided.

Without thinking, in my haste, I struck a match and immediately blew it out.

In spite of petrol being rationed, Dad always had petrol in a few jerry cans somewhere in the garage.

A sudden shock of fear went down my spine as I remembered Dad constantly warned me; "never, have a naked flame in the garage".

I was pleased that I had corrected my error before I had blown Dad's garage up and me with it. I carried out my experiment in the garden. Once alight, the gas created by the wet carbide allowed the lamp to work perfectly. If not ignited, the smell from the gas made by the crystal getting wet, was vile. The smell was such that it would have been repulsive to anyone except a schoolboy.

Surely a smell as bad as that must be worth money. Delighted with the result of my test, I extinguished the flame by removing the pipe from the jet and placed the lamp on a shelf in the garage:

Although electrical lighting was known before the 1914-18 war, in the main acetylene lighting, from carbide granules was used on almost all vehicles prior to 1927. A few companies, such as the Swiss 'Motosacoche' and the American manufacturer of the 'Indian' Motorcycle incorporated a dynamo in their lighting system.

Acetylene lighting depended upon water dropping onto granules of calcium carbide, which in turn produced a gas. The gas was piped to a burner jet in both the headlamp and the rear lamp. The flame, to produce the light was controlled by the rate at which the water dropped on to the carbide granules. I took a quantity of carbide crystals out of the tube. The next day I took them to school. I left the tube at home, not wanting any of my potential customers to realise how I come to be in possession of such a commodity. Having spread the word around in my classroom that I had some super stink bombs for sale, I was ready to commence business.

My price was the exorbitant sum of a penny a lump the same price of a weekly comic but much more fun. During playtime, eager buyers surrounded me and during the first playtime of the day I had sold all I had. My new wheeze was an instant success and unbelievably rewarding. I had sold about a quarter of my 'half a crown' tube; my profit was enough to buy another two. I was never top of my class in maths but it did not take too much of my brainpower to calculate I had made a seven fold return on my investment. The next break was the lunch period that gave me enough time to get the bus to Brixton and buy twice as much as I had on my first visit. I now had two unopened tubes and an opened tube three quarters full. I had only spent my profit so the cost of my investment remained at two shillings and sixpence.

After a few days of hectic trading, I realised one lad was buying more from me than the other lad. To my surprise, I discovered he was selling my pieces of crystal and making a profit. Was I was selling too cheap?

The two most popular areas at school for making a pong were in the toilets in the playground and inkwells in the classroom. As business ventures come and go, mine came and went quicker than most but upon reflection, I don't know how I got away with it for as long as I did. It lasted nearly two weeks. Sometimes, inside and even outside the school the smell was terrible. It was obvious it could not last.

My exorbitant enterprise came to an abrupt end when one of my classmates, put a small piece of carbide into his inkwell. His timing could not have been worse. It was during a maths lesson. I had learnt from experience the worst type of teacher to upset is a maths teacher. I came to the view that maths teachers were always violent and they never missed an opportunity to exercise it. Before the smell began to invade the classroom, the teacher had his back to the class, chalking on the blackboard. As the froth increased, from the inkwell, so did the smell.

Attempts by my colleague to stifle the smell, the giggles and the froth were in vain for the teacher must have heard the boys at the same moment he got his first whiff of the stink. As the teacher turned to face the class I knew I had sold my last piece of carbide. The teacher, at that point must have 'made his mind up' to not only find the culprit, that was obvious, but to interrogate the class until the supplier was found. His first reaction was to open a draw in his desk. From the open draw he produced a long cane and slammed it across the surface of his desk with such ferocity that his pen, pencil and chalk recognised his fury and scattered in all directions and papers fluttered to the floor.

The colour of his face turned scarlet and his eyes looked as though they were about to pop out of his head, he didn't say a word. He pressed his lips tightly together and his cheeks bulged as though he was competing for the world record of how long he could hold his breath. The giggling stopped. To say the teacher was annoyed would be too simple, it would be more correct to say he exploded.

The unstoppable frothing carbide spewing from the inkwell had no respect for the teacher's wrath. It continued to spread in volume across my classmate's desk.

The teacher moved towards the now terrified boy, who stared in front on him. The teacher stopped at his side.

"Anything to say boy, before you are impaled on the school flag pole".

The school did not have a flag but impaling, rather than caning, was this teacher's favoured threat.

I am sure the boy next to me wanted to speak but his answer was a muted gurgling. Like the rest of his body, his voice box had become momentarily paralysed.

"What was that boy? Did you say you don't want to be impaled just yet?"

The teacher had now returned to his normal composure and began to enjoy his power. With finger and thumb around the boy's ear, who now had tears rolling down his cheeks, was pulled up out of his sitting position and guided to the front of the class. They stopped at the big desk and with the theatrical timing of a professional actor the teacher faced the boy, and said: "Say goodbye to your friends".

They then both left the classroom. It felt an eternity before the maths teacher returned, when he did so, he stood at the door and shouted out "Pross!"

I replied in the most polite and innocent manner I could: "Yes Sir?" I answered, as though I had no idea why I was being called.

"Come out here".

I was escorted to the headmaster's office and entered alone. I was surprised to see the other boy was not there.

"The boy in here before you received three of the best and has been sent home. What do you think you deserve for something much more serious?"

"Nothing sir" I replied.

His smug composure changed and his voice gained an aggressive edge.

"You sold him that foul compound didn't you?"

"It was carbide crystal sir, to be used in an acetylene lamp, sir".

"Don't take me for a fool boy. I know what it is meant to be used for".

"I didn't tell him to use it in school sir"

"I am tempted to give you a good thrashing here and now for your insolence alone, but I am not".

My relief was short lived.

"I am allowing you to go home, at the end of the lesson, to allow you to stew in your own torment but don't think you are going to get away with it that lightly. I shall save your punishment until tomorrow. I am going to make an example of you. You will be caned in the hall, during assembly, in front of the whole school".

I was dismissed from his presence and I returned to my classroom only to find it was empty. The door was closed but the vile smell was seeping through the gaps between the woodwork of door and frame and contaminating the corridor. I rejoined the lesson that was now being continued in the hall.

The rest of the day passed without further incident but as I walked home, after school, I wondered what tomorrow would bring.

I was concerned my very profitable business venture, albeit small, was about to come to an abrupt end but it was no greater than having to face the headmaster's anger the next day:

I was not an aggressive boy and contrary to what my deeds may suggest my nature leaned towards timidness. When the morning of the headmaster's retribution arrived I went to school with more than just a little trepidation.

The news must have spread. My greeting as I arrival in the playground was not that of a pariah as I had expected. I felt I was being looked upon as a hero.

I had become a celebrity that nobody wanted to associate with. I sensed, as I should have done, this was not going to be a normal day. I realised my new status with my peers had also been noted by the teaching staff which could increase my degree of punishment.

At first I missed my classmates not approaching me to buy something. I was being ostracised* and that was of a psychological* importance to me;

At the time I didn't think in those terms, nor would I have known what either of the words meant.

This sudden change in my popularity affected my attitude of that what awaited me. The fear I had endured during the night, for the teacher's punishment was now replaced by anger and defiance:

It was customary and accepted by society and many people still do believe that parents and teachers had a right to physically punish children. I have considered, since my attempt to bully the wrong person, people should not be allowed to hit other people. More so when it is adults versus children: My radical thinking for twelve years old maybe questioned. The reader must not forget, however, it is not so unlikely for all children to take this view for they all have a vested interest. In my case, maybe I was not so radical for I was less than average height and weight for my age and a good target for an aggressor.

Before I walked into the headmaster's office I assumed he had made is mind up that I was going to be caned.

While I was in the playground, my thoughts were disrupted when a young pleasant looking female teacher approached me and asked me to follow her:

This was before the bell went for school to commence. She must have been waiting for me to arrive. She tried to console me and appeared to be sympathetic to my plight but knowing what awaited me, I treated her with contempt. She was on the side of the enemy. I was led again like the day before, to the headmaster's office but now I was given a lecture and told my behaviour was unacceptable and I deserved a good thrashing. When he had finished speaking, he asked had I anything to say for myself. I believe he was expecting to hear an apology and thereby my admission that I deserved to be caned.

If that was the case, I must have surprised him. My tears and a plea for forgiveness were not forthcoming. I was now genuinely angry and, I guess, driven by fear, I launched into a verbal attack. I told him I was being treated as I was because I was a child.

"I am twelve years old. If I was grown up and bigger than you are, you wouldn't dare attempt to cane me for fear I would retaliate. My father has never caned me".

The headmaster allowed me to continue. He appeared to be speechless.

Due to my uncontrolled anger, I then began to cry and between sobbing and trying to catch my breath, I told him he was a bully and I had done nothing wrong.

"It is not illegal to buy or sell carbide. If it had been, I would not have been able to buy it. Making a profit is not illegal. The shop had done so".

That was the theme of my scrambled but logic defiance. I refused to say I was sorry and challenged his authority to inflict any form of punishment upon me:

Attitudes have changed since then but at the time teachers did have the authority and from his point of view my revolutionary attitude had to be beaten out of me.

Had I have spoken in a more respectful manner and humbled myself, maybe the outcome would have been a little different but only a little. The headmaster was clearly taken aback by my unruly defiance, cheek and admission of selling.

But I had challenged his authority and that had been a silly thing to do, I believe, I was instrumental in sealing my own fate. The maths teacher escorted me from the headmaster's study to the assembly where my audience awaited. I was guided to a spot on the stage with the same procedure as I imagined as being led to the guillotine during the French Revolution. I also considered it seemed not that long ago I had taken the same steps to receive praise for painting my war savings poster.

Then, like now, I stood by a piano that was the instrument that triggered my short time of glory. On that occasion, I was being praised for my talent but now that meant nothing, I was about to be punished for another talent. From painting a picture to producing a pong - what a dramatic change of fortune two years can bring.

Between the headmaster and the maths teacher, I was escorted onto the stage. The headmaster stepped forward and spoke to the collected assembly. The speech seemed to go on and on but I do remember a little of it: The headmaster may have considered what I had said in my disrespectful rage. He concluded his speech:

"I do not approve of children buying and selling during school time and turning the classroom into a market place in principle. I am prepared to 'turn a blind eye' to moderate trading during playtime, I know that comics, marbles and conkers, etc, often change hands. I do not consider that to be a caning offence. This young offender before you all is, therefore, not about to be punished for his enterprise but for his impudence and bringing a toxic evil smelling substance into the school and disrupting a lesson. I hope that is clear to everyone".

I received three heavy vicious strokes of the cane across the palm of each hand and three as I was bent over, just where the bottom of my short trousers met behind my knees.

I was caned for impudence, disruption, and lack of discipline and for not accepting any punishment for my actions. Not for selling. It was a hollow victory.

After the caning, I was instructed to return to my classroom. As I walked from the stage the edge of my trousers rubbed against the area where the cane had come to rest. When I was out of sight, I turned my trousers up to ease the irritation. My legs felt as though they were on fire. But my punishment had the outcome opposite to that which was intended. I lost all respect, albeit through fear, I may have previously had for teachers and the authority they held. My punishment enforced my defiance. I ignored the headmaster's instruction to return to the classroom. I held back my tears of anger until I left the hall. I ran into the playground, locked myself in a toilet and cried alone. I cannot recall returning to the classroom that day.

I secretly continued trading in carbide, in small quantities, outside the school premises until I sold all of my existing stock. Just by chance, another 'money maker' emerged on the scene: The saying 'when one door closes, another door opens' has proved to be true in my case, not just at school but all of my life.

A new pastime of making bracelets from electrical plastic covered cable became popular at school and within a week or two developed into almost a craze. The bracelets first came to my attention after I saw a couple of boys wearing them in the classroom. With no more than enthusiasm and small amount of the capital, that was a part of the profit from the now diminishing carbide business, I was able to 'get in when the pickings were at their best'.

One evening, I mentioned to Pat of the new bracelet fashion. She told me they were also being made and worn by the girls in her school.

Pat wanted to make one for herself but she did not know were to obtain the cable: Dad had nothing like the requirement in his garage. All he had was a very thin multi stranded rubber covered automobile cable. The cable I required was ordinary 13amp single core plastic covered electrical household ring main cable. It was stiff and stayed in any chosen position. Pat offered to show me how to make one if I could get the cable.

There was a small electrical shop in Clapham Park Road within walking distance from my school. It was there the following day I made my enquiry and purchased four different coloured lengths of cable, enough to make one bracelet. I took the wire home and Pat showed me, in one night, the very simple manner in which they were made.

The electric cable was in the usual electrical colours red, blue, green, yellow, black, brown, green with a yellow tracer, and brown with a black tracer. The following day, I took the finished item to school and 'showed it off' during playtime The interest the bracelet received was a surprise to me, more so when I mentioned I knew where to buy the material and the few pence it would cost:

I had made my own list from the prices I had been given in the electrical shop but because of the spontaneous enthusiasm I had given little thought of my profit margin, I just multiplied the cost by a factor of two. What made my new line of activity most attractive was the fact that unlike my previous ventures I was now collecting orders and buying the merchandise with my customer's money.

On my third consecutive daily visit to the electrical supply shop, the shopkeeper suggested it would be much cheaper for me to buy small reels. The shopkeeper's advice was sound. I bought one reel each of the four most popular colours.

I paid the shopkeeper but as I lifted one from the counter I was surprised how heavy it was. I arranged to collect them on the next afternoon on my way home from school. The next day I went to school on my bicycle and collected the four rolls of cable.

I followed the same procedure each time I needed a new roll. Rather than carry the roll of cable to and from school each day, I cut off pieces of different colours at home to order.

I had no plan of future income while I was running down my carbide racket but within the week I got into 'full swing' with a new source of pocket money.

It would be an understatement to say train spotting was popular. Before the Summer School holiday period began, the most popular subject of discussion and activity in and out of school was just that:

When the school summer holiday break began, train spotting became a most serious pastime. Nearly everyday, Benny and I travelled to all of the London main line stations:

Waterloo and Victoria Stations belonged to the Southern Railway, SR, which served all of the South, South East and South West of England.

King's Cross Station belonged to London North Eastern Railway, LNER, served the East Midlands, Yorkshire and the Eastern side of the country up to Central Scotland. The Great Western Railway owned Paddington station. GWR served Cornwall in the West Country. Wales, Birmingham and The Midlands. Euston station belonged to 'The London, Midland and Scottish Railway', LMS, served as their title suggests all of the industrial cities and towns North of London.

Not all train enthusiasts were children. Men of all ages were part of our large friendly and informative fraternity.

The older men were a 'mine of information'. Old men of retirement age, sixty-five years plus, would tell some wonderful train related stories, of the late 1800's. Benny and I were 'suckers' for a good story, which filled in our waiting time before an expected train would arrive. It is more than likely most of their adventures and nostalgia of accidents and difficult labouring tasks were not all true but they held our attention 100%.

Often, while we were waiting on a railway platform, another train spotter would join us and 'tip us off' where one particular locomotive could be seen. Armed with direction we would rush, on our bicycles, to another location to get a glimpse of a piece of rolling stock.

We waited many hours on main line stations, in all sorts of weather but most of our 'spotting' time was spent in the marshalling yards at Nine Elms in Battersea. Large steam engines arrived just to go through the large washing tunnels:

Nine Elms 'loco yard' was a massive site covering many acres of sheds, sidings and turntables. There were always an abundance of assorted locomotives, some pulled passenger carriages, and others just shunted goods wagons.

Some of the wagons were full being positioned ready to begin a journey. Odd shaped metal cylinders on wheels to carry various forms of liquids and oils were constantly being shunted to and fro.

Every locomotive had at least a number others also had names. The names and numbers were listed in a pocket book form and sold in newsagents all over the UK.

These pocket sized directories, one book for each of the Big Four rail companies, was the driving force for the mass interest:

I understand the idea of producing the publication came from a railway clerk. He submitted the idea to the railway authority and when his idea was rejected, he gained the copyright to publish. He did so. The clerk's name was Ian Allen and his new little books were an immediate success.

One group of locomotives that took my attention in particular was the 'Merchant Navy' class belonging to the Southern Railway. Each one of the locomotives in the group were named after a character from the story of King Arthur and his knights of the round table:

King Arthur, Queen Guinevere, Camelot, Lancelot, Maude, Merlin etc, etc.

I sat for my eleven plus exam before the summer holiday period began, unfortunately I was not made aware at the time the consequence of obtaining a pass mark but I doubt it would have made much difference, had I have known.

My failure to pass, determined I was to continue attending the same school after the summer holiday break. My failure did not appear to surprise Mum or Dad, it was more likely to have been a greater disappointment for some of the teachers who would have preferred me not to have stayed. On returning to school I discovered, had I have passed, I would have qualified to have moved onto today's equivalent of a Grammar School.

After a few weeks into the Autumn term Mum and Dad, were informed by letter, that although I had failed the examination, I could still be considered for a place at a more senior school because I had a technical aptitude. I discovered that I had, in fact, achieved the fourth highest place of those that had failed. In turn, the parents of the three boys, with marks higher than mine, had also received a similar letter. They had declined the offer. Dad was proud of me and immediately responded with a letter to my headmaster accepting the offer.

The letter made no reference that I recall, to the fact that I had originally failed and I was a 'fill in' for a spare space.

Only a few days passed before another letter arrived offering a date to attend an interview at the suggested school in Black Prince Road, Kennington:

I knew exactly where the school was and what it looked like. Since getting the official letter from the London County Council that a place had been provisionally reserved for me at the school, I had

309

carried out my own inspection. I travelled by bicycle with my regular companions, Benny and Beechy.

When the day for my interview arrived, I travelled with Mum in my best clothing. We got off the tram at the Gaumont Cinema at the junction of Kennington Cross and Black Prince Road, walked down the tree-lined road and found the school on our left hand side.

It was not in my nature to be nervous so the proposed change of school did not bother me a great deal. One positive aspect about the appointment for the interview was that I did not have to attend school for any lessons that day.

When Mum and I arrived at the school we were shown to the Headmaster's office by a teacher who, by chance, entered the school at the same time we had. On entering his office, we were offered a seat and the headmaster went through the customary niceties of an introduction. I felt comfortable during his 'getting to know you talk' and went very well until I was given a pencil and paper and a page of questions on mathematics to answer. The friendliness shown by the headmaster put me at ease, and caught me off guard and mentally unprepared to sit a sudden written examination. Consequently I was unable to answer most of the questions. From frustration, I started to cry.

Before my allotted time was up, the headmaster, seeing that I was not going to continue, sympathetically suggested that I could put my pencil down and let him look at what I had done. Up to that moment, most of the conversation had been between the teacher and Mum. I handed him the paper and after only a glance he put the paper back on his desk and looked totally at me. I knew he could not have been very impressed with my effort and my normal cheeky bravado deserted me. I felt the poorly educated wretch that I was. He then told me there was an emphasis on training for Technical and Engineering occupations and I would have to improve on my mathematics and treat my studies seriously if I wanted to qualify for a certificate. He read from some notes that were in front of him, as he read, I wondered what my present school had written about me. I held the opinion that my interview would be successful: I could not imagine my current school giving me a detrimental report if they wanted to be rid of me.

By way of terminating the interview, the headmaster rose from is seat and Mum shook his hand he had offered. As we approached the door he asked me, it seemed as an afterthought, "Ronald! Can you give me the definition of an hypotenuse?"

I knew that it was the longest side of a right-angled triangle.

"Yes sir", I said full of confidence, "It's the same side as a window cleaner's ladder, resting on a flat surface, leaning against an upright brick wall".

"Well, it's not a wrong description and you obviously know what it is", he chuckled but that is not the answer I was expecting in practical terms it is correct and a splendid one. I must compliment you on your originality".

He then looked away from me and while still smiling he spoke to Mum.

"Well Mrs Pross maybe we will be able to teach Ronald to explain that a hypotenuse is the side of a right-angled triangle opposite to the right angle".

In parting, Mum was told she would receive his decision in the post. On the way home, Mum told me she didn't understand the teacher's definition and thought my explanation of hypotenuse was better than the teacher's. We returned home not knowing if I would be transferred or not.

I returned to normal school activities the next day and continued with the same routine for another couple of weeks more until the expected letter arrived. I had, by this time, conditioned myself that I wanted to move. Although I was not thrilled at the thought of going to *any* school at *any* time, when the letter of acceptance arrived giving a start date I was delighted, as was Mum and Dad,

I had been told by Mum the family had not seen a banana since before the war and I was aware it was regarded as a luxury item.

While I was in the paper shop one Saturday morning putting my round in my shoulder sack, I could not help overhearing part of a conversation between the shopkeeper and a customer.

"A lorry load of bananas has been delivered to Roberts greengrocers in Brixton this morning and they are going on sale as soon as the shop opens".

I knew where this particular greengrocer was so when I had completed my paper round with an extra spurt of energy I ran home to tell my mother where I was going and took a ration book. Without stopping, I boarded a 45 tram outside Stockwell underground railway and got off at the Odeon Astoria cinema at the junction of Brixton Road and Stockwell Road. The greengrocer was established in a corner shop in Atlantic Road, Brixton, opposite Electric Avenue.

When I arrived I could hardly believe my eyes. The queue was so long, I could not see the end of it. I walked to the end of the side turning but the queue continued on into Brixton Station Road, the adjoining street. The queue must have been four hundred yards long. Disappointed but still determined I joined the end of the line of people and prepared myself for a long wait, the time was eight o'clock. At ten o'clock a man from the greengrocers walked passed me while counting people in the queue. When he was about twenty people further on he stopped, put his arm into the orderly line and facing down the queue I heard him say "we will definitely be sold out of bananas after this person".

The crowd responded in varying degrees between disbelief and sad humble acceptance to a defiant mini rebellion. Some people shouted abuse like that to a footballer that scores an own goal at a cup final. One lady further down the line wanted to have a fight,

"Why didn't you tell us sooner, I've been waiting in this bloody queue for over four hours". I understood her disappointment but I had been waiting two hours and I was in front of her. I wanted to tell her not to tell lies but she was a big heavyweight ugly woman so I thought better of it and kept my mouth shut.

"Sorry lady, I didn't know any sooner," he said as he walked off.

Content with the news that I was going to get bananas I joyfully observed the scene: At first some swearing came from behind me from potential revolutionaries that refused to leave the queue but in a short while the moaning and groaning settled down. Some stayed while the remainder just drifted away.

People, from the very far end of the queue filled the gap that had been made by those vacating it. Not wanting to believe what they had just heard they must have been working on the theory that now there were fewer people in front their chances must have increased,

More time elapsed before the greengrocer came into view again and by this time the queue had got as long as it had been when the shopkeeper had come along the first time.

As he approached I heard him repeating "extremely unlikely, extremely unlikely".

He carried on down the line of people, repeating his forecast, like an old gramophone recording stuck on a scratch. Without stopping or changing his stride his voice faded has he walked farther on. "Extremely unlikely, extremely unlikely."

Nobody left the queue in front of me, so I stayed put. At eleven o'clock, I had been in the queue for three hours. The railway arch was now behind me, I had rounded the corner and I could see the shop in front of me still selling the exotic fruit. At eleven thirty and with only four people in front of me, waiting to be served, the 'extremely unlikely' man shouted out 'bananas all sold out.'

I was stunned, I felt as though I had taken a kick from a horse. My thoughts of going home with a prize had been dashed. At that moment, nothing was more important to me than a bunch of bananas. My throat was so tight I felt too choked to cry. I would have given my entire weekly paper round wage that was in my pocket, to have gone home with a fruit that none of our family had seen for four years.

Even Dad, working for The NAFFI couldn't get bananas.

I read in a newspaper later that 10million bananas were being unloaded at Bristol Docks and were about to be distributed widely throughout the country.

On my last week and my very last chemistry lesson at Haselrigge Road School after the lunchtime break, I joined a queue of boys waiting for the teacher to arrive to open the locked laboratory. As I waited, my attention was drawn to a group of my classmates in the queue in front of me. They had broken the school disciplinary code of waiting outside a classroom in an unorganised pack. It was a rule that teachers liked to impose upon boys.

Boys that were doing nothing looked unruly if they were not standing in a straight line. Why did male teachers act as though they had never been children once themselves? They had no understanding of schoolboys. Or maybe they remembered only too well.

The group had compressed more to a rugby scrum. My first thought was that a boy was trying to pick the lock on the lab' door but the rowdiness was a little too excitable for such an operation. My curiosity was aroused as to what was causing the disturbance so I moved nearer to join the throng. The direction of the onlookers gaze was on just one boy. I realised it was something he was doing closer to himself, rather than to the door, that was the centre of attraction.

As his back was towards the door and facing the group it ruled out the lock picking thought. As I pushed closer, I thought I saw him moulding something, in front of him just below his waist level. Yes! It was a long fat length of plasticine.

But no it wasn't.

I was amazed when I realised he was caressing his willy. The performing boy encouraged a couple of other boys, near to him, to also expose themselves. He then displayed the method of exercising for making it larger. Gripping his willy he began to rub it backwards and forwards, instructing his new admirers to do the same, telling them theirs would also grow. The small group increased to an excited crowd, so much so that the corridor became blocked. Some gasped

314

and some laughed but the majority, like myself, were mesmerised by the extended length and girth of the flesh that had grown in his hand. The more he rubbed, the more it appeared to grow, like the genie emerging from Aladdin's lamp. When at it's largest it looked, except for the colour on the end, like the pastry cook's rolling pin in my Gran's kitchen. One of the boys had been influenced by the magic act in front of him, so much so, had unbuttoned his trousers and he also exposed himself in a futile attempt to be competitive.

While the champion continued his stroking action he waved it around for all to see and boasted he was the only boy in the school that could pee over the top of the toilet wall in the playground without wetting the wall on the inside. There was laughing, heckling, pushing and shoving from the boys behind me to get a better look. It was like Sunday school when free sweets were given out.

One of my classmates, in the crowd directly behind me exclaimed; "That's bigger than my Dad's willy".

The first boy, with his very own personal truncheon in his hand, rather aggressively, as though he had been offended, said "Can't you see properly? This isn't a willy this is a cock. What you've got is a willy":

If that part of the anatomy was categorised in Latin and named relative to size then I thought my one would most probably be labelled 'willy minus'.

The sound of the chemistry teacher's footsteps coming up the stairs put an end to the impromptu biology lesson and we all rapidly returned to a semblance of an orderly queue as though nothing had happened.

For a month or two later, the enormous size difference in the boy's appendage and mine constantly returned aggravatingly to my thoughts. Each night I went to bed and conscientiously exercised in the manner the boy had recommended.

I rubbed up and down, almost automatically. Erotic thoughts were not included in the instruction. I employed my right hand, in a casual manner, while completing my homework with my left. Sometimes my arm and wrist ached to such an extent it felt as though both were about to drop off but I continued until sleep overcame me.

I kept my programme of bedtime exercises a secret I did not even share my ambition with my two closest school friends.

With no reward to see from my effort of nightly rubbing, my enthusiasm to own such a robust instrument soon passed. I was to learn some years later when I went into the army that nature had not 'short-changed' me. The dimension of my appendage, I observed, was no less than a good average:

I had read, during a history lesson of the American civil war, the then American President, Abraham Lincoln, 1809-1865, had been credited with saying "all men were born equal".

Of course, he was not referring to what was tucked away inside a man's underpants but in any sense, the statement was nonsense. The monster owned by the boy at school displayed to me that even nature could be unfair in its distribution of attributes.

Too soon my schoolwork for the first time in my opinion, had to be taken seriously. Learning became a greater priority than playing and even earning pocket money but I made no conscious decision to stop my antics in any moneymaking schemes, my new school environment forced the change.

My new school, 'The Borough Beaufort Technical School for Boys, insisted that each pupil wore the school uniform: Grey flannel trousers, grey cap, navy blue blazer, white shirt and school tie and not least a magnificent, light blue and gold on navy blue, badge for cap and breast pocket.

My first day at 'The Borough' was the first time I had ever worn all new clothing from head to toe at one time.

My new school had been built a little before the second world war, circa 1937. It had a modern purpose built carpentry and a metal workshop both on my preferred subjects list. For each subject the workshops were used for a whole afternoon. In my previous schools, with the exception of music and art, I had one class only and sat at my own desk for all lessons. A different teacher would come into the class for the period set aside for a subject and then vacate to another teacher that taught a different subject.

Now the procedure was the other way around. The teachers remained in one class while the pupils had to attend a subject classroom. At the end of each period all of the classes would empty and armies of boys would be on the move and passing each other in corridors to get to their next respective lesson.

My new classmates were different from my previous school, they were eager to learn. The adult manner of most of the boys had an influence on my behaviour. I gradually became 'almost' a reformed character.

All of my previous 'earners' had been unplanned they came to fruition only by the initial action of someone else. Again, my initiative in a new piece of dealing was due to satisfying the demand in the popularity of American comics:

American comics were by far superior in their content than English picture comics. For comparison American comics were in full colour and designed to appeal to an older reader with a, stupid, adult story line, albeit, the main theme was science fiction. They were in fact designed to appeal to the adult market. Superman, Spiderman, Batman and Robin were but a few of the titles obtainable in America.

With the exception of non cartoon type boys weekly comics like: The Adventure, The Rover and Wizard English comics had foolish, simply and childish, antics and sold for the amusement of children only. I cannot recall how I was able to obtain these rare American comics but they regularly came into my possession. I very soon gained the reputation of being the 'one with the comics ' for sale or exchange.

Not wanting to clash with any ruling the school may have had regarding money changing hands, I kept the whole business on a low profile.

There were some features of my new school that I had not encountered in previous schools: The Borough Beaufort had a common study room/

library/ reading room where no teachers entered. The school also shared the facilities of a sports ground in Croxted Road, near West Dulwich railway station. Sports day was every Thursday afternoon.

Although I was now finding most of the lessons enjoyable and accepting school with all of the discipline it entailed, sports day was my most favoured, it never came quick enough.

One sunny afternoon at The Dulwich Sports Ground, while playing cricket, I was positioned as wicket keeper. The batsman had hit the ball with such a powerful swing I could see it was heading for a boundary. As the ball travelled without a chance of being stopped I called to a teammate fielding at square leg. As he did not understand what I was saying, I raised my arm with a flat palm as though pushing the wind. He then understood I was telling him to field further out. He then acted accordingly. While my instruction was going on, the fielder at long off had now recovered the ball and seeing my raised hand threw the ball hard for me to catch. In that instant of my lack of concentration I managed to catch that well aimed ball. Full on the nose. It wasn't a knockout but there was no more cricket for me that day. I had to endure the ridicule. A week at school with two black eyes can be a very long time.

Art, a much safer pastime than sports, was a half-day lesson that was taken at The Borough Polytechnic. The building now has the title of The London University.

Mathematics, English, Geography, History and Natural History were compulsory subjects. Religion was also compulsory but I must have been taught the very minimum required by law for I cannot remember being bored by the subject.

During one lesson, in the carpentry shop, as the session was coming to an end, the teacher called for the class to gather around his bench. We were informed that over the coming weeks, starting the following week, we were all going to make a wooden stool.

The school would supply the timber for the seat but we were asked to bring to school any odd lengths of 2" x 2"pine that would be used for making the legs:

Wartime restrictions were still in force and building materials still were in short supply. I disregarded the 'pine' and the following week I took to school the correct length and gauge but in pieces of ex coffin oak. Although the teacher rejected my timber for the task in hand, he thanked me for my contribution and put my offering in the timber store for a future project.

When my stool was finished for a small fee, to cover the cost of the material, I was allowed to take it home.

I also liked the metal work lessons but the teacher was stricter on workshop discipline than Dad was in his garage. He was as strict as a maths teacher, for example: the teacher insisted that while anyone was at the bench with a metal saw or filing, goggles were to be worn. The class was instructed to clean, with a wire brush, the metal filings from a file after each lesson.

Being clean and tidy also meant putting tools back in their respective places after use at the end of each lesson. When the time came to sweep our benches and put the clean tools away, the teacher would place himself in the centre of the workshop and loudly ask: "What is a tidy workshop?"

From the very first lesson we had all been programmed to shout out the answer. We responded in chorus; "A tidy workshop is a safer workshop sir".

My first project, that took about ten weeks to complete, was a calliper gauge.

An important part of working with metal, I learnt the method of tempering steel and at a particular temperature, how to treat metal with oil, to protect it from oxidisation. I was again allowed to take my completed piece of work home. It became a useful tool in the garage and it never went rusty.

In the mathematics department I began to get 'a grip' on the theory of numbers and with that came an enjoyment of algebra lessons. My previous belief that substituting letters for numerals was stupid was dispelled:

The manner in which any teacher teaches is the key to the students' absorption rate.

My math's teacher, unlike others bullies I had encountered, was skillful in both knowledge of the subject and his ability to teach. His method must have suited my thought pattern. He was skilful in teaching transposing a fraction to a percentage and the value of shifting a decimal point for easy calculation. But I never completely overcame my failing to recite a 'times table' like poetry, it remained a problem for me, albeit to a lesser degree even to this day. My difficulty is consistent with an awful memory to remember poetry. I had no problem of giving the answer to a question on multiplication, for example: What is four times nine? Nine being one less than ten, I automatically thought of four times ten equals forty and then deduct the four 'ones' to give the answer of thirty six. I was able to give an answer with my method as quick my school friends using the 'poetry system'. I found my system much easier than trying to remember the rhyming of saying once nine is nine, two nines are eighteen, three nines are twenty seven etc. In attempting to say a 'times table' I would get a mental block of remembering the number I had last said. I am not suggesting my method is better than that which has been tested by time but it was better for me.

Rest periods were a feature that I had not encountered since my first infants school. The first piece of work on the first day of each new term was to copy a weekly work schedule. There were usually two rest periods of half an hour per week, which we were allowed to use for extra studies or for checking homework.

I spent many hours in the Common Room, CR. That was another feature that was very new to me.

During spare sessions, I was taught how to play the game of chess by a school friend and spent many hours playing the game. Had I have not changed schools and remained at Haselrigge Road School, I would have spent that time in the playground playing with marbles, conkers and flicking cigarette cards.

For the first time, I began to understand the value of knowledge, that school was a place of preparation for adult life, rather than somewhere to be while parents went to work. That is not to say there was a new master plan for children of working class people. There was no escape from the 'factory fodder' principle that still remained. The system was not changing. I was.

The street parties that had taken place to celebrate the end of the war in Europe had softened the fact that lives were still being lost on a daily basis in the war against Japan.

Despite the massive air raids by U.S bombers on their cities, the Japanese Military Government refused to follow Germany's example to surrender. On one air raid on Tokyo alone it was estimated 100,000 Japanese civilians were killed. The Japanese military confronted with these devastating casualties did not waiver. They were determined to fight to the end:

Between 1942 and 1945 the Japanese were driven, not without bitter fighting, from all of the territories they had captured during the first six months of the war in the Pacific.

On the 30th July, with the war almost at its end, the US warship 'Indianapolis' was torpedoed by the Japanese in the Indian Ocean and sank in twelve minute. From a crew of 1,996, only 316 survived. Because of the Japanese resistance to surrender history entered a new era.

In the early afternoon August 4 1945, the crew of an American Boeing B29 bomber led by Col Paul Tibbetts assembled for a briefing. They were told they would be flying a special bombing mission, code name 'Littleboy, to drop one bomb. Not until their return were they told they had dropped the world's first atomic bomb:

The Atomic Age had begun.

When 'Boeing' first unveiled their new bomber, in the early 40's, it was the intention of the manufacturer for it to be known by its code number of B17. But when it first went on display for the American press, one American newspaper reporter, due to its large amount of armaments, referred to it as a 'Flying Fortress'. The name stuck.

Before the war finished a larger version was introduced and coded B29 but referred to as a Super Flying fortress.

On 6th August, while peace negotiations were taking place between America and Japan, the Atomic bomb was dropped on Hiroshima. One bomb did not end the war.

The explosion was equivalent to 12,500 tons of TNT. It was estimated that between 70,000 and 100.000 Japanese died instantly and another similar amount died in the ensuing months from burns and the exposure to radiation.

It was not until the second atomic bomb was dropped, three day later, did the Japanese government agree to the American unconditional peace terms.

The second target had been Nagasaki and another 75,000 civilians were killed outright.

On 14th August, the American President, Harry.S.Trueman, formally declared the Second World War was over.

Between the war years, most people had at least one member of their family posted abroad on active service or had been taken prisoner. Some, while retreating through France in 1940 had been in captivity for five years. Others serving in the Far East would have had a similar time span without seeing their love ones. Coloured bunting that had been decorating the streets since May, to celebrate the victory over Germany, had remained in place to celebrate the anticipated capitulation of Japan.

The singing and dancing in the streets that had taken place to rejoice in the victory in Europe was just a 'dress rehearsal' for the Japanese surrender and for the expected return of 'the Forgotten Army'.

In addition to the Union Jack, coloured flags of the allied nations and other flags of all shapes and sizes adorned almost every house and shop. For a couple of days while the celebrations were taking place it was normal to see people, that appeared to be strangers, stop and kiss in the streets, perform a couple of steps of a dance and continue on their journey in opposite directions. Understandably, people in uniform were heroes:

Demobilisation pay for 5 years war service for a private in the British army was £61.18 shillings and sixpence. As I write, this value would represent no more than a day's wage for a person on a poor salary. In 1945 it represented, something like, ten weeks wages. It was an amount of money that most working people had never previously had in one lump sum.

My Sister told me, in one of her letters from Australia some forty years later, that we both went to a victory party in Courland Street, Clapham where my Aunt Lou lived. But my most vivid recollection of the celebration was a tour of the West End Dad took us on in the part-restored Triumph car.

My memory of this occasion remains sparkling bright, not because it was the end of hostilities, as one would immediately think but because of the vehicles exhaust fumes. Our motorcar would have won first prize, if any had been given, for the biggest contribution towards producing a new form of smoke screen.

The whole of The West End was one big car park, cars, buses and coaches were nose-to-tail. Each time there was a slight movement and Dad slipped the car into gear a cloud of black smoke came out of the exhaust pipe.

The worn engine, that Dad did not want to spent more money on, gushed out clouds of bluish oily thick smoke every time he put his foot on the accelerator to move forward a few feet. We were stationary for long periods and each time we moved it was little more than a cars length. The traffic was so slow it would have been much quicker to have gone by public transport to Waterloo and then walked. We didn't realise it at the time and never witnessed it before that bumper-to-bumper traffic conditions were a taste of what was to become normal.

Football league fixtures returned proper and during November, a Russian football team, on a goodwill tour, arrived in England to play three matches. 'The Moscow Dynamos' received a hero's welcome at each of their games.

They brought a new style of football to the country. They won two games and drew one. They played Chelsea FC at Stamford Bridge. The game was a draw at 3 - 3. They played Cardiff at Ninian Park and gave them a 'spanking' with a finishing score 1 - 10. Their last game of the tour was against Arsenal at Highbury. The visitors won 3 - 4. It was unfortunate the game was allowed to be played. The fog was so dense for most of the game; the ball could not be seen. Not only did the crowd not see the ball, most of the time the referee didn't nor most of the players.

During the winter months, when there was snow on the ground, like all children, my friends and I got involved in the traditional snowball fights. One morning I awoke with surprise at the brightness of the daylight coming into my room. I got up, looked out of the window and saw there had been a heavy snowfall during the night.

Good fortune had scheduled the snow to arrive during a school holiday. I immediately made plans to travel with Pat to North of the River Thames to throw snowballs from an area I frequented many times:

When there was plenty of snow on the ground, on previous winters, I had cycled with my two constant companions to Westminster and along the Victoria Embankment, on the North side of The River Thames. We got off our bicycles at the traffic lights at the junction of Northumberland Avenue and threw snowballs at the pigeons. One of us had the bright idea that we extended the terror of our snowballs from pigeons to people.

We left our cycles at the base of a column of the Hungerford footbridge, then walked up the spiral concrete steps:

Hungerford Bridge caters for both pedestrians and railway traffic. The railway line terminates at Charing Cross railway station. The bridge crosses the river Thames, between Westminster Bridge and Waterloo Bridge.

When we reached the top of the steps, we walked along the bridge towards the south side of the river and positioned ourselves directly above the main road. We were also above the foot traffic going to and from Charing Cross Underground Station. With an abundant supply of snow we pelted our unsuspecting targets with a barrage of flying lumps of snow. That was in the past.

Now, Pat and I entered Stockwell Station, both of us, complete with a scarf and gloves and came out at Charing Cross Station. As we made our way up the concrete stairs we heard the rumbling of a steam train departing from the station above us. A high, heavy gauge wire fence separated the footpath from the railway lines.

On the pedestrian bridge we were able to observe the trains passing in and out of the station, we also had a good view of the road below. Once we were directly above the pedestrians I immediately started making snowballs and pelted the passing unsuspecting vehicles and people below.

Pat, influenced by the joy we were both getting from my misbehaviour, soon joined in the fun. She started gathering her own piles of snow, formed her own snowballs and, copying me, dropped them over the bridge onto pedestrians' heads. Pat selected a horse and cart as a target and after a second attempt, made a direct hit and knocked the drayman's hat off. He made it clear he did not think it as funny as we did and responded with angry words and an aggressive gesture. Pat was so disturbed by his displeasure she decided not to throw anymore. But it was only the coldness seeping through my hands and arms that brought our mischief to an end.

Rather than encounter someone that we may have annoyed we chose not to go down the steps to street level immediately below. We walked along the length of the bridge, across the River Thames, and descended on the south side of the river. We had enjoyed a good day's outing. We boarded the underground at Waterloo Station and made our way home.

Other than playing games in the street and listening to the radio, going to the pictures was still the only means of mass entertainment.

325

Pat and I joined the Odeon Cinema Saturday Junior Picture Cub.

Most Saturday mornings during the winter months and less in the summer we travelled to our preferred cinema, the Odeon at Clapham South. I think the entrance fee was sixpence. There were always a number of American cartoons but the main feature was always a serialised story with over a dozen or so episodes. Superman and Westerns were most popular, but the Superman stunts were obviously animated and were poor when compared with modern computer aided skills: All the flying sequences were drawings superimposed upon a live background.

When my Uncle John was seventeen, he registered for National Service by claiming he was eighteen: The compulsory National Service commitment was two years. John joined the Royal Air Force as a cook and signed on for an extra year, which increased his salary for the whole three-year term.

The period before Christmas when business in the garage had reduced to no more than tidying-up coincided with a plan, appearing in the latest issue of 'Hobbies' magazine, to make an Eskimo style kayak. Without delay, we made a start by shaping the ribs from 'Ashtons funeral parlour' best quality off cuts.

Dad had all of the remaining necessary materials on hand: Boat builder's varnish and a roll of heavy black out linen substituted for seal skins: Dad had bought the linen to cover the interior of his WP Motors sidecars.

TEN

DODGY HALFCROWNS AND A PAEDOPHILE

For a long time Mum was very ill and extremely weak with an ulcerated stomach. Mum's daily diet was solely that of egg custards. If anything else passed her lips she would be violently sick. I became aware of how serious Mum's condition was when, during the winter of 1946, she became so weak she was confined to bed for months. When the Easter holiday period arrived, she was still very ill and spent more time in bed asleep than anywhere else, Mum's poor health had become so normal that I gave no second thoughts about going on a cycling holiday.

I packed a small two-man tent on my cycle and with 'Beechy' we cycled to Lancing, West Sussex and camped out for two nights. We had no space on our cycles to take blankets or provisions, the only extra piece of clothing I had with me was a woollen jumper. Beechy had done likewise. Before setting out we had not considered a precise place where we would sleep but we didn't worry we knew we would find a piece of open ground to pitch the tent.

We cycled to Shoreham, crossed the bridge over The River Adur on the A259 and travelled west along the coast until we reached Lancing. At South Lancing at the T Junction of Brighton Road and South Street A2025 we stopped at a cafe, opposite The Three

Horseshoes pub', for a cup of tea. Between the seashore and the main road was a deep grassed hollow: The hollow, I was told, was there to act as a defence to stop the road from flooding during periods of high tide: A few years later it was used as a local council refuse tip and over a period of a few more year was totally filled in up to road level. It now boasts a smartly manicured grassed area, part of which is a car park.

As the cafe was so near and so convenient for breakfast the following morning, we decided this was the spot to camp for the night.

During the first night, we were so cold we had little sleep. In addition to our normal clothing, we wore our rainproof cape and trousers.

Early next morning, being so close to the sea, we decided it would not be proper if we did not go for a swim. In just our trunks, we ran up the slope, onto the beach and continued running straight into the sea up to our knees and plunged in. The sea was very cold and we were very stupid. It was so cold it I was unable to breathe. We could not get out quick enough: My breathing was not restored to normal until I was out of the water and running up the pebbled beach.

Shivering with the cold and without a towel to dry ourselves, we ran along the gully until we were dry enough to get dressed. It had been a foolish act but at least we had our morning wash. In the cafe across the road, we each had two slices of toast and a cup of tea, which reduced our misery. We walked back to our tent, locked our cycles together inside our still erect tent and, by bus, took a ride into Brighton.

At midday we treated ourselves to a beans on toast banquet. Our luxury meal took some of the money we had set aside for our return bus fare, with no alternative we walked back to Lancing. It took hours. During the long walk we collected old newspapers from roadside waste bins to cover over us for extra warmth for the coming second night. The second night was colder than the first. In spite of the pile of newspapers that covered us we were still cold. I cannot understand why we just didn't give up, after the experience of the first night and return home.

We got up early again on the second morning, without considering getting near the sea to wash. At the time we knew the cafe would be open, we walked across the road for a cup of tea and to thaw out. We had enough money to buy one slice of toast to share between us. We had half a slice each and covered it with thick tomato sauce. We joyfully broke camp and started our way back home. Our joy was not from the experience but in anticipation of sleeping in a warm proper bed. The two very cold nights plus having had little sleep took their toll on our endurance. The return journey was hard going but it was still daylight when I got home.

As I cycled down the side path of the house to put my cycle in the garage, I was greeted with the news that Mum had been admitted to hospital.

That evening I joined Dad and Pat to visit Mum at Kings College hospital, Denmark Hill, Camberwell.

I didn't recognise Mum as she lay in bed. She was so thin and pale she looked dead. She had a plastic tube up her nose and another in her arm, both coming from suspended bottles behind the head of her bed:

Less than six hours earlier Mum had undergone an operation to remove a duodenal ulcer. She was still under the influence of the anaesthetic. She looked so fragile she was barely able to speak. When she saw me she gave me a weak smile and mumbled something that I could not understand.

"Mam asked if you had a good time Ron?" Dad said.

I held her hand and lied. I told her I had.

Mum went back to dreamland and we all said goodnight to her sleeping form. I walked out of the ward and as I turned my head and looked back I wondered if I should expect to see Mum alive again. I had never seen a person that looked so dead before other than my baby sister Beebie and she was dead.

As the following week passed, Mum made a remarkable recovery. Her condition improved so well she was soon discharged. For a month or two she convalesced at home while making daily visits to the hospital for penicillin injections. Not only did Mum recover fully from her operation, she also survived severe penicillin poisoning.

Miraculously Mum was soon looking in a better state of health than I remember her being for many years. She was able to go to work.

She got a job with her younger sister, Rose, working for The London County Council in a school for children with learning difficulties:

Mum and Rose, assisted in the kitchen with the cooking and serving. The school was on the same site as the school that Pat attended in Priory Grove but totally separated by a brick wall.

I could make the statement that from the age of thirteen I had free school bus tickets and commented no further. But, it is worth expanding on because upon reflection I find it amusing and it is just another small piece of my history of petty 'dodgy dealings' I involved myself with.

As I have illustrated I was always alert to make or save a penny or two or take advantage of any moneymaking situation be it legal or not.

Regarding my free travel: Officially because the distance, between home and school was within five miles I did not qualify to travel free. Mum gave me tickets that were originally designated for use by other children:

Most of the, approximately 40, children attending the special school that Mum and Rose worked in had to travel a greater distance each day than they would have had they attended a 'normal' school. For this reason, the children were allowed free bus tickets.

Because some children lived within walking distance, obviously, bus tickets were not issued. Nevertheless, tickets were supplied by the London County Council, at County Hall, relative to the number of children on the school register.

One of Mum's many tasks included distributing the tickets to the children that had to travel by bus to get to school. It appeared there was no monitoring or regulating of the quantity of tickets supplied. The tickets The London County Council, LCC, supplied were relative to the total amount of children on the register irrespective of absentees or local walkers. So there were always spare tickets.

Every Friday, after school, Mum brought her housecoat home to wash. She would place the contents of her pockets on the mantelshelf. One Friday with her packet of 'Players Weights' cigarettes and a box of matches, there were a small bundle of tickets which I had not seen before. The tickets in front of me were, of course, the undistributed ones.

As Mum placed the tickets on the mantelshelf, above the fire, I asked her what the unusual looking tickets were used for.

She told me the tickets were only for use on buses and why she had them in her possession, she warned me, they were not for me and I must not use them. It was a challenge for me to overcome.

The weekend passed and on the following Monday morning, I noticed the cigarettes and matches had been removed from the shelf but the tickets remained.

As I left the house for school, I took a couple of the tickets and put them it in my satchel. On reflection, maybe I didn't give Mum the same credit as I would have given Dad in the shady deals department. It is quite possible Mum saw the potential the free tickets had and was one thought ahead of me. It was a way to save her giving me bus fare money. If that was her plan, she left me to work the details out for myself.

It was my intention to use the ticket on the journey to school but I was unable to muster enough courage.

Through the day, during school hours, my thoughts were more with rehearsing how I was going to deliver the ticket to the conductor than listening to the lessons. I could not stop myself from imagining many different scenarios that could take place and how it could go wrong but I made up my mind to be bold and chance using a ticket for the homeward journey.

I decided to present the ticket in a casual manner hoping I would not have to answer any questions other than the simple ones I had prepared myself for. When the school period came to an end I walked to the bus stop at the junction of Kennington Lane and Black Prince Road and anxiously waited for my bus to arrive. While I waited, my mind working overtime, I had a silent argument with an imaginary bus conductor.

When my bus came along and stopped, I got on quickly and ran up to the top deck, chose an empty seat nearest to the stair opening and waited for the conductor to arrive.

I sat and nervously listening to the conductor's footsteps. I then began to get misgivings. While I was considering postponing my fraudulent act, I was startled to suddenly hear:

"Your fare please".

The 'moment of truth' (truth being related to honesty, suggests that I have chosen the wrong expression but it fits the bill,) had arrived. The conductor was standing beside me holding out his hand. I boldly offered my ticket. While I held the ticket up for his acceptance, I placed a book on my lap and pretended to read. I did not have the courage to look him in the eye. The conductor took the ticket from my fingers, without a word passing between us. I felt myself shrink during, what felt, the long time he took to put the ticket in his punch machine buttoned to his jacket and produced the traditional 'ping'. The conductor, without giving me a hint that he was suspicious, returned my ticket with a small hole in it to indicate the bus stop that I had to get off.

My tight knot of fear dissolved into joyful rapture. I was pleased I was alone for I could not contain my pleasure transforming my face with a silly smile.

When I returned home, my first priority was to 'pocket' the remaining tickets that Mum had left on the mantle shelf.

My confidence, to use the tickets, grew daily and by the end of the first week it was solid and I was using them as though they were a legitimate allowance and I had used them for years.

Two weeks elapsed before my supply of bus tickets were exhausted. I realised Mum must have forgotten about the supply she had left on the shelf for not once did she question me of their whereabouts. If I wanted to continue with my little 'scam', I had a dilemma

How could I approach the subject to encourage Mum to give me more tickets?

During the next weekend I decided to 'come clean' and tell Mum that I had been using the free tickets without incurring a problem. I hoped I could convince Mum to allow me to use another lot. I was surprised, to say the least, that she offered no resistance to my request.

The following Monday evening, with a warning to be careful, Mum gave me a fresh bundle of tickets. Mum kept me supplied with the bus tickets until I left school.

It did not take me very long to wonder if Mum had not deliberately planted the first batch of tickets on the shelf to see if I would take the bait.

As a result of my now, slightly more, serious attitude towards schoolwork and a reduction in my penny activities, I began to develop acute symptoms of 'pocket money deficiency'.

My lack of buying and selling and making money at school, however, was soon compensated by my realisation of all the moneyboxes on the underground, like unattended banks needed attention.

They were, of course, the automatic ticket machines sited on every station. One little problem did exist. I had to overcome their design. They were meant to work one way only, to take money.

My new plan was born when one Saturday I went with Dad to the surplus store to buy materials for his sidecar manufacturing. While making the purchase, in addition to buying a large quantity nails, screws, nuts and bolts Dad bought washers. Dad's description of the size washer he needed was that of "about the size of half a crown".

We brought our shopping home and distributed them in their appropriate bins in the garage.

The large washers had a small hole in the centre, as all washers would have, but as luck would have it, they were not only about the size but exactly the same circumference as a half-crown:

A half crown, extinct since the introduction of decimal currency, would be the value of only twelve and a half new pence today. Not the sort of value one would consider breaking the law for. But when I left school to start work I only received £1.25 shillings a week in wages. To get some idea of the value in present day terms we have to think in percentages. Each washer, if they could become half crowns, would be worth one tenth of my gross weekly wage.

My plan was to use a washer in the half crown slot of ticket machine. My thoughts had progressed beyond getting free tickets. I had a preference for free money.

At my first attempt the plan did not work. The disc went through the slot into the machine but was not accepted and the washer was returned via the reject cup.

During the coming weeks while I was still in the process of trying to perfect my latest piece of unlawful activity, John, now eighteen years old and my mentor in crime came home on a weekend pass from RAF Northolt. When we were alone, I commenced to tell him of the difficulty I had encountered trying to perpetrate my intended fraud. Before I could finish telling him the details of my plan, he interrupted me and told me that the blanks would have to be, not only, exactly the same circumference and gauge, but most important, the disc would have to be milled around the edge.

He rejected my idea because of the time it would take. To cut out a piece of metal to the correct size and make each single lines around the edge would require a cutting tool with micrometer settings. Even if such a tool could be obtained it would be too expensive to buy and take far too long to make each one. He had not given me a chance to complete what I was about to tell him.

Had John have heard me out, I would have told him that I had the correct circumference ready made. All I had to do was to get over the task of finding a quick method of the milling. Later, still giving the task some thought I saw, in my mind's eye, the solution. I overcome the obstacle before it became a problem: I also discovered, a few months later, that even thinner round pieces of metal would still be accepted by the ticket vending machine. It was the milling that was critical.

In Dad's garage, I placed my first trial washer in the bench vice. I then ran a coarse file across the edge and with one stroke it looked like something I was trying to achieve, so I continued. I unclamped the jaws of the vice, moved the washer around a little more, I tightened the vice again and repeated the process until I had completely covered the rim to meet the point where I had started.

I was satisfied with the result but it was time consuming and at this point, I did consider that John had, most probably, been correct in his judgment. Not until I had taken the round piece of aluminium completely out of the vice did I notice the marks the clamping edge of the vice had made. A series of straight lines were left on the washer where it had been gripped in the vice and had left almost identical marks that I made on the rim with the file.

My second attempt was more than twice as fast: By placing the disc in the vice around the rim, instead of flat, I was now able to achieve the same result without using the file. I was also able to knurl two opposite sides with each single action. But the washer still only looked like a washer. I would not be able to spend it in a shop, unless I met a counter hand that happened to be blind and unable to feel the hole in the middle.

I lost no time to test my homemade coin. I walked the fifty yards from the garage, in the back garden, to Stockwell Underground Station. Without hesitation, I slipped my pseudo half crown piece into the slot and pressed the button for the cheapest ticket: It must have been for a tu'penny, 1p, ticket. There would have been no reason for me to have selected anything but the cheapest.

To ensure I was still unobserved, I casually glanced over my shoulder as the soft alloy disc slipped into the slot:

Had I have given any thought of the consequences of getting caught maybe, I would not have had the courage to perform the swindle. But I had reached the point of no return. I could not reverse the law of gravity. As the washer dropped and tinkled down into the bowels of the machine, I wondered, had it made a different sound?

I was certain it sounded nosier than normal. Maybe it did, maybe it did not but the machine supplied the ticket and the change rattled out into the returned coins cup.

Without bothering to count my 'winnings', I scooped the money into my hand and took the ticket. I tried to act like a normal passenger that had just bought a ticket but in reality I was controlling an urgent need to laugh. As a precaution against the chance of having been observed, I confidently walked passed the ticket office alighted the escalator down to the trains.

While I was waiting on the platform, I gave a little more thought as to what my next move would be. I had a ticket that was stamped in bold print STOCKWELL the station at which I should commence my journey.

The ticket allowed me to travel one or two stops either North or Southbound. I reasoned it would be unlikely that the ticket collector would examine my ticket but nevertheless, if I were challenged I would look a little foolish trying to explain why I was getting out at the same station as I had come in. At worst, it could have appeared I had travelled a return journey with a single ticket.

I was sure I had not been seen, so I thought it reasonable not to continue an unnecessary act of deception. I decided I did not want to spend more time by travelling on a train to somewhere I didn't need to go. I had to use a different ticket.

When the next train stopped at the platform, I joined the throng that alighted and walked with the flow of people heading towards the exit. I rode up the escalator to street level and offered, not the ticket I had just bought but, one of my second hand tickets from my collection.

I was thrilled at my cunning and the simplicity of the best money making scheme I had yet devised. It was so easy. I chose to overlook that I had committed a crime.

At the cost of a few minutes labour in the garage, producing one disc, I was rewarded with enough cash to buy two tickets for seats in a cinema. Although I wanted to boast to uncle John and close friends of my colossal achievement, I contained my euphoria and kept it a secret, for fear my simple little earner would be exploited by others. I did not want to kill my 'Golden Goose'.

During my last full year at school, the thrill of riding free on the underground railway just for the sake of it diminished. A new pastime captured my attention.

When the new season started, I started going to watch professional football matches every Saturday afternoon with Benny. We alternated between watching Chelsea play at Stamford Bridge and Fulham at Craven Cottage. We only travelled to the home ground matches. The Saturdays that Chelsea played at home coincided with Fulham playing away and vice versa. The star of Chelsea was Tommy Lawton. Ronnie Rooke was the star at Fulham:

Football league fixtures were mainly played on Saturday afternoon. The Football Association controlling league football, had not yet approved fixtures to be played on Sunday, nor had floodlights yet been used.

Motorcycle speedway became very popular for a few years immediately after the war. My favourite team, only because it was the most convenient to get to, was Wimbledon where speedway and greyhound racing events took place once a week after normal working hours .

A large following of motorcycle speedway or cinder racing was of teenagers too young to hold a motorcycle-driving license. These young enthusiastic motorcycle racing followers emulated their racing heroes by replacing a motorcycle with a pedal cycle and raced around home made circuits. Cleared bombed sites in every city in the country had made plenty of space available.

The open spaces were ideal to mark up racing circuits without cost. Each race meeting attracted a large crowd of non-paying spectators.

In the late 1940's dirt track cycle racing craze 'took off' in a big way. Teams, divisions and leagues were organised. Meetings were advertised in advance. Teams had their own 'home ground' and racing colours. In fact, the motorcycle version was aped wherever possible:

To allow the cycle rider to sit lower than a conventional pedal cycle and imitate a speedway frame the cycle frame had to be made lower: The crossbar, the two back saddle stays and the saddle to the bottom bracket tube were cut to allow the saddle to be lowered. The crossbar was then curved, to meet the new lowered height, about eight inches from the saddle tube, likewise the rear stays and then welded.

In the early 1950's, as the post war housing rebuilding programme gathered momentum the open spaces became scarcer. The sport had been destined for a short life but the young riders discarded their adapted cycles and took to the roads on motor scooters. The dying of one pastime gave birth to another. The riders of the new scooter and motorcycle era were going to be called 'Mods' or 'Rockers'. But this is still 1946 and pedal cycle speedway had 'taken off'.

Dirt track cycle racing never captured my spare time; I liked conventional cycling on the road.

My cycling got me to places where I wanted to go, with pedal power speedway the rider went around in circles and only finished where he had started.

Cycle speedway became so popular one cycle manufacturer, Phillips, built and retailed a frame to emulate that made by the amateur enthusiast. The factory made cycle had only a limited success.

I chose Sunday mornings to prepare a dozen or so washers to cash them in over a period of a couple of weeks on a once-a-week journey of the network. There were times it became tiresome, like going to work. I would much rather have spent the time cycling.

My shameful act of theft gave me pocket money that replaced my previous financial school activities.

I realised when the ticket machine was emptied sooner or later my activity would attract attention from the railway police. To make detection less easy I was cautious enough to cease using my local, Stockwell station.

I would normally travel on the Northern Line and get off at Bank Underground Station, where the City, Central and District Lines converged.

On one occasion and only once, with a ticket from my second hand collection, I travelled half the entire length of the Central line. I got on the Eastbound train at Bank station to the terminus at Ealing Broadway before commencing my fraud. When I reached the end of the line, I went up to street level, surrendered my high value but secondhand ticket and walked out of the station. I then walked into a newsagent adjoining the station and bought a newspaper. I walked back into the station and used my first aluminium dummy half crown of the day. I acquired the cheapest ticket that would take me to the next homeward bound station. I got on the train and got off at the next stop, West Acton. I surrendered my ticket, went out of the station and came back in again and with another one of my prepared washers I bought another ticket to take me to the next station, North Acton. I was constantly alert that I was not being observed and I repeated this action until I had emptied my pocket of washers and substituted them for real money. It was, of course, time consuming but the reward was much greater than an adult would expect to earn for a weekly wage in full time employment.

I was only thirteen years old at this time and not for the first time I must have had more pocket money than my father.

Because my counterfeiting was so easy it became regular and my only source of income. But even with the easy and high profitability of my crime I became discontented with my self-imposed discipline. It was the routine of travelling to too many different stations that I found tiresome. For fear of detection, however, I never allowed myself to become too confident. Later to reduce the time factor, I modified my method of 'coin collecting'. I began to carry a prepared washer with me at all times in the lining of my jacket. A little riskier no doubt but I reasoned if I wasn't 'caught in the act' there was no chance of me ever being questioned or searched by anyone with authority. With a prepared washer always on my person I could spend it in an underground machine anytime during my normal travelling whenever the opportunity presented itself. Although the cost for me to travel was not only free but also profitable, I still used my bicycle a great deal. Would I be believed if I said money isn't everything?

Benny and I were still using the cycles we had recovered from the garden shed while the war was on. We became very deft in stripping all the parts down to the frame. We painted them a different colour regularly, sometimes as often as once a month. All of the paint that we used was also from our wartime collection, stolen from unattended sheds.

Bottles of ink and blotting paper were standard and obvious equipment in all schools and offices. Then came along a simple invention to eventually change the scene.

1946 was the year that pens with solid ink and no nibs first appeared on the market. The first ballpoint pen was named after its Hungarian inventor, Ladislas Biro: The nibless pen was a wonderful invention. It was first used in the UK by the Royal Air Force and the Royal Navy and banned from being used in schools by the education authority. It was feared it would spoil handwriting skills. Ballpoint pens were still not allowed in my school when I left to start work in 1947.

Biro is one of only a few Hungarian words to be used in the English language. Goulash needs no explaining. The only other word 'coach' comes from Kocs, the village in Hungary where horse drawn coach-like vehicles were first made.

Another 'brainwave' came from Louis Reard, an engineer turned fashion designer, He demonstrated his first 'Bikini beachwear. He named it after the atomic bomb test site at Bikini Atoll in the Pacific Ocean. He introduced it as being highly explosive.

The captured Nazis on trial, accused of war crimes, at Nuremberg in Germany lasted through to 1946. Twelve of the twenty-two accused were found guilty and sentenced to death. Three were acquitted. The remainder were given long prison sentences. The trial was known as The Nuremburg War Crimes Trials:

William Joyce broadcasted propaganda from Germany during the war was charged with treason against Great Britain. Joyce's broadcasts were listened to in the United Kingdom with humour and not taken seriously as intended. He was nicknamed 'Lord Haw Haw' by the British press. During his trial he claimed in his defence to be an American, which would have made the charge of treason against Great Britain technically incorrect, but it was found he had held a British passport. He was found guilty and hung in Britain on 3rd January 1946.

Although Rudolph Hess spent nearly all of the war years under guard in England, he was given a life sentence, which he served, in Spandau Prison. Spandau Prison was in the British Zone of divided Berlin. The occupation forces shared a twenty-four hour guard on the prison's main gate. During the later stages of his life, because of his ill health, there were many protests supporting his release but the Russians always resisted the pressure.

Through the war years, the world's first television service had been suspended. The BBC resumed television transmission in 1946 and introduced a £2 licence fee. There was still only one station, which was in black and white only. The cost of a television set was very expensive, unreliable and, like pre-war days, very few people owned one. Our house, like the majority, still only had a radio.

For me, television could have been nonexistent for we had no contact with it. I believe when programmes first resumed it did not commence until about seven o'clock in the evening and closed down about ten o'clock at night. The total week's viewing came to 25 hours. The small nine-inch screens were housed in very large veneered cabinets. The quality was such that the picture could only be seen while the room was in darkness.

One afternoon, walking away from Brixton market, after Mum and Dad had completed shopping for vegetables, Dad stopped to look in a window of an Electrical store in Atlantic Road Brixton.

Next to the electrical shop was a small grocery and provisions store and forerunner of self service, regularly boasted special offers. The store had an enter door and an exit door and designed so as the customer would have to pass all of the shelves before reaching the till. This method of selling was criticised for placing all of their special offers nearest to the till and exit.

It was suggested, correctly, customers would buy more than they came into the shop for.

The shop was called The **TE**a **S**upply **CO**mpany from which the name TESCO comes, now the country's largest food supermarket chain.

In the electrical shop there were a number of low priced radios and record players on display. One radiogram in particular attracted Dad's attention, without commenting, he went into the shop to make an enquiry about easy payment terms. He came out, spoke to Mum and walked back in again to put a deposit on it. The salesman in the shop had promised him it would be delivered within two weeks after his financial reliability had been investigated.

Two weeks elapsed but Dad received no contact from the shop regarding delivery. He returned to the shop to complain but the salesman gave him some poor excuse why the radiogram had not arrived. Dad went into the shop angry and came out feeling no better.

Week after week Dad returned to the shop and engaged in angry words with the salesman. Eventually the radiogram *was* delivered and the portable box 'windup' record player was relegated to the junk cupboard under the stairs.

To initiate the new radiogram Dad bought a 'Brunswick' recording of Bing Crosby crooning his way through 'Golden Earrings'. On the 'B' side was another recording of Bing singing 'Mandy is Two'. I believe the 'B' side was more popular with Mum and Dad for it reminded them of my dead baby sister Bebe.

I have no doubt, having the luxury of an electric driven record turntable in the house, urged me to buy some recordings of my own.

'East Street', a small side street off the Walworth Road, is a market for licensed stallholders only. Stalls were pitched in designated plots along each side of East Street and allocated by the local council.

There was no access for wheeled traffic on market days. The Sunday market was so popular the tightly packed shoppers could only shuffle along, shoulder to shoulder, at a slow pace.

Bicycles, baby's pushchairs and prams were frowned upon by most shoppers and frequent arguments erupted after a wheel of a pram or a bicycle pedal was accidentally pushed over someone's foot or the skin from an ankle or lower calf or shin was removed by a pedal or a wingnut.

The costermongers sold mainly fresh fruit and vegetables but other goods ranging from confectionery, ice creams, bread and cakes were also sold. A number of stalls sold clothing.

In neighbouring side streets collectively known as 'Club Row' people with a full time jobs during weekdays set themselves up on Sundays in any space that was available along the pedestrian walkways selling in most cases junk.

Cleared sites of wartime-bombed houses were set aside for larger items such as second-hand cars, motorcycles, bicycles and large pieces of machinery. Smaller articles including clothing, motorcycle spare parts, tools and household items were in another area.

Dad was not a regular visitor to the Sunday market but when he did go, he travelled by motorcycle. When Pat and I accompanied him Pat sat in the sidecar and I sat on the pillion seat. Mum usually stayed at home to prepare the Sunday midday dinner.

The reason for Dad's visits was to rummage through the heaps of motor spare parts and other oddities that were offered for sale.

A few vendors used a blanket spread on the pavement to

denote their boundary. Most other sellers were not that particular, they just placed their piles of junk on the pavement and waited for anyone to show an interest.

During one of my market visits, I bought the first of many gramophone recordings from a second-hand stall. I was attracted to the recording not because I knew the song but because I liked the humorous title; 'I hate you 'cos your feet's too big' by Fats Waller.

The first time I played the record I was immediately 'hooked' to this style of jazz. I played it with regularity and learnt the lyrics word for word. It was the first of what became a large record library.

There were many Sunday mornings, when Dad could not spare the time, I went to the market with Benny on our bicycles. Benny also caught 'the bug' of record collecting.

During the year, I built a collection of pre-war gramophone records that I was proud of. Among a wide selection of blues, boogie boogie and big band swing, my favoured type of music was Dixieland jazz.

Most of the records were by the star musicians of the 1920's and 1930's: Cab Calloway, Nat Gonella, Joe Daniels, Louis Armstrong, Roy Fox, Harry Roy, to name a few but many others were by lesser known bands and vocalists.

On one visit to the market I bought an ex Salvation Army base drum. I can't remember the price, but it must have been cheap for me to have made the purchase. Not until I commenced the walk to my padlocked bicycle did I begin to wonder how I was to get it home. I had no options, the drum had to go on my back. Without consideration as to what I looked like, I tied a piece of string to each side of one of the many skin adjusters at the top and bottom of the drum and made a loop for each of my arms to go through. I put it on like putting on an overcoat, cautiously straddled my bicycle and slowly peddled home.

Another Sunday visit to the market, a few weeks later, after making a regular purchase of one or two secondhand gramophone records, I caught sight of a small kettledrum and copying Dad's style of haggling, I made the purchase.

On each subsequent visit I kept a sharp look out for any piece of percussion instrument that may be on sale. I purchased anything that could be useful.

Within a couple of months I had a complete drum kit. My budget collection of noise making instruments, albeit scaled down, cost me pennies. It consisted of a kettledrum with a clamp and stand. An ex boys brigade hip marching drum, which I adapted to be used with snare and brushes. Accompanying the base drum a padded pedal, a pair of cymbals on a stand with foot control and a tambourine with side jingles. I bought a new snare to attach over the tambourine and a pair of wire brushes. I made my own drumsticks and brackets, to hold it all together as one unit to complete the kit. On some of our musical evenings I accompanied Dad with ukulele on my midget drum set with Mum and with Pat joining in the vocal accompaniment, we would sit around the fire and have a 'sing song'.

During the school summer holiday of 1946, I frequently played with my two mates along the footpath of the River Thames. We often cycled to Kingston upon Thames by the main road and then on to Hampton Wick via the riverside footpath.

One of our favoured swimming areas was the river at Walton further along the river passed Hampton Court.

On one occasion, while we were swimming at Walton, I accidentally got out of my depth. I am sure I came very near to drowning. I swallowed a lot of water and it was only the result of flapping my arms and kicking my legs in panic that propelled me into shallower water that I survived. On another weekend, Dad took Mum and Pat to Walton on Thames by his motorcycle and sidecar while Benny and I set off earlier on our bicycles. We met later at a prearranged grassed parking area along the riverside. After we all had finished our simple picnic lunch, Benny and I went of to have a swim in our favoured nearby creek. We soon got bored with splashing around and while still wearing our swimming trunks we decided to construct a raft from the long thick reeds that were growing along the riverbank. We collected, what we believed to be, a sufficient amount of cane and leaves but greatly underestimated the amount of reeds that was needed for buoyancy to hold our combined weight. After a couple of hours of continually adding and testing to ensure our primitive transport would hold us above the waterline, we bound the reeds together, sat astride our craft and pushed ourselves out from the safety of the creek into the main flow of the river.

It really was a very stupid thing to do but we were well qualified, we *were* very stupid. We paddled ourselves not only into deep water in the middle of the river but we were in the same lane that was used by large pleasure boats. Sure enough, as we should have expected, within a little time, from a bend in the river, a large river steamer came into view.

The person in the wheelhouse of the approaching steamer attracted our attention by giving a loud blast on its horn. The sudden noise also alerted the people relaxing by the river edge. We paddled furiously to alter our collision course but the speed the boat was travelling reduced the distance between us at an alarming rate. Our joyful excitement was replaced by serious fear. I was not so afraid of being tossed into the water and I am sure Benny shared my thoughts but more concerned of the possibility of being struck by the boat or the propeller blades.

I was aware of the passengers looking over the safety railing on the boat, shouting instructions and willing our escape. Having abandoned their picnics, people came running towards the riverbank possibly preparing to make a rescue attempt. It all happened in a few minutes. As the large boat came alongside, we could see, from our retreating area, the steep white side of the boat. I am sure I could have reached out and touched it. As the distance between us increased our fear and total concentration was replaced by laughter. It appeared to us that we were no longer in danger but for only a few seconds, our excitement was refuelled by the high waves as we were suddenly caught by the

346

boat's wake.

The large waves pushed us up and down but we hung on tightly until we were dashed upon the riverbank. As my feet touched ground, I found I could hardly stand. My spent energy combined with fear had sapped my strength. I noticed Mum and Dad were also in the crowd of relieved onlookers.

As 1946 progressed, I saw less of Benny but accompanied Beechy on our bicycles, and frequented the banks of the River Thames, between Kingston and Hampton Court,

It was during one of my now less frequent outings with Benny along the river, that I later realised, I had my first encounter with a man that was sexually interested in young boys:

Benny and I were engaged in a bit of fishing and throwing stones into the water when a man approached. He sat down on riverbank, some distance away but near enough to be within talking distance. He wasted no time to make conversation about fishing. Very soon he was sitting next to us but his talking point shifted to his house that, he told us, was near by. He then invited us back to his house to have lemonade and cakes. Normally, at any given time during daylight hours, an occasional casual walker would not be far away, with or without a dog, walking the riverbank. This day was no exception.

Only a short time had passed before we made any decision, when another man walking along the path appeared. When, he was at the nearest point to us and still on the path, he stopped and called out to our new acquaintance sitting by our side. "Clear off, you dirty bastard, or I shall call the police".

The man stood up and, without a word of protest, briskly walked away. We were both puzzled and could not understand why the second man was so verbally aggressive to our new companion and why they had both acted as they had. As the first man retreated, the second man walked nearer to us and told us to be careful of talking to strange men. He informed us there were some men that preferred to be with boys than with ladies.

The man he had shouted at, he told us, was one of *those* men. He was no more specific and did not go into any details about sexual perversion in anyway.

Sex education was beginning to be taught at some schools but only for fourteen year olds. Sex education for children was a very controversial subject and I was thirteen so I was still one year away from any adult knowledge of that nature. I certainly had not been told about sexual perversions. I was not aware of the word or of the act of homosexuality or of course, paedophilia and did not understand what he was telling us.

I am sure that a boy aged thirteen in the 1990's would have been aware, but this was in the 1940's. We were none the wiser what the man was talking about after he had left us.

On another occasion and one of a more pleasant nature while in the same area, Beechy and I were packing up our fishing gear when a lady with a young boy sat on the bank not far from us. The boy, about five or six years old, immediately took his shoes and socks off and ran down the bank and splashed into the water. He wadded in but before the water had covered his knees, he slipped, fell forward and submerged himself with only his head showing above the water. In shock, he remained stretched out in the water but raised enough effort to cry out.

Because only the boy's head could be seen out of the water it appeared, from the riverbank he had fallen into a deep hole. The woman cried out in alarm that the boy was drowning and shouted to me, or anyone, to save him. I quickly rolled my trousers up to my knees and barefooted I ran into the water, grabbed the boy's hand and simply walked with him back to the bank.

Not by any stretch of the imagination could I pretend either of us, the rescued or the rescuer, were in danger but as I walked back to the riverbank, I trod on something sharp in the water. The offending object was an L shaped piece of glass from the bottom end of a broken bottle. As I put my weight on the bottom part the top end cut downwards and across the top of the toe next to my big toe. I thought it must have been a deep cut because a cut is not normally painful. In this case I could feel the pain where the glass had cut between a knuckle joint.

The distressed woman did not witness my gallant rescue. She had held her hand across her face not daring to look. Still believing the boy was about to drown. She was hysterical and did not recover her composure until I returned the boy to her side. She cuddled the boy and while doing so she noticed blood was now covering a large area of my right foot:

Due to the fact that my feet were still wet, the blood from the cut blended with the water and spread over the rest of my toes and foot. The cut appeared to be more serious than it was and her attention was instantly transferred from the boy to me. She quickly got a handkerchief from her handbag and as she dabbed and fussed, trying to arrest the bleeding, she said I was very brave and she would always remember me for my courageous deed in saving her son from drowning.

Had she been a little more observant, she would have noticed my clothing was still dry and therefore would have deduced I did not have to get into deep water for the rescue. For my part, had I not been concerned about losing one of my toes, due to the excessive loss of blood, -a whole toe full! - The episode would have been funny. It did not stop me later, however, from boastfully lying that I had saved a life and 'embroidering' the event, as the boy's mother believed she had seen it.

I still had the perfumed handkerchief wrapped around my toe while I cycled back home. With my right foot shoeless and covered with only the once white linen handkerchief, the bleeding could easily be seen seeping through the improvised bandage.

We had used the same route many times and knew the area well. As we cycled homeward and passed Wimbledon Chase Railway Station, I remembered there was a small cottage hospital a little further on.

The hospital was one of the many voluntary run hospitals up and down the country that relied solely upon donations to keep it viable. I decided to stop there to get further attention. I cycled up to the front door and with my friend I dramatically limped into the reception area. A nurse escorted me to a cubicle and attended to me immediately. After I had been asked my name and address I was invited to state what had happened. I told the nurse the sensational fictitious version.

As my toe and foot was being cleaned, I realised that I had more than one cut. I also had another large cut on the pad of my big toe. After the toe had been dressed I was given, an anti-tetanus injection in my bottom. There was no charge for my first aid attention.

I assisted Dad to make good progress with the Kayak and satisfactorily completed the timber framework. When the motorcycle repair business started to pick-up again, Dad made two rope loops from the garage roof and stored the half finished boat until the next opportune moment to continue the build.

One of Dad's regular customers, the Welsh soldier, Taffy, was a sergeant instructor in The Physical Training Corps.

One day, while Dad was working on Taffy's motorcycle, he arrived at the garage to enquire if Dad had found the cause of his concern. After a brief description of Dad's findings, their conversation drifted to everyday events.

As Taffy was a Physical Training Instructor, PTI, they began to talk about health and fitness. Dad mentioned his concern, about my intermittent stomach pains and although I had a medical examination no explanation for cause or cure had been given. My frail anaemic looking condition was evidence of Dad's concern. "Next time I call I'll bring some weight lifting equipment with me. Ron can use them. That will put him into shape" Taffy promised.

While Dad continued working I heard Taffy say: "Other than being under developed, there may be nothing wrong with him. Plenty of young lads, older than Ron, come into the army looking the same. We should get him started on some weight lifting exercises that will build him up".

A month or two elapsed before Taffy arrived at the house again and true to his word he delivered a complete weight lifting set comprised of: a bar with two end and two inner clamps, two weights at five pounds, ten, fifteen and twenty pounds and two at fifty pounds each and a typed schedule of a personalised training programme.

He showed me how to lift the weights correctly and advised Dad that he should enrol me with one of the many body building postal courses that were often advertised in the national press and magazines.

I followed his training instructions and his advise to do repetitive work with the smaller weights rather than trying to lift the heaviest weight. I also made a point of looking out for any advertisement that could increase the size of my skinny body.

One advertisement caught my attention: 'You too can have a body like mine in seven days' just by spending one half hour every day', it claimed. A picture of a man with tremendously large muscles accompanied the slogan. The advertisement was in a magazine appropriately called Superman Comics.

The suggested seven days was deliberately misleading it was an advertisers gimmick. One week did not mean from one Sunday to the following Saturday. What it actually meant was if one worked out for half an hour every day and then calculated how many half hours there were in seven days it would take three hundred and thirty six days. The advertisement would have been less deceiving but also understandably less appealing if it had read one year.

I answered the advertisement and sent the completed application form to 'Boris Dmitre, Bodybuilder' and anxiously awaited a response from him from his gymnasium at Leigh-on-sea, Southend. A week elapsed until I received a reply. When I opened the envelope I was, at first, disappointed to read the cost. I was not expecting the course to be so expensive but as the fee could be paid monthly, I decided the London

351

Underground ticket machines could afford it.

Included with a small booklet, explaining the cost of the course was an application form for me to complete. I was requested to write down my age, the nature of my employment, a history of any physical disabilities, illnesses and diseases.

I was able to answer about half of the questions in the boxes to show the ailments I had recovered from. With Mum's guidance I answered the remainder, all but one.

I have had Measles, Mumps, Chicken pox, Malnutrition, Appendicitis and a number of other diseases that had either escaped my memory or I was not aware of: I had not had Diphtheria nor Tuberculosis:

These two diseases were then high on the list of common ailments and illnesses in the world, which caused many premature deaths.

I also had to complete the measurements of my neck, biceps, triceps, wrist, chest, waist, hips, thighs, calf and ankle measurements. I came back to the question I had missed.

'Do you have any bad habits'? The remaining question asked.

What a daft thing to ask. I did not understand the relevance. I asked my mother how I should I answer it. "Ask your father" Mum said.

"Dad, do you know what this question means?"

Dad took a look. "What do you think it means?"

"I don't know. It means a lot of different things I said. Mum tells me I have a bad habit of always leaving doors open. My teacher tells me it is a bad habit being regularly late for lessons. But they have nothing to do with body building, do they?"

Dad answered in the best way he knew. "It's asking if you go to sleep as soon as you get into bed, or do you stay awake reading or doing something else?

Innocently, I tried to encourage Dad to expand on the 'something else' but without success.

"If you can't think of anything just put no " Dad said "it will make no difference to your exercises".

"That's exactly what I thought"

After I posted the completed form with my first monthly instalment, I waited another week for the reply. The long awaited envelope arrived one morning while I was eating my breakfast; it was too large to go through our letterbox. Mum answered the door to the postman's knock and returned with my parcel and placed on the table in front of me. She waited while I opened it to see what I had received. I pulled out the contents. In front of me was a disappointing simple piece of equipment, which comprised of a one-inch wide band of white canvas, about the thickness of tent material with an adjustable buckle, like that on a shoe. The other end had a dog collar clip. There was also a book of exercises and a second smaller book telling me how to get the best out of the equipment:

My bodybuilding course became a subject of conversation eight or nine months later when I had started work. One of the motorcycle salesmen told me that the question referred to masturbation.

One of the lads at work of my own age told me: "It means do you give yourself a wank. You should have put 'Yes' 'cause everyone has a wank"

After being told the meaning behind the question I realised I should have put yes. I would not have wanted to have had admit to the truth, so I believe my answer would have remained the same. It was still, at this time, regarded by society that masturbating was an activity that was responsible for a lot of the ills in the shaping of ones character. I believe this view is driven more by religious and spiritual bias than scientific fact.

It was, for instance, believed that it was the cause of bad eyesight, it stunted growth and made one slothful etc.

One evening during the summer, Ted Bell, Dad's ex-wartime lorry driving colleague, arrived at the house. He greeted me with "hello".

I instantly knew him as the man that Dad had given my dog to when our house in Studley Road was bombed. He had come to ask Dad to give his newly acquired car, a fifteen-year old Austin, a service.

After 'Ding Dong' had left, I overheard Dad tell Mum that he would still have the car over the coming weekend and to ask Gran' and Grandad if they would like to join us, weather permitting, in a drive out to the countryside.

During the next few days Dad spent some time working on, in and under the car and completed the service by the following Saturday.

It had been a pleasant sunny morning on the Sunday of our outing so we had an early midday meal scheduled around the feeding times of Grandad's rabbits, birds and chickens, Mum also prepared a simple picnic for the afternoon's countryside tour which would have consisted of no more than a few sandwiches and a flask of tea.

John, having come home on an unexpected weekend pass from RAF Northolt, joined us. While we all sat in the car waiting to go, with engine running, Dad had his sleeves rolled up, head under the bonnet, making a last minute adjustment to get a ' nice tick over'.

Pat and I sat squeezed in the back with Gran, Grandad and John. Dad, satisfied with the result of his 'tinkering', closed the bonnet over the engine, wiped his hands, got in the car and drove us off. We headed south along the Clapham Road. The large Austin was black and a very grand limousine:

Just after the war, it would have been very unusual to have seen a new car, more unusual to see a new car in any other colour than black. Although the result of peacetime production of new cars was now reaching the showrooms, the majority was produced for the export market only but they were all pre-war designs. The new post war models would not appear in the car show rooms until 1947.

Inside this ' Big Austin Ten' it had red leather upholstery, pull down blinds trimmed with lace on the back and rear side windows. There was also a sliding glass partition between the driver in the front and rear seats. Inset in the back of each of the front seats was a small wood veneered panel. Dad had reminded me, on more than one occasion, before we set out, not to interfere with any of the fittings as the owner had spent a lot of money getting the car restored. I sat in one of the back seats because Dad could not see me from his driving position; I defied his instruction not to tamper with anything. I could not resist pulling out one of the panels in the back of the seat in front of me. I discovered a tray that when unfolded became a table. Secured by clips, inside the backrest of the seat were half a dozen wine glasses and drink decanters.

After we had spent a couple of hours driving around Surrey, Dad pulled over onto a wide grassy verge away from the main road and parked. After our picnic we lazed around and Dad took some photographs. It was not long, however, before Grandad got fidgety and reminded Dad that his birds would soon need feeding. For Grandad to have wasted his time by relaxing was rare. His timetable dictated that any spare time was grooming time.

His prize birds and rabbits were always, or so it appeared, being prepared for a private sale or the next exhibition. I do not recall him, other than going to work, ever spending time that was not related to his hobby. On our return home, Dad mentioned to Mum that the car was running perfect. He was very satisfied that the service and adjustments he had given the car had improved its performance.

Ding Dong came to our house again during the following week to collect his car. Before his departure he invited us to visit him and his wife at his home along the Kingston by-pass. We visited them the following weekend. We travelled in our smoky old 'clapped out' Triumph. His house, being on a main road, was found by Dad without difficulty: It was a nice semi detached house with an integral garage. The low, waist high, wrought iron gates had been left open to allow Dad to drive our old Triumph straight up in front of the garage door. We got out of the car and were greeted by Ding Dong before we had shut the car doors.

The moment I entered the house I was impressed. I compared the house against our house. They had beautiful carpets, as opposed to our pieces of broken lino' with nails surrounding the breaks to stop anyone tripping and making it worse. There was bright clean wallpaper and every piece was stuck to the walls without one single tear, gap or dirty mark.

Although Ted was also a handyman, he couldn't have been as

good at it as Dad, none of their furniture had been hand made. Another wonderful feature in the house, was a real three-piece suit, it had been bought from a furniture shop. In contrast to our settee, Dad had made our one from the back seat of an old scrapped Ford V8 Pilot limousine, mounted on oak that came from our favourite timber supplier. Although all of the clean furniture was a sight to behold, it could not boast of being upholstered with real leather like our ex Ford sofa.

Another item in the house that helps me to remember the visit so well, was the most unusual sight of a bar in their lounge:

With the war at an end, most civilians but not all were released from their 'directed labour':

Coal miners are one example. All men that were directed to work in the mines earned the nickname of 'Bevin Boys', named after the wartime Minister of Labour, Ernest Bevin.

They were now free to find an occupation of their choice. Dad chose his preferred pastime and returned to being a motor mechanic. 'Ding Dong' had found employment as a drayman with Watneys, the brewers, delivering barrels of beer from the brewery to public houses.

Behind the bar, in his lounge was a gas cylinder and a barrel of beer. A hand pump, on the surface of the bar top allowed a pint to be drawn just like being in a pub'. But the star attraction was a television set in a large wood veneer cabinet.

Spread out in front the open coal fireplace was Jumbo. He was no longer the cuddly little puppy that I had expected to see. He was now a full-grown Spaniel. As though out of politeness, rather than recognition, Jumbo lazily raised himself but paid no particular attention to anyone of us and after we had sat down he returned to his reclined position.

Dad complimented Ding Dong on how he had set up the bar and how he had prospered. He told Dad he got a very generous discount on the beer. They both laughed heartily. A legitimate discount would not have warranted such laughter. I assumed that he was referring to the same type of discounts that they had got when they both drove for NAFFI.

The Autumn had nearly passed since our visit to Lancashire,

when Mum told Pat and I that one of Dad's distant relatives, Aunt Alice, would be staying with us for a short holiday:

Alice was the Mother of Dad's Aunt Olive. Olive was the sister of Stylo's first wife.

At the time of our invitation to spend the week 'up North', Mum and Dad had given no thought to the possibility that we could be going for more than just a visit. Our invitation, it now appeared, was the first stage of a strategy planned by, and for, a much longer holiday for Aunt Olive. I believe, Mum and Dad did not realise they were being 'set-up'. They had no reason to be suspicious of Aunt Alice coming to visit. They were unaware that Aunt Olive had not planned an end date. They were unwittingly agreeing to the future permanent housing of Aunt Alice. Sporadic letter writing had taken place between Mum and Aunt Olive over the past twelve months. Now the seeds of the correspondence were about to germinate. But where could she be fitted in? We did not have enough room for ourselves.

We had progressed in our living space by 100% since the end of hostilities but that still only gave us two rooms, plus the shared semi-basement kitchen in the house:

One room served as a dinning room and lounge. The second room, on the second floor, was the bedroom for the four of us. I cannot understand how Mum and Dad allowed themselves to be persuaded to take Aunt Alice in. But they did and that meant a major upset in who resided in what room. Any changing of rooms had to have been with the agreement from Gran and Grandad.

The three hitherto unused rooms on the top floor of the house, including the attic room now had to be included in the reshuffle.

I spent the best part of one Sunday helping to move small pieces of furniture out from Gran's front semi-basement room up to the top of the house.

Some consideration had to be employed to overcome, what would have been an almost impossible manoeuvre to shift Gran's iron sprung bed. It had to pass two sharp narrow180 degree bend half way between each floor. The solution was found by taking the bed frame out through the basement side-door, into the front garden and with block and tackle, hoisted it up to and through the top window.

Aunt Alice arrived one weekend bearing gifts. I believe I came off best with a present of a hand carved ivory chess set. I can't remember how many months she stayed with us but however many it was it was too long. I am sure she was bald and wore a wig.

While out on one of many lone Sunday cycle rides, I stopped for a cup of tea at a little roadside cafe on the A23. I was cycling south on my way to Brighton. The cafe was in the small village of County Oak, between Horley and Crawley. The village of County Oak has now lost its identity by the growth of The Crawley Industrial Estate:

Crawley, like a number of other small towns for instance, Basildon and Billericay, Essex and Swindon in Gloucestershire etc were part of a massive post war building programme to accommodate the slum clearance in London that was yet to take place.

The cafe was a timber structure and is no longer there. On the site now stands the headquarters of 'First Choice', travel operators. It was the first time I had used this cafe and upon entering, remembering this was now more than a year after the war in Europe had ended, I was very surprised to see, only ex German or Italian solders in POW uniforms. The counter was situated the furthest point from the door. I had to walk the full length of the 'hut' to the counter to order a cup of tea. I felt all of the occupants ' eyes were upon me. It was more like a rest room than a cafe. I felt as though I was intruding into their private quarters. Some had the odd cup of tea in front of them and talking while others were just reading, but my attention was immediately drawn to the quality of the woodcarvings that were hanging on the walls. Some of the patrons were whittling while in conversation, others sat alone and concentrated on the objects they were working on. I assumed the wall decorations were all the work of the men now sitting in front of me.

The fact they were our very recent enemies and still prisoners, their ease and apparent relaxed attitude surprised me. I was too young to be deterred by their presence, and still walked up to the counter to purchased a cup of tea. For want of more seating space and a little bravado, I sat amongst them. Before I had taken a sip of tea, one of the prisoners asked me, in very clear English, if I wanted to buy a hand carved souvenir. The only thing I bought was the cup of tea. I was soon on my cycle again on the second half of my journey to Brighton.

Benny and I were always looking in the windows of cycle shops, comparing frames and newly arrived pieces of equipment. On one widow shopping expedition we saw some very unusual cycle frame transfers. We bought a set each that brought the time around quicker than normal for our bicycles to get another strip down to clean and paint. Because we had the new transfers, the cleaning and painting received special attention.

When the job was done our bikes sparkled. Delighted with our effort we had to try them out. We cycled to Clapham Common and on the return journey we changed over. Benny rode my cycle; I rode on Benny's. As we got to Clapham Common North Side, we both started racing home. With my head down I raced in front of Benny, I looked up just in time to see a stationary bus in front. I was only just in time to see it. Not enough time to avoid it. I smashed into the back of the bus with such a force that I pushed in the rear panel of the bus. The driver nor the conductor were aware of the collision and as the bus moved off, I remained sitting in the road with Benny's front forks and frame bent backwards and front wheel a buckled mess. Except for a bump on my forehead that fitted the shape of the dent in the back of the bus, there was no other damage. Benny stood over me transfixed as he looked at his cycle that was now beyond repair. I tried to reduce the seriousness of the wreckage by telling him although the new paint was scratched, the transfers were still OK.

When I got home, I noticed, protruding over each end of the roof rack on the Triumph, two long lengths of heavy angle iron and on the back seat two wheels with pneumatic balloon tyres. Dad had bought the wheels from one of his favoured shops, the ex- government surplus store.

Dad was not at home for me to ask him what the wheels were for. I wondered what he was going to make next. Within a week I was helping to build a caravan. I forgot about Benny's bicycle problem.

I didn't get over excited about the world boxing scene but I was interested enough to listen to the fight between Freddie Mills and Gus Lesnevich, the light Heavyweight world champion title holder. Freddie Mills failed to beat the count in the 10th round and failed in his attempt on the world title.

ELEVEN

A PROPER WEEKLY WAGE

The winter 1946/1947 was extremely cold over all of the UK. In some parts of the country the temperatures were the lowest since 1881. At the end of January 1947, some areas had to endure temperatures as low as minus 20 degrees. Heavy snowstorms and fuel shortages brought the national economy to its knees. Thousands of homes were without water, heat and lighting. Due to the freezing condition water became a precious commodity. The radio and newspapers christened the period 'The Big Freeze'.

The extremely low temperatures lasted about two weeks. When the thaw came, the frozen water pipes in houses burst and, because of rivers flooding, some people were forced to leave their homes. The demand on the plumbing trade was exceptional and widespread.

Continuing from the war years coal was still rationed and still in desperately short supply. For reasons unknown to me, coke, being a by-product of coal, remained unrationed. More extraordinary, bread, unrationed during the war years, was only obtainable with a ration book.

On a number of early mornings, before Dad went to work, I accompanied him on his Ariel motorcycle and sidecar to the Gas, Light and Coke Company on the South side of the River Thames at Vauxhall. On each journey we managed to load two 1/2 cwt, 56lbs, sackfulls of coke into the sidecar.

The detached house next to where I lived had also suffered internal damage from incendiary bombs during the war. The house, 2 Binfield Road, had also been unoccupied through all of the war years and was still without residence seven years later.

When we moved in, next door's back garden was in the same neglected and overrun condition as our garden. Another two years growth had occurred since then. It was overrun with shrubs, tall nettles, brambles and naturally sown saplings had become a jungle that would not have been out of place on a film set.

Half way down the garden stood one tree far higher than any other it must have been over a hundred years old. This monster had grown so large it was taller than our three storey house. The trunk, with a girth of something like five metres was pushing our dividing garden brick wall at an angle to such an extent it was in danger of collapsing.

In the garden, the first half of the hundred feet rear garden was Dad's; his garage took half the width. The remaining portion of the first half was grassed. The second half was Grandad's birdcages and rabbit hutches.

I cannot be certain what the driving factor was that caused Dad and Grandad to agree that the tree had to be cut down. I doubt the dangerous condition of the wall was uppermost in their minds. My guess is it was a combination of the very cold winter and the scarcity of coal that called for drastic action. To substitute coal, the tree was a plentiful source of fuel and became the target for corrective safety treatment.

One weekend, with no let up of the cold conditions, Grandad climbed almost to the top of the tree. He tied himself loosely to the tree with a stout piece of rope and started sawing. The top branches came down first in rapid succession and then the trunk in pieces of about a metre in length. Obviously, as he progressed shortening the tree, the trunk got thicker and the task got greater but he was a 'powerhouse'. By the end of the second weekend the tree had been reduced to half of its original height.

One day while he was up the tree cutting, Dad was on the ground sawing the long lengths into logs and splitting them with an axe small enough to put onto the fire indoors. I helped by sawing the smaller branches. While the tree cutting was taking place, the garden wall had received some heavy blows by the large pieces of tree trunk and branches that had fallen onto it. The garden wall eventually gave up defying gravity and had collapsed into the garden to join the twigs, branches and sawn logs.

When about only four meters of the tree remained Grandad decided it was short enough to fall in one length. The wall was no longer a barrier and started cutting at ground level.

After a couple more hours sawing and many stops to spit on his hands and get his breath back, Grandad put the saw down and with Dad and I assisting, gave a push. The tree gave a creak and a moan but resisted our first effort. With another few saw cuts and more pushes the tree finally gave up. With a slightly greater sway the tree made an enormous 'crack' as the timber fell across the garden and hit the ground with an earth trembling thud. Grandad's part of the job was done.

Looking up the garden from the back of the house more than half of the now horizontal, tree trunk was hidden behind Dad's garage.

To make Dad's task of sawing the tree trunk into logs easier, it was decided to raise the trunk onto a sawing horse. With this in mind Dad and Grandad cradled the trunk in their arms and lifted as high as they could. As previously instructed, I quickly placed a sawing horse into position under the tree trunk and pushed as near to the centre as possible. Satisfied with the result, Grandad lifted his cap from his head and, with his handkerchief, wiped the sweat from his forehead. The once proud tree stayed in that fallen position until the next weekend, when Dad again resumed in reducing the length of the trunk.

Dad had already commenced sawing behind the garage, when I went into the garden to get my bicycle out of the garage. As I came out of the garage, pushing my cycle, I heard a thump and a crash followed by a painful groan. I rushed to the rear of the garage not knowing what to expect. I was shocked to see Dad spread-eagled and pinned down to the ground by the, still, large and very heavy tree trunk.

Dad lay still and quiet and looking rather peaceful on his side in the grass, until he uttered a croaking noise followed by a soft moan. The trunk was across his legs at the knee joint. In addition I believe he must have also hit his head on one of the garage uprights for he remained frighteningly motionless.

He mumbled the same words I was thinking, "You won't lift it Ron, and you'll have to get Grandad".

Without hesitating I formed a mental picture how to free his legs. I visualised a seesaw and ignoring Dad's instruction, I rolled a freshly cut log that was near at hand in the gap, between log and ground that was created by Dad's legs and pushed it as close as possible to his left knee to make a seesaw. I then dragged a heavy piece of tree and rested it upright, against the high end of the seesaw and gradually lowered the length of timber across the offending tree trunk. When it made contact I was able to transfer my grip to push downwards. To my delight, my seesaw worked with no effort. As my pushing moved the trunk downwards, so the other end, trapping Dad's legs, obviously, came upwards. Although by no more than an inch or two his legs were no longer in contact with the tree. To secure the log against falling back onto Dad's legs, I then rolled another large sawn log under the raised end. I anxiously asked him if he was now able to move his legs. He was still in a semi-conscious state and answered me with an unintelligible mumble. I pushed his feet to bend his legs at the knees but he gave a louder moan of pain. There was still too much obstruction but now I realised the round log I had pushed under the trunk to act as the centre of the seesaw could also act as a wheel. By pushing the end I was now able to roll the whole trunk away from his sleep like form he now had the freedom to move, if he was able to.

"Are you OK Dad?", I asked,

He seemed to have recovered his senses, as I touched his shoulder he turned on to his side.

"How the bloody hell did you lift that tree by yourself? I can't believe it," he said.

I felt proud to the point of tears. Still in shock, Dad sat up, as he did so I noticed a nasty, freely bleeding gash on the side of his face.

"If you can stand up Dad, I'll help you to get indoors," I said.

I helped Dad to stand but one leg appeared more damaged than the other. With one of his arms across my shoulder and wincing with pain with each step he hobbled towards the house.

Dad was still in a state of shock as we reached the steps into the house. Without expecting an answer, he kept repeating, "I can't believe you lifted that bloody big tree by yourself Ron. You must have had some divine intervention".

I had never heard Dad make a religious pronouncement before or after this event. It was a 'tongue in cheek' comment that suggested to me Dad was returning back to his normal self. I was proud I was able to come to the rescue but it had nothing to do with my strength, it was just pure and simple engineering science. Dad suffered no permanent damage and within a few weeks he was back to normal.

With encouragement from Dad, I completed an application form to join his cherished organisation. The Cyclists Touring Club, CTC:

Cycling in the 1940's was big time. There were many more cycles on the road than petrol driven vehicles, which made cycling much safer than today. Immediately after the war there were still more horses and carts than motor vehicles: Bread was rationed and delivered by The Co-op by horse and cart. The Co-Op and The United Dairies delivered milk by horse and cart. Coal was still rationed and also delivered by horse and cart.

By return of post I received my CTC lapel badge, an embroidered breast pocket blazer badge, a map of Southern England and a monthly journal informing me of my section's meeting place for Sunday outings. My meeting point could only have been nearer if my Clapham cycling group met me outside my house.

We all met, about fifteen of us, each Sunday morning at The War Memorial opposite Stockwell Underground Station.

I found my new cycling companions just as Dad had suggested they would be. Although all of them older than me, they were a pleasant and concerning group of people. I should have felt out of place, for they were all well spoken and worked in middle class employment, banks or offices. They were a good steadying influence and looked after me like the child I still was.

Each Sunday outings usually covered about thirty-five to forty miles round -trip and all at a steady pace. Every cycling trip with the CTC that summer was memorable, I do not remember one occasion that it rained.

One young lady and her boyfriend in addition to cycling, spent their leisure time performing in amateur dramatics. They were forever singing songs from a hit stage show, 'Oklahoma': The show had newly arrived from America. Although I liked music, I had no interest in musical shows on stage.

One evening, during one of Stylo's weekly visits to the house, he gave Mum some complimentary tickets to see the stage show at the Strand Theatre in Kingsway, off The Strand, London which no longer exists. Mum accepted the tickets and when she told me it was to see 'Oklahoma' I eagerly awaited the outing. Being totally ignorant of the theatre, I thought we were all going to see a western film. What a disappointment! What a bore! I had not connected, before seeing the show, they were the songs my cycling colleagues sang.

I hastily add I no longer hold that view. There are many musical shows I like but I have a preference for Guys and Dolls and a special appreciation for Cole Porter.

One Sunday, not wishing to go out with my CTC friends, I cycled to East Street market and purchased a second-hand Nat King Cole Trio recording of 'I'm just a shy guy'. All of Nat Cole's previous recordings I had purchased had always been second-hand and non-

366

vocal. He was a talented pianist but I was surprised to hear, on this recording, he also sang.

The record had been released two years earlier in 1945 but I had not heard it before. It was the beginning of a new career for him as a solo ballad singer. A week or two later I bought Nat Cole's recording of 'Route 66'. Thereafter, until I went into the army, I bought every vocal recording he made. Of all the popular ballad singers he has remained on of my Top Ten list of all time great vocalists. He was a heavy smoker that may have added to the quality of his voice, but the smoking undoubtedly shortened his life. He was 48 years old when he died in 1965 from lung cancer.

In 1947, the Official school leaving in the UK was fourteen and remained that way until the 1950's.

Upon returning to school after the 1946 Christmas holiday period I felt disenchanted with the whole concept of learning by sitting behind a school desk. Although I was happier at this school than I had been at any other I was getting increasingly unhappy at the thought that I had volunteered to put off going to work until I was fifteen.

It seemed an eternity since Mum and Dad had received the London County Council letter telling them I had qualified for a place at 'The Tech'.

At the time, Dad had been delighted and I was aware, knowing how he felt, that if I was going to try to leave school earlier than I was now committed I would have to make my feelings known gradually. Almost daily Dad would enquire about my progress. Rather than tell him, what I knew he wanted to hear, over a period of a few weeks I began to make him aware of my growing displeasure of staying at school for another year.

One day during my unsettled period I read on the notice board in the school study room an information sheet offering engineering apprenticeships.

Although it was intended for applicants to apply after reaching the age of fifteen it set a though in motion that it could be just the lever that might interest Dad enough to agree to let me finish school at fourteen. My fourteenth birthday and the Easter school holiday was only a couple of months away. I needed to make my mind up fast what I wanted to do.

The first weekend after reading the notice I mentioned it to Dad. Although I had not considered any strategy my timing must have been perfect. While I was helping him in the garage 'grinding in' some valves on an engine rebore job, I brought up the subject of an apprenticeship.

To my surprise, Dad did not seem unduly disturbed by my words of discontentment of remaining at school for another year.

"Is that really what you think you would like to do Ron? Do you always want to have dirty hands and grease under your fingernails like me? I thought you wanted to qualify to be a Draughtsman".

"I think I don't want to work in an office all day", I replied.

"Well before we go any further, we'll get Mum to write to your headmaster to find out if he will release us from your promise to stay the extra year".

Although for the next few weeks the subject was a constant topic of conversation I did not get involved with the politics and administration of leaving school.

It must have been early in March that Mum showed me a letter that agreed to allow me to leave school at fourteen. I was delighted with the news. Since I had begun to think of leaving school my daily lessons became a chore.

Meanwhile, unknown to me, Dad had been doing some homework himself looking into the company offering the apprenticeship. With the last few weeks remaining before my fourteenth birthday, Dad showed me a letter inviting me to go for an interview with a specialist motor racing and sports car manufacturer. The company was Allards. They had their main office and factory in Keswick Road, off the Upper Richmond Road, Putney.

I was thrilled. I took the letter to school to show the headmaster and he appeared to have no problem with excusing me from attending school that day.

When the big day arrived Mum fussed around with my clothing to make sure I looked my best. She hadn't considered that motor engineers never look smart.

For all of the attention I received from Mum, when I left the house, I still looked like a schoolboy.

From my cycling adventures, I knew the area well and I did suggest that my transport should be by bicycle. Mum was insistent, however, that I used public transport.

I travelled by tram to Clapham Junction and then a trolley bus that stopped outside the factory and office entrance. I had never at this stage of my life travelled in a taxi, had I have chose to I could not have got nearer to Allards.

Once inside the building in the reception area I was escorted to an office and told to go through the open door. I had no problem with nerves and felt comfortable when the man behind the desk ask me to take a seat.

"You look very young! How old are you?"

"Fourteen sir"

"When are you fifteen?"

"Next year sir"

"Is that not when you leave school?"

" No sir. If I get an apprenticeship my headmaster will allow me to leave a year early".

Your father's letter did not tell me how old you are. Because you are attending a Technical School, I assumed, because you are leaving school this year, you were fifteen".

He paused still looking at me.

"No sir" I said to break the Silence.

"Well I am very sorry young man" he began.

I knew he wasn't about to say sorry you've got the apprenticeship. My heart sank I couldn't say a word. I was so disappointed I could have cried. On leaving home I felt so cheerful and confident I had no doubt that I would not be awarded an apprenticeship. I thought my journey was just a formality. I was making the visit to be told how much money I was going to get and when I was going to start.

I missed part of what he had been saying but he was still talking when my brain started telling my ears to listen. I heard him say:

"That is why our apprenticeship scheme commences, for our boys when they are fifteen".

More insignificant words followed before he reached over his desk to give me a piece of paper.

"Take this voucher to the cashier at the end of the corridor and she'll reimburse your fare. I will write to your father to explain everything. I will keep you on our waiting list and if you are still interested when you are fifteen you can apply then".

I didn't feel like being civilised but I got up out of my seat, walked to the door and manage to remain polite. "Thank you". I said.

I closed the door behind me and followed his direction to redeem my voucher. I collected my fare money from the cashier and left the building. I thought my life had come to an end. I went home.

The next day at school I was asked by a number of my classmates how I had got on. I didn't want the humiliation of letting it be known in school that I had not been successful. To evade telling a lie, I told those that asked. "I am leaving at Easter".

I hadn't considered that my unfruitful attempt to work at Allards could prejudice me leaving school a year early. The pretence made me feel better and as the day progressed I was happy again thinking of nothing other than leaving school:

It was possible to have a telephone installed only if it was for business purposes. Dad had been working for himself for about two years and had been on the waiting list for about twenty months before it had been fitted, which was a week or two prior to my Allards interview. Upon hearing of my rejection news Mum rang Pride & Clarke Ltd, on our new telephone:

Pride and Clarke Ltd. Automobile Distributors, was one of the largest new and second-hand motorcycle dealers in the country.

Mum arranged for me to attend an interview and like the little boy I was she came with me. We sat through the interview together but between Mum and The Company Secretary it was agreed I would commence work on the Tuesday after the Easter holiday period, which was now only about two weeks away.

It was in my mind, had I been considered for a similar position I had sought at Allards and Dad had accompanied me to P & C's, I am sure I would have started on a better status than a Tea Boy. Before Easter a letter from my potential employer arrived addressed to me, confirming my start date, where to report and my salary. My weekly wage was to be one pound two shillings and sixpence. This was on a par with the winnings I was picking up each week, although unlawful, from underground ticket machines.

For my fourteenth birthday Mum and Dad bought me a nearly new 'Dawes' sports cycle with a 19inch frame and 26inch wheels. It was an unusual size: The normal smallest adult frame was 21inch. It was one of my very few possessions from Dad that he had not made. The colour was light powder blue. I was so pleased with the cycle within a few weeks I had taken it to pieces and repainted it.

Until the past few weeks I had not considered I would one day not be a schoolboy to continue to enjoy the reckless activities I had been used to. The day had arrived for a new phase of my life to begin. Maybe I was still only a boy and maybe, as I get older, I will still remain a boy but I was and at least about to become a full-time working boy.

To be continued.

ABOUT THE AUTHOR

The author was born in South London in 1933 and educated at Hazelrigge Road Secondary Modern, Clapham and more thoroughly at The Borough Beaufort Technical School, Kennington.

He completed his National Service in 1953 after serving with the Royal Irish Fusiliers in Goettingen in Germany, and Berlin.

After completing his two years in the army he trained as a butcher and remained with a National Supermarket chain for 19 years. He has also worked as a Telecommunication Engineer, Life Assurance Agent, Performance Analyst and Contracts Manager with an International Electronics Company.

He is retired and lives with his wife in Billingshurst, West Sussex. He has two Daughters and four, adult, Grandchildren,

The Penny Entrepreneur is his first book.

COMING SOON

HE BECAME A SOLDIER
Is the sequel to The Penny Entrepreneur.

A post war adventure.
BY RONALD W PROSS

He Became a Soldier continues the events where *The Penny Entrepreneur* ends. It commences with his first employment after leaving school, his 'called-up' and completion of his two years national service in Northern Ireland, Berlin and Gottingen in Germany.

It chronicles some world history including IRA activities in Ulster N.I. the partition of India and Pakistan, the civil war in China, the conflict in French Indo China, now Vietnam, the Korean War and the race between the USSR and the USA to launch a vehicle into outer space it could also be of special interest to those students interested in social history of the period.

ISBN 142511259-5